Mote House

An inherited past

Julia Botterell

First Published in Great Britain
By Julia Botterell

Cover and book design by Julia Botterell

Other books by this author
Denbigh Lacquer
2009
Maidstone Maid
2010

Printed by Book Printing UK www.bookprintinguk.com
Remus House, Coltsfoot Drive, Peterborough, PE2 9BF

Printed in Great Britain

ISBN 978-0-9563647-2-2

A brief note about the author

Julia was born in Kent in 1950. She is married and lives in North Wales on the outskirts of the village of Hawarden. After 34 years in teaching first in Kent and then coming to Wales in 1974 she wrote a family history Denbigh Lacquer in 2009 about her somewhat eccentric aunt and then completed Maidstone Maid in 2010 about her own childhood in Kent during the austere 1950's. Family history always intrigued her and has, to a large extent, continued to shape much of her writing.

Since retirement she and her husband Allan have enjoyed some far flung globe-trotting whilst continuing to enjoy a variety of interests including theatre, reading, food and drink, having friends around for meals, studying wildlife, art, looking around historic properties, researching family tree history and more recently learnt the art of sugar craft flowers to decorate wedding cakes...oh yes..... and being completely hooked on the iPad.

Church

Vicarage

Mote House

Mote Lake

Kings Arms

General Store

Post Office

Drewe & Son

Ticehurst Bakery

Simmons Hardware

Village Hall

Village Pond

Papermaker's Arms

Bank

Ivy Leaf
Cottage

stream

apple orchards

Headmaster's house

hop gardens

School

farm

Estate workers Cottages

Kilndown Woods

Kilndown Manor

cherry orchards

Cranesbury

Railway Station

Rosemount Villas

Staton Master's

house

Lodge House

Railway

Cranesbury Village

Cranesbury Village 2009
Rosie & Ellen

When she came up the path to the house I knew then that it was the beginning of the end. My past and her future would finally fuse together as they had always been destined to do. She, in her innocence, had already instigated the painful process of unravelling our shared history whether I willed it or not. I suppose that I had always been waiting for her, waiting to greet this moment. And now that she and the moment had arrived, I dreaded them, yet felt compelled to welcome them.

One half of me was desperate to meet her at last, but then, I'm ashamed to admit it, the other half was quite afraid to face the exposure, and the part that I had played in our shared history. Sitting quite still I could feel a swirling of ungovernable emotions as my heart drummed against the constraints of muscle and skin and its echo pounded in my ears. Where was my vision, my clarity of purpose when I needed it most? I, who had once so skilfully manipulated and controlled, now reduced to this pathetic state; so silly to get worked up. I tried to steady my nerve.

As if the past could be changed now.

Her hesitant knock had still made me jump, although I had been sitting here all morning waiting for her to come. From my window I had silently watched her cautious, yet graceful, progress towards my front door as she thoughtfully avoided the drooping flower heads of the herbaceous plants which spilled untidily onto the path. And my tea, which I had just at that moment poured, carelessly flowed from my overturned mug, slowly spreading an annoyingly large dark stain across the scrubbed grain of the beech table.

Then, after another slight hesitation, she knocked again before I had even reached the hallway.

"I'm coming, I'm coming" I muttered to myself.

1

In her hand she carried a sheaf of papers. I had to clear my throat before I could speak. It's so often like this these days; as if my voice is reluctant to be heard. And when it does speak I hardly recognise it as my own. When did it change? When did it become so timorous, so tired and ancient?

"Yes?" I managed to sound querulous, impatient, even to myself.

"I'm sorry to trouble you. My name is Ellen, Ellen Sumner."

Her young voice was clear.

"I'm looking for some information about Mote House and I was told to come here………," she hesitated, "I've been asked to look into it you see. We came across some documents. There seems to be some discrepancy over the names on the Land Registry." She offered the papers that she was holding as evidence but I did not take them from her. Not yet, not so soon. I looked instead at her open face. How breathtakingly beautiful youth is; I had forgotten how beguiling it is. That soft unlined skin, her cheeks slightly tinged pink with embarrassment, those clear grey eyes, her hair a glow of burnished gold in the sunshine, and a face that echoed the past.

She frowned, unsure, and withdrew the proffered sheaf. I glanced down at my own blue veined hands and a thick band tightened across my chest.

"You had better come in."

∞

I've been living in Ivy Leaf Cottage since, well, for a lifetime now. It's still a lovely house although the upkeep is so expensive. Having the thatched roof is the main reason for the costs I suppose. Trying to find men who are still able to do a good job, and getting good quality straw thatch all adds to it. It was built around 1910, a nostalgic nod I always thought, to a past age of rural life favoured by the Arts and Crafts period. The herringboned brickwork has weathered considerably over the

2

years and needs some repointing work, but the colour is lovely, a warm rusty golden brown. It has always reminded me of that farm house in Thomas Hardy's novel 'Far from the Madding Crowd', Bathsheba's house. Mind, it could have been the aunt's house, it's a long time now since I took up with books.

And the name! Ivy Leaf Cottage. Such a ridiculously whimsical one I've always thought. I've no idea who chose it, perhaps it was the Latterbridges. What is it that the Baptists say about their faith? That it should cleave to them just as the ivy clings to a wall. Isn't the ivy leaf a symbol to them of this? I'm sure that I read it somewhere. Anyway what does that matter now? I've been clinging to this house for years now so perhaps I have become the ivy; although with me it's a symbol of tenacity not faith. Where was I? Oh yes. The windows are small and latticed which doesn't allow for much good light in all the rooms, and they are a devil to keep clean, but when the evening sun catches them the colours are ethereal, quite exquisite.

As for the main features, well, all the fireplaces are the originals, but there is an efficient oil-fired central heating system which was installed some time later, so I rarely bother with them. In fact I can't remember when I last set one or had the chimney swept. I suppose that they are both due for a spring clean but I don't seem to get round to organising things these days; just keep writing lists to remind myself why I am still here! Anyway it's not as if the Queen is coming to stay.

In fact I have been on my own now for as long as I can remember, but I keep it tidy and don't have much help except the window cleaners who come round once in a blue moon when they remember where I am. I did have the rooms downstairs redecorated a few years ago. Father and son they were. The lad was as daft as a brush and the father not much better but they did do a good job, although it took them a week longer than they had first estimated. In the end I was glad to see the back of them.

3

My shopping is brought in from the village by van, and I more or less have the same things each week, and then ring the shop if I think of something different. And I also use a laundry service for the bedding, which gets dropped off each week as well.

A few years ago I had cats that had strayed into the area and adopted me but the place has been without an animal for some time now. I miss the sight of a comfortable curled-up cat on the chair, but there we are, things change. I have always been self-sufficient and independent, a bit like the cats that came and went. Still it would be nice to be treated and have someone putting out my food once in a while. I never did give the cats a name. They just came and went as they pleased. I didn't control them. No, I did too much of that in the past and learned to regret it. Still that's another time; can't change the past.

Inside there's a lot of space. It is bigger than you would have first thought. Quite deceptive really. Probably the kitchen is the best feature. I used to think it was so old fashioned. Edwardian cream fronts with cupped handles to the drawers. But then times change don't they? Things come round again. The old Belfast sink is original too and the scoured beech draining boards. Of course some of the cupboards have seen better days; hinges a bit wobbly, the usual sort wear and tear, nothing really major, although there is a bit of black mould under the sink. Half the time though I don't notice it.

Upstairs there are three good sized double bedrooms, and the bathroom along the landing has the old enamel bath with its big taps; a toilet cistern that empties Niagara Falls into the pan when the chain is pulled and a square basin which has a lime scale stain running down towards the plughole that I have never been able to shift due to the cold tap needing a new washer. That washer has been on my 'to do' list for years.

Downstairs there are two more reception rooms which I rarely use. These days I prefer to stay in the kitchen which faces the garden path; being south facing it has the sun for most of the

4

day. Anyway the drawing room, or lounge as they are wont to be called these days, has a well upholstered suite, the fireplace has a blue and yellow lily flowered tile surround and there is a low beamed ceiling but the room faces north and it's a devil to keep warm.

Ancient old books are kept behind the glass doors of the bookcase; there's nothing contemporary or remotely modern on the shelves. Even when it was first stocked, most of them were never taken out, or have seen the light of day since they were purchased; bought just for pure show, for the look of the expensive leather bindings lining the shelves. Some are silly old romantic novels, 'The Beloved Vagabond', 'Anne of Green Gables' and the like, then of course most of the obligatory classics including some Dickens, Austin, Willkie Collins, EM Forster, Trollope, Bronte, and Hardy. There's an odd bit of murder and mystery, 'The Hound of the Baskervilles', 'The Turn of the Screw' and such like, then some miscellaneous reference stuff, the usual dictionaries, a few well-thumbed children's books, 'The Railway Children', 'The Water Babies', a tattered copy of 'Alice In Wonderland' and an odd book or two of the local photographic history of Kent which I did look at a few years back, probably when I had nothing better to do.

One of the best rooms is the dining room, but as I said, I have no reason to use it now, having no dinner guests. The table is lovely; I do keep that well-polished. That and the chairs are probably worth quite a bit now. I think that they were made by an old London company; Heals and Son I seem to recall.

I used to keep the outside fairly tidy, but Mother Nature has long since reclaimed her land. Once upon a time I could afford a gardener who weeded the herbaceous borders but as I don't go outside much I don't see the point of doing it. As long as the pathway is clear for the groceries and whatnot to be delivered, that's the main thing.

Still enough about the house, I'm just putting off the inevitable. My visitor this morning, oh yes, I knew that she was coming. You can scoff, especially as she made me spill the tea. But there we are. I knew that one day she would walk up that path and ask about the house.

She and I have a connection you see, one that she is just beginning to feel. It's inevitable. And once she and that house come together, time will be stood on its head, and then I will come tumbling down. There will be judgements made. All those years when I had to manage those situations, to ease people through the tangles, to help them find their way, you can call it meddling and manipulation. I know. I know I regret so many of the consequences, but then what would have become of them if I hadn't seen and understood those consequences? Wouldn't it have been far worse?

All my life this special gift, this Cassandra's sight of mine, has been both a blessing and a curse. It's not something that I could just turn on and off. And don't think that I have suffered from it too. Hard decisions had to be made and sometimes, well, perhaps sometimes I did stray too far. The temptation became too much, but then I was also young and headstrong. I wanted my life to be my own as well. Was that too much to ask?

Oh yes. I have paid for my past mistakes as much as those whom I sought to help also paid. But power is such an addiction. I would defy anyone to resist the craving that I had then. It's hard to describe my ability to know, to feel certain of what will be said, who will appear, or how someone will feel, even when they take pains to disguise it. You can call coincidence, telepathy, or that I have premonitions if you want, if you want to put it into a little box. You have probably even felt it yourself. Standing in a queue and having an overwhelming sense that someone is staring at you, or thinking about someone and suddenly the 'phone rings and it is them on the line. Well imagine that ten times over and far more powerful. I have their conversations inside my head, as if someone is speaking to me directly. I can hear their thoughts and answer them as if they have spoken out aloud. It happens with objects too, I might be wondering about something and it will suddenly be on a shelf, on a table when I hadn't seen it there before. You understand about coincidences, that they are just strange and random? No, not for me, my life has been filled with such phenomena. I expect them, just as you expect to see a rainbow through the sun- filled raindrops. And they have coloured my life as far back as I can remember. Yes, coloured it, distorted it and twisted it until there was no going back. No way back.

Some people sleepwalk into disaster; they allow themselves to become puppets, having no vision, no sense of positive choices or of taking up the opportunities. I could see so plainly the right course of action, but by their stubbornness and by being so contrary they stepped aside from the path that I had mapped for them. Of course I couldn't prevent them falling once they had made such disastrous and catastrophic decisions, decisions made without any applied logic I might add.

 Did money did come into it? Oh yes, a good deal of it. There was never enough then and certainly there isn't enough of it now. Were crimes committed? No not by me, well not deliberately. Yes I knew of the crimes of passion, those against liberty and love. I saw the betrayals and the injustices. Yes indeed I witnessed the blaming and shaming, the unfair judgements that were made and secrets that were kept. I could still keep those secrets and choose to exonerate myself. Even now I still can do that, but I want it to end. I want it all to be at an end, over and done with once and for all.

In the past I prided myself on my eloquence which was often complimented on. I have had years to put things into perspective and to blame myself. Others that could have taken their share, their due portion, are no longer here to lessen the burden. Could things have been different if I had not intervened? Well of course, but would their lives had been happier, more fulfilled, I think not. They would have made similarly absurd choices, misunderstanding their own needs and allowing gossip and innuendo to govern their lives.

Am I passionate? Do I sound passionate?

Well I was once.

Oh yes, once I was inflamed by life and by those around me. I watched the moths fluttering around the flame and wanted to join in the dance. I can almost smell those days. If I close my eyes even now I can still hear the beguiling low laughter, smell the swirl of cigarette smoke, acrid hot tar on the roads and fresh wet woodland grass flattened beneath me and feel his urgent strong arms enfolding me, crushing out my breath.

But for now, finally the events will have to unfold, to unravel and I will allow her to follow her vision as I once did, and she will, although her gifts are as yet untrained.

Still, enough of her for now, all, as they say, will be revealed, but it has to be in my own time. I need to put my life in context, both hers and mine, within this village which has been both my playground and my fortress.

It is a pretty little spot, this little village of Cranesbury. We still have two good public houses, the only difference now being that they both serve food. That's a sign of the times. Once upon a time it was just the old one, 'The King's Head' hotel, the one on the left past the duck pond at the very top of the hill, which had a formal restaurant with rooms.

Now the other pub, with its white clapperboard frontage, once known as the Papermakers Arms, has food. It's that pretentious, nouvelle cuisine kind of food that they have there. Clever of them to serve so very little but to charge their customers the earth, but then that's fashion. This pub is at the far end of the pond with their entrance around the other side away from the road, facing the water.

Then there's the old village sign that hangs by the pond probably obscured from view at the moment. I think that the overhanging branches of the trees sometimes mask it. They need cutting back a bit more. I have always like that sign. It's prettily done; the entwined cranes both looking out in different directions. Something almost heraldic about the style I've always thought. Some wit said that we villagers were just like those cranes; we could never see eye to eye!

At the crossroads there are still one or two shops left. There once was a really good butcher, Robert Drewe and Sons, he used to sell such a lot of game. There was always a queue in his busy shop. As a child I can remember seeing all the soft limp white rabbits, with their tied back legs and glazed eyes, hanging forlornly in a row, together with the lolling necks and small bodies of the brightly feathered pheasants. Fresh golden sawdust was scattered on the floor each morning but by the end of the day it became spotted with dark red blood. All his meat hooks, gleaming knives and butchery paraphernalia were hung behind his counter and he had a leather strap attached to the heavily scored bench where he used to sharpen his knives. Such a big man he was. His straw boater with a blue and red band sat squarely on his head. I never saw him without it except on a Sunday at church and then he would be wearing his bowler hat so people never knew exactly when he went bald.

On the right of the butcher's was the hardware shop, owned by old Simmons who was always in his brown dustcoat. He was a thin as Drewe was fat, 'as thin as his broom handles' we kids used to say. But for all that he was a nice man. Drewe had a temper on him but Simmons seemed to find the positive things in life, although he did have hard times, and a lot of worry about his wife whom we rarely saw as she had some kind of chest complaint, which was especially bad during the winter months. We used to love wandering into his shop. He never seemed to mind that we didn't buy much, if anything at all. I think that we

9

must have been a nuisance trooping in, but we were morbidly fascinated by his mouse traps which he used to demonstrate to us, pretending that he had lost a thumb in the process as the steel spring snapped shut. And he knew where every last thing was in that shop. It was an Aladdin's cave of shelves lined with tins, packets and pots. Brooms, buckets, and tin baths were hung outside. Garden twine, spades, forks, wicker baskets, fishing rods and wriggling live bait managed to edge a space for themselves, and bird cages, laundry drying racks and meat safes were perilously suspended from the ceiling.

On entering his shop the tinkling of his bell always set off his talking Mynah bird which spoke once you were safely inside. Even now I can hear its raspy voice. 'Hello, who's your lady friend?' And 'That'll be tuppence please!'

Simmons must have sold some things over time and yet when you went inside it seemed as if nothing had changed its position. Boxes just became a little more dilapidated and crumbled and other items faded blue whilst sitting in the sunlit shop window, despite all the yellow cellophane sheeting that he used to protect the stock in the hottest summers.

Further on the hill on the left hand side was our local bakery. Pies, pastries, buns and tarts were laid out in the front whilst the bread was lined up along the back wall. Enticing smells would waft out into the road from the bakery early each morning as the slatted bloomers, fat puffy cottage loaves, and crusty rolls found their place on the shelves. Mike, the baker's boy would routinely leave his bike propped up against the side doorway oblivious to the irritation of customers and Ron who constantly reminded him about putting it round the back. "Or you'll end up with a clip round the ear if I catch you leaving it there again!"

Mike waited for the exasperation to reach its climax before he would give us a wink and wheel the offending obstacle away. As a child I was in love with both the beguiling smell of fresh bread, and the baker's boy. His eyes opened wide with astonishment when the shouts got louder as if he was genuinely surprised by the often repeated charade. And then the wink drew you in, as a fellow conspirator, to share the joke, smiling at the bluster of the baker Ron Ticehurst.

I could read Mike. And he knew that I knew of things that he hadn't shared with others. There was his dalliance with Ron's foolish assistant Mary. I saw her look away. Her silly lame attempt to ignore him only showed me how much she cared for him. And he, with his confidence in his ability to make her yearn, also gave only the slightest acknowledgement that he had seen her standing awkwardly behind the counter. I saw the trouble all along and knew what he would do then and much later, leaving her with double trouble.

But I am going ahead of myself. Situated just on the other side of the road to the village pond and standing in its own space to justify its importance was the National Provincial Bank's black and white timbered building with large imposing mullioned windows, quoin blocks at the corners, and three tall twisted chimneys. Each Tuesday and Friday it was especially busy when the village seemed to fill with farmers from the surrounding farms. Then come Wednesday afternoons and the village would close early and quietly rest from its weekly duties.

Twice a day the cream and brown village bus came into the village, except on Sunday when there was no service, depositing an assortment of fractious children with their harassed mothers, impatient teenagers and a few weary travellers down outside Drewe's shop. Even in 1928 when I was six, when we had particularly heavy falls of snow, the bus managed to get through although it had to have some help reaching the top of the village before wending its way around the narrow roads, passing the pole lined hop fields and orchards as it trundled on towards Maidstone.

Of course we had a Post Office together with its General Store side, which was just below the bakery and then there was the

Norman church St Ethelbert's, with its vicarage, which were tucked behind 'The King's Head' at the top of the hill, affording wonderful views across the fields to the west. Mind, it could also be a windy spot which gave no shelter for the shivering congregation when they spilled out after the long service on a cold March morning. Our old stone church's claim to fame was having two huge sixteenth century brass plaques, depicting saints, which had been laid on the floor to one side of the pews. An army of church cleaners ensured that those brasses gleamed in their somnambulant prostrate position. As children we were instructed to step around them for we were routinely reminded that it would result in 'pain of death' if we were ever to accidently tread upon them.

Then there was our village school, the old elementary board school, which took in boys and girls from the age of five to eleven. This was situated towards the bottom of the village, past the duck pond, and down the hill past a few cottages on the left hand side of the road. Alongside the school lived the school headmaster and his wife. Tall red bricked walls with the small ivy-leaved toadflax clinging to the mortar, hid the small yard from view and the high windows ensured that no child looked out, and by the same token no one could see in. Two side entrances were marked, BOYS above one doorway and, GIRLS above the other door, then on the wall between the entrances was an engraved stone plaque.

CRANESBURY ELEMENTARY SCHOOL
THIS PLAQUE COMMEMORATES THE OPENING OF THE SCHOOL
IN 1892 BY THE BOARD:
COUNCILLOR GERALD RANSOME,
COUNCILLOR ARNOLD PARSONS
REVEREND MATTHEW BISHOP
MRS LAVINIA ALLSOP
"FERREUS OPUS ERO REMUNEROR"

And that was more or less the extent of the village centre. There was an old village hall down the lane behind the Bank that had been much neglected over the years. It's covered in bindweed and brambles now. Far too costly to do up I expect. The old board school was bought some years ago and turned into a house and the Post Office and general store are struggling to make a living. Years ago poor old Simmons's hardware shop went under and is now converted into a house although the butchers and the bakers still seem to prosper, frequented by a few townies who have plenty of money for 'country fare' and don't seem to bother about their inflated prices. The bank has become an estate agents and the bus only comes once or twice a week. Progress is a wonderful thing. There isn't a car park so cars line the village and cause traffic congestion in the summer when people are making their way to the coast. We haven't got a village bypass so even the large articulated lorries have to negotiate the narrow roads.

If the weather has been particularly fine I have ventured up the lane and sat by the pond, but not recently. And then of course there is the big estate, further up the lane, hidden from view. I suppose that I need to talk of Mote House. But after so many years it is difficult to know where to start. As soon as I think of the first thing to say I find that something else needs to be explained. Perhaps it would be easier to begin when we were just children, Milly, Jack, and Thomas and I, all together. We were inseparable playmates then. We shared everything once upon a time; confidences, games, secrets. Yes, there were many of those. Then we grew up. Things changed.

Jack was my brother. He was born in 1920, and I came two years later. We were very close and yet as different as chalk and cheese. We were both born at home in the rooms above at the Papermakers Arms. Our father Archie Minton was the licenced landlord and, I have to say, very well suited to the job. He was loud, gregarious; good with all the customers, generous, good-looking and well-liked by those who enjoyed a laugh and a joke. In company he excelled, it really brought out the best in him. But when he was with just us and our mother things were different. He lost his sparkle. Times were hard and he had not imagined that he would have to eke out a living that was so precarious. He had a greed for life which had not included long hours in the pub supporting an antagonistic wife and two wilful and demanding children.

He had met and married Ethel, our mother, just a bit after the war, in 1919. War took the wind out of his genial sails. During his spell in the army he had risen to the rank of Sergeant when fighting in France with the Kentish Rifles. The shock of those years had made him hunger for some home comforts and then he met pretty, slender, Ethel on coming home. He was at once smitten by her demur, alluring, coquettish attitude, encouraged when she shyly allowed more passionate intimacies on each subsequent date and thought that it had merely masked a natural zest for adventure and fun. He had imagined long romantic nights of passion, which Ethel had seemed to promise. Her furious rejection of his affectionate advances which continued long after the birth of Jack in early 1920 had at first puzzled him, and then frustrated him. He had been careful with her at first, realising that a nursing mother needed time and was bound to be tired. He took his duties as a father seriously providing her with practical support, wanting her to feel cherished and loved, hoping that she would reciprocate his devotion. Attempting to encourage and woo her again he generously presented her with small romantic gifts whilst kindly seeking to reassure her of his love. For well over a year he had resorted to pleading and coaxing her, but all his best efforts failed. Finally his patience snapped and he changed forever.

I never knew that easy loving man that had been Jack's father. The decision to demand his marital rights without her consent finally resulted in another pregnancy and I was born in 1922. It was as if Jack and I had two different fathers. Ethel punished him with interminable bouts of silence and then thinly disguised hatred when he forced himself on her. Her obvious distain of his treatment towards her and his 'needs' drove him from being a modest drinker to drink more heavily which, in turn, made him more dangerous.

By the time that I was five I came to accept the pattern of the day. The final drink, 'one for the road' as the last customer left and the sound of his clumsy step on the stairs as he lumbered upstairs. The bruises, carefully marking areas that the public would not see, served as a reminder to Ethel that he was still the man of the house and that he would have his way with her whether she cared or not.

Having lost all respect for her he sometimes surprised himself in moments of reflection when remembering that she had once been his darling girl who had stolen his heart. And then having thought of those earlier times he cursed the day that he had set his cap at her and ruined his life. He told other women that he had been a stupid fool to believe that the 'frigid bitch' like her could have ever been 'the one'.

Ethel saw, but had fiercely resented, Archie's natural easy love for his son Jack that he had enjoyed in those first few years. Perhaps she too, in her hidden reflections, acknowledged with some faint nod to unbidden guilt, that she had deliberately and perversely changed the man she had married. But stealthily over the years she sought to put a wedge between them, engineering grievances where there were none. Cunningly she overruled his spontaneous, firm but fair, fatherly guidance. Doting on Jack she spoilt him at every opportunity, intimating that his father would not like or approve of certain things. There were actions and decisions that required disguise and secrecy. She drew him into her confidence and slowly, to her utmost satisfaction, the boy rebelled against the man. 'Give me a child until he is seven I will give you the man'. Ethel used the Jesuit mantra as her own. Such a strong weapon that she skilfully wielded.

By the time that Jack was seven he was indeed quite out of control. Arrogant and indifferent to the feelings of others, greedy for all the rewards that life had to offer, outwardly he appeared to emulate the gregarious quick witted nature of his father, but inwardly, hidden, there was a fearful confusion. The natural generosity and open-hearted warmth inherited from his handsome father had been subsumed under Ethel's careful watch. He was a child of many parts which constantly warred against each other.

As much as Ethel spoilt and doted on Jack she resented and ignored me. I was the physical result of her pain and she ensured that I was kept at a distance. I was clothed and fed and sent to school, but she didn't allow sentiment or motherly feelings to cloud her aversion to me. At first I just sensed her hostility and then as my powers grew I began to hear her thoughts and to know of her intentions. Finally I was able to revel in her dismay when her plans were thwarted, but I never allowed her to see my triumph. All that I too kept hidden.

Jack, like so many others, witnessed my sixth sense, but he, like they, dismissively put most things down to sheer coincidence and sibling familiarity and I did nothing to persuade them or him otherwise. It suited my intentions. It kept their minds open for me to read. I played the game sometimes deliberately misunderstanding them when it all became far too clear and apparent to me. I played the fool but made fools of them all.

For most of our childhood Jack and I rubbed along together. He enjoyed the older brother, protectorate role and I went along with the charade. We shared most adventures and when it suited me to help his cause; he was naively appreciative, not suspecting the extent of my involvement. And as we grew up my concealments became expertly honed. I excelled in my deceptions.

I knew of my father's involvement with other women. I saw what they did together. I knew about the assignations. I watched and listened, providing alibis when it suited me, without him being aware that I did so. So many times I would carelessly suggest that I thought that I had heard him say that he had gone to watch a football match, or to have some shoes repaired when I knew that he was meeting Beatrice Latterbridge or Roseanne Parker. With some of them, like the amorous Roseanne, our barmaid, it was just a fling, a flirtation that suited them both but with Beatrice Latterbridge something more developed. Her vulnerability and loneliness had at first seduced him and then consumed him. Ronald, her husband was a difficult man to like; he had an overbearing air. He liked to bend things to his will, being most happy when in the garden, pompously regimenting the flowers, admiring his efforts, regarding the artistry of nature as his own work. At the bank he appeared to work hard but his aspirations began and ended at his desk. His ambition as a young man had been to acquire money. That Beatrice was unfulfilled and lonely was beyond his comprehension. He didn't consider her whilst he was a work and once home when they were together he didn't think to ask how she was or about the pattern of her day. She became used to being invisible. She kept the house neat and tidy, she was on the church cleaning rota, but her life was stagnating and suffocating her. Even then she didn't have the energy to appraise her situation. The exhaustion of an empty life had deadened her thoughts; she was sleep walking her life away. Although a neighbour, living in close proximity, one whom Archie had known for years and seen her going about her business or walking to the church, he had never considered her. In his mind's eye he had thought of her as being aloof and straight-laced despite her youthful trim figure and blond curls. In fact before that particular day he couldn't have vouched that they had had a conversation or that he had ever exchanged more than a cursory routine 'Good morning'. Their worlds revolved around different axis. His constant enjoyment with Roseanne was providing ample satisfaction. He was looking forward to the end of the evening when he would change more than the beer barrels in the dimmed light of the cellar. Ethel had no desire to stay up late and see the bar empty of its regulars.

Papermakers Arms 1927
Archie

Archie squeezed Roseanne's soft rounded buttocks. His fingers gripped her flesh as his groin drove into her. Roseanne's smile widened as she allowed his hands to fasten around her. Deliberately she pushed back into him; feeling him hard against her.

He was impatient for her, now that the shutters had been fastened and the front door locked to ensure their privacy. There was no need now for pretence between them. No romance. No sweet caressing words; just a compelling animal need that arose in them both. She could feel her wetness and his hardness compelling them both down the well-worn cellar steps. Their dance was well rehearsed. He grasped her full breasts, pulling them roughly towards him. Her fluttering stomach contracted into shudders of desire. Her breath came in snatches as he pulled up her grubby blouse and then, exposing her breasts, he took the dark circles between his lips panting heavily as she writhed against him.

"Oh, yes, yes" he wanted more of her as her hardened nipples filled his mouth.

She clung fiercely to him allowing his urgent manhood to penetrate deeper into her, filling her, joining together in juddering thrusts. Wordlessly lost together they surrendered to their own passion. Then it came to them in one explosion of exquisite pleasure. For her it continued in waves of sensual bliss juddering and peaking as it consumed her body. For Archie his mind was numbed, his whole body had fused into her; fire and heat gripping into him, a molten ball burning him. He was lost inside himself; she no longer existed for him. There was just the blinding pounding in his head, and then it was over.

"Bloody hell Archie you were quick!" Roseanne's satisfied smile gave lie to her accusation, as she pulled together her blouse and straightened her skirt.

"Anyone would think there was still a war on!"

He grunted, unwilling to answer her. He watched her dress, aghast that yet again he had played such a shallow part and that had he allowed himself to debase them both. He had already begun to tire of her, of their ritualistic game that had led him on and then emptied him so quickly. She existed for him only in parts; he no longer wanted her as she was. He saw her merely as a vessel. His need of her body and its yielding flesh was real, but her aimless chatter, shallow thoughts and her base needs wearied him now. Once, when it had first begun, he had enjoyed the chase, the frisson of pleasure touching her as he brushed against her whilst she served the customers. The thrill as she had exposed her large voluptuous white breasts from the constraints of her tight undergarments had caught his breath as they had finally consummated their desire. The dark circles around the firm strong nipples had mesmerised him as had her casual consent to their coupling.

Then he couldn't have enough of her. His addiction had driven him on. Each illicit encounter was as a new adventure. He learnt what most excited her, discovering what would bring her to him, just as a ripening flower helplessly opened to the probing bee. At the beginning he had wanted to possess her, to become a voyeur of her florid secrets.

But all that had happened; the routine game of physical adventure had been played out too many times. Her small mind wearied him. They were compatible only in the act itself, and for the rest of the time she was nothing to him. He couldn't recall one conversation, one moment of meaningful connection. He was disgusted of himself and of what he had become. And at times of quiet reflection his guilt spilled over when he considered how he betrayed the image of the man he had wanted to be. He

20

could then appreciate his baseness towards Roseanne. He had taken advantage of her simple nature. He knew that once he had held himself to be superior to some of the farm lads who displayed such loutish behaviour, but when he judged himself against them, he now found himself wanting.

∞

Roseanne was perplexed as she pulled on her coat and started on her way home. During the walk she began to feel aggrieved. Archie was too easy to take her these days, too quick to take her and then let her go. He never spoke to her as he had done in the past. He used to say how beautiful she was and that she was his honey bee, his queen, but now he couldn't get his trousers down and get it done quick enough. He still performed well but he had grown apart from her. He didn't joke to her as he had done no tender intimacies to show how important she was to him. Perhaps she had been too willing. She should have made him work harder.

She made up her mind as she neared the house, Archie would have to change. She was resolved. No more shenanigans unless he mended his ways. Roseanne, you have made yourself too easy my girl, he's had it too easy for far too long. And if he didn't play ball then his missis could be used as bait. And he's had it all for free; the realisation of her situation, her lowly status horrified her. Not one penny more had he ever given her! It was about time he offered something in return for services rendered. He had treated her as some kind of slave, free for his taking, whenever he fancied it. Things would be different from now on. She would see to it tomorrow first thing.

∞

21

Archie looked around the deserted bar. Was this the sum of his life? Was this all life had to offer him? A quick fumble with a grubby barmaid? An illicit romp which gave him nothing but the moment of relief and then the gnawing numbness of their empty coupling? She had probably had all the men around the area and then more. He nursed his resentment, as it grew inside him. A frigid wife and a bawdy barmaid to service at will. When did it all go so badly wrong? Where was his pride, his fulfilment in life? When did his hopes and dreams die? He had been cheated. Robbed of home comforts by his shrew of a wife and then shamefully debasing an ignorant barmaid. He had had enough of it. His self-pity gnawed at him, the fingers of doubt curled around his heart, and he found that he had to gasp for breath.

My God this life is draining me away! He was astounded and horrified by the fear that his life could be so summed up in such a brutal fashion. It had reduced him to insignificance. He had a failing business with more debts accumulating every year, a son who was becoming a mummy's boy rather than a real son to him, a daughter who appeared so remote: in her own world, and then there was their mother, his wife. A wife in name only. She was to blame for his ills. Had she been a loving woman he could have made a success of it all. She was the cruel deception that made his life a caricature. Reaching out across the bar he grasped the nearest bottle from the shelf. Someone would have to pay for his misery. Tipping the bottle towards his lips he drank quickly; the fiery liquid feeding his wrath and resentment.

When he looked at the bottle again he noticed with some incoherent surprise that the contents had been consumed; it was empty. In anger he banged the bottle on the bar and staggered to his feet. Upstairs Ethel heard his heavy unsure footsteps as he lurched across the landing. Her top lip turned down in disapproval. As usual he would be too drunk to find even the door handle, let alone his bed. She bristled in indignation and disgust. Let him fall over and lie where he fell. She went to turn over to sleep and then in fear realised that his hand was on the door. He lumbered into the room. She sat up aghast.

"You drunken fool!"

Archie saw her defiant dull eyes, then her face turning away from him in disgust. A bolt of searing blackness numbed his brain.

"You vicious woman. You scheming, bloody woman!" he sneered as he managed to grab the brass bed rail.

"Think yourself so bloody high and mighty, you blood sucking cow." He growled as he pulled at the covers to bring himself closer to her, and then as she attempted to shrink from him he caught her hair in his hand and drawing back his hand he let the full force of his arm arch across the air and thud into her face. The blow knocked her back into the pillow and the bright red blood flew across the bedclothes

"I'll bloody teach you to respect me!" Archie lost all sense of time and reason. Only I heard the sounds of his anger, but not once did I hear mother cry out. She, like Archie was insensible to the outside world. His first blow had rendered her unconscious. She did not witness the first ferocity of his attack. Her unresisting body lay defenceless before the onslaught. And this time she did not have to shrink from her neighbours to hide the bruises on the following morning. It had gone too far for that.

∞

And it was me at the tender age of five years who went into the still silent room and saw the utter confusion that he had created. Sitting on the floor beside the bed he was caught in the trailing bedclothes that tangled around him. I didn't need to look at him to know that he was crying inside. He didn't hear me come in but I could hear him, I could hear his voice inside my head.

I can't go on like this, it has to end. I can't be here. What have I done?

He longed for escape but first I wanted to catch him and imprison him to make him pay. I could hear his self-pity and then his guilt and fear and then his crashing sense of sadness and loss. But then I too felt his sadness stealing over me.

Mother was still breathing. The blood still trickled from her nose. One eye brow was mottled blue. A makeup artist had overdone her palette. Her breath came in laboured bubbled gasps from swollen lips.

Only the bed in disarray and the crumpled rug beneath Dad gave sign of the assault, the rest of the room had stayed neat and untouched. A whirlwind; the centre of the storm, had been contained in just one place. Against the back wall stood their swirled walnut veneered wardrobe with its one worn door knob and door that always refused to close properly, allowing the contents to peep out. The badly scratched pine dresser still held the delicate leafy etched water jug carefully placed upon a lace doily. Even the dressing table with its angles at odds to the slope of the floor still displayed mother's pots of cream and powder. Her pink glass set of containers were neatly set to one side, and the matching rectangular glass plate held her hair pins and her single string of faux pearls. Over the end brass bedstead with its bulbous knobs her skirt and jumper still managed to hang from the rail but the tangled underclothes had slipped to the floor.

Perhaps there was one person whom he could summon; just one co-conspirator who could perhaps be prevailed upon to cover his tracks.

"Daddy?" I had pulled at his hand trying to shake him back into the world.

"Daddy!"

He looked at me, bewildered, as if shocked that I was at his side. He shook himself and gasping the side of the bed pulled himself to his feet. He looked down at Ethel and his breath caught in a deep sigh of horror. I listened to his thoughts,

*I've been and done it for good this time, my God what have I
done?*

He turned to me his hands held in front of him as if to surrender
to his offence.

"Daddy?" I was unsure of holding my face together; my lips felt
wobbly, his fear had drawn itself to me and tightened against my
chest. I could feel my pulse jumping and thudding at my throat.
His panic and confusion gripped me in a tight vice. I was being
overtaken, trapped in his web of desperation and torment.

Then a light of recognition appeared in his eyes, he saw me in my
nightdress, barefoot on the cold wooden floor.

His self-pity gave way to the horror, suddenly realising that I
knew of his night's work.

He stretched out and gasped my arm as if to interrogate me, his
dank breath in my face. I squirmed away from his hold. I could
not let him know of my power, my gift. There could be no
exposure of that. He was just too close at that moment, too
aware; I needed a diversion, some semblance of
misunderstanding.

"I can't sleep. I feel sick, is mummy sick too?"

I gave him time to collect his thoughts, letting him believe that
my presence was a result of the confusion; of my childish panic
at being unwell.

And then he could see a way out. Finally, yes, his wife was
unwell, had been unwell too. Mother and child both sick. She
needed help.

"Did she fall over and been sick?"

He accepted my statement. *Yes there had been a terrible
accident. She had tripped against the bedside cabinet trying to
get up too quickly as she was feeling sick. Gripping the cabinet....
causing it to fall against her. Yes it had happened that way.
Knocked herself unconscious in the process. And then he had
found her like that. Even the child had seen the rug; she had
known that Ethel had felt sick. Just an accident. Hadn't she just*

25

said so? That's how it had happened. Anyone could ask the child. She knew the truth. He rehearsed the version until it sounded right.

"Go back to bed now; mummy's had a bad fall. She'll be alright though. Right as rain in the morning. Don't you fret, I'll see to her. I'll come presently. Off you go now."

I could feel his release, his heart began to slow. I was dismissed from the awful scene.

Archie believed I knew little, that thankfully I had not seen what there had been to see; to bear witness to his awful brutality. But I had. And I knew all the truth and I had placed the story in his head and he readily accepted it as his own, congratulating himself for a quick thinking solution. So be it, there was an end to it, and I had done what needed to be done for now.

As for Archie, he had no need of other voyeurs, coming in to their bedroom, seeing the results of his dirty work, being exposed in their eyes. There was enough complication already. The story needed to be straight and Ethel cleaned up. He prayed that there was no internal bleeding, no bones broken. *How hard did I go at her?* She had always recovered before; strong as old boots despite the look of her. He would tend to it. He would straighten things up, sort things out. Good old Archie. Always ready in a crisis. Good old dependable Archie.

Why then had he not called a doctor to her? He pondered on a satisfactory reply. Meeting enquiries with humour could defuse them, why then, she was adamant that he didn't. Hadn't she said that she was fine? Insisted it was just a stupid accident? Just a nice shiner where she had knocked herself on the cabinet? And of course she always bruised easily. And then, despite him trying to argue with her, hadn't Ethel said to him *'anyone looking at me would think that I had been beaten up!'* Yes that was the way to go, meet the thing head on. But now there was a night's work to be finished before the daylight shed its beam on him.

26

Papermakers Arms 1927
Roseanne

That was the night that changed so many things. When Roseanne went back the next day there was a stillness about the place, as if something or someone had died. Dirty glasses were still on the bar, an empty whisky bottle had rolled onto the floor and smashed, and door to the upstairs that was usually half ajar was closed.

Roseanne stood with one hand on her hip uncertain, unusually hesitant, and determined not to break her resolve.

If the old devil thinks I'm doing all this on my own he can think again! She sighed and bent over to retrieve the pieces of broken glass, her own actions defying her will.

Drunk as usual and good old Roseanne will tidy up the mess. The whole family are a piece of work. There's Archie who is nice as pie one minute and then like the very devil when he thinks no one can see what he's up to. Then that skinny dried up scrag-end of a wife of his who thinks that the world owes her a living. No wonder he's desperate for me. Can't get enough, like a man thirsting for water in the desert he is. And then, once he's taken advantage, once he's had his fill it's, 'bugger off home now Roseanne'!

Well this time things are going to change. And he thinks I'm so stupid that I don't see what he's up to with her upstairs. Too handy with his fists when there's a drink inside him and her pretending that she knocked her head against the door, an accident, my arse. Well she must be a very unfortunate kind of person then. As soon as one eye opens another one closes. And what does she really think that the folk in the village think! They're not as daft as she thinks they are.

I should have taken up that job with the Parsons. Get out of this trade, with more money, and a deal more respect than here, a nice little earner and no late nights. They say that he does a lovely spread every Christmas up at Mote House, and it's for all the employees, no expense spared. There's real peaches that grow in the conservatory, and oranges and lemons. They put up some tables in the kitchens and it's laden with all kinds of expensive food from the city. Our Walter's mate Arthur brings some of it down from Billingsgate, and he said that it's all good quality for the family and those who work there. No difference at all.

He plays this huge grand piano better than a professional up at the Palais and she has lovely dresses from France. She goes to all the exhibitions and art galleries and thinks nothing of spending a small fortune on paintings for the house. Then there's the garden, full of colour, winter, spring or summer. It's Henry Forrester their head gardener who lives in the Garden Cottage, with his five kids who does it all, well then he has four men under him just to do the lawns and what not.

To think that I didn't go up and see about the job because Archie said that he needed me. Yes I'll say he needed me, for a quick fumble and no mistake. And me, too loyal and soft hearted to say no. I've got others who have been begging me for a chance, but I've not let them have a go for ages now. I won't say that Archie hasn't been good in the past. He's got a real way with him when he wants to turn on the charm and oh my, he can make your insides turn inside out and no mistake, the handsome devil that he is. But it's time to call it a day.

Then those kids of his. There's young Jack. Well he was given the right name, a real little thieving jackdaw, can't resist shiny things like those birds. I can't say that I've ever caught him at it but things do go missing when he's been around and never do seem to turn up. Mind, a spit of his father, a real chip off the old block, he's got the same kind of charm. Those lovely eyes of his would melt a block of ice. He's going to break hearts one day. But the daughter, well, she is a queer one. Not a looker for sure that one.

I don't know what it is about her. I can't seem to put my finger on it. My gran used to call it being fey. Such a little slip of a thing and yet her eyes go right into you. You feel as if as you've been pulled through a mangle. She says something just when you had thought of it. I think she must spend a lot of time up to no good, listening at keyholes and then finding out things that she shouldn't know. It's a wonder that Archie and I have got away with it for so long with Miss Nosey Parker around. Mind she's so secretive she probably wouldn't say boo to a goose anyway or let on what she saw. I've never trusted her. It's not natural for a child to know so much at her age when she should be playing with her dollies. 'Been born before' my gran used to say, lot of nonsense still very strange. Rosie, short for Rosemary, now is that for remembrance I can't think?

Roseanne by force of habit moved around the bar putting chairs on tables still covered by dark circles and overflowing ashtrays. She drew back the stiff wooden shutters and the morning sun rays caught the fine dust as it moved languidly around her exposing the brown stains on the worn velvet benches in each alcove. A single strand of cobweb disturbed by her movements in front of her wafted at her cheek and she caught it with the back of her hand, irritated by its intrusion, and to find that she had unthinkingly fallen back into her old ways.

She stopped, staring without seeing; facing the small heavy framed dark shadowy prints that had once depicted vibrant hunting scenes. Men in red jackets astride large ill-proportioned horses surrounded by a mêlée of impatient brown and white dogs, but that were now hidden behind cloudy filmed thin glass. On the opposite wall were similar frames but these prints were of romantic pastoral scenes showing sturdy women and small children in their jackets and bonnets, grappling the thick trailing twisted ropes heavy with their hop blooms in the foreground, with picturesque white oast houses set against blue skies behind them.

Seeing a small child's jacket hanging at the door leading to the back room caused her to turn away and still in her unbidden reverie she dreamily picked up where she left off, picking up a stool and setting it down tidily against the wall

Still those kids, they are all thick as thieves, with that Beatrice's daughter Millie and Fulwood, the station master's lad, Thomas. Now Thomas, I will say that he's a nice lad, a real little diamond. I've got a lot of time for that little lad. A real little sweetheart, and clever too, but in a nice way. He's just quick on the uptake, always willing to help. Run errands and such like. They say at the school that he works hard, keeps his head down but not showy. He will go far or there's no justice in this world. Mind where he got his brains from is a mystery. His father is not exactly a shining light. A bit too pompous for my liking, perhaps it's a bit of shyness to be fair, still in a grown man you expect them to have grown out of it by then. I don't much care for Alice either she can be a bit standoffish. Probably thinks that being a station masters' wife makes her something special.

The door banged open. Archie stood before her, staring as if he had seen a ghost. She wondered at his surprise, and found herself to be irritated by his vacant expression.

"Well who did you expect to see at this time of the day, the Queen of Sheba?" Her lips closed, and she waited, the curtain at the door wafted with the change of air flow. Stale beer and acrid old pipe smoke accompanied the fluttering curtain's dance.

"You're lucky that I'm here at all after everything last night". Her accusing tone drew tight fingers across his forehead. He could feel the pounding of his heart pulsating in his ears, a loud roaring, waves crashed in his head as his hand went out to steady himself, reaching across to the sticky surface of the bar.

Ethel lay still above them. Her face bloated and luridly discoloured. *After last night? What did she know? How can she have known?* He needed time to think. His brow felt damp, he breathed in deeply.

"Now, now, my lovely Rose, Roseanne, light of my life, can't a fella have a lie in without getting blasted out first thing in the morning?"

His light bantering tone and easy smile took away her resolve. Her rehearsed reproach began to fade. She attempted to gather her thoughts before his disarming manner unnerved her. She hated confrontation, afraid that she would not have the right words to do her fighting for her.

"If I wanted a shrew I could climb up these stairs and find one, but how could I go when there is a such a magnificent woman standing here before me?"

Roseanne smiled in spite of herself. It was true the comparison was obvious. She held a finger to her lips.

"Shh, now don't you start using your weasel words on me and trying to get into my good books. Once you've had your wicked way you just......"

But he had circled her waist, his fingers pulled her towards him and he breathed against her throat.

"You don't know how beautiful you are. I can never get enough of you woman. Why would I want to let you go?" His hands moved lightly over her blouse and then holding her against him he billowed up her skirts and began to caress up towards the softest part of her warm smooth thigh.

"No you don't Archie Minton it is ten o'clock in the morning. Now then, stop!" She wriggled away from him.

You've got work to do, and I've come to tell you that I've had enough of all this funny business between us.... and I'm going for another job!"

Her announcement, so unexpected, caused him to step back against the bar. His hands fell away from her.

Thank god, he thought. That's it! She knows nothing of last night. And she will never know that I wanted this to end, that I have had enough. My deception can be over, it is finished. I am free of her.
He caught her hand and held it in his.

31

"Roseanne, now, now. Don't be so hasty my dear. If you want it to be over so be it. I don't know why you've come to this. I blame myself. I've expected too much of you. But surely we can be old mates still, after everything that we have been to each other?
Roseanne frowned, shaking her head slowly from side to side in her confusion.
"Damned if I know what has happened to make you think this way? If there's another chap I won't stand in his way. But surely we can still work together Roseanne we make a good team you and I."
He heard his own protestations, almost proud of his presence of mind, as his head continued to pound a warning drum of fear. *She does not, must not know how I feel or what has happened, please god.* He prayed for his sanity to return.
Rosanne hesitated again. This was not the way things should have gone.
"No I haven't, no it's not that! Archie you are twisting things. You well know what I meant to say.....how I feel. It's not me wanting to end things; it's you...... you that have used me Archie. I've been too soft".
"You don't want to end us? I'm confused!" He smiled as if soothing a disgruntled child.
"No! Yes! I do want this to be over." Roseanne caught her breath, trying to find the words
" It's you..... you haven't.... you don't care for me like you should have, and that..... that makes me feel like I'm nothing. You never say you love me, care for me, not properly".
She put up her hand to silence his reply.
"No Archie, I'm having my say once and for all. I've got the offer of another job and I'm going to take it."
"A job, where?"
"Well, I could have a job if I wanted it. My cousin said he thinks that there's a job going at the Parsons place, that they will be offering a good position."

32

"A position, as …..?"

"Well I'm not exactly sure yet." She was irritated. She had been too hasty. He had caught her out; just when she had wanted time before announcing that she could improve herself, distancing herself, making him realise just what he was missing, and her making a life without him.

"I see. " Archie spoke slowly, "so at the moment you find yourself between jobs?" He showed his concern at her predicament.

She nodded. She felt deflated, wanting all this to end as she had first imagined. She should have lorded it over him. Not like this. There was no sense of satisfaction.

"Look. Well why not stay on here, no strings attached until something comes up? Perhaps a little improvement in wages would help? When things pick up a bit here? And I wouldn't want to hold you to anything against your will. It is a loss that I will have to bear. You know that I could never replace you, but….."

A rueful smile faintly lit his face and he spread his hands out, his soft palms upturned, as if desperate to placate her.

His generosity after her rejection of him as her lover overwhelmed her. He was taking it very well and more money too, this was unexpected. She tried to disguise her surprise.

"Well for the time being, yes. But I expect to see more than a bob or two by the end of the week Archie, and it's only as soon as I hear about the position at the Parsons then I'll be off."

"Absolutely my dear, of course."

Archie moved along the bar and carefully began to clear away the sharp fragments of broken glass.

Looking down from their bedroom Beatrice watched as Ronald moved between the herbaceous beds. His creamy straw boater sat proud on his head exposing a small thin pink neck. *He's caught the sun, and that will be sore tonight*, she thought. He was attempting to tie up tightly the blue delphiniums that had been caught by the wind, too heavy with their bright blooms to stay upright unaided. He will need more string, she observed. Why did he never take care to stake them up first with proper stakes, before they gained too much height? Every year it was the same. Delicate heads twisted and snapped.

His awkward ineffectual movements irritated her. His fussy, careless invasion of the untamed garden frustrated her.

I wish, I wish for this life to end. I am trapped by this foolish man, with his little bank clerk job at the little stuffy bank in this little dreary village. I am twenty two years old and feel fifty two. Where is my life going? Where will it end? I shall become old and crabby, shrivelled up alone and unwanted. To be free of it all, to go away. I need to ask mother if she and father are thinking of another Italian trip this autumn.

Was it only four years since she and Ronald had married? It seemed a lifetime away. Then she couldn't wait for him to return and ask for her hand in marriage. He looked so elegant and romantic in uniform, tall and lean. She had only met him at the ball that previous year and knew that he was The One. How hopelessly wrong she had been. He had come up to Mote House with his friend Peter Harrington who was an old family friend of the Latterbridges and her own parents. They were going to join up for drinks and Bridge with her mother and father that evening but Ronald had said how hopeless he was at cards and so she had taken him for a tour of their house and gardens instead, after he had had enjoyed a whisky and soda.

What a perfect fool she had been. A silly naïve seventeen year old who had never even been kissed before Ronald came on the scene. He said how much he loved poetry, what inspired him to write, and then had proceeded to quote large chunks of his verse to her. Totally obtuse and unintelligible, and some vaguely familiar but she had smiled and murmured at the correct places it seems, and so he was able to proclaim that he had been captivated both by her beauty and her ability to appreciate his verse.

And now she was here at Ivy Leaf Cottage, given to them by her parents as a wedding present, and Ronald established in the bank, again a position found for him by mother and father. His education and ability to quote his awkward parodies of Tennyson appeared not to have been sufficient for him to have found gainful employment on his own.

And at first she had been happy to play the housewife and an adoring wife. Her mother had given her every opportunity to be well versed in running a household and she had revelled in her ability to run a household, budget the accounts, produce pretty meals and dress each room. But much as Ronald was able to be stimulated by romantic verse, his ability to be excited by her fell disappointingly short. And as she had no way of knowing how their love making should be conducted she grew increasingly frustrated by the sense of emptiness. It was as if he was physically repelled by her, it being all over in an instant, as if he had performed a mere duty rather than to cherish her. There were no sweet words of endearment or of love. He gave more thought and attention to the flowers, which she viewed from the window, than to her.

Her parents had said that she had been far too young to embark on a marriage but she closed her ears to their advice to think and wait. And Ronald was already thirty two, ten years between them. There had been many who had not come back from the war and she had been concerned that the short supply of eligible men would deny her a chance of romance and marriage. Some of her old school friends had lost suitors and she had seen the fear in their eyes too. She had been frightened that her chance would disappear and so she brushed all her niggling concerns to one side. And she had been proved to be so wrong.

What she thought had been dreamy romance was merely his thoughtless ineffectual nature, his inability to make decisions, or deal with the real world. He wasn't artistic or talented, clever or caring. He bullied people. Increasingly she saw his fussiness. *Look at him now, still tangled with the flowers, he is just creating more mayhem than tidiness.* She chewed her lip.

She leaned further from the window watching his slow progress leaving a trail of broken stems in his wake. His stuffy acceptance of their world was just a mirage, it served to cover his failings, his inadequacies from others. But she knew, and oh the realisation had been grim.

Where would we have been without mother and father's help? She shuddered to think. Their kindness and love for her had for once clouded their judgement and worked against her. They had wanted her to be happy and as their only child they had invested all their hopes and dreams in her, although early on her father had had the sense to realise that Ronald could not provide for her.

Ronald's trust fund inheritance from the old Lady Faversham had been fast running through his fingers. She should have realised from the start, looked at the facts.

His mother, Sylvia, drifted from one crisis to another, dismissive, and totally unpredictable. Roland, his father, still believed that recognition and success was just one painting away. In the studio his canvases littered the walls collecting dust much as the rest of their house was doing. Their two Afghan hounds came and went as they pleased, uncontrolled and now uncontrollable. She had been aghast when she first visited the house. Once fine chairs, shabby elegant French furniture all covered in dog hairs.

Exquisite Persian rugs threadbare and dirty and everywhere a pervading smell of grubbiness and wet dogs.

She had been given tea in unwashed, chipped gold- rimmed china, the stains quite apparent once she had consumed the contents. Sylvia made no attempt to put her at her ease or to initiate conversation. Her attention wavered, showing that she felt Beatrice to be insignificant and unworthy of her darling Ronald. Even the ash which she casually flicked from her long cigarette holder seemed to hold her in contempt.

Good heavens perhaps that was why she had fought to have him! Because he was coveted by his mother! The irony of it all! Her prize was so unworthy. She had thrown away any chance of real happiness.

And then 1920 had come and gone and her heart had been broken. Ronald would not speak of it. And all she had to remind her of him were the little garments that she could not part with. Tucked in the chest of drawers in what was to have been the nursery. And then there was his little headstone, a small simply inscribed stone at the far end of the churchyard behind St Ethelbert's at the top of the hill. Only five months old and yet nothing could be done. He slipped away from her and it was if he had never been in the world. Her memory of him faded each year until she could hardly remember his face or form. A bit more of him was lost to her with each passing year but the stone in her heart grew heavier. Time, which is said to heal, was doing a lamentable job.

And what to do with herself? How to take up the monotonous hours of each day? She was educated, skilful and business-like. She could arrange flowers, organise events, follow politics, was aware of world events, and could manage people but she could not marshal her emotions or subdue her own despair. The church relied on her to assist with the rotas, the carol singing, the harvest festival and the Easter parade of floats. The village looked to her to help organise the stalls for the fetes. She could galvanise the reluctant, and steer *the* inspired, but her heart was heavy as the days grew longer.

She moved to look at her reflection in the large oak framed mirror in her own bedroom. Yes, her own room, not to be shared by the warmth of her husband's frame unless the appointed hour had come. How had it come to this? Was there something in her that was not attractive to men? She was aware of the winks and whistles that followed other women. Was she too earnest or too serious? Or was it that her grief was still too apparent that it frightened people from her? They had no adequate words of comfort and so did not wish to intrude.

The face in the mirror looked back at her. A face framed by a thick head of burnished gold hair, catching the rays of the sun as she turned from side to side.

The eyes widened and studied themselves. Clear grey eyes, nothing startling there. A mouth, whose lips had been recently rouged, a full bottom lip but both lips set in a serious line. Her top lip curved to smile and lighten the face; she pushed her hair away from her forehead. Smooth, no lines to be seen yet. She tested her brow with her fingers, drawing them across it, it felt cool to her touch; a strong brow still clear. Then she saw a long elegant neck and again her fingers ran down and stroked her throat. She breathed in deeply. Yes she held herself well.

She stepped away from the mirror to study her figure. But was she pretty? Did the sum of all her parts constitute an attractive woman? What made men go weak at the knees? She had rounded breasts still firm and quite full, perhaps a little smaller these days. Her waist was narrow and so were her hips, and her limbs were fairly long. She stood five foot eight inches in her stockings. Was she getting too thin?

She leaned closer to see her cheeks. They were quite sharp, two hollows had developed, when had that happened?

Suddenly she moved away from the mirror and back to the window. Ronald was now still wrestling with some hollyhocks that had already flowered.

She knew what would save her. She wanted another child before it was too late. He could not just appear now and then as a distant figure. It had to be now, and then again, until she could feel the stirrings of a child within her.

She called out to him, her voice startled his revelry.

"Ronald we need to talk. I want to speak to you."

∞

He looked up at the window, shading his eyes from the sun, uncertain as to whether he had heard her call out to him or not. Then deciding that he had imagined her voice he turned back to his task. Really the garden looked at its best now; it didn't really need much attention. He had worked hard this year on the beds. Earlier in the spring he had discussed the planting with Henry Forrester who had in turn supervised one of his men from Mote House and together they had produced a good show this year. He was pleased with the effect, but then he had always had such a good eye for detail. Some good colours blended well together. Cornflowers in front and the meconopsis poppies with the delphiniums and hollyhock behind made a nice arrangement. Thinking about it, it was probably an artistic talent that he had inherited from his father. These gifts often run in families. He could always see the larger picture, could visualise the end result which many folk were unable to do. Of course Forrester had to be guided by him initially, to see the vision first, and to be fair; the man had more or less pulled it off.

He had tried to describe the different floral scenes that he wished to create and had wanted far more sweet peas and a large buddleia or two, but Forrester had said that there wasn't room for that size bush which was a load of codswallop. Still, you sometimes have to give workers and tradesmen a bit of a free reign. And of course the trick was knowing when to reign them in, which fortunately he was able to do. Forrester had gone off muttering but then that was nothing new. Arnold Parsons gave his men way too much leeway, and then they found it difficult to obey orders. They forgot who was master and that set a dangerous precedence. It unsettled the natural order of things. But then Parsons hadn't had his experience in taking command of men. Thankfully his experience of war had given him a deeper understanding of how men like Forrester ticked; invaluable at the bank too.

"Damn it!" Ronald stepped back suddenly; the hollyhock that refused to bend to his will snapped off and unbalanced him.

"Didn't you hear me call?" Beatrice stood behind him.

He was surprised by her tone, indeed quite unsettled by it. She had appeared from nowhere and now was interrupting his work. He felt caught out, discarding the damaged hollyhock stem on the pathway.

"Can't you see that I am busy?" His indignation at both the wilful plant and her unnecessary interruption caused his voice to sound plaintive.

"Blasted Forrester planted these further back than I wanted and now they have gone over."

Beatrice looked at the trampled cornflowers, the flattened flowerbeds and the delphiniums that had been caught too tightly together.

"I called you and I know you heard me but you didn't answer. I said we need to talk." Her tone was flat and she stared at his moist pink face, his dark hair lank under the brim of his damp hat and her eyes narrowed.

"Well can't it wait, is it that important? You can see that I am in the middle of something here." He attempted to gain control, to demonstrate the importance of his work.

"I need to talk to you Ronald." She ignored his dismissive tone and looked at him again, hugging her arms to her chest.

"You are just making a mess of it all Ronald."

He gaped at her, his mouth dropped. She saw beads of sweat slowly streaking their way down his cheeks, dripping from his fine nose. His carefully laundered shirt was covered in spots of dust.

Beatrice turned and walked back to the house, and the herbaceous borders that Ronald had not yet worked upon swayed in an easy profusion of delightful riotous colour.

Her kitchen was cool and suddenly dark after the light and warmth of the garden. She sat down heavily at the large beech table. Her gleaming copper pots and pans hung suspended from iron hooks on the walls. As she waited for her heart to return to its normal rhythm she surveyed her domain. The immaculate surfaces were devoid of clutter, the cream cupboards were tidy, the pantry was stocked with her carefully labelled preserves and pickling jars. There was nothing that needed to be dusted, nothing to be tidied away. No silver even requiring a polish. It was as if no one lived here. It was an empty museum, too precious, a house waiting for life, for the joy of laughter, for some spontaneity. Well she would set it right.

She could remember when they had first come to Ivy Cottage. Such an exciting time! Suddenly she was in charge of her own house and could choose how things should be. Well-proportioned rooms were each set with a nice fireplace surrounded with decorated glazed tiles. The porch entrance to the hallway had a sturdy timber support on which small white clematis now trailed, mingling with a yellow climbing rose. A tall iron umbrella stand fashioned into a heron held two black tightly furled umbrellas. The kitchen overlooked the gate and the herbaceous pathway leading to the front door.

When they first had the house she and mother had gone up to Heals and Son's in London and had decided upon the table and set of chairs for the dining room to be sent down. The drapes had been made up locally after she and mother had selected the fabric from Paris. Ronald had chosen expensive sets of handsome books with matching gold embellished leather bindings for the large glass fronted bookcase.

Father had sent up some men to hang wallpaper in the two bedrooms and then set their furniture in place. Ronald's father Roland had generously given them a large unsold canvas as a wedding present. The subject was a dainty shepherdess with her swarthy swain accompanied by a small flock of very white sheep. It had taken some time for Ronald to decide on where to place the work of art which her own father had then arranged to be framed for them.

Beatrice moved over to the range and filled the kettle ready for tea. As she turned to put the cups and saucers upon the tray on the table Ronald appeared at the doorway. He looked at her sharply when she appeared not to notice his entrance and had not stopped setting the tray with plates and a sugar bowl.

"Well, what is *so* important that I need to be called away from the garden so suddenly?" There was a faint sneer to his pedantic tone that caused Beatrice to wince. She placed the milk jug beside the teapot.

"I merely asked to speak to you Ronald. It has been some time since we …. since I…. have had the opportunity to discuss things with you." She spoke slowly as if listening to her own voice. "I did not wish to disturb you but…." she looked up at him and watched as his nostrils dilated, his half-closed eyes not meeting hers. She shrugged helplessly.

"Sit down Ronald and have some tea."

"Not now Beatrice, I need to have a wash and get changed." Irritated he threw down his hat onto the chair and disappeared into the hallway. She heard the creak of the stairs as he made his way to the bathroom. His hat had missed the chair and retrieving it from the tiled floor she set it on the table. She did not move to pour her own tea but sat as if mesmerised by the hat as it danced in and out of focus.

A lump had settled in her throat, and she suddenly felt very warm. Slumping forward she cradled her forehead in her hands. *I am almost at the end,* she thought. *I almost hate him.* She flicked way the hat and it scudded across the floor towards the sink. Is there any way back from this? How can we have a child together when we are so far apart? He can barely talk to me these days. We are almost strangers. I no longer recognise this man. We do not talk or discuss, we do not laugh together, we do not share our thoughts, our secrets, our desires, and the longer we spend together the further we are apart. And in losing him I am losing myself too. I cook, I clean, I arrange the flowers in church, then we sit together in the evening when he reads and I sit and sew. We are like two old shrivelled people at the end of their lives. When did we last go for a walk, go up to London, or visit a friend? And what friends have we here? I have old school friends that I see from time to time but they have their own lives, their children and their families to consider. Ronald goes to work each day but I know nothing of his work, his colleagues or what they say. If I ask him he always says, 'not much, or nothing to interest you'. As if he would know what would interest me! And when I tell him about my day he nods and nods and then asks nothing, as if a necessary duty has been performed, that I am not worthy of attention.

Oh, when I think of him when I first saw him. He hardly paid me any attention the first time he saw me. He was so striking. Tall, pale blue eyes, slightly lidded, which gave him a mysterious look, and a fine long Roman nose inherited from his mother and her pale skin, sharp cheek bones and dark hair. I was just seventeen then. He had come home on leave that first time. And then the next evening when father was discussing business and his plans to expand, Ronald asked me to step outside afterwards so that we could get some air. He asked me to be his guide around the grounds that he wished to explore. And two weeks later he told me that he had fallen madly in love with me and couldn't go back without a promise of my commitment to him. He announced that he would ask father for my hand in marriage if he managed to survive until the end of the awful show over in France. By then I was so in awe of him. He was my hero. I wrote every day and he to me. I read and re-read his long flowery poetic letters, proclaiming undying love, and then was caught up with arguments with father and mother who kept insisting that I had not had time to know him properly.

But eventually my tears wore them down. However father would not agree to anything until he had found out what income Ronald had and how he intended to keep me. When Roland announced his substantial inheritance from his maternal grandmother, father was reassured and gave his consent. It was only after the wedding that it became clear the inheritance had dwindled somewhat between the time that Ronald had received the fortune and the few years before our marriage.

There was a furious row between father and Ronald. Father claimed that he had been duped and poor mother was distraught. Ronald refused to discuss the situation with me unless I could act as a loyal and supportive wife. Stupidly I thought that Ronald had my best interests at heart. That there had been a terrible misunderstanding and that matters had been taken out of Ronald's hands. It was just a matter of a legal dispute; a family tangle that Ronald was trying to resolve. He said that he had had to support his parents, and that some investments had been badly advised. He had tried to hold on to shares hoping that the market would pick up, but it hadn't happened. He had been unfairly judged by my father and called a liar which was blatantly unforgiveable. I believed him. Yes, I admit that I wanted to believe him, but this caused such a rift between my parents and Ronald. In the end I had to choose a side and I chose Ronald.

Ronald had already agreed to purchase Ivy Leaf Cottage, indeed had signed a contract before father realised that there were no funds to cover the purchase. Father stepped in and announced that he had always intended to buy the house as a wedding present. I think that he felt the shame of it all. He was mortified by the whole affair, having never reneged on a business transaction.

We had two years of it all, furious rows followed by half-hearted reconciliations. By then I was heavily pregnant with our son. He was born in the autumn of 1920 but never lived to see the spring. At first the doctor said that it was just a chest cold and then as he failed to thrive after Christmas and began to lose weight, father called in a senior man. He told us that his lungs had been weakened and that the infection had spread affecting the tissues surrounding them. It was too far gone and he died of pleurisy that February just as the snowdrops bloomed. I put a small bunch of them on his grave; they were as white and delicate as his cheeks had been.

Perhaps Roland's way of dealing with it was to close up, but I needed to share my grief and he wouldn't let me. So, yes, I do hold him accountable for my despair and yes, I do hold a grudge against him. I cannot forgive his coldness towards me. As if I failed to make his child, our child, thrive. I took on the blame and now I also cannot forgive myself. What a tangled web we weave!

A thump from upstairs roused her from her revelry. She heard him moving above the kitchen in his bedroom banging cupboards and closing drawers.

"Why is nothing where I left it!" he shouted down to her.

"What are you trying to find?"

"My grey flannels that I had on yesterday."

"They are hanging up in your wardrobe."

"Well I left them on the chair."

"That's why they are now in the wardrobe."

45

She heard the door of the wardrobe opening and then closing with a whack.

Good grief he will have it off its hinges. She picked up the teapot and emptied the contents into a basin. Filling the kettle once more she returned to the table to sit and wait for him. I will not stir, or cook or prepare anything until he has heard what I have to say. This time we will have it out in the open.

The kettle boiled, the steam causing it to whistle just as Roland came back into the kitchen.

"I am making another cup of tea. Would you like one?" She kept her voice light, conversationally cool.

He grunted and sat at the opposite side of the table. Then frowning saw his hat on the floor.

"What's it doing here?" He grumbled.

"It must have fallen," she did not turn round.

He stared at her back, uneasy, unsettled by her tone.

"Can't see how it got there." His voice was petulant again.

"Oh for goodness sake Roland, it's just a hat."

He went to speak again but her sharp look quelled him and being so unused to being chided, for once he was lost for words.

Beatrice carefully made the tea, poured out a cup for him, and passed it to him. He took it without speaking. Then there was stillness, a silence, which hung in the air like a reproach.

"Well. What do you want to discuss." The question was a challenge. He could not wait for her to break the silence; he needed to gain the upper hand.

"I want another child." She spoke so quietly that he almost asked her to repeat it. And then as if she knew that he had not understood, not wanted to hear her, she said again.

"I want another child Roland. We will have another child. I will not be kept waiting for ever. You will give me a child."

"Oh just like that!" He snapped his fingers, attempting to be flippant, to pass it off as a joke, a trifle.

Beatrice ignored the provocation. "It has been two years since Stephen was born. I have missed a child in my arms for so long now, and you have never sought to help me Ronald. You have never enquired about my needs and about my wants. You hardly come near me and when you do you scuttle back to your room without a word. I have rights as a wife, as your wife. I will not be denied this." Her cheeks grew hot and she pressed her knuckles to her lips and held an upturned hand towards him to prevent his interruption.

"I have been a good wife to you. This house is kept clean and tidy. You have good food on the table. I take care of you and your needs. I see to the domestic arrangements, our bills are paid on time, I don't squander your money....."

"Oh so I do nothing I suppose!" Roland snapped back. "My hard slog at the bank every day which provides you with the money to pay those bills. So I do nothing huh?" his indignation was manufactured.

"It was my father who saw to it that you had work ..... that we had a roof over our heads."

"Oh, oh, so that's going to be thrown back into my face is it? I should be eternally grateful. Down on your knees Roland, is that it? A touch of the forelock to the Squire, eh?"

"Don't be so childish Roland."

She rose to stand over him and he quickly stood to face her, pushing back his chair so that it fell back against the cupboard. Only the table stood between their anger.

"Well?" he sneered. "Let's to it then. Will the kitchen floor suffice or does my lady have another option?"

Beatrice gasped. "My God Roland you stoop too low this time. I will not be treated like this."

"You wanted a child, then you shall have one!" he shouted and his spittle flew and hit her cheek.

She crumpled before his anger. She had never witnessed such rage and it frightened her. She sat down with a hard bump and suddenly she was sobbing, finding it hard to breathe, breathless, gasping for air, as if drowning, drowning in her own despair. Ronald looked down at her suddenly weary. Have we come to this? Where will it end? But he made no move to comfort her, could not bring himself to touch her. Her words had cut deep into him, they had stung him. He was aghast at finding that he had lost control. She had reduced him to a state that he had not realised he was capable of being. She had shamed him, she had humiliated him.

He turned away and left her at the kitchen table disgusted at the scene.

Languishing on the horsehair filled couch Roland surveyed his cluttered studio. The north facing window gave the room clarity of light that he had desired. It was a perfect room in which to work, but earlier in the day he had abandoned his brushes. All day he could not bring himself to work. He now lay slumped, his mind wandering, trying to focus. Sighing he rose from the couch as if the effort exhausted him and walked across to the canvases stacked against the wall. He turned one of the larger pictures towards him. Sylvia stared back at him, her heavily kohl lined eyes inviting him to desire her, her lips slightly parted, the eyebrows slightly arched. Long perfect limbs and a smooth body merged against the folds of embroidered satin. Her chin rested lightly on the fingers of one hand, the elbow supported on a cushion whilst her other arm raised itself holding the back of her head, allowing her dark hair to cascade down her neck, coal black against the milky whiteness of her translucent skin. Her creamy-white heavy breasts were traced with light delicate blue veins and a dark hue encircled her nipples. A heavy gold chain suspended from her neck hung between them and encircled itself on the fabric whilst a long ostrich feather fan lay carelessly across her thighs. Heavy gold bracelets entwined themselves, dangling at her wrists and then bound her crossed ankles as if chaining her, weighing her down.

She was perfect, his Egyptian Queen. He had painted this one of her when they had first met, when she had been just eighteen, and couldn't bear to part with it. Their long intimate nights of passion had been wonderful. He wondered if he could ever paint such with such fervour again. He had been as if possessed by her. He stepped back to look again. It was his best work still. It was if she could step from the canvas and claim him as her lover all over again. The power of her gaze mesmerised him. Many times during the painting he had to fight off the desire to lay down his palette to consume their desire for each other. At night they would lay exhausted together, her pale skin slightly rouged from their lovemaking, his fluttering, beating heart trying to rest. Later again as they lay together she would hold his gaze and then his hand would gently stroke her thigh and belly until her murmured acquiescence, delighted, and encouraged him to begin again. She raised her breasts to him, arching forward as he caressed her, feeling her pleasure as he held her fast. Then raising each firm nipple to his mouth he could feel her expand until she groaned unable to resist. But he could not stop; he needed to make her strain at his will. Then as he delighted in her as she shuddered beneath him writhing in her pleasure.

He carefully cradled her head leaning her neck to kiss her moist skin and then her full lips, causing her body to curve away from him. He needed to consume her, to penetrate deep inside her and taste the exquisite beauty of her. Her panting acceptance of him drove him madly on as she writhed in ecstasy beneath him. She opened, unfurled, stretching to allow his total invasion, her arched back strained to raise her up to accommodate his caresses, until finally she flooded with passion and he knew it was his time. And then he entered her urgently. Her heavy white breasts shook in rhythm to him as he towered and heaved above her, and he continued the benign assault, invading and advancing, faster and more powerful with each push, gathering speed to a crescendo of shuddering movement. And finally it was over again, the crest of passion had been reached, and the waves of relief rolled back and forth lulling him to contentment. She was utterly his and he hers. Then, bemused by their serious passion, they became suddenly shy of each other. His fingers softly traced the contours of her face; she was his own complete love.

And so his picture had captured her intense beauty, her long body, full breasts, those serious eyes, flushed face, her full lips

50

still reddened from his passion, with only her maidenhood delicately hidden from view, carefully veiled by the long silky feather.

Roland sighed. What kind of future did he have now? His unsold paintings served as a reminder of the bleak market forces. Large country homes had stopped sending him commissions, and some had already reneged on commissions previously placed. He had tried to continue producing pastoral landscapes and still-life compositions but two galleries had closed and others were not showing new works.

Poor Sylvia used to money and privilege had no idea how to budget or keep a house. She had become pregnant within weeks of their first meeting, when she first posed for him. He had counted the months on his fingers. They had met in the early spring and young Roland was born in November.

He had only just become known, still wet behind the ears but feted by an interested London gallery who had glowingly reviewed his work. Arriving back from Paris he had already had a couple of introductions, sold some work, and received a serious promise of a few more commissions. All ready to set the world alight with his talent but now reduced to churning out populist trash. He had squandered his gift and reduced them both to being paupers.

He shuddered at the thought. My poor, beautiful spendthrift wife, who still lights up the room when she enters, and who is my life. And it is entirely my fault that we are still scrabbling around for money. She should have inherited a fortune and married well but then I came on the scene and spoilt it for her.

I can still see her mother, Lady Lavinia, white with anger standing in the drawing room barely able to speak.

"And how long did you think you could conceal it…….have you no shame……….how could you Sylvia? Your father is distraught; he does not want to see you. And as for you, you loathsome little man with your easels and paintbrushes!"

51

∞

She turned Sylvia out when she began to show signs of her condition so that their friends would not suspect. They had rented rooms in Eastbrook until Ronald was born and after a while luck changed and he had some work hung in London which attracted some interest and things were just beginning to pick up. He was selling well, producing good work.

Poor Sylvia had a rough time though. Ronald had been a large child and she was such a slender thing. The birth took so long and she lost so much blood. The butcher of a doctor that saw to her made such a mess of it all. He thought that he was going to lose them both. And since then they had not been blessed with children. They long suspected that she had been damaged after Ronald, but didn't have the courage to have it confirmed, wanting to live with some hope.

Probably for the best now that we can hardly maintain what we have. Our accounts with the tradesmen are currently in dispute! Yes currently suspended, until we can find some means of paying off some of the debt.

Ronald tried, bless him. After the trust fund on him was announced, and that was a real turn up for the books, he tried to settle as much as he could for us. Made things straight for this house so we didn't have to lose Rosemount Villas, but then some of the shares that were reinvested for him took a real nose dive and then, suddenly, there was nothing left.

Next thing he was announcing his engagement to that Parsons girl. The father involved in all kinds of business and properties, no end of money in that household. I never heard him speak of her until he suddenly came to the house, looking like a ghost saying that he was going to get married. Not that her father was too pleased either. I thought that history had repeated itself, that he had gone and made her pregnant. A war time fling. Can't say that I would have blamed him. None of them knew when their time would be up. But no, they set up house which the father coughs up for, and the next thing is Ronald was working for the bank. Not his line at all.

And no sign of another child at all, apart from that first one. Of course it was a tragedy for Roland, losing his son. He tried to bear up but his mother and I could see that he was broken, poor lad. As for his wife Beatrice, well she carried on as if nothing happened. Always busy in the village doing the church flowers, organising fetes and whatnot. Nothing better to do I suppose. A cold one that's for sure. Oh she is pretty enough, I suppose I can see how Roland fell for her. Sylvia was heartbroken. She had seen that he was wasted in that line of work. He was always a free spirit so like his mother. Well his wings have been clipped now.

Roland walked to the window. He did not know what to do. The weight of their situation hung heavily on him. To carry on as they were was no longer an option. He couldn't paint, unless he over painted his existing canvases. Although he had a small amount of stock it wouldn't last for long and he couldn't purchase more oils, anyway who would buy his work? The large estates had gone. He didn't have many small canvases to hawk at fairs. And those around here wouldn't give him the price to recover his labour or the materials. He would have to sell them at a ridiculously low knock down price. Even if he did it wouldn't stem the tide of debt threatening to overwhelm them.

He chewed his lip and reached for the cigarettes lying amongst the debris of his shelves. Perhaps he could do some local sketches of the towns and villages, attractive for a tourist to buy. He snorted at his own idea. How many tourists had he seen in the village recently? Could he set up a portrait studio, and then what?

He drew the smoke into his lungs and exhaled slowly. No. He needed some employment. He needed to turn his hand to trade.

Painting and decorating, odd jobs for the home? Walk from door to door asking for work? He shuddered to think that it had come to this.

The air moved and he was aware of her in the room before he heard her.

"Roland?" She put her hand on his shoulder.

"What's wrong my love?"

He turned and pulled her toward him.

"Oh just a spell of blues I suppose."

He smiled at her and kissed her lightly on the cheek, breathing in her familiar scent as he did so.

"Well come into the drawing room and I will pour a drink to cheer you up."

She caught his hand in hers and guided him away from studio, as if helping a child to find his way, and pressed him down in his chair.

"What will you have…. malt….. brandy?" Her light voice smoothed him.

"Oh you choose for me …. no I'll have the malt, and perhaps just a dash of water?"

"Mmm watered down, not often you have that." She smiled down at him and went to fetch the water.

When she came back she saw that he had closed his eyes, his head slightly tilted to one side. How she still loved the man. He had gained some weight in the intervening years since those giddy days when they had been mad for each other but he still retained an air of elegance that she had found so devastating. His dark brown hair was streaked with grey and slightly thinning on the top but his lovely soft brown eyes still held her in a spell. She had never regretted their life together and those sad years when they had tried so hard to have another child.

When they had first met he had been so shy and she of him. He had been so careful with her at first, their first romantic intimacy so chaste. He had caught her hand in his and brushed her lips with his. And it was if he had set her on fire. He had brought such warmth and light into her life. And when it finally came to their first act of lovemaking, he had been so solicitous of her needs, tender and kind. She had no experience of how to conduct herself, but he had gently brought her to him, concerned for her happiness, worried if he had hurt her, and constantly reassuring her of his love.

She had been so surprised by her own body's response to his caresses, and delighted that she could arouse such passion in him, exalted that she could excite him. And as they progressed, more trusting and understanding of each other's needs, they were able to lose any remaining inhibition, abandoning themselves to the pleasure of love. She had not known that passion could be so consuming.

She stroked his hair careful not to wake him. He had looked so worried, so weary, quite worn out when she had gone to the studio to see what had kept him so late.

And she had watched him staring at her picture. Her darling man, who had painted a siren, had seen in her such beauty, she had been so proud to have been his muse, to have been such an inspiration to him. But of course he had seen what he wanted to see. He had widened her eyes, catching a vibrant luminosity by changing the dull mauve and providing each iris with a wonderful violet rim. Her skin, so translucent in the painting had not had that extraordinary glow; he had elongated her neck, shortened her thin sharp nose, and made her breasts so full and voluptuous. She smiled ruefully, if only she had been so wonderful. But he had seen in her something that she cherished all through these long and often difficult years. His commitment to her had at first overwhelmed her and now she felt thankful that they had shared such an extraordinary love. It often frightened her, the thought of losing him. He was her raison d'être, a soul mate who had given up so much for her. His talent, given a free rein, without domestic encumbrances, could have given him so much more.

Even before Ronald was born he had found that she had no idea how to keep house or cook so it had been him who had patiently guided her. She had never seen food preparation, or learnt to set a fire. Their servants had seen to all that. What happened below stairs was a mystery that she had never sought to unravel. She had no need to know. She knew how to choose good fabrics for her dressmaker, and what was in vogue. She understood how to sustain conversation and to ensure that her parent's guests felt comfortable at dinner. She had been taught the latest dances. Her etiquette was faultless. She had some embroidery skills, but these were of no use to them in their tiny rented rooms, living on the pitiful amount of money that Roland had saved from the sale of his work.

 She had had such little energy towards the end. It had been an effort to move as she swelled, the weight of the child, and the long sleepless nights wore her down. It took over her life. She felt numb and her brain shrank into a tiny kernel; she could not think .And all the time Roland carried on quietly, patiently, seeing to all the domestic arrangements, ensuring that they had food on the table, their clothed were washed.

And when her time came, and the midwife that he had fetched could not help her, frightened by the complication, and the doctor who had to be summoned seemed more interested to know if he would be paid, it was then that Roland finally broke down. And she knew that she had nearly lost them both, the child and the man. He had wept and she had been unable to comfort him. Lying helplessly in the bed she watched his misery as if through a distorted mirror and as his image swayed she felt the knots of fear binding her tight.

All this had made them stronger. When the nightmare had ended, and she began to recover, and the child survived, they seemed to become even closer. Their passion continued but it

56

evolved into something deeper, they found compassion, joyful affection and also devotion in their love.

When she considered her own parents and their stiff manner to one another she wondered if she had ever seen a sign of affection. Her childhood had been punctuated by discipline and dutiful expectation. Their large manor house was cold, dark and dreary, a mausoleum. Each room had been cluttered with ornate jet black furniture and the heavy drapes at the window afforded little light to enter. It was a soulless place. Had there been laughter? She couldn't recall. It was such a long time ago, a different age, a different world away. The maids scuttled about afraid of their own shadows, everything and everyone had its place.

She still felt the shock of that day when she had been summoned to the drawing room. Had seen Roland standing by the table, his back to the window his face set, hands clenched by his side. Her mother's face had been contorted with rage. Terrible words had tumbled from her. She was caught up in a maelstrom of fury. At first she had not made sense of the wild pronouncements, not believing that she was about to leave the house, that a Gladstone bag had already been packed with her belongings and now sat in the entrance hall.

Her young brother who had unwittingly entered the room was sent away, as if her mere presence would contaminate him. There were vile words, bastard, harlot, damnation, serpent, that she and that vagabond, that filthy scoundrel, had defiled their house and good name. She had disgusted them. All their care in her privileged upbringing had been thrown back in their face. That she would no longer be part of the family. She would not see a penny more from them. They would no longer recognise her as a daughter, that as a harlot with no morals she was only fit to live on the streets.

A bell rope was pulled and the butler and her father's valet swiftly appeared as if they had already been alerted to attend.

There was a brief scuffle as they advanced towards Roland, ready to manhandle him away, and then she too was bundled from the room, shuffled into the hall, instructed to take her bag and leave. And even when they were sent word that her life was in danger there had been no response. It had been unforgivable.

The war had changed so much. Her young brother, Sebastian, had been killed within the first year of the campaign. They had no idea that it would claim so many, their young lives stolen from them on foreign soil. She shuddered at the memory. It had destroyed so much and had taken away Roland's livelihood. Last week when he had sent word to the big house, that the commission had been completed, he received a reply that it was no longer required. The agreement to pay a required fee seemed now to be defunct. It was an outrage. She was still seething at the criminality but it seemed that nothing could be done unless Roland sought legal assistance to recover the money.

She had known that other staff were being let go, there was talk of it in the village. Those who had retained their lives in war were now seeing their livelihoods destroyed. How ironic.

And her parent's inheritance that was to be settled on Sebastian was placed in the hands of the solicitor. They would not, could not, discuss it with her. They said there were some legal issues; the matter was complicated. There were other trust funds, some legal interpretation and further investigations that needed to be resolved before there could be a hearing that could be brought before a high court. She had made no sense of it. That Ronald had received monies from an earlier trust fund when he reached the age of twenty five had also made no sense. Unless her mother had, at some time, a change of heart and decided that a child was innocent of the crimes of the parents? That it was a way of demonstrating how much she, her own daughter Sylvia, had lost by taking up with Roland? Had it been a calculation of twisted cruelty? She could not understand it.

And Ronald had been so good. They had thought that they would have to lose this house but Ronald would not hear of it. He paid off the remaining loans and saw off some creditors as well. Then within no time at all there was hardly anything left. He had spent a little unwisely perhaps, but as a young man that was to be expected, and then he did make some hasty investments but in two years the bulk of it had more or less disappeared. Then, out of nowhere, he suddenly decided to get married after all. Beatrice had had a good catch in him. Such a talented boy just like his father, but then Parsons put pressure on poor Roland. Probably as a grocer, because that's how Parsons started, in trade, he saw the bank as providing a respectable job. It was hardly a profession and not what they had in mind for Ronald. Ronald had so many ventures that he could have overseen in the city. He had studied law for a while, but she supposed that he wanted to keep his new little bride happy. He had already brought their little cottage by then; a sweet little place from the outside. Mind she'd hardly been allowed set foot over the threshold. Beatrice was not the most hospitable of hostesses. She found conversation difficult. When she had come here, she would just sit and stare. Perhaps, she supposed, that it had been rather daunting for her to adjust to the intellectual level that we had always assumed was commonplace.

Ronald said that she had almost a compulsion to clean and polish. He would put down a shirt and the next minute it would have been laundered and hanging on the washing line. Well maybe a little exaggeration, but the place never seemed lived in. Not a place where a man could relax.

Roland stirred and she rose from her chair to take his drink to him.

"My Roland, you must have needed that nap." She smiled at him. "Hungry?"

"Mmm what's on offer?"

"Well we have some cold tongue in the larder and new potatoes that the boy brought up yesterday, if you fancy that?"

She made her way to the door.

"Oh and I think there are some apples that need to be used up, I could stew those? I was going to make something with them but then didn't. Think I forgot they were there!"

When he didn't answer she turned.

"Are you alright Roland? Still worrying?" And she saw his hand pass over his eyes. Her heart missed a beat. She went over to him again and bending down drew his head onto her chest.

"Don't worry my darling. Something will turn up. We have been through worst days haven't we?" And she kissed his lips and cradled him in her arms.

Ivy Leaf Cottage 1922
Ronald

Banging the door behind him Ronald strode down the path and in turning right walked swiftly up the road. Anger raged. A white fury enveloped him. He needed to get away from her. How dare she! She was a mad woman. Making ridiculous demands; I want a child! Always what she wants, not what we want. I've given her too much of a free hand. Well he would not tolerate it any more. And then bringing up that business with the father. Why, Parsons's old man George had only been a common labourer, an uneducated farm hand, only fit to dig ditches and mend fences. Probably couldn't even write his own name! For years he had worked on grandmother's land, hadn't even got a tenancy. Then his old wife Sarah, had been drudge, just a domestic, worked as a scullery maid up at the manor.

Them and their brood of snivelling kids!

And Arnold Parsons, he snorted, Parsons who now thought himself so high and mighty, swanking about in Mote House, had been one of ten, living in that rundown old tied cottage of theirs. He'd just got lucky; yes just bloody good luck that's all. Story was that he had started with just a hand cart in Covent Garden selling fruit and veg and whatnot then got in with a Jew boy, and suddenly they were running a string of grocery businesses. Money came to money and no mistake, just a lucky break. No real business brain there, just some murky investments and some cheap property that happened to come up in the right place. In those days you could buy anything if you knew the right people to cosy up to, new money and no class, all of them together, just common trade.

Then he'd gone and had a Palm House conservatory built on the side, and then had the heating system installed. That must have cost a small fortune. How many palms had he greased to afford that? Ronald smiled at his wit, his clever word play. My God he was wasted in the bank!

Last Christmas when he and Beatrice had gone for luncheon, Arnold had had a huge fir tree put in the entrance. The whole swanky thing decked out with candles and whatnot. A wonder it didn't catch the place alight all that wax dripping around. Again that was all for show, had to get the biggest. Then that hideous monstrosity that he had put as a water feature in front of the house, water spouting from some crudely fashioned fish or some sort of gigantic sea creatures with bloated lips. Appalling! Beatrice thought that it was, now what had she said? Enchanting! He snorted again, enchanting, he could think of another word.

Ronald reached the Papermakers Arms, went to pull at the door handle and then stepped back. He was in no mood for conversation. But just as he stepped back, Archie came to the door and opened it.

"Don't often see you around here at this time of day." And Archie moved aside to allow Ronald to come into to the smoke filled bar.

Wrong-footed and not quite knowing how to extract himself he went towards the bar.

"What'll be your pleasure?" Archie smiled at him. "Pint of my finest?" he offered.

Ronald nodded and placing his foot against the support bar he watched as Archie grasped the porcelain handle towards him and deftly filled the glass with the swirling foam topped golden brown liquid.

"Put hairs on your chest…. that brew….how's things?"

Ronald looked around the room. Two of the old villagers whom he vaguely recognised but whose names he could not begin to remember, sat by together engrossed in their game of dominoes. One looked up and nodded in his direction before settling back to the game.

"Oh you know, fair to middling." And Ronald tipped the glass and drank greedily, then with the back of his hand wiped his mouth.

"That good huh?" Archie's smile broadened. Leaning towards him held up his fingers to indicate a shared confidence.

"Between you me and the gatepost I shall be glad when this day is over, what with her upstairs in her condition."

Ronald shook his head bewildered by the supposed shared knowledge that he did not have.

"Your wife?"

"Yes cor blimey, be glad when she drops this one out an' no mistake."

"Oh, oh yes I see" Ronald recovered his composure, "Oh yes quite." He nodded to prove his grasp of the situation. "Your wife, Ethel isn't it!" He was pleased with himself to have dredged up the name from the recesses of his mind.

"Expecting another little nipper, another addition to the household? Congratulations must be in order then." He stared at Archie uncertain how to sustain the conversation.

Archie came to the rescue not appearing to notice his faltering exchange.

"Last time there was such a to-do." Archie stared into the middle distance. The two men silently considered the statement; only the click of dominoes broke the silence.

"Another?" He pointed to Ronald's near empty glass.

"Don't mind if I do, and yourself?"

"Why not, very generous of you Sir, anyway we'll be soon wetting the baby's head if she carries on like this." Archie shook his head and raised his eyes as if to indicate the beams above them. Ronald looked up at first considering the beams before slowly realising that Archie was alluding to the situation of the expectant mother in the rooms above them.

"Women, huh?" And slowly shaking his head he pulled two more pints, pushing Ronald's towards him. The thick foam on the beer shook and then settled as he slid the glass towards him.

"Can't live with them, can't live without them! And how is your good lady wife?" Archie leaned conspiratorially towards him inviting his confidence.

An image of Beatrice swam into Ronald's mind and he quickly drained half the contents of his second pint before setting it down on the counter, looking at the empty glass with some amazement.

"Didn't realise I had such a thirst!" he tried to emulate Archie easy banter before frowning when once again the thought of Beatrice and the recollection of their heated exchange rose up before him..

He breathed in; "Well they do get themselves in a state don't they?" he was uncertain about sharing a confidence but the desire to vent his anger and frustration was becoming irresistible. Archie looked at him expectantly.

Ronald turned to see that the other drinkers would not catch his words.

"Oh I don't understand her. Says one thing and means another." He shrugged. Tipping the glass towards him he loudly savoured the last few remaining dregs in the glass.

"A good brew I must say landlord."

"Call me Archie." Archie downed the contents of his own glass, and smacked his lips in appreciation. "Oh yes can't beat it." Pointing to the glass he looked at Ronald and smiled, "Another?"

"Yes, rather, why not. It's been a hot day."

"So, says one thing, does she?" Archie sought to draw him out.

"Mmm." Roland screwed up his eyes conjuring up her scornful face, remembering her spiteful words. Her father this and her father that!

"Yes," he spoke slowly. "It all gets so complicated doesn't it? They can't order their thoughts like us. Go off on tangents, start on one thing and then goes off on another."

Archie nodded his agreement.

"Never know what's going on in their heads." He pursed his lips. "Can't discipline themselves, stands to reason inferior intellect an' all that, not like us chaps.

"And so she said?" Archie waited, distracting the directness of his enquiry by taking a cloth and polishing a glass, holding it up to the light to inspect it.

Ronald took another long ruminative drink and sat the glass a little heavily on the bar, the remaining contents waved from side to side.

"One minute she's criticizing, moaning about bills and money, and how much there is to do in the house and the next starts on about having another child! You see no logic applied at all!" He stretched his head back and allowed the rest of the golden liquid to pour down his throat.

"What's a fellow to do huh? I suppose I've given way to her too many times, allowed her to have her head. Trouble is I've always been there for her, too much mollycoddling, wrapping them in cotton wool and not providing enough rigour. In the end it doesn't do 'em any favours, give them the requisite ammunition to think for themselves. Shield them from the world too. No indeed. Seen it with the squaddie chaps in the army too, same there, have to mother them, sort out their problems. Not got the right backbone, half of them illiterate too, incapable of making decisions, have to be led, exhausting work all the time. And no thanks for it in the end. That's the thing you see...see them through thick and thin and then end up being resented. Don't like to admit that we are superior. Stands to reason. Bigger brains that's what we have, can't argue with that can you... though they would if they could!" He snorted, shook his head and continued.

"It's just as nature intended things to be. Leaders and men, masters leading donkeys... the natural order of things. A man's wife should bend to a man's will but some seen to have forgotten the vow of obedience, modern ideas, just muddy the water!"

Archie shook his head in sympathy.

They sat quietly, each lost in their own thoughts with only the sound of the clock ticking ponderously, the murmur of the players and dominoes lightly tapping the table to disturb the silence.

"Well the way I see it." He lowered his voice and leaned in toward Ronald.

"You need to put your foot down, be master in your house. They respect a fellow who makes up their mind for them!" He winked at Ronald and at their shared conspiracy.

Ronald attempted to bring Archie's face into focus then pointed at his glass with only the remnants of a band of foam.

Archie slowly refilled it and set it back before him. The wet glass left a ring of liquid on the bar and as Ronald took the drink to his lips Archie stood back taking a clean glass from the counter to polish, and watched his customers carefully.

Ronald stood back on his heels, rocking slightly to maintain his balance.

The players began another new game, shuffling the spinning dominoes around the worn table.

Ronald finding that he needed some extra support slumped onto the vacant bar stool, and stared into the distance. Images of bottles and glasses swam in and out lazily. He breathed deeply and burped. He was at peace with himself. All was well. It was gratifying to find a man who understood and could follow his argument.

"Might have to put her on her back to get off mine...." he smiled at Archie pleased at his audacious wit.

Archie nodded.

They beamed at each other, pleased to find that they had some common ground between them, that they had so expertly solved a little mystery. And they stayed together, comfortable, finding no need for talk, lost in their own reverie, the long afternoon only disturbed by the sound of the dominoes spinning on the table, as the clock ticked softly accounting for each second of time.

A shout from the room upstairs jerked them away from their newly formed camaraderie.

The door to the upstairs' rooms flung open and a wild eyed toddler stood swaying uncertainly before them.

"Daddy, daddy!" He looked as if he had been crying.

Archie swung away from the bar. "Christ almighty! He's come down the stairs on his own, Christ almighty! Alright! Alright, now my son, there, there."

He went to the child and lifting him clasped him in his arms, covering his little face with wet kisses and gently reassuring him. "There, there, little lamb," soothing him. "Now you stay put here." And he carefully set him down again.

He trod the stairs heavily holding on to the rail as he went. Ronald was nonplussed uncertain how to respond. He looked giddily around at the two players who had been disturbed in their game.

One spoke, his Kentish accent thickly disguising any consonants that could have been present

"Shez abar to drop um?" He cocked his head and nodded to Ronald.

Ronald shook his head and for a moment the silence hung between them and then finally he understood.

"Ah yes she's about to drop, yes, she about to have the child yes, yes I think so." He nodded at them and they turned back to their game, dismissing him.

The little boy still stood by the doorway. He was a slight child with large eyes. An attractive boy Ronald thought. He struggled to recall his name, had Archie mentioned it?

"What your name then lad?"

"Jack." The boy spoke in a whisper as if his words would create further catastrophe.

"You know what's happening don't you?" Ronald sought to reassure him. His own tongue had become thick and unwieldy in his mouth.

"All quite natural …. you're going to have a little playmate, a little brother or sister did you know that?"

The child nodded his little head rising and lowering faster and faster.

Boy's had a shock, Ronald thought, he wondered what to do.

"Come here lad and sit with me. You tell me a bit more about yourself?" Ronald wafted an unsteady hand indicating a chair by a nearby table.

"How old are you then?"

But child would not move and shrank before the man drawing away from his reach.

"Hey, it's alright little man, no one's going to hurt you. Your daddy will be back soon. Ronald hoped that this would be the case since there seemed no one else around to look after the child.

And then the door opened and Roseanne walked in. She saw Jack and then Roland and raising her eyebrows said.

"So what's happened then?"

Ronald swallowed, and attempted to clear his throat, still finding that his tongue felt suddenly unnaturally thick inside his mouth.

"Erm." He began. "I think the landlord's wife is going into labour and he's upstairs with her now.

He pointed uncertainly at Jack. "Not sure what needs to happen to this little chap." He hoped that she would take control.

"Right oh." And she turned to the dominos players. "Time gentlemen please, let's be having you. Need to close up early today. Drink up. Sorry luvs. Shoo!"

She ushered them from their seats and then shooed them towards the door as if they were reluctant geese.

"Come on, come on, haven't you got homes to go to?" She smiled at them but they could see that she would brook no nonsense.

She turned to Ronald.

"Well perhaps you had better stay." Her eyes seemed to suggest more.

"Now let's get this little fella sorted."

And she swung him up to her ample chest, and then turning back to him said," I won't be long I'll just take him up the road and get Ron's wife to look after him. You stay here, just in case, until I get back, I won't be long."

Ronald held the door open for her and could smell an earthy musk as she brushed closely past him.

"She turned and smiled again, "Won't be long," she promised.

Upstairs the sound of moans grew alarmingly louder.

Ronald stood alone in the bar, his head felt light. Roseanne. He had never really looked at her before. Quite a woman in a grubby kind of way he mused. Wonder how many of the lads she has led down a dark alley. Put him in mind of the kind of woman that followed the men when they were out in France, always ready and able they were. He had only known a couple, a couple of French tarts who wanted money up front. Disappointing though, the pair of them; cheap tricks, lucky not to have got the clap, most men did. Mind, had far better in the East End. They'd certainly been up for it.

He hoped that she would return soon. He didn't know why he should remain; it wasn't as if he could do anything. But now he couldn't just leave, without saying that he was leaving, it was awkward.

He couldn't decide whether he wanted to stand or sit and in the end just wandered unsteadily around the bar staring but not looking at the various prints and pictures that swam in and out of focus on the wall.

The bar door banged open and Roseanne came in.

"Oh still here." She smiled as if he had made the decision to be there on her return.

"Well yes. I'll go now." He stood to pass her.

"Well I hope I'll see more of you." She spoke softly. "It has been a pleasure meeting you." And she left the suggestion of intimacy as she pouted her lips and blew him a kiss.

Ronald walked awkwardly back to the cottage. His mind was in a jumble of thoughts and the air seemed to wrap his head in a tight cotton wool band.

Beatrice opened the door just as he was about to do so, and stood looking at him in surprise.

"Ronald?" she questioned. "Are you alright ….are you…" But she didn't finish the question.

He ignored her comment waving away her words as if batting a fly from his face.

He grasped her hand, and pressed it to him. "We shouldn't argue." The slight rhythmic pounding in his head seemed to soothe him. He felt light and easy, outside his own body.

"Come." He held her hand tighter and started to push her back into the hallway.

Beatrice frowned at him, awkwardly trying to loosen his hold on her but he looked straight through her, his eyes glazed and unseeing.

She turned so as not to trip against the stair and then found him roughly pushing against her.

"Ronald?" Beatrice attempted to break away, to pull her hand from him, but he held her more firmly and then taking her waist he propelled her up the stairs.

"Ronald. No don't Ronald, you're hurting me." She tried to wriggle from his grasp but nearly fell against the higher step.

He did not hear her protests; she was merely playing the game. They almost fell in to the bedroom at the doorway and then he pushed her onto the bed down amongst the pillows.

Beatrice tried to find her voice to make him listen to her. His eyes would not focus on her; it was if he was possessed.

But he saw Roseanne before him, her welcoming smile, the sensuous full lips pouting at him, 'well I hope I'll see more of you. It's been a pleasure'. It was a pleasure, and he would see more of her. And as her full soft lips came towards him he gloried in his mastery.

Cranesbury Village August 1922
The Storm

It was just past midnight when the villagers heard the first rumble of thunder. Some had been unable to sleep, as the oppressive heat which had sapped their energy during the day, now seemed to suck the very air from the rooms leaving them restive and fitful, turning uncomfortably under their bedclothes. In the distance, a farm dog barked, fretting at the incoming storm, and his bark set off another closer in the village. Then there was sudden stillness, a suspension of sound, utter silence as if the earth had stopped revolving and every living thing was waiting an onslaught.

Archie sat exhausted in the bar as his wait for the unborn child continued. He had such a raging thirst. He had gulped some lukewarm water cloudy with swirling chalk deposits but it had done nothing to quench it.

He leaned forward his head dropping down onto his arms on the table and his back heaved and shuddered with his grief. For most of the day and throughout the evening Ethel's torment had continued. She seemed no nearer to being released from her agony and this time he was fearful that she would lose the battle. Ron's wife had come when summoned, leaving the child Jack with her husband. She had arrived, bustling with energy and optimism. She had been with Ethel during her first confinement and was competent and kind, but when he last went upstairs she had not met his eye just shaken her head at him and pushed him back towards the door.

Ethel lay swathed in sweat her hair streaked in set strands across the pillows, her eyes were closed.

"I'll come and tell you when to get the doctor if she carries on like this. You can't help by being up here just in the way. Now go back downstairs. There's time yet"

But that had been a couple of hours ago; an eternity had passed since then. Images of his life and the things that he had done and said swirled around his head, he had been a heartless bastard, no getting away from it, and now she was paying the price. Self-pity, recriminations and shame overwhelmed him.

Betty's sudden shout roused him.

"Archie go and fetch Doctor Sutton now, tell him I think the baby's turned."

Archie pulled himself away from the table and lurched towards the door, ducking back again to snatch his coat from the peg behind the bar.

He pulled at the handle and banged the door shut heavily behind him almost relieved to find respite from his inaction.

As he swung down the street his figure was suddenly illuminated by a flash of lightning followed by almost instantaneous thunder and the rain that had waited to fall released its torrents creating a wall of water in front of him.

∞

Beatrice watched the frenzied flash that forked past the window instantly lighting up the sky in daylight brilliance and heard the angry roar of thunder that seemed to shake the very foundations of the house.

Ronald lay insensible beside her. She looked at him with revulsion. How could he sleep through this? At first she had been unable to even rouse herself and to move away from him. Her shocked body had been stupefied, refusing to respond. Then a second splintering flash lit the whole room and immediately another heart shuddering demonic crack roared and boomed in its wake; a thrashing dragon feeding on its own fury.

God, she thought, *I feel like death, let the storm come and take me now. Let it bring the house down, and him with it!* Her own anger now raged with the beast of the storm.

She flung back the bedclothes, suddenly galvanised into movement, and went to the window staring into the ink blackness before the next blinding flash zigzagged across the sky leaving an imprint of fireworks inside her head. And as she looked out, the village was swathed in a blanket of light, houses, lanes, hedges, trees, garden, laid before her, as an intimate theatre set, displayed just for her. And just before the black night folded back on itself she thought she saw, through the driving rain, a bulky figure racing down the road.

"Mr Minton!" she wondered. "Was that Archie Minton?"

And the wrath of the dragon roared its reply.

∞

Ron tried to soothe the little lad. He had woken up screaming, frightened by the storm and the day's events no doubt. He had put him in with little Gwen, his sister's little lass, who had come to stay for a couple of days, and, before Jack's shouts, had lay asleep quite unperturbed by the storm but now both children were wide awake. Gwen was unsettled at not finding herself at home in her own bed and Jack's little face was screwed up in terror. Ron had forgotten how fearful children could be of storms.

"There, there, nothing to worry about. It's just God has got himself in a muddle and has started to rearrange his furniture again." But both sets of eyes looked at him without comprehending his metaphor, it merely caused them more anxiety and Gwen began to sob, both children's cries reaching a crescendo.

Ron was unused to coping with children on his own; he was long out of practice and had thought that Betty would have been back by now. He looked at the clock. Half past twelve! What was keeping her? It should have been long all over by now, he fretted.

The white lightning lit the bedroom, and the children's pitiful faces looked ghostly in the reflected light.

"Come on the two of you, let's be having you downstairs and we'll have ourselves a nice warm drink." He couldn't think what else to do. Betty did all the cuddling stuff and whatnot. He was a shy man not used to showing his feelings.

He picked up Jack who was as light as a feather in one arm and helped Gwen disentangle herself from the sheets.

"Come on the pair of you scallywags." And he led them to the stairs; Jack tucked securely under one arm with Gwen trailing in their wake.

The cat who had been nicely and comfortable attached to the kitchen armchair found itself indignantly vacating its warm bed as Ron set both children together in the space.

"Right, now for some nice warm milk it'll cheer us up."

Gwen was distracted by the disdainful cat who now sat some distance away from them, watching them surreptitiously, before deciding to furiously wash the furthest part of its back to prove that she had not really been bothered at all by the insult and the loss of a warm bed.

Gwen attempted to call the cat to her, but Jack's loud renewed cries caused the cat to abandon the washing facade and with flattened ears escape the room.

Ron set down the pan of milk and came back to the children, "Now then now then lad, don't take on so. You'll soon be back home."

But the thought of his home, instead of placating the boy only made things worse.

Oh lawd, thought Ron, what a to-do! Come on Betty how long are you going to be?

Finally the milk warmed through and he managed to coax them into having a sip, taking turns from the same cup, trying to make a game of it.

"One for Gwen and one for Jack. That's it all gone!" And he turned the cup down in mock horror that they had drunk it all. "None left for me!" and the children in spite of themselves found themselves amused as his big eyes opened wide and his mouth turned down to resemble an unhappy clown. Encouraged by their response he whisked a teacloth from the stove and wove it about his head as a bonnet holding the ends under his chin.

"Oh lawd what are we do!" and his falsetto shrieks and mimicry of an old washer woman caused the children to giggle.

Mincing around the room his large frame filling the space and putting one hand on his hip he twirled around fluttering his eyelashes at them and the children now found themselves engulfed in helpless laughter. And as he stopped, puffed by his sudden exertion, steading himself against the arm of the chair he heard their cries in unison.

"Again, do it again!"

And unwilling to let the children become fearful, Ron took up his act again, exaggerating the walk and wiggling his bottom at them, until their peals of laughter and giggles reached a crescendo.

"Now then, Now then!", he adopted a policeman's stance, twirling the copper stick as an imaginary truncheon before them, as if remonstrating, before tucking it neatly under his arm.

"What's all this jollity I should like to know. Children should be seen and not heard you know. No more giggling on my patch, or I'll have your guts for garters!"

The children were now so soothed and distracted that they did not at first realise that Betty had come in.

She stood at the door, smiling at Ron.

"Well fancy keeping the children up at all hours Ron Ticehurst!" Her coat that she had thrown over her shoulders was soaked, and she took it off and hung it dripping over the second kitchen chair.

"Let's have these children back upstairs now. Come on you two, time for bed sleepyheads." And they allowed her to shoo them in front of her before she bent down to carry Jack up the stairs. "Come on my little solider. Let's tuck you in or it'll be morning before you know it."

"Have they settled?" Ron asked as she reappeared in the kitchen.

"Yes I think so. And the storm has quietened down a bit now." They both sat facing each other, cocking their heads to listen to the distant grumblings of the storm.

"Mm it's going away now."

"My lord it has been a long, long, night and no mistake."

Ron waited for her to expand.

"I had to send Archie for the Doctor, I thought that she'd breached."

He nodded, allowing her to tell it in her own time.

"She poor thing was quite worn out, could hardly do a thing at the end." She sighed, weary herself.

"The doctor had to use forceps, so the little thing is quite back and blue, looked a right old state. Still at least she's in one piece. More than could be said for Ethel poor love. The Doctor had to stitch her up, she'd been that torn. Oh a right old mess! Ethel was adamant all day that she wouldn't have a doctor kept saying that they couldn't afford it! And I said to Archie that I would leave it as long as I could but I daren't risk it in the end. We could have lost them both!"

She moved uncomfortably in the chair.

"Oh dear lummy, my back's quite gone. Anyway, I said to the doctor that she had had it bad the last time. Not really got child bearing hips that one. But we both thought that it would have been easier for her this time round. Just goes to show you never know."

"Whatever is the time?"

They both looked towards the clock on the mantle in dismay.

"Oh dear, and you need to be up again in a couple of hours Ron!"

They heard the last murmurings of thunder as they wearily undressed for bed.

"And I thought that the storm would clear the air." Betty sighed as she tried to waft some coolness down into their bed with the sheet.

"It's so close, it'll be just as hot tomorrow, and my, didn't it rain! I thought that it would never stop." Her phases punctuated the flow of the sheet.

"Come here woman. Keep still, you're making it worse instead of better."

Ron reached out to hold her, and she finally acquiesced, allowing him to surround her, holding her to him, her curved back nestling against his large chest and loins, comfortable with each other. Quietly and gently he stroked her arm, soothing her, until they both fell into a light fitful sleep, knowing that their slumber would have to be disturbed by the next day's early responsibilities.

∞

The next morning the storm's damage was all too apparent. Two barns in the next village Chitterhurst had been struck. One had almost been empty, waiting for the new harvest to be stored inside but the other had been closely stacked with hay. The fire engine from the station at Cranbrook had been summoned but the road had been blocked by the flash floods so they couldn't get through.

In Easthurst some cows had taken fright and gone through a hedge careering though the next farmer's field, trampling down part of his crop which had been ready to harvest, ruining much of his barley. Some of the orchards had lost their cherries, the heavily laden branches had been broken off, and the strawberry fields in Westbury had been stripped of their plants as a torrent of water had swept across leaving bare patches in its wake. Closer to home a tree had crashed through the side panelling of the Palm House in Mote House. The servants awoke to glass and debris everywhere. But most people in the village counted their blessing, finding themselves untouched by the night's work.

The air had not cleared. It made children fractious and parents irritable. Earlier that morning Ron had set to his baking and the heat of his ovens caused him to feel faint and unsteady. He was particularly put out by Mike and uncharacteristically gave him a sound telling off when he saw him lounging by his bike having a quick puff of his cigarette.

"You lazy good for nothing! Get that bread delivered or you'll be feeling the back of my hand lad!" he yelled.

Mike turned to him in surprise, immediately sprang on his bike and pedalled furiously away down the hill. His legs flying out as he turned the bend.

"And mind the bike you dolt! But Mike had ridden out of earshot by then.

∞

Ronald woke with a jolt. He rolled over awkwardly not quite aware of surroundings but realising that he felt distinctly unwell. A sickly acid rose up in his throat and his head thudded relentlessly.

He tried to draw himself up noting with some confusion that Beatrice was not there by his side and that he was in her bedroom.

"Beatrice!" the house was quiet.

He groaned and struggled from the bed unwrapping the clinging sheets; prompting his legs to take him unwillingly and shakily to the window. Grasping the open window he looked down as the garden haphazardly rose up to meet him. He passed a hand over his face. It felt wet. He wiped it against his thigh. Disgusted with his inability to steady himself he gripped the window sill. As the garden came into focus he saw that it appeared to be mown down. All the tall plants lay flattened and scattered in pools of water.

"What the devil!" he shook his head in disbelief and the action caused his head to thud harder.

"Oh my God." He staggered back to bed, and as he lay back the room danced and twirled around him.

He tried to remember how he had got there. There had been a row. Beatrice had caused a row. Then what? He trawled though the fog that had once been a brain. Ah yes, he seemed to remember something. He had seen Archie, been in his pub, they had had a drink. Then what, then what? How had he got here? His memory refused to co-operate, somehow he had lost time. Then Roseanne swam into his mind. She and he? He could not think. No it couldn't have been. He waited for the jumble for thoughts to settle themselves and turned back to the pillow. I need to sleep, he thought.

Beatrice sat at the kitchen table. She had not dressed. Her dressing gown fell unfastened at each side trailing on the floor. She chewed her lip. Already the room was flooded with light and she felt sticky with the heat.

I am done with him. She thought. I cannot bear him near me. He is despicable, and to think that I wanted a child with him; a future together. She frowned at the recollection of the night and suddenly an awful thought took hold. What if? She dare not think it. She would not let the thought take root. She needed to be free of him; it could not be now, not that. And her neck bent and she cried silently.

∞

Roseanne turned over shifting the bulk of the man away from her. The bed was a tangle of grubby sheets and her foot was caught fast. Irritably she tried to disengage herself but in so doing disturbed him. He grunted and then a smell of rotting cabbage wafted up from the depths of the bed towards her. She put her hand to her nose.

"Bleedin' hell Bert; where's your blooming manners?"

Annoyed she sat up and surveyed the jumble of the room. His trousers and her underclothes lay strewn about the floor. The wash stand basin still had dirty water in it causing a grey rim to form. She frowned at the scene.

"This place is like a bleedin' pigsty!" she announced angrily.

"Come on, get up," and she pushed the man roughly to rouse him.

"Hey Roseanne, not so hard, just give me half a mo."

He heaved himself up, propping himself against the hard brass bedstead, and burped.

"Pardon I'm sure!" and he winked and smiled at her.

"Now I'll have none of that!" Roseanne found herself smiling in spite of herself.

He saw he soften and reaching out he attempted to hold her to him.

"Now that's enough." She sounded firm this time and wriggled away from him.

"You had enough of that last night."

"Good though wasn't it?" he seemed to ask for her approval.

"Well fair to middling, 'specially in this heat." And she sighed heavily.

"Thought that storm last night would put an end to it, but now it seems even hotter this morning." She grumbled more to herself than to him.

"Still not sure if I need to work tonight what with that carry on with Ethel last night, ' speck that Archie won't want to open today, 'tho suppose she's had it now, certainly took it's time coming."

Bert had not listened to her as she rambled on; he lay back, staring at the cracked ceiling, lost in his own thoughts.

She looked round at him. "Come on shake a leg, haven't you got work to go to?" and gave him a gentle push.

He sighed deeply and heaved himself up again.

"Alright, alright, I'm moving!" and he swung his legs over the bed his feet touching the bare wooden floor and coming into contact with an odd boot that had found its way to the side of the bed.

"Cor, this is a mess Roseanne, can't find a thing with all your frillies in the way."

"My mess! Don't you be so cheeky Bert or it will be the last time you get an invite to my bed!"

"Thought that you were desperate for it, just doing you a favour girl." He grunted as he had to lean forward to gather up his shirt and trousers.

"Desperate!" Roseanne was piqued by his clumsy humour. She pulled on her drawers and fastened her shirt, buttoning the blouse breathing quickly, suddenly unsure of herself.

"Well, I could find a lot better than you." She attempted to bring him down a peg of two.

"Roseanne, are there many left that haven't had a go?" He pulled his belt and fastened the buckle and looked round for his cap.

She felt a flame of anger lick her face. "You go too far Bert."

"Well you know where to find me." And he ducked as he went through the doorway, his large frame filling the space, holding both boots in one hand. And she listened as he stomped down the stairs and heard the door as it banged to.

I can certainly do better than you; she consoled herself, plenty more fish in the sea. And she went to the wash bowl before making her own way down the stairs.

As she waited for the kettle to boil she allowed her mind to wander, and she found her thoughts returning to Archie and Jack and the scene at the Papermakers Arms and then of Ethel's confinement.

She found Archie attractive but was at times strangely unnerved by him. He kept his distance, always joking, but then he did that

82

with everyone. She knew it was his loud way of making them feel at ease with themselves but she could see that he held something back. He wasn't all that he seemed to be. She couldn't put her finger on it. He had charm and knew how to flatter. He was a good listener, the regulars always said so. And yet although he did appear to listen, she felt that it was an act that he put on for them, a show that he never let slip before them. But when they were on their own and there were no customers left and she was putting up the chairs ready for the next morning's clean, she'd sometimes catch him with a faraway look on his face or deeply engrossed in a book. His face would soften and although looking quite serious he seemed somehow at peace with himself. And if he caught her watching him he would toss it carelessly to one side as if it was of no consequence and wink at her.

Then there was little Jack. He doted on the child, always catching him up and smothering him with loud kisses, causing the child to have fits of uncontrollable giggles and to squirm in happiness. His love for the child was wonderful to see. There weren't many men around here who would like to be seen showing such affection in public. Perhaps they did behind closed doors, but not for all to witness. But somehow it didn't matter to Archie.

But recently she had seen such a change in him. As Ethel's time had got closer there was an anxiety about him. He seemed unable to settle and yet still played the clown with the regulars. There was a brashness about him that she hadn't seen before, and a sometimes even a sense of menace. And he was drinking more these days.

Mind with Ethel it was enough to drive anyone to drink. She and Ethel had never got on. She always held her lips together as if she had been stung by a wasp. In fact she should have been a wasp, because when she said something, it often had a nasty sting in its tail. Just ordinary things but you knew what she meant.

"Have you cleaned up in here already?" really meant, "why haven't you cleaned it properly, it still looks a mess." Oh yes she had the measure of her and usually tried to keep out of her way. But my, oh my, it was so hot today. There was no air to be had. Even the dogs were quiet this morning, none of the usual barking.

It needed another storm to try and clear the air, she thought, as she walked out into the glare of sunlight and ambled down to the public house to see if she was needed.

All around him lay shattered glass and shattered wooden frames but looking up at the roof it seemed undamaged.

"Forrester, what do you think?" he beckoned the man to him.

Forrester picked his way through the crunching glass. He had removed his waistcoat and looked unfamiliarly casual without the garment.

Well Sir, I think that it looks a deal worse than it is. I know that we have lost quite a bit of the vine and a couple of the peaches but really it's just part of this side that's gone. The structure is intact, and the roof is sound".

Both men peered up. Arnold mopped his brow.

"When I've had the men clear the branches and they've sawn the main trunk, I think that we'll see that it's not too bad."

"But about the water system." Arnold was anxious, it had been costly to install.

"Difficult to see at the moment Sir, what with all this around," He waved his hand over the broken pots, mangled plants and splintered branches covering the partly flooded flagstones.

"It seems fine but well only know for sure once we turn the water back on, then we can see if there are any fractures to pipework. I've had Roberts to look around and he can't see any breaks. It seems to have missed them. I think this water is mainly rain from the storm Sir."

Arnold pursed his lips together.

"It's a damn shame, just when we thought how well it was looking Forrester."

Forrester nodded, hoping to be soon released so that he could start organising the clearance and get on with the work, but Arnold was still troubled, fretting at the chaos.

"And poor Louise had set her heart on hosting the garden party this weekend. She sent out the invitations and got some extra help in to sort it all out. And we wanted to show the Palm House off, our own bit of Kew Garden! "

Forrester nodded again, "Very sad Sir, but it will be right as rain once we manage to clear out all the debris. We'll be able to see our way clear to replacing the frames and then the glass." He looked about him uncertain about how long he would be detained.

Arnold became aware that the conversation was becoming a little strained.

"Yes of course Forrester, silly of me I'm holding you up aren't I." He backed away, and came back, having had a second thought. "Let me know your assessment first before anything is done. I want to know if we should change anything, and if we need some new specimens."

"Absolutely Sir, as soon as the men have done that I'll get back to you. I'll contact some local nursery men as well."

"Good show!" Arnold began to feel more like himself again. His enthusiasm for another venture started to grow. It could work out even better than he had first thought. He had heard that there used to be some good varieties in Chatsworth, before they had to close their glass houses down during the war. And perhaps he could look at the grounds again. Make some extra water features, after the success with his first fountain. Arnold loved the garden. It was his piece of heaven.

He had already proudly acquired a nice collection of horticultural books with exquisite picture plates, and regularly took the Curtis Botanical magazine with its superb illustrations by Lilian Snelling and news of Lawrence Johnston's exciting work at Hidcote. Louise's aunt who lived in Tunbridge Wells had been the matron at the boarding school where Lilian had boarded and had said that the girl was always painting, had a real talent for it. Then Louise was always pleased to have the flowers available for her house arrangements.

86

As he walked back to the house, noting that the roses needed some deadheading, he could feel the oppressive heat, beginning to perspire as the unrelenting sun beat down. Two reclining stone lions at each side of the front entrance watched his approach without interest.

When he stepped inside the coolness of the large entrance hall was relief. Louise came from the drawing room.

"I thought I saw you coming," she noted his damp forehead.

"Well how bad is the damage? Can the men do anything?" she enquired anxiously.

"Yes, Forrester seems to have everything in hand," he breathed more easily now that he was away from the heat.

"My word I can't remember when we last had it like this!" he took a large handkerchief from his pocket and dabbed at his brow.

"Forrester says that he will get Roberts to look at the pipes but he doesn't reckon that they are too bad. The men will start clearing today and then we can see what needs to be done. I've told Forrester that I want to know the extent of the damage before he starts getting men in."

He sighed again, "Still, wonder how the Bedgebury estate has gone on. Should think there has been a fair bit of damage one way and another down there. Shouldn't wonder if some of those tall ones would be a target for a lightning strike. That giant fir that Beresford had planted all those years ago is a size already, must be the biggest around here."

Louise smiled indulgently, "oh no, I know what you're thinking. A Palm House is one thing, but a Pinetum takes up acres of land, which we haven't got. And I don't want all those dismal pine trees around us, they make things look gloomy. The house would lose its views. And look at the state Lewis left Bedgebury in, costing a fortune. No wonder he had to sell up."

Louise led him to sit. "Once the men have sorted out the pipes then perhaps we could plant up some borders along the back. I'd like some more foliage, it helps to compose my arrangements, and keeps a nice shape."

Arnold allowed her to settle him. The cost of the repairs had started to niggle with him again. His plans to expand would have to be temporarily suspended if the work proved to be too costly and he was impatient to start. If only his old folk could have seen the house and the land that he had acquired, they could have seen how far up in the world he had come. Louise had made such a good job of the rooms. They looked opulent, that was the word, opulent, and to match any fine house that he had seen in the magazines that she had shown him. They had good taste; he was beginning to acquire a taste for some good wines. He smiled at Louise's loyalty to her sweet Grants Morella Cherry Brandy. Still it was said to be quite medicinal.

He loved the spring when the cherry orchids produced glorious pink tinged dense white blossom clouds that seemed to stretch as far as the eye could see. He cherished this land, his land. It was the reward of his hard work and graft.

He enjoyed watching the itinerant pickers scaling their tall flimsy ladders, whose narrow tops would lose themselves amongst the tree branches, as the trees enveloped both man and ladder. And then their little children running in-between them wearing bunches of cherries as ruby earrings, their grubby aprons stained red. And the horses fastened close to the wagons. How he loved it all.

And there was his wealth. He would lie awake at night sometimes gripped with the fear that his castle and everything in it could all come crashing down. That he would wake and find himself back with his old folks. George worn out before his time and Sarah thin and worry lined. If only they had lived on and he could have made their lives so different, to have saved them from the constant fear of being turned out of their tied cottage by the farm manager, when they were no longer useful to the estate. And then to be looked down on, perhaps that was always the hardest part, to be thought of as being of such little consequence, little better than a beast of the field. A labourer, a hired hand, a worker, never to rise up in the station of life. The horizon of the land merely signifying the extent of a dream. A solid, uncompromising existence.

 But he had raised himself. He had bettered himself. By his own endeavours he had carved out a life for Louise. Provided her with home comforts that they had never thought possible and still he had plans for their future as long as the bubble didn't break.

They had given Beatrice a solid education. But then she had gone and met Ronald.

Arnold felt a cold lurch in his chest. How could she have fallen for a chap like that! Such a cold character. His father was a decent enough fellow, in a funny sort of way. Probably talented enough, he had seen some of his work, not quite to his taste but looked well enough but that was no way to provide for a family. Far too reliant on fancy folk's whims, and, since the war, not many of those still around to want pretty pictures.

Beatrice! His mind's eye could still picture her at home; he could hear her laughter ringing. Such a happy good natured girl. Now whenever they saw her she seemed to have faded. A faint shadow of herself. And Ronald had done that to her; a girl who could have set her cap at any lad and made a man proud. And a clever head on her shoulders too.

The hardest part was suffering the distance between them. It was as if Beatrice had decided that she had to choose and had turned her back on them. Louise had been heart broken. When the bad business with the cottage came about they had been horrified. Ronald had duped them all. His own good name could have come crashing down if he hadn't stepped in and bought the property. Then it was if Beatrice blamed them for interfering! Still the business with the child was tragic. Another time when they hadn't known about how bad things were getting until it was too late. Perhaps if they had been able to call in some expert help sooner it could have all been averted but again they had been kept at arm's length and only by the time the child was at death's door were they told of it. And it had been going on for weeks. You would have thought that a situation like that would have at least brought mother and daughter together but if anything it seemed to push them further apart.

Beatrice hardly ever came to the house, to see what work he was engaged upon, or answered any of her mother's invitations. It was a bad show, no mistake. They hadn't brought her up like that, but then his influence was too strong. It was as if their presence would contaminate them all.

Arnold bristled at the thought of Ronald and his ability from afar to rock his own self-belief. He could feel his roots return to unsettle him. A son of an illiterate labourer, was there no escape, would self-doubt always be there to torment him? How fragile was this existence.

He worried about how to effect a change, how to bring her back into their lives. When Beatrice had first set up home Louise and she had gone about choosing bits and pieces for the house and it seemed to be fine. So Ronald must have said something to have squared the pitch. Something must have happened to have set them so far apart. If only he could put his finger on it. Mind it could have been that mother of his, Sylvia. Now she was born with a silver spoon in her mouth and then thrown it all away. Scandal had followed her and Roland for quite a while.

Probably couldn't stand to see her perfect son married to trade. Her own family were so used to ordering people about without a thought for their feelings, so it must have been a shock for her to find that he could hold his own and more. That he would not be trifled with. She was so used to dominating that poor husband of hers and thought that she could play the lady over him, well when it came to it she couldn't and then had seen him putting everything right. That must have stuck in her throat, to have known that her son needed to be bailed out. What a weak individual he had been, even had to put pressure on the bank to find him a position. Funny how money oils the old wheels and a threat of a removal of funds brings people to their senses. Mind, it was not a part that he had enjoyed playing. It still made him uneasy. Always good to keep people on side, never know when you need to call in a favour. Keep your friends close and your enemies closer.

Arnold looked up, suddenly aware that he had been daydreaming, and that Louise was not in the room. Getting up from the chair he stood, unfocussed at first, at the window overlooking the lawn, as the gardener walked back and forth ungainly pushing the roller grass cutting machine that had recently been delivered. Neat lines formed in his wake. The young gardener, feeling the heat, had turned up his shirt sleeves to his elbows exposing his brown forearms, whilst his loping gait seemed to suggest that his boots were slightly too big for his feet.

Arnold smiled, and the young lad, who caught sight of him at the window, touched his cap momentarily, let go of the handle and then frantically grabbed it back again as the machine threatened to veer from the line that he had set himself to take.

Admiring his newly mown soft green lawn, framed by the generous herbaceous borders, which in turn were protected by neatly trimmed short young yew hedges helped to restore Arnold's equilibrium. The sun's rays had been softened, having to filter through the broad leaves of the horse chestnuts and limes trees that delineated the top lawn from the small orchards and walled vegetable garden beyond his field of vision.

Louise was right. He needed to concentrate on the Palm House before thinking about some new specimens for the borders. He was lucky to have such a reliable source of coal for the heating from Chislet Colliery despite the previous strikes when the supplies were patchy.

Arnold turned away from the window and went into his study. Sitting at his desk he looked at the ledgers in front of him. He needed to get back to business, and to arrange a trip to London to see his wholesalers. Then he had to find a way of bringing Beatrice back to them. Perhaps he could tie the two things together, kill two birds with one stone. He pursed his lips and started to examine the accounts.

Cranbrook   Autumn 1927
Archie

Archie looked up at the sky. It had been threatening rain all morning and now the brooding clouds darkened the day, dousing the natural light, turning the white clapper-boarded houses grey. He turned up his collar and tucked his neck further into the folds of his coat. A wind had picked up and it caught the front of it causing it to flap against his legs. He hurried on down the street, past the church and turning the corner crossed onto the other side of the raised pavement mounting the steps and keeping close to the shop fronts to lessen the effects of the wind. Having tucked his head down, he did not see her until they had almost collided. And as he stepped back he put his hand out to steady her.

"Heavens!"

"So sorry!"

They spoke together, both embarrassed to have nearly caused an accident.

"I wasn't looking!"

"Nor I"

"The wind, I think I have .." and she fluttered her hand across her face, blinking rapidly and rubbed her eye.

"Some grit?"

"Not sure. It could just be.." and she tried to smile shaking her head,

"Such a nuisance, this wind."

They were awkward now, not quite knowing how to end the conversation, aware of being rude, wanting to add something else, but at a loss as to what to say. There was a need to explain, although why they both couldn't decide.

He looked at her flushed pink cheeks, reddened by the wind and her confusion. She had closed one eye, holding it closed with her gloved fingers, and she shook her head.

93

"Oh it will be fine, so annoying!" She tried to dismiss him, but he held her gaze, his frown demonstrating his concern, and was aware that he was still holding on to her arm. She glanced down at his hand and Archie following her glance, quickly pulled his hand away.

"Sorry!" he tried to apologise for the offence, for touching her.

"No, no!" She was now aghast, she had been rude. He was only being kind. She attempted to smile still squeezing one eye shut. Goodness what must I look like, she thought, I must look a fright! Archie took a large handkerchief from his side pocket and offered it to her.

"Here do you want me to take a look?"

But another gust of wind leapt at them both and she had to reach up to steady her hat, turning her head away.

"Oh dear it's getting worse." She smiled ruefully up at him again. "And I'm sure it's trying to rain."

Archie made a decision.

"Let's go over to the church, Mrs Latterbridge, and then I can take a better look at that eye of yours."

She allowed him to lead her by the elbow, easier now that proper formalities had been established. They reached the church porch and paused together.

"No it's too dark to see." And he grasped the metal handle and pushed it so that the heavy wooden door swung open.

The quiet stillness of church made then aware of them being together, bringing back the awkwardness that they had hoped to avoid. They felt themselves on view, to be watched, and a strange sense of impropriety engulfed them.

"Sit here," Archie indicated a pew and Beatrice sat quickly obedient to his request swallowing nervously.

"Oh I'm so sorry to be such a nuisance!" and she attempted to laugh away her discomfort. But Archie slowly shook his head. And she realised that she had never looked at him before. Why, she thought, he is like a different man! And she watched him trying to avoid looking directly at her, realising that he too was just as embarrassed as she was, although making a better job to disguise it than she was.

"Look up!" and gently cupping one hand under her chin he took his handkerchief from her and carefully stroked the edge across the lower eyelash.

"Look away!" and as she moved her head to one side he leaned closer to her raising the top eyelid up and taking the tip of the handkerchief delicately wiped it towards the bridge of her nose.

Why, thought Beatrice, he is treating me with such tenderness as if I were a little child

"There!" he announced triumphantly and displayed a tiny dot of grit on the white cloth for her inspection.

"No wonder it was smarting." And he grinned down at her, pleased with himself.

"Well, quite a surgeon Mr Minton!" she found herself caught up in his success, allowing herself a measure of contentment as he lowered himself onto the pew close to her.

"Wait until it clears."

She could smell his warm tobacco scented skin. Dabbing her still smarting eye she tried to adjust to her wavering vision. And they sat together in their conspiracy of happiness as the leaded bejewelled saints stared down at them in veiled understanding.

"So, what brings you to Cranbrook?" Beatrice unwillingly broke the silence; her own quiet voice resonated and echoed back to her.

"Oh this and that." Archie shook his head and frowning he looked away staring into the distance. Shutting her out, he seemed almost offended by her question as if she had intruded.

Beatrice stood up, suddenly offended by his dismissive tone.

"Well I won't keep you." A sharp note entered her voice making it higher than normal.

"Thank you for your assistance. I'll be on my way."

Archie stared up at her, slightly bewildered and then rose himself.

"Oh I'm sorry Mrs Latterbridge that sounded very rude. I didn't mean to …."

He spread his broad hands in front of him trying to appease her. Beatrice shook her head accepting his apology, but wanting to show that it was a misunderstanding. She felt ridiculous, that he must think her silly and spiteful. How mortifying! She breathed in.

"Beatrice, please call me Beatrice."

And as he pursed his lips his eyes widened, drinking her in, staring into her troubled young face and a slow satisfied smile spread across his face.

"I will indeed Beatrice, and it's Archie at your service from now on."

He tipped his hat and she bowed her head and as she raised it back to look up at him their hearts missed a beat.

They turned and walked out of the church, Archie swung the door back to closing it with a bang, and the rain splattered up from the pavement and against the porch.

"Oh goodness." Beatrice was piqued and they turned back to each other in dismay.

"It may only be a shower," Archive raised his eyebrows at her, pushing out his bottom lip in a clownish fashion and she felt an unfamiliar warm bubble surge up inside her. Looking up at him she threw back her head and together their glorious laughter chimed in unison.

Once their laugher subsided he stared down at her thoughtfully and then, without a word, took her elbow and keeping her close he strode down the high street steering her towards the little tea shop before finally announcing.

"Come along my Mrs Latterbridge, I'm going to treat you to a nice cup of tea", he held her tighter, "and when it stops - then I'll let you go!"

Bemused she allowed herself to be propelled up the steps and settled at a small gingham covered table. They appeared to be the only customers there. Beatrice looked around feeling a little conspicuous, as the waitress in her white cap and apron approached their table. But Archie ignored her.

"Let me take your coat to let it dry."

And she found him helping her out of the coat and then handing it to the girl.

"Could you hang this up for her please?"

He took off his own coat and hung it over the chair before setting back on the seat.

The young waitress disappeared into the back of the long room, and once more there was just the two of them.

Archie studied her. Her hat covered and crushed her hair but some golden curls had managed to escape. The carelessly draped silk scarf across her throat caught onto one shoulder seemed to frame the picture. It was as if an artist had had a hand in her composition. Her serious grey eyes watched him scrutinising her. One eye was still slightly bloodshot.

"Oh goodness do I look a mess?" and she tried to affect a dismissive laugh, but his study of her almost quelled her enquiry before it had had a chance to be heard.

"Far from it, far from it." he murmured softly almost speaking to himself.

Beatrice could feel her colour rising.

"Except for that hat!"

Before she had a chance to reply he had dashed the little box hat that she had thought so fetching from her head and set it on the table before them.

"There!" He announced with a twinkle.

"How impertinent you are Mr Minton! I'll have you know that was, that is, my new hat!"

And as she laughed her soft smooth cheeks became flushed and her grey eyes lightened.

My word, Archie thought, as her thick swathes of bronzed curls cascaded to her shoulders, why have I never noticed her before, she is quite marvellous!

"Well I would ask for your money back then."

The waitress approached them with her note pad and they smirked at each other, conspiring, as if two naughty children caught out in a misdemeanour.

"Tea for two with extra water please." Archie gave the order, and he winked at her.

My goodness, thought Beatrice, I am allowing myself to get carried away by this man. What is happening to me?

She raised her eye brows at him before assuming a casual air.

"And do you often take tea here Mr Minton?"

"Only when there is a beautiful woman to share it with."

And she smiled, unable to contain her delight in his flattery.

"Oh, so you often bring women here." She was pleased to find that she was able to parry him with her own thrust.

"Well Mrs Latterbridge! You've got me there, that little tongue of yours could sharpen knives."

"Yes it probably could."

As they sat drinking their tea their short banter petered out, both were uncertain and unwilling to bring their meeting to a conclusion, but fearful that they would only be disappointed once the tea ceremony was over.

"So," Beatrice decided to restore some distance.

"So Mr Minton is it impertinent for me to ask again about your business here in Cranbrook? Or should I mind my own business and tell you why I am here instead?"

He merely shook his head and shrugged his shoulders.

"No, nothing of great interest I'm afraid. Just a little meeting with the bank, very mundane, very.."

And he seemed to slump down a little in his chair, not noticing that he had not finished his reply. He looked at her sadly and his eyes became quite hooded. There was a sudden air of despondency and he stared again into the distance as if searching for an answer.

"Oh I see." Beatrice sat quietly. Their moment was over. They had become strangers again. The silence unsettled her.

"I erm, I came to find a little coat for Millie... a winter coat." And she nodded to herself as if he had already replied to her. But he merely sat waiting for her to continue.

"Millie my little girl? You know her? She is nearly four and a half now you know."

Archie roused himself

"Of course ah, yes, yes, quite a bonny little thing."

"I was going to bring her with me today but as we were waiting for the bus Betty called out to me. She could see that Millie was playing me up. She didn't want to come shopping, children can be so difficult when they have to be dragged around the shops. Anyway she had Ron's niece, Gwen, staying with them for the day and asked if Millie wanted to stay with them and be a playmate for Gwen. I was quite relieved especially with the weather looking so uncertain!"

He nodded, screwing up his eyes as if to recall her image, and then it came to him, the girl with a head of blond curls dancing along with her mother, chatting animatedly. Of course, little Millie! Looking back at Beatrice he saw her sad face staring back at him.

"Why if she grows up like her mother there'll have to be a beauty competition in the village!"

And he watched as Beatrice melted, her shoulders straightened and as her smile flooded her face he felt his spirits suddenly rise up again. Leaning forward he whispered.

"And then whose heart will she break?"

But they both knew that he was not referring to her daughter. He reached across the table and held her hand lightly.

"You take care of yourself Beatrice. It has been a real pleasure. You have brightened up my day. Thank you my dear."

His warm hand had only held hers for a moment but it had touched her heart. He had found a secret key to unlock a longing that she had never known she had. How could such an ordinary man do such extraordinary things? She could not allow it and yet she would not let it go.

Losing herself in the business of putting on her coat and securing her hat allowed her to find some composure. Without realising it she had been holding her breath.

"Thank you for the tea Archie, and for my eye. You have been most kind."

But before she could pull on her glove he reached out and held her hand as if to shake it, then with his other hand he enclosed it, cradling protectively in his grasp. She could feel the pressure of his grip holding her fast. Without a word he slowly released her, gently allowing her to withdraw her hand and pull on her leather gloves. Leaving the tea shop the little bell tinkled and they stood together on the step both reluctant to be the first to leave.

"It seems as if it will brighten up." Archie peered up at the sky.

"Every cloud has a silver lining." Her voice was steady, but still she felt a little breathless.

"Yes indeed, a wonderful silver lining." He touched his hat.

"Well, need to get on," he said briskly, business like giving himself a little shake like a dog who had received a wet shower. Then as he faced her their eyes held fast to one another as they drank in the image of each other

"Until we meet again!" He offered the words carelessly but his serious glance denied his flippancy as he turned away.

"Goodbye Archie."

She stood watching him walk away from her. What had happened today? Here was this big, almost clumsy man, with whom she had hardly ever passed the time of day, dismissing him as just the public house landlord and as such, of no consequence to her. She had hardly ever really noticed him before. But now, causing such an upset in her! It was silly. She was a married woman. She continued to watch him passing by The George but he did not turn around. Soon he was at the corner of the street before finally disappearing from view.

Archie walked briskly towards the bank. His thoughts were raging against each other. He was annoyed to find himself so confused. What a complete fool he had made of himself. She was probably laughing at him now. What would she think of him? Idiotic behaviour, he wasn't some school boy. Surely he should have learnt his lesson with Ethel. She had bowled him over all those years ago and look where that had landed him. Now that the awful mess with Roseanne. It had only been weeks since he had managed to free himself from that shameful muddle. He hadn't come out of that smelling of roses either. It was pretty shabby how he had been with Ethel. He could still see her face. He shuddered. He was a brute; too handy with his fists. How had he become like this? When would he learn not to get tangled up with women? Trouble all the way. He would steer clear of Beatrice, no, Mrs Latterbridge from now on. She was another man's wife, and he had his own responsibilities to attend to. No it was finished. There, he had decided. There was nothing in it, just a friendly cup of tea, nothing more.

He looked up. He had reached the bank. *Well Archie you need some luck now. If ever there was a time for the gods to pity you, let it be today!* He gave up a silent prayer and pushed open the door.

Mote House 1926
Arnold

Arnold's study never saw the morning sun and so he usually waited until the afternoon before embarking on his business in there but today things could not wait. He held the latest copy of the British Gazette in front of him and the news it contained troubled him. It had confirmed his worst fears. There were going to be blockades. Damn Churchill and his meddling with the blasted Gold Standard! Why couldn't the man see the error of his ways, he had gone blithely ahead, ignored all the good advice and look where it had got the country! It could have been over with the miners if the Government had sorted out the owners. Now even the Kent miners were contaminated by it.

Arnold rubbed his temples trying to clear his thoughts. They had already started getting in the army at the London Docks now that the dockers had gone on strike and that meant even more pilfering. They had always taken their cut. It was common knowledge that half the goods walked off that dock every day under the noses of the bosses and now the army lads would be doing the same, he had no doubt. And the officers wouldn't have a clue!

He needed to protect his food supply to Convent Garden or he would be going under next.

Arnold had always had sympathy with the miners; he'd always spoken up for them. It was a dirty business, all the lockouts and beggar wages but he could not afford to be caught up in their struggle, he had his own men to pay. He hoped that they would not be picketed. They would drag them all down. There would be anarchy.

On the front page the newspaper printed the latest headline, the report that the Flying Scotsman had been derailed in Newcastle. Nothing but hooligan behaviour! Arnold shuddered.

He still had a good supply of coal for his Palm House from the Chislet Colliery and the word was that Betteshanger would come on stream soon, if the reports were to be believed. At least the worst of the cold weather was over but it still needed heating. Arnold had been recently approached to set up his own haulage company. However it wasn't a simple business. Investment of lorries was one thing but finding enough suitable men was another and he didn't like the idea of employing a gang of men that he didn't know. There were stories of scabs being set on and it could all backfire once people came to their senses. Some had long memories especially of perceived injustices and certainly he could see that there had been injustices. He had been told, from reliable sources that the poor blighters in the Kent mines were far worse off that than those up north, or in Wales, working in dreadful conditions, terrible conditions. But getting caught up in all that dubious communist business was another thing entirely it could jeopardize his whole business. He relied on connections, word of mouth, agreements. It was a fragile enterprise and one bad deal could set it all tumbling.

Arnold shivered. How many nights had he dreamt of his pack of cards tumbling down? He didn't have a fairy godmother to right them, to stack them up once they had fallen.

Where would it all end? He'd seen some of it on the Pathe News. That hadn't been encouraging either despite watching all the troops marching past. It was said that there were over two hundred thousand men in the new Civil Constabulary Reserve but that couldn't be right. Even the government couldn't have worked that fast. Then the Cavalry Regiments had been organised but what role the Royal Horse guards would take up he had no idea. Troops against the ordinary working man stuck in his throat. That would only result in a blood bath and no mistake. He rubbed his chin. Only this morning the paper had reported, 'Either the country will break the General Strike or the General Strike will break the country', how he hated all this jingoism.

Looking up he saw that Louise had come into the room.

"Mr Minton is here to see you Arnold. I believe you asked him to come?"

She was curious. Arnold hadn't mentioned it to her and he had always shared his concerns with her. Louise felt a little put out.

Arnold frowned and grimaced. He didn't want to let Louise know how worried he was this time. He didn't even know the extent of it himself.

"Yes, dear, yes," and he tried not to meet her interrogatory glaze "Show him in here will you?"

Louise threw him a long hard look and pressed her lips together, but she went out into the entrance hall as requested.

"Come this way Mr Minton, my husband is expecting you. Would you like to take some tea now or shall you wait until later Arnold."

They came in to the study together and Arnold was stuck by the differences. Louise looked quite small and fragile against Archie's robust frame

Archie came forward and shook Arnold's hand.

"Please take a seat Mr Minton. Would you care for some tea?"

Archie shook his head.

"Perhaps later, no need for the present," and he turned to smile back at Louise.

"Thank you all the same."

The two men faced each other across the tooled leather desk. The room smelled of wax polish and pipe smoke. Arnold was at a loss of how to begin, and played for time, absentmindedly turning over his Parker fountain pen causing a small spot of ink to stain his fingers.

"I suppose you have heard about the business at Tilbury docks, strikes and what not?" he asked slowly watching Archie carefully.

"Yes a bad business." Archie was unsure how this involved him.

"We don't seem to have suffered; our supplies of ale and stout are still coming through from Fremlins Brewery." He shrugged a little.

"Not sure if they will be affected by all this."

He waited for Arnold to expand and while he waited he glanced around the room. It was an impressive room, but neat and business like. A globe stood at the far window, and there was quite a collection of books lining the shelves.

Arnold cleared his throat.

"As you may be aware Mr Minton much of my business is London based. I operate in and out of London. Covent Garden, Billingsgate, the docks...."

He paused as it allowing Archie to absorb this information. Archie nodded.

"I run a tight ship. The men whom I employ I have known for years, indeed in the early years I was one among them." He smiled.

"You follow my drift? I was like them in my youth, started at the bottom and worked my way up. We operated as a family Mr Minton and still do, I trust them and they trust me. I pay fairly and I get their labour and their loyalty. "

Archie nodded again.

"And some have risen with me; we have formed partnerships. Expansion has brought in different areas of commerce, property. Modestly I have to say these ventures have been, are, successful, very successful."

Archie watched the man thoughtfully.

"So where do I come into it?"

"I need more eyes Mr Minton, I need to be assured that there is no infiltration. A rotten apple rots the barrel."

"If new men are working on the docks if different men are manning the railways, if transport men run the food supplies, if the haulage companies want different rates how do I know how many fingers are exploring the pies, taking a slice of the cake do you see?"

"I'm not sure what expertise you think I have to offer Mr Parsons."

"I know, I know, it's a tricky business. I need a man on the ground, to see what is being said, and then to be able to relay that back to me. I need a common man. Oh I mean no offence when I say common Mr Minton. I merely mean to say that as an ordinary man you would not stand out in the crowd. I have heard that you were a very able army man. Organised, focused, that sort of thing. The men who were with you, said that you were respected for getting a job done. I remember them using the words, efficient and keeping a cool head."

"I don't know who you know." Archie was taken aback." I haven't been in contact with any of them, not since demob days."

"Ah well, people do talk Mr Minton, or may I call you Archie?"

"Yes, please do."

"Well you would have the right credentials to speak to certain people there, having to run a public house you would need to see that your supplies are secure. You could come and go without arousing any suspicion. I merely need to know what is the topic of the day, what is being said, Just that. To be my eyes and ears, see if anything has changed, that sort of thing. I think a man of your intelligence would pick things up and could sound things out. Your listening skills are legendary so the locals tell me. And what you hear stays with you. You are a man's man Archie. Just the sort of man I need."

"And you want me to go up to London, how often would I have to go up there?" Archie was bewildered.

"If you are talking about the topic of the day I would have to be haring back and forth."

"Well no, of course you couldn't do that, but a couple or more visits every week could just be enough just so that I can join the dots together so to speak. And it could all blow over in weeks or go on for months, we are rather in the dark on that score."

"And what if there is nothing to report? Are you offering a financial arrangement, to keep me away from my business?"

"Mr Minton, I would hardly ask you to come here and do this for the good of your health. Of course there would be remuneration. I would pay you any expenses you incur, and there would be a substantial sum on completion of this venture. I am talking two or three hundred pounds, more if this goes on for months. I would stand to lose a significant sum if any of my businesses failed. Think of it as a protection policy, with profits. "

"Who would I talk to, what would I ask?" Archie saw the possibility of writing off some of the debt that was persecuting his sleep at night.

"I will furnish you with the details Archie, what to look out for, etcetera. I need to know if there is any intimidation, men working in gangs that kind of thing. Stock left unattended, any money passing hands without dockets: fraud and pilfering as I said before. I need hardly spell out the practice of things disappearing from the back of a lorry, you understand my drift."

"And if there is nothing to tell or if I fail to see something that is happening right under my nose?"

"Archie, if there is nothing, well that is to the good, and if you miss something so be it, I am not going to hold you accountable. I am willing to take the risk. I do not enter lightly into any enterprise. Usually I am a good judge of character; I take a pride in that. During these years my nose has not let me down. It has been a faithful barometer."

And Arnold smiled at his analogy pointing to the long stick barometer hanging on the wall.

"It has been my fair weather friend much like that piece." and he stood up to bring to an end the interview.

"Think it over Mr Minton, but I would appreciate a speedy decision, time is of the essence in this matter."

"I won't keep you waiting Mr Parsons, you have been straightforward with me and I have been flattered by your faith in my abilities. I will accept the proposal, with expenses, but I would not be happy to take your money if things go badly with you. I would feel some blame and do not wish to place myself in such a position. I will accept your money if at the end of the day we agree that things are as they should be."

"My word, such a man of principle! I didn't quite anticipate such qualms!"

They smiled at each other and leaning across the desk they shook hands.

"Tea Mr Minton?"

"I will thank you."

Arnold led the way crossing the entrance hall. He felt a weight had been taken from him.

"Louise!" he called "Mr Minton is staying for tea." And he led the way to the drawing room.

They both settled into a chair and Arnold watched Archie appraising his surroundings.

"It's a nice room don't you think? Gets the morning sun on this side, and has a nice view of the garden."

Arnold felt pride in his home, Louise had made things comfortable, modern, not like the clutter had had seen in other houses of his contemporaries. They had not moved with the times as they had here. The room was light and airy, good furniture, some nice Hooker lithographs on the wall. A man could relax in a house like this.

Archie saw a brightly painted dome shaped doll on the table by Arnold. Arnold followed his gaze.

"A Russian doll. Ever seen one before? It's child's toy." Arnold reached over and offered it to Archie.

"Take a look."

Archie examined it and then smiling shook his head and handed it back.

"A toy? What does it do?"

Arnold twisted the doll, dressed in an apron, a scarf tied under her chin and carrying a chicken tucked under her arm, until the two parts come apart. Inside was a slightly smaller doll, still wearing a scarf but this time holding a broom. He placed the two pieces in the table showing Archie the second doll.

"First the Rooster girl, now this." Twisting the second doll he exposed another smaller doll.

"Well I'll be blowed!" Archie smiled.

"Ah but there's more." And Arnold proceeded to twist and separate the remaining dolls until the last doll emerged as a baby in a crib. Then he lined up the completed family in order of diminishing sizes for Archie to view.

"Our Beatrice used to play with this for hours. Been here ever since, just collecting dust!"

Arnold looked thoughtfully across at Archie.

"You've got a little girl haven't you?"

"Yes our Rosie, she's a funny quiet little thing."

"Here you have it, take it home for her."

Archie started to protest.

"No I insist. The wife was going to give it to Beatrice's child but Beatrice decided against it for some reason, can't think why, and so take it for your little girl instead. If she's a quiet one it would probably suit her."

As he spoke he put the dolls one inside the other together until it was reassembled.

"Here she's yours."

Louise came in carrying the tea.

"I thought I would come and join you men." She explained.

"What are you doing with the doll?"

"Just showing Archie the toy. I have said that he can take it for his little one, you don't mind."

"No of course," She smiled at Archie "We had thought to give it to Millie our granddaughter but, well, it wasn't required." She shrugged.

"Parents have different ideas these days don't they?"

But Archie watched as Louise glanced over to Arnold and saw the sadness pass between them.

St Ethelbert's Church 1927
Beatrice

It was such a beautiful day. Beatrice looked up at the sky, it was cloudless, such a perfect clear azure blue. The sun warmed her skin. How is it that the sun can make you come alive? She thought. It lifts my spirits. She stood before the large horse chestnut tree which had cast its shadow near her. The ground was covered in prickly conker shells. Most had already shed their shiny contents and been carried away by the children but there were one or two new ones that had fallen since the last raid. Millie ran over to her.

"I've got a lovely one look Mummy." She proffered up the shiny brown unblemished conker, the polished sheen of the nut glinted as it nestled in her hand.

"Why yes that's a beauty! Let's put it in my basket." and she held the basket towards Mille who triumphantly dropped it in with the others.

"It's the biggest one yet," she announced proudly.

"My one is the biggest one isn't it mummy?"

Beatrice nodded. "Mmm.... well done!"

The child skipped away delighted with the praise, kicking the grass peering down, and then brushing the over the spent casks to find another trophy.

Beatrice watched her bemused by her enthusiasm. I must have been like that at her age, she thought, how simple life was then. She put her hand to shield her eyes against the low sun's rays. Usually the field contained a flock of sheep but they were nowhere to be seen. The farmer must have moved them on or they had decided to find a different stretch of pasture. There were just the scattered black pebbles here and there to denote their recent grazing.

"Careful where you walk Millie, there are sheep droppings everywhere," she warned. But the child appeared not to notice she was so absorbed by the hunt.

"Another!" Millie stood up holding the conker aloft, before running over to her.

"Well, my lady I think we have plenty here, now the basket's nearly full. And it's time for dinner."

Millie pouted. "I don't want dinner."

"Well you may not but I do, we can always come another day," she tried to bargain.

"Come on we can have a race and see who gets back first!"

As she allowed the child to skip away in front of her she thought about the evening. It had been such a while since she had been up to Mote House; she almost felt some trepidation in going with Ronald. He made things so difficult. And she wanted to get the display ready for the church this afternoon.

Ron had asked her to collect the harvest loaf. It always made such a wonderful centre piece. She loved the sheaf of bread, had always done so even as a child. To see one thing shaped to resemble another was still magical, bread into wheat, from wheat the bread. It was a circle of life. Complete. She had loved the stories as a child, the sheaves of golden wheat bowing down before David, such vivid pictures came into her mind when she had first heard them and still now those same pictures flickered in her mind's eye.

Bread of heaven, unleavened loaves, feed my people with loaves and fishes, and He broke the bread and said eat, this is my body. The language of the bible still held its power over her.

The harvest service was always well attended. The school children had been asked to collect some fruits from the fields, in little paper baskets to remind them of nature's abundance. She smiled, reminded of the odd assortment of little rosehips and squashed blackberries that had been collected last year.

"I won!" Millie swung at the stile, her little cheeks red with the exertion.

"Well you certainly did!" She helped her clamber over the wooden bar and then they walked back to the village.

Ron saw them passing and beckoned her in.

"I've had Mike take it up to the church for you save you having to carry it."

"Oh thanks Ron that's good. I've got quite a bit to take myself and thought that I would have to be going back and forth quite a bit. That's lovely thanks."

"And how's our little lady today?" Ron swung the giggling child up.

"Careful Ron, she's getting to be quite a weight now!"

"I'm four!" announced Millie breathless as he brought her back down.

"No!" Ron gasped in mock amazement, "Never four, well, well!" Millie nodded urgently wanting him to believe her.

"I am, aren't I mummy!" she turned to Beatrice to confirm it was true.

"Yes." Beatrice laughed "I don't know where the years have gone Ron."

"Oh, a four year old princess in my shop," Ron held his apron out to curtsy before her.

Beatrice watched as the child held her little hands to her mouth to try and stop herself from giggling.

"Ron you really have a wonderful way with children."

His good humour was infectious, she felt herself caught up with it.

"Come on Millie I have lots to do today."

As they turned to leave Ron called them back.

"Do you want to leave her here with Betty, little Gwen is coming over this afternoon. She can have a bite here and you can come for her after you've finished at the church.

"Oh Ron you are a life saver, I was wondering how I could occupy her this afternoon. She would have got so bored up there. But are you sure?"

"No problem at all, my pleasure."

Beatrice turned and looked down at Millie.

"Would you like to stay here and play with Gwen when she comes?"

Millie nodded vigorously.

"That's settled then, thanks Ron." and she went out into the sunshine.

The cool of the church after the warmth of the sun outside made her shiver slightly. Across the pews the stained glass windows cast their magnificent kaleidoscope rainbows, bathing the church in different hues.

Rev. Martin came up to greet her, pressing his hands together.

"So pleased that you could come Mrs Latterbridge, you always manage to work you magic for us, so grateful for your help."

I wonder if you know how irritating you are, she thought, but she smiled putting her head to one side.

"No trouble at all I enjoy it."

"Jolly good show" and he nodded his head up and down.

Goodness you are becoming a caricature, just go away and leave me alone! Beatrice remained standing by the font smiling as he backed away, as if departing from an ancient queen, still murmuring his thanks.

I'm going to call you Uriah Heep from now on, you silly little man, go on, go on, just disappear! She remained there until he turned and opened the door, stepping down into the vestry.

Good, now perhaps I can begin. Spreading the flowers and foliage on the floor she fanned them out, surprised at the plentiful supply donated from the villages gardens and pleased to find that the gold and orange chrysanthemums and dahlias were such good specimens. These are so much better than last years, she thought as she wove the trailing foliage around the empty baskets and tubs, losing herself in the task as she balanced shapes and colours, blending and contrasting, fashioning them to create an autumnal mosaic. The fiery reds, burnished gold, vibrant yellows and warm amber, mingled with the subtle architecture of oak, beech, variegated laurel, and the berried rowan foliage. She scattered fattened rose hips and delicate lacy hops towards the front of her display, moving them about until she was quite certain of the composition before finally stepping back to survey her work.

All that was required now were the fresh vegetables and fruit, the jars of jam and bottled fruit to surround her centre piece of fashioned bread. They would arrive tomorrow, her work had been done. She sat down on her heels and squinted at it, pleased with herself and her floral tapestry.

It was so quiet in the church and being a Saturday some of the shops had closed for the afternoon. Drewe the butchers always closed before twelve and Ron followed suit at two. The thick stone walls of the church shut out any sound of traffic; it was as if she was alone in the world. She could hear her own breath, the silence. Then suddenly the heavy church door grated on its hinges and a babble of voices flooded into the church; young high voices quelled by a deep baritone.

"Will you boys be quiet! This is a church not a training circus!" The choirmaster forged ahead scattering the jostling boys in his wake as he attempted to take the lead.

"Brown, Peters, Renshaw will you quieten down! When I want your contribution I will ask for it!"

He turned and saw Beatrice who had quickly risen to her feet and stood protectively by her display.

"Oh I beg your pardon! Mrs Latterbridge! I didn't see you there." Turning to the assortment of boys jostling in the aisle his voice modified to a more melodious tone.

"Now then lads, quieten down. Quiet. Now then, now then, we need some order here. First, are you all here?"

"I am." A voice returned, and the boys sniggered.

"Renshaw, I'll have none of your cheek, your mother will hear about this, if this carries on."

"Sorry Sir!" Renshaw's apology was somewhat compromised as Beatrice saw him winking at his fellow choristers, their well-honed conspiracy to wind up the choir master quite evident. Beatrice found herself smiling in spite of herself and she attempted to clear her throat to disguise her reaction.

"Now lads, mind Mrs Latterbridge's work of art. We need to rehearse our walk from the aisle, to your positions in the stalls, which I want to be completed in an orderly fashion, not some pathetic barging about as it your usual a modus operandi, do I make myself clear?".

"Yes Sir!" The instant chorus of agreement did little to reassure him.

"Now line up. Peters you take the lead on the left and Renshaw to the right. NO!NO! I said the right, Renshaw!"

Smirking the boys jostled and pushed each other around, digging each other in the ribs as they watched the choirmaster's impatience grow.

"How many times have we done this! What's the matter Jameson why are you hanging back?"

"I usually go behind Renshaw but you've told him to go right but I'm on the left."

"S'right Sir, I do go left usually Sir, shall I change places Sir?" Renshaw's innocent attempt to assist did not fool any of them. Another outbreak of giggling commenced.

"No you will not, stay where you are. Jameson follow Renshaw, Fenton behind Peters. Right, er now where's Dickens?" Looking around he surveyed the boys.

"Well where is he?"

"Here Sir, I'm on the right side Sir, your said right now Dickens." A small boy held his hand aloft to show himself.

"No boy, I said where were you? Not go right! You go behind Fenton don't you."

 The boy nodded his agreement.

"Well go there then! We'll be all day at this rate."

The boys tittered.

"Quiet! Quiet" He quelled the noise but breathed heavily trying to compose himself, realising with some horror that Beatrice was there watching the charade.

"Now the order of music.....stand still Dickens, stop hopping about! We'll start with 'We plough the fields and scatter,' all verses, then 'For the Beauty of the earth, All things bright and beautiful,' 'Come ye thankful people come,' and we'll finish with 'All creatures of our God and King'. I might put in 'Glad that I live am I', but I'll check with the organist...."

As she walked down the aisle to the door of the church the sounds of the choirmaster battling against the boy's rude humour followed her until she reached the porch. Hesitant she stopped and blinked allowing her eyes to adjust to the sudden glare. Before her the village showed itself as a picture postcard. The road wound down the hill, white clapperboard houses and window fronted shops either side until the crossroads where the pond nestled beneath the weeping willows. Mallard ducks had settled for their afternoon siesta their heads firmly tucked down whilst the timid red beaked moorhens stayed close to the tall bulrushes keeping out of sight.

Screwing up her eyes she started on down the hill, the slight decline of the road trying to dictate the pace and quicken her step. Reaching the crossroads she stopped realising that in her revelry she had gone past the bakery, and as she turned back she was aware of a figure emerging from the Papermakers Arms. He glanced up and saw her and for a moment she was uncertain of how to act. It would look at as she was deliberately avoiding him if she turned and walked away to go back up to fetch Millie. She was embarrassed. He had not moved. If she carried on down she would have to speak to him. Beatrice decided to continue on.

"Hello Mr Minton," she called out carelessly, but finding that she needed to explain herself. "I've just been to the church to do the harvest display."

He nodded signifying that he had heard her but still he said nothing.

Why this is just embarrassing! She thought, will you just speak man and then I can go back for Millie.

Although Archie saw her confusion he couldn't trust himself to respond, he struggling to keep himself close, to keep firm, but her look of awkward resignation caught him. He breathed deeply.

"Mrs Latterbridge, how are you keeping?"

"Well, very well thank you."

"And your little girl not with you today?"

"No, no, she, she's with Mr Ticehurst. Gwen's with them, she's playing with her." Her words stumbled catching in her throat.

"Oh I see good, good. A lovely afternoon isn't it?"

The banality of their discourse horrified them both.

"I'm just going back for her now... I just came down to look at the ducks." She gestured at the sleeping birds and then looked down at them. Bright peacock green necked males surrounded by their entourage of soft beige females.

Before he could stop himself Archie found himself moving closer towards her as if drawn by a desire to view the birds for himself, casually, as if she had invited him to share the innocent moment.

"The males are so colourful aren't they?" Standing at the pond's edge she could smell his warm scent, but could not meet his eye. She breathed in, drawing his scent down into her lungs.

"Aye, always like to surround themselves with the ladies." Archie stood closely at her side. Beatrice put her hand on the old iron railing that fenced the road side of the pond to steady herself. Stems of delicate white flowered convolvulus had twisted

118

themselves around each post anchored fast, their tenacious green tentacles encircling each other in their race to bind themselves together.

Archie looked down mesmerised at her small hand so close to him; within his grasp, and he fought the overwhelming desire to lay his hand on hers.

"Not that much difference between ducks and the Homo sapien species then." Her words skimmed across the water and as she turned she saw his smile fade and his face darken.

"Maybe, maybe not, I'll not keep you then." He swung round heavily to face her.

"I'll say good day Mrs Latterbridge. My regards to your husband." It was as if he had stung her. Her face lost its colour and she pressed her lips together to prevent any words tumbling from them.

"Yes good afternoon Mr Minton." Cold and haughty Beatrice straightened herself, standing tall before him before backing away and hurrying up the hill.

I'll never understand that man; she fumed as she quickened her pace against the gradient of the hill. He blows hot and cold. Friendly one moment and then can't even be civil. And to think I didn't want to hurt his feelings. Well I shan't be worrying about him any day soon! And her anger propelled her forward.

Damn woman, Archie thought, butter wouldn't melt one moment and then as deadly as a sneaky adder the next.

He walked heavily back to his pub, kicking a stray stone into the gutter before stepping inside.

Harvest Supper 1927
Archie & Beatrice

Rows of dancing lights flicked from the candles secured inside the jam jars which Robert Drewe and Joseph Simmons had tied to the tall wooden stakes which they had banged in at intervals along the lane leading to the village hall. All afternoon there had been a frenzy of activity with harassed mothers and excited children getting under their feet. Trays of sandwiches had been cut, pies baked, cakes and buns decorated with cream and icing sugar, toffee apples dripped surplus toffee onto the trays, jellies had finally set and the men were trying to erect the trestle tables between the bales of hay. Orders were being given but each group seemed intent on organising themselves. Exasperated by the chaos Betty shouted.

"Stop everyone! Mr Latterbridge, Ron, everyone stop!"

Surprised to hear a shout there was a moment of calm and everyone turned to see who it was.

"Now then, we need all the tables together up here at the far end for the food, and then bales to each side. Then there will be more room down here for dancing. No, Mr Simmons, we don't need more bales over there!"

Robert Drewe chuckled. "Watch out lads we've got the sergeant major in."

The men looked sheepishly at Betty.

"She's quite a formidable woman isn't she Ron!"

Ron rubbed his nose, "Well you've got to let them take the lead now and then!"

"Ron Ticehurst I heard that!" Betty marched down the hall.

But the men obediently took her lead, and following her direction the hall finally started to take shape.

An assortment of oil cloths covered the tables and then Archie appeared at the doorway rolling a barrel before him. A cheer went up at his arrival.

"Mr Minton, can you bring that up to the front and then give a hand with the bales? How many have we still got to fit in?"

"That's the lot now."

"Where are you putting the band?"

Various suggestions were given simultaneously, and a crescendo of discussions took place, each man trying to make his voice heard above the rest.

"Last time they stood at the front."

"No they didn't, they sat over here on the bales."

"Aye that's right they did."

"Well there are only three of them this time. Mickey can't play this year."

The news was greeted with a groan. "And he's the best one of 'em!"

"You'll never notice once you've had a couple of pints."

"Cheeky bugger!"

Outside it was dusk and the little line of candles in their glass houses took on an extra brilliance.

They sauntered out. "See you later!"

"Bring your own tankards lads."

∞

When the light had finally faded, the black velvet sky displayed its own set of flickering dots which, when watched for long enough, seemed to travel in one direction, but when viewed again appeared to be back in the same place.

Already the hall was packed. Men crowded together at the bar, the children slid on and off the bales and the women patted their hair with one hand and smoothed their long skirts surreptitiously checking to see who had the trimmest figure, the nicest blouse. Beatrice stood to one side with Ronald. He had not yet gone to the bar.

121

"Drink?" He enquired lethargically looking above her head towards the front of the hall.

"Yes please Ronald, lemonade with a dash of something in it. I don't know what they've got."

"I'll see what there is," he spoke again to the space above her head and sauntered away from her.

The hall was beginning to heat up as more bodies crowded in. I'm sure there are more here than last year, thought Beatrice and she studied the room looking to see who was there. Roseanne was surrounded by a dense group of men who only gave way momentarily to allow one of them to peel away, with their beer glasses raised high above their head, clasped firmly between two hands to prevent themselves being jostled or the beer to be spilled.

"One at a time lads, the barrels still full, no need to…."

"Whoa watch your backs, mind your backs!"

"What's your poison?"

"Get em in lad, just a half for me."

She watched their good natured thumps on each other's backs and bear hugs as they greeted each other as if they had been parted for years. Their easy good natured shouts and banter caused other standing groups and couples to raise their voices so that they could hear one another. Ronald stood on the periphery of their tight circle attempting to get closer to the bar. One turned and saw him but swung back unwilling to give way to him. Why, she thought, even although they have known him all the years, he is not one of them, he is still an outsider, they do not like him.

One or two of the bystanders watched their children becoming more daring in their play, taking turns to jump from the bales and play a game of tag.

"Careful there young'un!" A fallen child was scooped up and set back down on its feet, but the next moment it had darted off eager to resume the game.

"They'll all be worn out by bed time!"

Betty came and stood at her shoulder.

"Pardon?" Beatrice strained to make sense of her words.

Betty cupped her hand to her mouth, "I said at this rate they'll all be worn out!"

"Has Millie had anything to eat yet?"

"No I was waiting for Ronald to get us drinks first," she raised her voice for Betty to hear.

"Looks as if he's got a long wait then!" and Betty jerked her head towards the bar. Ronald appeared to have made no headway in penetrating the wall of men.

"Ron!" Betty called him over. "Come here."

He wove his way around groups towards them.

"What love?"

"Beatrice still hasn't got a drink; can you give Ronald a hand?"

Ron smiled down at Beatrice, "What's he getting you?"

"I'm not sure," she laughed," something nice and cool I hope!"

Ron swung away from them and as he approached the bar she watched as he placed one hand on Ronald's shoulder and then, like the Red Sea, the men parted for him to take his place alongside them.

Beatrice felt her face redden. Betty was saying something to her and she nodded without wanting to ask what had been said.

"Yes." She replied.

And Betty carried on her one sided conversation only stopping when she was distracted by Gwen who had tumbled off a bale.

"Oh goodness!" and she hurried over to rescue the child.

Ron had reached the front of queue, dragging Ronald along with him.

Beatrice looked around for Millie and saw her chattering alongside Rosie and Jack. They were sharing a pork pie, with Jack obviously attempting to demonstrate how much he could stuff into his mouth at one go.

"Jack Minton, you'll be choking to death if you carry on like that!" She had pushed her way through the throng and bent down to speak to them.

They looked up at her and giggled.

"Jack's being a piggy wig!" Said Millie,

"Yes he's eating our porkie pie!" Rosie nudged Millie in the ribs. And the three dissolved into giggles at their joke. Jack turned red, then spluttered and finally spat out chunks of pie.

"Oh Jack's being sick!"

"No I'm not!" he choked indignantly, "the piggy's trotter got caught down my throat!"

Beatrice found herself caught up in their easy camaraderie.

"Well young man, I hope that you don't turn into a little pig yourself eating like that. Now where are your manners all of you." but she smiled as she remonstrated. "No more of that thank you."

"Now do you want a drink yet?" the three shook their heads vigorously wanting to be left to themselves.

"Are you sure?" and all three nodded energetically.

"Well I'll go and see where your father's got to, now behave, and that means all three of you."

As her back was turned she could hear them giggling again. She turned in towards the crowded room searching to see where Ron and Ronald had got to but as she couldn't penetrate the swell of people. Goodness it's even more crowded than before. She tried to turn and as she moved away a man stepped heavily backwards onto her foot.

"Ouch!"

"Oh sorry love." He turned apologetically, "have I hurt you duck?"

"No, no problem," but her foot was burning and she wanted to sit down to rub it. She managed to squeeze through and limped over to the wall but there was nowhere to sit.

Ronald was still nowhere to be seen so she waited; standing on one leg and rubbing her foot against the calf of her other leg. "There you are!" Ronald bumped up against her. "Where have you been I've been looking all over the place? Why didn't you stay where you were?" His indignation marred his fine features. "I wanted to make sure that Millie was alright and then someone trod on my foot!"

He glanced down at her foot without remarking on it, and then at her, "Anyway here's your drink, what's left of it. It's like a bun fight in here."

Accepting the half full glass of tepid liquid she swallowed thirstily.

"My, it is hot in here now."

"How long to you want to stay?" Ronald sipped his drink.

"We've only just got here; we've hardly been here two minutes! The children are having a nice time, I haven't eaten yet and I want to hear the band. It's ages since we had a dance."

Ronald sighed. He looked around the room, "It's not really my cup of tea you know."

Beatrice chewed her lip. He was so insufferable at times. He turned the nicest occasions into a wake.

"Well I shall be staying."

Ronald raised his eyebrows. "What did you say?"

"You heard Ronald. I don't want to leave yet awhile that's all."

"As you wish, though how you think people are going to dance here beats me, there's no room to throw a cat."

"It always thins out once the food has gone. You know that" There'll still be a long wait." He was determined to dampen her enthusiasm.

"Oh Ronald!" She lost patience. "Go if you want to, but you'll have to take Millie when you do because I want to have a dance."

Glancing away from him she saw the Reverent Martin bearing down on them.

"Look the vicar's coming to have a chat with you, how nice." and before he could answer she had pushed her way back into the crowd leaving him open mouthed.

When she looked back he could see him trapped against the wall, nodding vaguely and holding his head down to catch the flow of the vicar's insistent monologue.

Serves you jolly well right! She suddenly felt light hearted, pleased with herself and her artful escape, she breathed in and smiled.

Archie saw her across the room. He saw her close her eyes, throw her head back and stretch her shoulders as if she were releasing a heavy burden. He searched for Ronald, puzzled that she was alone and then as a group moved to one side he caught a glimpse of a tall dark headed man. Ronald stood stiffly against the wall, his pale face wearing a look of ill-disguised weary impatience. Then as he continued to watch he saw the cause of his discomfort. Ronald was trapped by a smaller slighter figure talking animatedly at his side. Archie smiled. So that's why you're looking so pleased with yourself Beatrice!

∞

Once most of the food had been eaten, Margaret, Betty, Ethel and Mary took up the table coverings whilst the men set about dismantling the trestle tables, turning them on their sides to stack against the wall. Tired children were being buttoned into their coats as the band arranged their makeshift platform, placing the boards at the front of the hall. Discordant notes filled the air as they tuned their instruments. Some couples sat waiting on the vacated bales whilst others grouped some chairs around the edges of the room in between the bales.

"We need some space to dance."

"Keep them closer together they're in the way there."

The bar was still surrounded by a happy group of men.

Beatrice knelt down to finish fastening the buttons of Millie's coat.

"Time to go home, jiggery jig!"

"I enjoy myself," Millie announced

"Good that's nice, isn't it Daddy?" Beatrice lifted her face up at Ronald who stood apart from them impatient to move.

"And did you have enough to eat?" Beatrice stood up.

"I did. I had jelly."

"Lovely."

Betty came up to them. "Thought you two wanted to stay for a dance."

"No, I was, well, we decided to get back for Millie," Beatrice started to pull on her own coat.

"Look if you two want to stay I'll take Millie for you."

"No, no we couldn't let you do that." Ronald held out his hand for Millie.

Beatrice stared at him.

"It's no trouble at all, really it's not, and she's always as good as gold."

"Well if you're sure." Beatrice turned away from him avoiding his eyes.

"No Mrs Ticehurst, we couldn't impose on you again. Anyway I'm quite bushwhacked myself."

Betty saw her fleeting look of disappointment.

"You young things! And Beatrice in her lovely new frock! Look, you stay for a couple of dances and then come on up for her. I'm not going to have no for an answer. Come on Millie. Let's go and see what the cat's been up to whilst we've been away."

She held out her hand to Millie and the child took it. Ronald watched as she led her away.

"I see you've got your own way again," he sneered. Peering through the smoky gloom across the shadowed hall, beyond the swirl of dancers a lone figure caught his attention. Leaving Beatrice he walked towards the bar. Roseanne stood fanning herself with a piece of cardboard and as he came closer she glanced up at him and smiled.

Beatrice had lost sight of him in the melee of movement. Slipping off her coat she took it the tiny cloakroom and returned to the hall. Anger with Ronald had taken the pleasure of the evening away. Her resentment festered. All she had wanted was to dance and he couldn't even allow her that. Why did he have to be so difficult? She had taken such care with her appearance tonight and he hadn't even remarked upon it, not one complimentary word. In fact she couldn't think when he last said anything about how she looked. It was as if she were invisible. And she was still young! Enviously she watched other couples holding each other close, smiling into each other's eyes, moving together as one.

As one dance ended another began. Moving along the side of the hall she edged her way round to see if she could find him, trying not to collide with the energetic dancers. I am a wallflower, she seethed, and here I am hugging the wall, trying not to draw attention to myself. It is humiliating. He has deliberately humiliated me to get his own back. An elbow drove into her side, and she gasped to catch her breath.

"Sorry!"

She shook her head, indicating that no harm had been done, trying to appear unconcerned and laughing off their apology.

"Not dancing then?" Archie had put out a hand to steady her and then frowning into her serious face he was suddenly concerned. "Are you alright?"

Beatrice was mortified. "Oh yes. No, no, I was just going to get a drink, it's so hot in here."

He glanced down at her again and then turned his back against the dancing couples in the packed hall to try and give her a little protection, but his action merely caused them to be pressed closer together.

"Isn't Roland with you?"

"Well yes he was, but I seem to have momentarily lost him." She affected a casual air, trying to distance herself from it all. But Archie did not move away instead he put his hand against the wall above her shoulder to keep and give her space and to steady himself. But again the action brought with it an intimacy; it was as if she was enveloped by him.

Raising her head she looked into his face as he looked down at her. Her delicate beauty caught his breath. Their eyes met for a brief, almost imperceptible moment, his clear blue eyes darkened, as he drank in the look of her serious grey eyes. Next, bewildered, he turned away and shook his head. She thought she heard him catch his breath, before he turned back again, breaking the spell. He took his hand from the wall.

"Did you want that drink? Shall I fetch you one?"

"No, no, I wouldn't want to trouble you." Her breath came with some difficulty. She brought her hand to her chest. She felt a tight band gripping itself across her.

And when he saw her hand spread across herself as if she had been wounded, he reached out to her without a thought and pressed her urgently to him. She was held so close to his chest that she could feel his heart thumping against her. The strength of his warm embrace melted her. She felt that she was merging into him. It was as if she had always known him, that she was a part of him, and he, a part of her.

He buried his head into the pillowed softness of her hair, drinking in her intoxicating scent. He wanted to crush her to him; his need of her was overpowering. They stayed in their tight embrace, he unwilling to release her, and she lost in the powerful wonder of it.

The darkness of the hall and the dancers surrounding them sheltered their intimacy.

"My God woman!" His faint whispered breath came in hoarse snatches. "What have you done to me?"

And then suddenly it was over. He released her quickly.

"I am so sorry, forgive me. Beatrice I have no idea what came over me!" He was mortified by what he had said, of what she must have heard, angry that he must have appeared to her to be so ridiculous. He had made himself a laughing stock, acting like some love-struck boy. And now she would believe him to be a shallow philanderer, just an untrustworthy rogue. He should have known better. He was ashamed. He meant nothing to her, how could he?

"Let me find Ronald for you." He was desperate to escape from her.

Beatrice felt as if she had been ripped from him. She felt an awful fear that she had lost something so dear to her, so valuable and that it would tear her soul open, but she would not say those things, she could not let him see that she was breaking apart. She did not have the strength or the courage. How could she say this when they hardly knew each other? It was impossible. He did not mean those words. It had been pretence, just a game he played. It was just his way. He thought nothing of her.

Once more she stood alone in the hall. All her hopes for a happy evening were quite dashed. She pushed her way to the back of the hall, found her coat amongst the piles bundled on top of one another in the corner of the small vestibule and went out into the night. The lights on the poles twinkled in and out of focus as she fought against the need to give way to tears. Music and shouts of laughter followed her departure as a painful rebuke, reminding her of the happiness that she had not shared. Sadly she realised that Ronald would not even worry that she was not there. Her self-pity absorbed her, held her unmoving, as she stood under the black starlit sky. Her mind battled with confused images and shadows, replaying snatches of half remembered conversation. Finally her breath quietened and straightening her back she slowly wiped her face, feeling the coolness of her hand against the heat of her cheek. I am stronger than this, she thought fiercely, and with renewed determination she made her way up the hill to collect her child.

The Stream 1927
Rosie, Jack, and Thomas

It had been Thomas's idea to catch tiddlers that afternoon, or it could have been Rosie's. Someone suggested it. The children had started off at the village pond trying to see if they could see any fish but the ducks had stirred up the mud and the weed had become too thick. They trailed along the lane towards the apple orchards, Thomas led the way. Jack was in charge of the old wonky net which Mr Simmons had said they could have. He had forgotten that it was there and only just discovered it trapped under some boxes when he was having a sort out.

"I can't sell it." He had told them sadly, "it's almost parting company with its pole."

In fact the netting had become so frayed that it threatened to snap away completely but the children were pleased with the present of an unexpected trophy and were determined to try it out. Jack had tried to wind some wool around the perimeter of the net with little success.

Thomas used the strong stick which he had just found to swish at the heads of the stinging nettles along the path.

Rosie hung back. She was annoyed that she had not yet found a stick for herself and that both boys had said that they didn't think that girls could catch fish anyway.

Thomas looked up at the trees. They were groaning under the weight of the fruit. Some early ones had already fallen and had created a small lumpy carpet under each tree.

"Anyone looking?" Jack scrambled up the bank towards a small gap in the fence.

"I'll stand watch." Thomas stood on serious sentry duty in the middle of the lane holding his stick vertically to the ground and placing his body to face the fence so that he could keep watch both directions just by turning his head.

Jack squeezed through the gap, his jacket just slightly caught up by the prickles of the hawthorn before his was able to pull away. The children watched as his legs disappeared.

"Cor there are loads here, real whoppers." They could hear his voice on the other side.

"Just get a couple now and we'll come back for more later." Thomas was keen to get going.

Rosie knew that Mr Parson's motor car would be coming. She had seen it in her mind's eye long before it arrived. There was a way now for her. She wondered whether she should warn them but decided to wait for a while. She wanted the net.

"If I help you not get caught - can I have the net?" She sauntered over to the net that was lying at the edge of the lane and picked it up.

"Hey put it down," Jack's head appeared through the gap.

Rosie considered her position. Thomas still stood on sentry duty he still had not heard the car.

"If you get caught with those apples you won't half be in trouble, anyway I know something, Mr Parson's coming, and he'll catch you if you don't come out now. Let me have the net or else I'll say what you've been doing."

Thomas considered her. He smiled at her fierce determination.

"You are a funny thing Rosie."

She shrugged and went over to pick some long strands of grass and holding them between her lips she attempted to blow thought her thumbs as she had seen Thomas do when they were last out.

Jack had just started to wriggle through when he heard Thomas shout.

"Car, there's a car!"

Jack suddenly found that it had been easier to get in than it was to get out and struggled with renewed rigour to push himself back though, his coat snagging on the small thorns of the hawthorn.

"Give'us a hand, quick!"

Thomas grabbed the shoulders of his jacket and tugged desperately. Jack struggled and then finding himself suddenly free slid down the bank. The two boys sat by the bank as car gently rounded the bend in the road.

"I won't tell on you this time." Rosie announced, standing between them and the approaching vehicle, waving the net vigorously as the car slowed to pass them before proceeding on its stately way, "but it was me that saved you. Me and my net, I told you so, so it's mine."

The two boys looked bemused.

"We'll take turns okay?" Thomas grinned at her.

Rosie smiled, "If I let you." And then a sudden tightness caught her chest. She saw the dark water swirling and dragging Thomas away from her.

"What's up Rosie? I said fair turns, didn't I?" Thomas shook his head as he considered the serious set of her mouth.

"You are a funny thing!" and he turned away to catch up with Jack who had decapitated the cow parsley heads further up the lane.

"Wait up Jack! Give us an apple then." And he jogged away leaving Rosie behind.

She trailed further behind, allowing them to disappear from view. By the time she turned up towards the long drive there was no sign of either of them, but she knew that the ponds were hidden away down on the right behind the row of elms and the tangle of shiny large-leafed rhododendrons.

But she didn't follow the small path, but instead with sudden urgency continued up the drive. Her heart thudded, and there was a pounding in her ears, as she drew level with the car, now empty of its previous occupants, stood parked outside the front door.

Then, just as she was about to knock, the door opened and Arnold Parsons stepped out.

"Goodness young lady, what can I do for you?" And his jovial tone gave way to concern as he saw her pale face.

"What's the matter child?"

She seemed to shudder and then cried out, "an accident! There's been an accident! Thomas is in the pond! He's going to drown!"

Arnold recoiled. "My God!" He wheeled round and shouted back into the dark interior of the house.

"Louise, fetch help, get one of the men to meet me at the ponds. Get Forrester to bring some rope!"

He caught Rosie's hand in his as they started to run together.

"Show me girl, which pond?" and allowed her to signal the way before abandoning her to forge on ahead.

As he raced through the bushes following the small track down towards the water's edge he could see a boy floundering in the water, and another small boy shouting as he tried to stretch out holding a small stick towards his friend.

Then he turned as he heard Arnold's shouts. "Keep back lad. I'm here."

Jack screamed back, "he's stuck, he can't swim!"

Arnold slithered down the bank and found himself in the muddy edge of water, the boy was within reach if he could just take another few steps, but the mud held his boots fast.

"Damnation!"

He looked towards the frightened boy on the bank, and wildly around him to find some means of securing his position and extending his reach. The mud held tight entrapping both legs, he could see nothing that could be used and then looking back at the child in the water he could only see the top of his head in the swirling water.

"My God he's going!"

Arnold heaved one leg from the mud and placed it heavily back in, his heart pounding as he could feel his balance compromised in the black oozing mud. Desperately he lunged towards the area where the head had been and felt his hand make contact.

Grabbing and grasping with both hands he pulled the mass towards him and found that he had the boy's coat collar in a tight grip. The boy's head was lolling and sinking in front of his chest. He heaved the sodden mass closer to him but could not turn or move. His attempts to move fastened him closer to the mud threatening to pull him over.

Again he tried to turn to the bank to grasp the overhanging slender plants but the stems gave way as he wrenched them from their roots.

He thrashed in the swirl of mud, the stench of undisturbed rotting vegetation caught at his throat and still the boy made no movement, hanging from his arms as a misshapen scarecrow.

"Hold on Sir. We'll have him!" Arnold turned his head and saw, from the corner of his eye, the gardener's boy, with a rope hanging heavily over one shoulder running towards him.

"Don't come any further!" Arnold shouted. "Make a loop, throw it over us otherwise we'll both go under! I can't free my hands, I daren't let go!"

He tried to quell the fear that was threatening to overwhelm him as the mud continued to pull him down.

The rope snaked towards them but hit his back and slithered away.

"Again, throw again!"

His fingers were locked in the boy's clothing, and his breath came in shuddering gasps. He thought he heard a gasp, but was unsure as to who had made the noise. Again the rope reached him but failed to encircle them.

"Again boy!" he tried to steel himself against the panic that was gripping his heart.

When the thick rope splashed beside him, once again missing its target, he decided to throw caution to the wind and freeing one hand made a desperate attempt to grasp it. His fingers rounded in the rough twine of the rope's skeins.

"Don't pull!" He grunted. "I haven't got a proper hold." He twisted his hand, forcing the rope to wind around itself his wrist and desperate not to loosen his grip on both boy and the one chance of their survival.

"Now pull!" he ordered.

The boy wound some rope around his chest and leaning back began to pull but the grassy bank afforded no hold. He too slithered trying to keep away from the edge.

Then they both heard shouts. Forrester and some of his men came running over.

"Form a line. No, go further back." Forrester clipped orders, managed the men's position.

"Play out some of the rope but don't let go. Easy does it." He joined the lad at the edge.

"Step back, that's it." He guided the boy away to a firmer surface.

"Now lads, take the strain and hold." He turned and saw Jack with his nose running, his hand held to his mouth to stop the sounds that threatened to overwhelm him, and his red rimmed eyes staring wildly about him.

"Lad, go back to the house and ask them to fetch Dr Sutton. Now lad, go!"

The boy shook himself free of the awful spell of inaction and then bounded away.

Turning back to Arnold his formal tone changed, he lightened the moment with an encouraging smile.

"Not long now Sir and we'll have you out in a jiffy." And he stepped next to the boy and took a portion of the rope.

"Now lads go gently, I want you to take the strain and ease back, pulling as you go. That's it, keep it going and ease back." His low voice offered reassurance, calm and security.

Arnold felt the searing pain as the rope tightened around his wrist gripping his flesh in a heated vice. He held his arm to his side. The boy in his arm felt like a dead weight, and he prayed that it was not so.

Slowly he could feel that the sucking mud was releasing them. He squelched sideways and then hands were grabbing at his clothes and he was heaped onto the bank as a soggy mess of debris.

They pulled the boy away and started to pummel his back. There was no sound from him. Arnold felt a black despair threatening to overwhelm him.

Then, finally the boy choked, gasped and bubbling dark liquid escaped from his blue tinged lips. Arnold heard himself moan and his tears fell uncontrolled.

The men looked on aghast at the scene, then their discomfort was relieved as they heard shouts and Dr Sutton appeared at the brow of the bank carrying his bag, followed by the billowing skirts of Louise Parsons holding Jack's hand and Rosie trailing in their wake dragging a twisted fishing net behind.

"Arnold!" Louise looked from Arnold and Thomas and then back again.

"Thank heavens!" She shook herself as if to shake off the fear that had enveloped her.

"How is the child Doctor?" She turned to the prostrate figure masked by the doctor's coat as he worked over the boy.

"He's ingested much of the water but he is breathing." The doctor rested back on his heels.

"I need to check his lungs are clear but there is a risk," and he shook his head when he realised that the audience hanging on each word contained two shocked children.

"Carry him up to the house." Can we use a room?" He inclined his head to Louise, his request already expecting her acquiescence.

"Of course!" She bent towards Arnold.

"Can you stand dear?" Then she marshalled her thoughts.

"Forrester get one of your men to run back to the house, ask the maid to prepare the drawing room for the child; we need some clean towels and hot water for the doctor. My husband needs a warm bath and a set of fresh clothes. One of the men can go to

138

the village, use the car it's still on the drive. Maynard can drive him. Tell the landlord Archie Minton that there has been an accident and then go down to the Station and tell Mr Fulwood that Dr Sutton is attending to their son but that he's out of immediate danger. Bring his mother back if that is possible. Erm..."

She looked around trying to gather her thoughts. The men watched her, waiting to be released and to follow her orders. Jack and Rosie caught her eye.

"Ah yes, take the... take the children back to the house they both need some sweet tea for the shock. No, perhaps we need to get them back home. Take them back to the house first, and then when Maynard returns he can take them home."

Arnold stood uncertainly rubbing his wrist; the rope had torn his skin leaving reddened, swollen, bloody wheals. Both shoes had been sucked away by the mud but one sock had managed to cling to his mud coated foot. His lower clothes were unrecognisable as his garments; they were contoured in green weed slime and thick brown mud, giving them an appearance of thickened muscle and sinew.

Louise looked back at him. Her anxiety deepened the frown line between her brows, suddenly marking her age.

"Come my dear." She went to take his arm.

"No love, I'm a filthy mess. Leave me be, or we'll both be like mudlarks!" His wan smile apologised for the rebuff.

And stretching he arched his back. "Come let's all get back, then soonest mended."

They watched the odd assortment in the procession which preceded them, the two children trailing behind one of the men, foiling his attempt to take their hands. Thomas was being carried by another, with the doctor trying valiantly to keep pace, and Forrester with his arm round the shoulders of his assistant offering words of encouragement.

The forgotten rope lay curled untidily at their feet, a somnambulant snake wearied by its endeavours.

Ivy Leaf Cottage 2009
Rosie

I knew then that my heart would be broken. I had foiled the first assault on his life and would be powerless to prevent the next. But I would have lost him long before then. He would be taken from me despite my best endeavours to hold him fast. I kept him whole for another to take the prize. And despite my desire to hate her for it I couldn't. She too would suffer by my hand and so I finally let him go, as a penance for my guile.

We four children, Millie, Jack, Thomas, Jack and I were as thick as thieves, during those early days before the war. We were afforded so much freedom then to roam the countryside. Jack and I because our mother Ethel was pleased to have us out from under her feet, Thomas, because he was trusted to be sensible by Samuel and Alice Fulwood, and Millie because she wore Beatrice's resistance down with her insistence that it wasn't fair not to be able to play with her friends. Beatrice would make us give her our solemn word that we would look after her.

Jack was mortified that she had to tag along, reasoning that he already had the burden of having a baby sister in tow all the while. How things would change in a few short years. I was always determined to be wherever Thomas would be. He was the best of me. Had I played it differently, but there we are, I set the pattern of our lives and they too played their parts that I had allotted.

I watched Archie vacillate between the women in his life. Despite his best intentions, he still dallied with hapless Roseanne. He kept Ethel almost at arm's length unless the drink and her antagonism got the better of him, and then there was Beatrice. With her he was all at sea. They danced around each other, mesmerised and rebelled by turn. Frightened by their attraction and yet drawn ever closer by their need to be loved and comforted. Together they were the best of themselves, apart they were lost souls.

And I was to provide the catalyst. My actions that day did not go unmarked. Arnold and Louise were amazed to discover that child of such a tender age could have the presence of mind to warn of the impending danger.

"And she was merely a tiny scrap not yet six years old!" They were happy to add detail to the retelling of the event. I was invited to play at the big house with the toys that had been purchased for Millie. I became their darling, perhaps a substitute at first for the granddaughter who was still kept away. Being precocious I had learnt to read fluently by the time that I was six, and Arnold's library entranced me. Archie's small part in keeping Arnold's business secure added to their pleasure in having me there. Father and daughter were held in esteem; a clever daughter of a fair and astute man. Arnold approved of us both. And to be fair my father was a different man when he was with Arnold. I saw a side to him that he never showed at home. I could have almost loved him then if he could have allowed it. When I saw the library for the first time I knew how father too could be lost in that world, consumed by the words wrapped in the text of emotion and reason, astounding images, hearing thoughts and sharing discoveries, learning of secrets and dreams, colourful pictures, light and shade, an endless voyage. The magic of a created world made more vivid and more real than our own. Stepping inside a cocoon of knowledge, and cushioned by the salve, and caress of those words playing across the captivating pages. A powerful love affair of heart and mind.

I should have kept to the books and not tried to rewrite lives.

A year or so after our drama by the ponds Millie was finally allowed to come to the house to play. Not that I was happy with that, as it interrupted my quiet sessions in Arnold's library. Suddenly I was expected to be the friendly playmate. Things had changed for Beatrice and she was grateful to have Milly looked after, bewildered by her own muddled assignations, finding that she no longer knew how to control events that threatened to undo her.

Pretty little Millie was empty-headed at the best of times and she was mostly unaware of my half-hearted pretence to involve her in my activities, participation which only became apparent when there was a witness to our games.

Somehow during my time at Mote House softened me, I allowed my happiness to become magnanimous. I could see father and Beatrice forever circling each other, like two magnets constantly turning away and together, attracting and repelling in equal measure. I decided to allow their dance to unify.

I knew on that day with searing clarity that Louise Parsons was to take Milly to Tunbridge Wells for a new dress; that Beatrice would take her early to the big house ready for the trip. I suggested to father, as he finally unfolded his newspaper after coming up from the cellar that I had forgotten to say that Mr Parsons had urgently wanted to speak to him, and he had said that I could play with Millie. I knew that by the time we arrived, Mr Parsons would be out on business and that Mrs Parsons would have already left with Millie. My timing was perfect. As we arrived on the steps of the house, Beatrice opened the door to us.

∞

"Goodness I didn't know you were coming." She looked flustered and took a step back.

"I came to see your father; he wanted a word with me I believe." She shook her head.

"He has gone out to speak to the suppliers about new stocks for the orchard I believe. I'm not sure whether he will be back before luncheon. It may be later on this afternoon I'm afraid, he usually likes to see two or more to discuss the new varieties." Beatrice looked apologetic.

"I wonder if your appointment went out of his head, he has such a lot to think about just recently. Or maybe there could be a misunderstanding?"

Archie looked down at me and I shrugged.

I kept my eyes lowered and willed her response. *Invite us to come in, do it now.*

Beatrice swallowed awkwardly,

"Where are my manners, do come I now that you have come all this way. Can I get you some refreshment, coffee or a tea perhaps? The child..." and she waved her hand in my direction, "she may like to take a look in the library. I have heard that she is a veritable little bookworm."

Her nervousness made her speak too quickly. And she became more awkward knowing that she appeared so flustered.

"That would be very nice." Archie smiled and as I looked up I saw a man that resembled my father but was so altered and so warm that it caused a hard lump to stick in my throat so that I daren't breathe.

I trotted away to the library unwilling to break the wonderful spell that was cast over them.

I knew that her face would reflect that same radiance. I did not stay in the library. I wanted them to feel free, without the constraint of a child under the same roof. I made it known that I wanted to read in the garden, to the maid who came with a glass of lemonade, and so I gave them the large house, no cause to have to leave too soon, a time for them to fold themselves together and find utter contentment in their intimacy.

∞

Later that year Beatrice presented her husband with another daughter, and they named her Dulcie, and during that time Beatrice blossomed, not only with the pregnancy but her

144

happiness permeated every part of her daily routine. She became immune to Ronald's pettiness.

Archie's changes were more subtle. He certainly drank less but Ethel's ability to dull his spirits continued, as did her baleful watch over her two children. She became more spiteful to me and more accommodating to Jack's wilful behaviour. Where formally Archie had raised a hand to her, he now turned away in disgust. But with me I sensed a more benevolent side. He was not that loving man that gave himself to Beatrice but at least there seemed to be a truce, and a chance to rub along together. Beatrice's acknowledgement of my love of books had surprised Archie, he had not thought of it before and when he did it gave him a jolt to have missed such a thing in his own child. His sense of pride was marred by having to admit to himself that he had not seen it for himself. It diminished him and he felt a deep sense of shame which he hoped that Beatrice would not discover. When he started to explore his feelings about his children he realised with horror that his daughter had never really impinged on his daily routine. She had been a shadow that he had consigned to the outer extremities of his existence. He could not put a finger on it but when he examined their relationship and watched her more closely he realised that he knew nothing, they were strangers merely sharing the same home and the same mundane everyday events. Then when he happened to see her watching him, her serious penetrating stare that flickered away as if it had never happened, he felt inadequate, unmasked, as if she were the adult and he the child. It unnerved him and a sadness for them both settled in his heart, because he knew that he could never be the father that she deserved. He simply could not find it in himself to reach out to her. And he knew that she would rightly judge him for that failing. Then once he had allowed such intimate circumspection he consigned it to a separate place, a box that he would keep closed. Henceforth he played a public role that marked him as a solicitous father, and allowed me to settle back into the shadows.

Mote House   Spring 1929
Archie & Beatrice

When Beatrice opened the door Archie stepped back in surprise. He was so convinced that the maid would be standing there in her place that he felt embarrassed to have been so wrong-footed.

He allowed himself to be guided into the spacious hallway. A large vase filled with creamy double-petal narcissi, drooping red and orange tulips, and strong-stemmed yellow daffodils with short frilled trumpets sat on the table beneath the stairwell. To the left, a stand held some furled black umbrellas and two silver-topped walking canes on one side and on the top sat a little silver dish with an open box of calling cards. Two hats were held on the hooks astride a large oval inset mirror. Above the heavy door the stained glass window panels lent an ethereal light, staining the black and white tiles in a Turner seascape.

"Goodness I didn't know that you were coming." Her wide eyes fastened on his.

Archie swallowed: his mouth suddenly dry and his tongue felt thick.

"I came to see your father; he wanted a word with me I believe." He looked around him aware of the stillness and of his own awkwardness.

Beatrice heard her own reply, she saw the child and then they were alone, standing together in the hallway.

They breathed in, slowly adjusting to themselves.

"Please come into the drawing room." She led the way and he followed her long skirt and swaying hips mesmerised by the fluidity of movement and the soft sigh of his own breath.

"You didn't say, tea or coffee?" she did not meet his eye but indicated a chair.

Archie sat down but then stood again.

"I don't like to impose. You probably have things to do. I'll come again, when it's more convenient."

"No! No please stay Mr Minton. My father would think it ungracious if you had not received some hospitality in his house."

"Coffee then, I'll take coffee," he smiled but could not take a seat, he needed to be on his feet, and in a show of interest walked about the room admiring the pictures and porcelain laid out for display. Picking up one or two pieces and then, fearful of their value and fragility, placing them back carefully to their allotted place.

"A nice collection, your father has a good eye, or is it Mrs Parsons?"

His small talk jarred, clashing with his intention to be more, more inventive, clever, and witty. He realised with dismay that he knew nothing about fine china or pictures, and that she would sense his ignorance, the finery of the surroundings diminished him.

"The child...she may like to take a look in the library? I have heard that she is a veritable little bookworm."

And turning to Rosie, "Would you like that?"

Rosie trotted away and Archie watched her disappear grateful for a moment to collect his thoughts before they were once more alone.

After the maid had left the tray he watched her slowly pour the coffee, careful not to overfill the tiny gold rimmed cups. It was as if the moment was suspended.

Suddenly he knew that he could not stay. He was lumbering around, a bear in a china shop. Things would be broken and he would not be able to fix them. She didn't deserve this. He could ruin her life. What had he been thinking!

"Beatrice, Mrs Latterbridge I should go." He floundered trying to make his outburst more gracious.

Beatrice looked up, a small cloud of dismay flitted across her face.

"Why? What is the matter?"

They stared at each other. He looked at her smooth face, and then her pink lips parted in the utterance of her question. Her large eyes opened wider as she scanned his face, and she pressed her hand to her heart to compose herself.

"There is no need to leave so suddenly. Please, stay, enjoy the coffee, or the maid will be offended!"

"And you?" his voice was low.

"Of course," she smiled to dispel his anxiety. "It is a while since I have had the chance to enjoy a morning to myself."

"A chance to escape?"

"Something like that."

They sipped the coffee relaxing their guard.

Archie looked around as he settled into the arm chair. "I have never sat in here before. Are all the rooms furnished as well as this?"

"I'll give you a tour if you like Mr Minton."

"No... I... I wasn't .... That would be an imposition."

Beatrice laughed at his discomfort. "No they would be pleased to know that the house was appreciated, but you should also see the garden, the snowdrops have gone now but there is a meadow which should have a good show of daffodils by now. As a child I loved it when the carpet of bluebells appeared. It won't be long now. Forrester has worked so well. Some gardens take centuries to develop and yet he has already worked his magic in such a short time. The Palm House is a marvel, despite that storm damage a few years ago. Now dad has designs on the apple orchard. He wants to have new stock grafted, something like that I think. Why, whatever is the matter Mr Minton?"

Archie smiled. "No I was just enjoying you talk. I don't think that you have said more than two words to me in the past and now,

here we are, and you, getting lost in the wonders of bluebells
and apple orchards."

"Do you not enjoy gardens then?"

"Well I've never owned one, and have no idea about planting
and whatnot but I still appreciate beauty, wherever it is to be
found."

His blue eyes widened as he glanced across at her.

And the retort that rose to her lips froze as she drank in his
admiration.

She rose abruptly and shook, as a dog, freeing itself of water
droplets.

"Time for a tour then, house or garden or both, the charge is the
same," and she smiling, watched as he tried to extricate himself
from the deep recesses of the chair.

"You choose," he spread his hands out, "Your choice, I'm in your
hands."

"Well..." she considered glancing at the window, "as it is still a
little unsettled let's do the house first and see if it will get a bit
brighter." Then glancing at her wrist watch, "When do you need
to be back Mr Minton?"

They left the drawing room and entered the cool hall once again.

"Of course the library would be a favourite for you no doubt."

And she led the way across the patterned tiles to a warm wood-
panelled room and the door closed softly behind them. A
delicate stepladder perched itself precariously at an angle at one
side of the room and a large desk sat importantly at the far end
facing a heavily draped window.

"Oh I wonder where Rosie has gone." She looked around the
room.

"I thought that she wanted to delve into the books."

They both turned to look thought the window and glimpsed a
small figure with the maid walking towards the orchard.

Beatrice breathed in deeply and met Archie's smile. She
indicated the drapes.

"The red velvet was father's idea I believe. This is very much a man's room don't you think. There is such little light unless you pull them right back."

A shaft of faint sunlight played with the dust particles in the disturbed air. Archie watched transfixed as it created a circling halo around her golden curls.

She went to pull at the cord to part the drapes.

"No leave them."

He stopped her hand and held it and then with his other hand he encircled her waist and pulled her to him, burying her head onto his chest.

His words were forced in short staccato bursts from his lungs.

"Beatrice. You undo me. We have danced around each other for too long. Every time we meet. Every time we see each other. I've tried. God knows I've tried. But I'm not a good man….. I've wanted you for so long, watching you, and I've lost my reason. I shouldn't even be here. But now we're here I can't let you go again… watching you day in day out with that….."

And he couldn't go on, he held her tight as a drowning man clinging to desperate hope.

Drawing up her chin, he held the nape of her neck, crushed his mouth upon hers, parting her lips in his passion, drinking in the essence of her and feeling the shudder of her body as she folded herself into him.

They stood together swaying in their embrace. Then Archie straightened, and grasping her arms set her apart from him.

"Beatrice, I don't know how, but I'm falling in love with you. I have fallen in love with you. There, I've said it." He smiled but his brow furrowed and he anxiously searched her face, fearful of her response.

He reached out to her and turned her to face him, and wrapping his arms around her he soothed her and rocked her gently until he could feel the fear releasing itself from her.

"I will never let you down Beatrice", he murmured.

Beatrice stepped away from him, easing herself into back into the present, pressing her hand against her chest to catch the moment. Then there was such wonderful warmth as the euphoria of happiness overwhelmed her. She felt the heat and a pounding of an urgent pulse in her throat, in her head, pounding through her veins in rapid staccato. Then she suddenly laughed and catching his hand she kissed it quickly.

"Oh my word! Mr Minton! You've quite taken my breath away!" They grinned stupidly at each other, almost unable to take in the moment, and then Archie frowned.

"And you...your breath...is there...anything.....anything else that I have?"

And he suddenly grinned as he realised that she was still smiling at him, shaking her head slowly back and forth.

"Why..... what would you have me give? She teased, wrinkling her nose.

Archie drew her to him again and they folded into each other, content to feel the warmth of their bodies holding them together. Beatrice raised her face to his and kissed him gently. It was as if they had always known each other, a comforting sense of coming home to a safe harbour. Archie looked down at her, seeing in wonder the light in her eyes shine before her lips parted again, urgently meeting his passion with her own hard desire.

When they finally drew back Archie shook himself.

"Beatrice. You know nothing about me, but I promise you this...... I'm not leading you on."

Beatrice could not help herself grinning back at him. "Well no doubt I could say that I believe your intentions are dishonourable. I'm a grown woman Archie, not some slip of a girl."

"We both know that we have a different life apart....commitments..... wife....husband.... child." She shrugged her shoulders. "Perhaps we should just give ourselves a chance of some happiness Archie….before it's too late. I don't know…"And she spread her palms outwards to express her inability to convey her thoughts.

"All I know is what I am. What my life is like. It…well it…"she bit her lip and shook her head. "I want something more in my life…before it just drains away!" Her eyes glistened and she swallowed hard.

"Tell me about you Archie…..who you are….what your life has been. I don't need promises, just to know that what we have will sustain us….. help us to go on living… making everything more, well, bearable…" She tailed off anxious to hear him speak.

He frowned not quite sure of himself.

"Beatrice I…I'm not looking for a companion…a friend….I want more than that. You do understand? I want you…. desire all of you…and if we can maintain the charade of the ordinary part of our lives would you accept that? Are you willing to take that risk?"

Beatrice nodded. "I made such a foolish mistake in Ronald!" her voice caught and she breathed hard in order to continue.

"I thought… believed… that he was something that he was not. I have paid for that mistake. I do pay for it every day and I believe that you too made the wrong choice? It makes us into people we do not recognise."

Her voice lowered "I think that Ronald has never loved me. I have never known what it has been like to be desired until you Archie…"She shrugged her shoulders and her voice descended to a whisper so that Archie had to lean forward to hear her.

"I didn't know if I was even capable of feeling passion…. is it so wrong to want that?"

Archie took her hand and spoke slowly.

"We will have our time Beatrice, we will find a way you and I. Don't be afraid….this is not some quick affair. I have to tell you that I have not been faithful in my marriage. There is a side to me that I don't want you to discover in case I lose you…. but…. well…

153

I don't intend to throw my happiness away, not now that I have found you."

Beatrice looked at the clock. "Well…. I think that it is time for us to find your little girl…."She placed her hand on his shoulder.

"And I wasn't asking for you to be a saint Archie. If I wanted that I'd be on my knees in the church praying for salvation!" She grinned at him leading him out of the library into the hall.

∞

On the way home he watched as Rosie skipped ahead. What innocence there is in a child. When would her life change, and would betrayal and subterfuge play their part in her life he wondered.

Mr Parsons had not returned to Mote House although they had waited a while before finally taking a turn in the meadow to admire the ripples of canary yellow daffodils and then inspected the neatly cordoned fig trees that had been fastened around one side of the walled garden.

Rosie had been found in the Palm House sitting cross-legged on a cushioned stone chair with a book balanced on her lap and an empty plate and glass placed on the edge of a large urn that contained a young tree in a profusion of white star-burst flowers. As they passed Simmons hardware shop and drew level with the pond at the crossroads, a dull ache settled on him, growing heavier as they turned down the hill until finally they entered The Papermaker Arms.

But before he closed the door he couldn't resist a glance across the road, his eyes half closing to create an image of the cottage at the end of the small lane with Beatrice inside. He imagined her neat kitchen and the scent of fresh flowers before he turned back into the stale ale smell and the gloom of his bar.

Cranesbury Village 1930
Rosie, Millie, Jack & Thomas

"What are you going as?" Millie lay on her back looking up at the sky, not addressing anyone in particular.

"Going where?" Thomas was still trying to direct the sun's rays through his piece of glass onto the little heap of dried grass.

"Not where, what!" Millie turned over to see how the experiment was going, and in doing so felt a rip in her skirt seam.

"Oh bother!" She sat up and twisted the material round to examine the damage.

"S'matter Millieworm?" Jack was tracing the passage of the beetle through the grass putting stone obstacles in its path to see if it would go over or around them.

"What do you think this time Tom, round or over?"

"Dunno, what did it do before?"

"Over every time, except last time when it fell off, then it went round"

"Uh huh, in all probability I'd say that you have a directional beetle there then, rather than a wandering one, trained by Augustus Caesar." Thomas poked Jack in the ribs and they grappled together.

"Mind out! I'm trying to read!" Rosie shifted over to another space on the bank and tried to blank out their noise.

Millie stood up. "Well, I'm going as Little Bo Peep."

"Where?" Rosie shielded her eyes from the glare of the sun, and watched as Millie tried to poke the seams back together.

"Not where, I've just said haven't I! For the carnival next week, what are you going as?"

"Don't know yet. Mum hasn't started making ours yet." Rosie was evasive and turned back to her book.

"I didn't know that your mother sewed." Millie was suspicious; it wasn't like Rosie to keep quiet about things. She sniffed.

Rosie lay on her stomach, and breathing deeply she closed her eyes and waited as a scene appeared, unravelling, as she emptied her mind. And as she waited she saw the lantern hanging from the hook in the back porch of Mote House. Jack O Lantern! For Jack! But for her, she could see just a length of deep blue velvet. As she tried to bring it into focus the image disappeared.

"You'll just have to wait and see." She turned irritated, back to her book.

"So Tom." Millie tried again. "Are you going to watch the carnival?"

"Yep, 'spec so. Eureka!" Jack looked round to see a tiny flame curl and lick through the mound before it died leaving some shreds of blackened grass.

"Hey, well done!"

The two boys rocked back on their heels and admired the remains of the experiment.

"Didn't think that the sun would be strong enough, just goes to show huh?" Thomas grinned at his success.

"How's the beetle going?"

"Slowly!" Jack shrugged, "perhaps a bit of fire would speed it up a little."

"Don't be so cruel Jack." Millie turned to Thomas.

"Don't let him Tom." She pouted and her bottom lip protruded.

"Oh don't start crying on us." Jack was suddenly piqued, "I was only joking. Girls huh!"

Turning her head Rosie saw Thomas wrinkle his nose at Millie, witnessing his endearing smile, and she knew that at moment that his heart would always belong to Millie. Good dependable Thomas. Too good for the world. Then she saw a glass timer emptying the last grains of sand and shuddered at the image. She jumped up, "come on let's have a race.....to the beech tree and back"

"What's the prize?" Jack was on his feet.

156

"Winning is reward in itself." Rosie offered.

"No point then." Jack flopped down.

"A kiss from me!" Millie offered.

"Definitely not then!" Jack theatrically gestured being sick holding his throat and gagging.

The two boys rolled about together.

"Just because you know that I'm faster than you." Rosie challenged them both. "That I'll win hands down."

"Don't be daft Rosie." Jack sneered.

"We'll give you a head start, you and Millipede ." Thomas grinned. "We'll count to five."

"That's not fair, she's older than me." Millie objected.

"Would it help if we tied our legs together?" Jack turned away and went back to his search for the beetle that had scurried away during his absence. He was bored by the girls' presence. He wished they would leave them in peace.

"Why don't you go and play somewhere else, with dolls or something." And he poked through the grass with a thin stick finding no trace of insect life. "Reckon they've gone and hibernated. After all my training it's gone and vanished!"

"Probably heard about your plan to roast it alive." Rosie squinted into the distance.

"Ladybird, ladybird fly away home, your house is on fire and your children are gone." Millie flapped her arms.

"It wasn't a ladybird you stupid girl!"

"I'm not stupid; you're just a horrid boy!" Millie shouted back, and she got up and flounced across the field.

"Oh come back," shouted Thomas, "he didn't mean it."

"Yes I jolly well did!"

"Now I s'pose I'll have to go after her." Rosie glared at Jack, "Mrs Latterbridge said that we had to look after her, you are mean Jack. You always spoil things for everyone."

"Don't blame me, she's the one that gone off in a huff. And it was you that started it, talking about roasting things."

157

"I did not!"

"Yes you did, you said that I was going to roast the damn beetle, didn't she Tom?" Jack appealed to Thomas sense of fairness.

"Well yes but...."

"I did not START it, that's what I meant, as you well know. Millie is right, you are a horrid boy. I wish you weren't my brother."

"And I wish that you weren't my sister!" he shouted at her retreating back.

The two boys watched her race to catch up with Millie who had reached the stile.

"D'you know, she is quite fast!" Thomas was bemused and smiled at Jack raising his eyebrows.

"I know she is," agreed Jack, "why do you think she suggested it in the first place?"

"Come on, let's catch them up, perhaps Mrs Latterbridge will have some of her homemade lemonade, I'm parched."

Thomas picked up the book that Rosie had left in her haste to leave and the pair jogged across the field reaching the stile, just catching a glimpse of the girls as they disappeared under the bridge.

By the time they had caught up, the girls had already reached the orchards and together they followed the stream, climbing over the final stile at the lane.

"That sign's gone wonky." Thomas pointed to the signpost that was half buried by a tangle of young ash saplings and brambles. "Where's Kiln Man?"

The children giggled as he attempted to pull it upright and gaped as it came away from its plant anchorage and wobbled precariously.

"Well it least you can read it now." Thomas was embarrassed. The sign announced Kilndown Manor with its point denoting the direction.

"Yes but now it can't stand up on its own." Rosie added unhelpfully.

"Oh leave it." Jack was impatient. Mr Parson's men will see it when they come along.

"I know, you go back with Millie and I'll go up to Mote House and tell them." Rosie volunteered.

"Good idea." Jack was keen to continue, the lure of lemonade beckoned him.

"See you later!"

Rosie smiled back at them and as she walked up the long drive she thought of the thanks, and praise, the gift of the old lantern, and the blue velvet that Mrs Parsons would find.

∞

As the children trooped up the path, studiously closing the gate behind them, they saw Beatrice reaching down into the pram to lift the child out. Dulcie was vigorously waving her little fists.

"Oh goodness, she doesn't want to settle at all today." Beatrice lifted her up and jiggled her on her hip.

"Do you my little turnip?" and holding her high she nuzzled her face into the child's tummy.

But the baby would not be quieted and resumed her sharp protests. Beatrice sighed. "She's been like this all morning, I think she must be teething."

The children watched as she placed her back in the pram and attempted to cover her as Dulcie squirmed and kicked them away.

"I think I am losing the battle." She straightened up. I think I'll just leave her for a bit."

"Does she need rocking?" Thomas looked into the pram.

Beatrice smiled down at him. "She probably does Thomas but I can't be doing that all day long. I need to hang the sheets out on the line otherwise they'll never dry." She disappeared into the kitchen.

Thomas held the handle and with gentle pushes set up a swaying motion. The pram creaked in unison with the motion and Dulcie's piercing screams were punctuated with pauses and hiccups. She gazed at Thomas fixing him with a fierce stare, and then put her fist to her mouth and sucked hard. Thomas smiled at her, and she frowned back, demonstrating her mood with another flurry of kicks.

Then she took sharp breaths, and quietened, watching his face whilst waving her free arm. Thomas continued to push the handle up and down, and watched as her thin blue veined eyelids drooped and fluttered, her muffled gulps softened and finally the lids closed and she slept rosy cheeked and content.

Beatrice came back onto the porch.

"Well I never. I've spent all morning with that little madam and she hasn't given me a moment's peace! Now you...," and she smiled at Thomas.

"Go round the back and I'll get all of you some biscuits and lemonade."

The children walked around the side of the house and settled on the bench, Millie squeezed in between them.

"Biscuits AND lemonade!" Jack beamed at Thomas, "Well done mate!"

"And they're home-made," announced Millie taking credit on behalf of her mother.

"Shame that Rosie's not back yet though." Thomas said eyeing the plate of biscuits as Beatrice came round the corner.

"Where has she gone I thought that she was with you and Millie?" Beatrice looked around expecting to see her.

"No she went up to Mote House to tell 'em about the sign post that we'd found on the path. It'd fallen down." Jack munched on the biscuit and some crumbs flew from his mouth during his explanation.

"She won't be long," agreed Millie and they all viewed the last remaining biscuit as Beatrice went back into the house.

"Shame to waste it!" crowed Jack triumphantly and snatched it up.

"You should have shared!" Millie was indignant.

"It should have been Rosie's." Thomas quietly reminded them before Jack stood up and started coughing violently.

"Crumbs…. down the wrong way……!"He gasped hitting his chest.

"Serves you right for being such a pig!" Millie stood up and shook her skirt, "and you've covered me in crumbs you horrid boy!"

Winter had clothed the village in a covering of snow and the pink tinged grey sky promised that there was more to follow. The pavements had already become wet and slushy where footprints had trudged a series of tramline paths.

"Cor blimy, it's perishing." Jack stamped his feet and despondently looked around. There was still no sign of the bus and they had waited, first quite hopefully and now with a growing sense of doubt.

"Do you think it could have got stuck?" He pulled up his collar and then rammed his hands back into his pockets.

Thomas squinted, turning into the wind to look back towards the bank, hoping to see it turning the corner but the road remained empty.

"Nope, no sign yet but it could just be held up." He huffed out his breath to watch the vapour form a cloud, and then a series of huffs and watched as they formed a series of mini clouds before disappearing.

"I wonder if they'll start me on straight away today." Jack spoke to the street ahead not wanting to face the biting wind.

"What?" Thomas missed the words in his reverie.

"Rootes. I wonder if they'll start me today. I haven't had a letter back to say what's expected." The long wait had made Jack feel anxious.

"Probably just show you around then, tell who you'll be working under, that sort of thing."

"Thing is, said that I'd had a bit of experience." Jack felt the need to admit his disclosure, and shrugged, hoping for some reassurance.

"What, tinkering with that old bike that you found?" Thomas grinned."

"Well, No I'd said that I.... well that I'd spent a bit of time with Maynard. Y'know, old Parson's chauffeur, well I had to say something didn't I."

Thomas turned and looked down at Jack. Already Thomas had towered over Samuel his father. His arms had outstripped his sleeves and the hand-me-down trousers from his cousin would soon need replacing.

Jack had remained small and compact. With Thomas he was relaxed and more even in temper but with others, unless he steadied himself, he became edgy, unpredictable, and sharp. He already knew how to exploit his capacity to entertain, to be humorous and witty when he chose to be, but found himself less able to control his magpie greed. The draw for something not quite within his grasp frustrated him.

The job with Rootes had come about by sheer chance. They were employing young apprentices. His father had spoken to Parsons who knew William Rootes, having bought different motors from him when he had the business at Hawkhurst. Parsons learnt that he was expanding his business and setting up in Maidstone and happened to mention it to Archie.

Jack couldn't believe his luck when Archie asked Parsons to put in a good word for him. His wages, even as an apprentice mechanic, would be far better than anything that was on offer on the nearby farms. And then there was the chance one day of promotion, Jack had already dreamt of his advancement, and in his dreams he could see himself behind the wheel of the dazzling chrome and gleaming bonnet of his own motor. One day.... one day his day would come.

"Here she comes!" Thomas blew on his purple tinged knuckles. "At long last!"

They stood to one side as the passengers dismounted and then raced to the back of the bus.

The warmth of the other passengers had caused the thick condensation on the windows to drip and there was a stale smell of dampness, of old blankets and cigarette smoke. The outside world was obliterated as they jolted past fields of pristine white and the orchard trees wearing thick cumbersome snowy drapes. Jack rubbed his sleeve across the window and they both peered out.

"Think it's thicker here?"

"Dunno, s'pose as it's a bit higher it's bound to be."

The bus rattled on its way with the springs in their seats voicing their disapproval of the moment incurred.

"What's the Grammar like then?"

Thomas considered the question. He still felt a fish out of water. So many of the boys boarded; their superior air and arrogance spoke of money and position. That he had succeeded in gaining a scholarship did little to allay his feelings of inadequacy. Cranbrook had a fearsome reputation; even the fabric of imposing buildings spoke of refinement and tradition. Of course his parents, Samuel and Alice had been thrilled to learn that their son had surpassed all their expectations. But their pride in his accomplishment brought him an unwelcome weight to bear. He wanted to do well, he loved the challenge, the masters were fair and each day brought about a fresh desire to know more, but his new world was obliterating his old one. The new horizon beckoned him and as it did so it took him further away from the familiarity of home and past friendships, of old ways. It demanded change in him and he was fearful that the gain would be at too high a cost. He rarely came into contact with Jack or Rosie and then there was Millie. She was becoming a stranger and when he had caught sight of her he didn't know what to say. She seemed not even to notice him anymore.

"Thomas!"

"Oh I was just thinking. Yes it's great. Hard work though."

"I wouldn't thank you for it."

Jack stared unseeing out of the window. "All those boring old books to read, stuff to swot over, glad to see that back of all that sort of stuff." Then he nudged him in the ribs. "All work and no play makes Jack a dull boy eh!"

Thomas smiled back at him.

"You wait, they'll expect their shilling's worth from you when you start! No skylarking about there I bet!"

"Mmm." Jack considered his fate. "Still, will be bringing home a bob or two at any rate."

Thomas felt his insides contract. Yes there was the rub. The cost of his place at Cranbrook had cost his parents dear. He needed to do something, but it had to be discreet. To be in obvious employment would be frowned upon by his fellow students, and it needed to be part time, during his weekends. So far nothing had come up and Christmas was already looming.

He was going to try Kilndown Manor. The vicar had suggested it to him last Sunday although he had admitted that he didn't know if they needed anyone.

"Just a thought," he had said.

He would have gone today but he needed to go to the museum for his next assignment, their natural history rooms contained some very good specimens and he was anxious to deliver a good piece of work for the science master. He had been quietly informed that his science knowledge was 'a little below par' and that he needed to improve in preparation for the end of term exams.

Latin had been a challenge but he had begun to see its relevance as it crossed the different disciplines. History fascinated him and the English lessons had caused him little anxiety, and he was informed that he had a good ear and an aptitude for languages. As the school had put a great emphasis on physical prowess and team games it was fortunate that his size and strength had given him some advantage on the rugby field, despite his lack of skill. Suddenly he was knocked out of his daydream. The bus was labouring up the hill and making little headway in the slippery conditions.

"Reckon we'll have to get off at this rate", Jack said as they slithered to a halt.

The engine strained and the wheels turned but the bus began to slew round.

"I'm 'fraid everyone will have to disembark!" A series of groans met the announcement, and then people reluctantly thronged the aisle audibly grumbling as they made their way to the front of the bus.

"If I'd known what sort of journey this would turn out to be I wouldn't have bothered," said one woman to no one in particular as she clutched a large shopping bag in front of her, "and my varicose veins have been playing up something shocking!"

A fellow passenger tut-tutted her sympathy as they stepped down.

A straggling file of people made their way up the hill, some holding on to each other for support as they endeavoured to find a grip on the ice and snow.

"We shall be late getting in at this rate!" Jack was anxious now that the prospect of employment threatened to be snatched away from him.

The bus wound its way slowly up the hill, the gears grinding as the driver tried to engage a lower one, and then it gathered speed and passed them leaving deep ruts of dirty snow in its wake.

Finally it stopped at the crest of the hill and waited for its struggling occupants to reach it.

Thomas looked back and saw the woman with the large bag had stopped and was trying to catch her breath. He went back and held on to her arm.

"Jack, give her a hand!"

Then together they marched three abreast, causing her breathlessly exclaim.

"Lummy I didn't know that I'd end up with *two* nice young men today!"

Jack raised his eyebrows in mock horror but Thomas shook his head at him smiled down at her, both of them trying to maintain their grip on her stout body swathed in layers of outer garments. As they slithered and shuffled towards the bus a cheer rose to meet them from the passengers already assembled to climb aboard.

And finally they were on their way, passing the small newly built bungalows and bare elm trees lining the route, then on past the fire station as they crawled cautiously down the hill towards the county town.

Jack left Thomas still on the bus at Bishops Palace and made his way across the road towards the new Rootes premises built alongside the frozen River Len. He entered through a side door marked Office Enquiries, his air of easy confidence concealing the apprehension of his fluttering stomach.

A middle-aged woman seated at a tidy desk peered over the top of his glasses at him.

"Yes, can I help you?" Her manner did not convey the slightest intention of doing so.

He hesitated, already irritated by her air of superiority.

"Are you expected?" She waited and she held the frames of her glasses to look at him more closely, setting them further back on her nose.

Stuck up cow, Jack smiled back at her; two can play at this game. "Yes I am. And I think that you should be able find a record of my appointment. Jack Minton. Ten thirty today."

She looked back at him suspiciously, as he smiled benignly at her, and she registering the veiled insult implied by his cool tone.

Be careful lad, she thought you don't want to start off on a bad foot with me. But she said, as she turned away from him, "Wait there while I see who is available to see you."

Jack waited. He looked through the little window partition at her little empire. Taking prominence on her desk sat a large neat open ledger annotated with dates, names, and amounts of money. Small dockets were skewered on a thin steel pin, little cubbyholes held envelopes and stationary, and some smaller ledgers. There was an air of order and discipline, everything in its place and a place for everything.

Jack thought of his own father's accounts, papers jumbled together haphazardly, bills, orders, demands, and all a mishmash of utter confusion.

He wanted his life to be different; to be better. He resolved that he would make sure, no matter what, that one day his name would count.

Kilndown Manor 1935
Thomas

Lady Faversham considered him. He was a strong good looking young boy; tall with long limbs and an easy smile. She approved of him. His arms were already protruding from the sleeves of a well-worn jacket and the cloth cap that he held in his hand was frayed, but he was clean, as were the boots that showed the signs of a recent polish.

"So you're the stationmaster's boy." She knew he was of course but she gave him the opportunity to speak about himself.

"That's right your ladyship." Thomas hoped that this was the correct form of address. "My father, Mr Fulwood, has been at Cranesbury station for fourteen years now. They moved from Tenterden just after I was born."

She liked the sound of his voice, he enunciated well.

"So you have left school now?" Fifteen, she thought he looked older than his years, perhaps due to his height and so many of the village boys looked so undersized these days. When she considered her own Sebastian, so handsome, but she quickly dismissed the image before it took hold of her, it did no good to dwell. To her surprise Thomas shook his head.

"No I attend Cranbrook school. I started the term this September."

"Boarding at Cranbrook!"

"No, no, I am a day student."

"Oh," She was still unclear and leaned forward to catch his words.

"I was fortunate enough to gain a scholarship."

"Nothing fortunate about that young man, you have to work to achieve that. You obviously have some talent then." She murmured her approval

Thomas felt himself blush under her scrutiny.

"Well, well, a scholarship boy. I expect your parents are very proud." Her interest grew.

"And what do you propose to do. What future do you see for yourself?"

"I'm not too sure yet. I enjoy Latin and history." Thomas wasn't sure how much she really wanted to know or whether this was a normal polite way of conversation, of small talk.

"Mmm, have you considered university?"

Thomas laughed. "I think that is probably out of the question."

"Why?" She was genuinely surprised.

"Well, there are many things to consider." Thomas felt ashamed. He could not speak to her of money, the doors that it opened and the doors that remained closed through lack of it. She had probably no concept of it. He looked away. The grand surroundings of the drawing room, with its lofty ceiling and the delicate but faded Chinese wallpaper were a world away from his own home. A large bird with outspread wings, its feet fixed to a small branch, was contained within a dull domed glass jar. The mantelpiece held a selection of pretty blue and gold vases painted with roses and garlands of intertwining flowers, and a gilded clock held fast by two adoring winged angels took centre stage.

At every turn there was another marvel to admire. Set at each window were inlaid semi-circular tables each holding a small bronze statue. The portraits staring from their high vantage point around the walls, he supposed, were the long dead ancestors, and then there was a heavily ornate and carved sideboard topped with an immense silver serving dish with two wine coolers at either side. Every piece spoke of high value and long proud tradition. It was as if he was a stranger who had stepped into a foreign landscape.

Lavinia Faversham watched him as he took in his surroundings. "Do you approve?"

He turned back to her suddenly brought back to himself.

"Approve?" he didn't know how to answer.

"Do you like the room? Are there pieces that catch your eye?" She was suddenly amused as if they were engaged in a game of choice.

Thomas looked back to look at the bronze statues.

"They are extraordinary," he ventured. "They seem to come alive."

"Well chosen." Lavinia smiled. "They are of course French, as is the beautiful ormolu clock", she waved towards the mantelpiece, "but I am pleased that you have picked those two out. They are by the sculptor Clodion, Claude Michel Clodion, and my favourites too; we have something in common then. A good eye!" She breathed in deeply, considering the bronzes.

"Well now, back to business. We have a handyman at present but he has not been in good health for a while. I think we could place you to work alongside him, just for the weekends, you said?" She waited for his response.

"If you could relieve him of some of the heavier duties for the time being, you look strong, are you?" She prepared to dismiss him and rang for her maid.

"Take Thomas to Heyman. He's to work with old Bert. Ask Heyman to explain his duties and to inform him of the hours and remuneration for the hours that he will be working"

She turned back to Thomas, "Heyman is our butler in charge of all our men here. I've enjoyed our little talk. Most edifying."

∞

Rosie waited until Millie had retreated up the lane towards Ivy Leaf Cottage before she turned back towards the pond. Sitting on the bench under the oak tree she cleared her mind until she could see Thomas jumping the stile and walking up the lane. Finally he appeared.

"Hello Thomas." She called and at first he was so preoccupied that he didn't hear her. The air was still raw from the day's frost, and the ducks sat mournfully at the frozen edges of the pond, grumbling to themselves. They had trampled the snow, vainly trying to find some green vegetation and had left haphazard matchstick patterns in their wake.

"Thomas!"

"Oh hello, I didn't see you." He grinned as he drew level.

"You got it then." She couldn't resist, the temptation of knowing was too much.

"The job at Kilndown? How did you know?" He looked down at her, frowned and wrinkled his nose.

"A little bird told me." Rosie was pleased at his surprise.

"Well it must have flown here very fast 'cos I have only just been told." He shook his head, "I don't know Rosie, you are a queer one sometimes."

"And did she like you then?"

"Who?" he teased.

"Why Lady Faversham as you well know."

"Well yes, I think she did actually."

An image of two brown figures gently came into her mind and then faded. She felt a shiver of pleasure.

"It'll be a day that she will remember, and your good fortune, when her time comes." Rosie was transfixed by the powerful force of her knowledge; it held her for a moment, unable to rouse herself.

"You are a funny thing Rosie Minton" Thomas tousled her hair. "Anyway what are you doing here, it's freezing."

"Oh I was on my way back from Simmons, mum wanted some more candles but he'd closed early," she lied easily.

C'mon then let's go home." He slipped his arm in hers and together they tramped down the street towards the Papermakers Arms.

172

Mote House 1936
Arnold and Louise

Louise came into the gloomy study.

"Arnold you will strain your eyes! You haven't asked for the lights to be lit."

Arnold looked at her reluctant to leave the article that he was reading in his paper.

"If it's not one thing it is another," he sighed, "Look at this." He held the paper aloft and indicated the piece.

"We're in the middle of this blasted depression when business is so shaky and now this."

Louise took the ungainly sheaf of papers from him and seated herself at the chair opposite.

"The front page, the piece on Spain?"

Arnold nodded." Another bloody mess it seems. And there's talk of Germany rearming; the whole of Europe seems hell bent on war. You mark my words. We'll all get dragged in one way or another, whatever Baldwin and Chamberlain say about non-intervention."

"It might not come to that surely. These countries have always had their squabbles and the Mediterranean people are renowned for having hot blood. We've had one war. People wouldn't stand for it, not after last time, not again. What they do is their business not ours."

"There might not be a choice, Louise." He reached over and took the paper from her.

"But it calls it a Civil War; it's not as if they are fighting anyone else."

"Well if you read further down, even some of our people have gone over there, joining the resistance or something." Arnold tried to find the passage to quote. "It's here somewhere, blast, now where was it?"

Louise rose from the chair. "Come on Arnold, you can't change things by fretting."

But Arnold shook the paper straight and scanned it again.

"Now where is it? There's the bit about General Franco and the government and Germany and Italy having given him support. Villages bombed and churches ransacked. Nuns and priests, civilians killed, all kinds of terrible goings on Louise. It's a blood bath."

She went round the desk to him. "Come, it's late, you need to eat."

"If we get dragged in this time Louise, we might go under. If our import supplies are hit, or the men are called up again…"

"Or you worry yourself to death!" Louise was impatient. "Now enough! Put the paper away. We will have our meal without any more discussion about Spain or business or anything like that and we need to talk about Beatrice."

"Why Beatrice?" Arnold was surprised.

"If you come in to eat I will tell you." She said turning her back on him and leading the way to the dining room.

"What's this about Beatrice?" Arnold was nonplussed. "Is it Ronald?"

"Well yes and no." Louise waited until they had been served and the maid had left.

"Well?"

Louise breathed in and pursed her lips together. "Perhaps a mother notices more."

"Notices what?"

"It's difficult to know where to start…. I've had my suspicions for a while now, and I'm afraid that if I have noticed, then others might also…"she waved her hands to signify the helplessness that she felt.

"I have no idea what you are talking about."

"Beatrice and Archie! There!" She held her hand to her chest.

"Beatrice and Archie and…. you're not making sense Louise."

You must have seen how much happier she is now, more content."

"Well no doubt having the girls has done that" Arnold pursed his lips.

"For a man who understands business and takes such a keen interest in the world you are sometimes so blind Arnold," she shook her head in exasperation. "And since you have mentioned the girls, who does Dulcie remind you of?" Louise lowered her eyes and seemed to study her napkin, before glancing sideways at Arnold.

"Dulcie? Erm.... well she doesn't take after..."Arnold scratched his head, and started again. "She and Millie are very different I suppose with Millie having her mother's looks when she was that age."

"Exactly so!" Louise nodded.

"Why what's your point, I wouldn't say she takes after Ronald either if it comes to that."

"There you have it." Louise scrutinised him "You have hit the nail on the head, if only you had the sense to see it."

"Louise you have quite lost me. Stop talking in riddles."

"Dulcie and Rosie do you think they are alike in any way?"

"Well Rosie is much older than Dulcie but they have the same, well similar colouring I suppose, and Dulcie is certainly far more forward than Millie was at that age, she seems a clever little thing."

"And who does Rosie take after do you think?"

"Really Louise you seem to have a bit between your teeth this evening. I have no idea."

"Edith or Archie choose." Louise eyes narrowed as she delivered the ultimatum.

"On balance, if push came to shove, yes you can see that she favours Archie, same eyes, same sort of look that she gives you."

"Finally!" Louise raised her brow. "And can you not see how alike Rosie and Dulcie are? She is the spit of Rosie when she was at that age!"

"I wouldn't say that." Arnold frowned, "Similar, yes, but then children change as they grow."

"Arnold it is my firm belief that Dulcie is Archie's child, and no don't give me that look, hear me out." Louise's voice shook. "I am talking about my own child and my grandchild. It is my belief that Beatrice and Ronald live like strangers, so why is it that Beatrice is so much happier, that she is like our old Beatrice."

"You're obviously going to tell me."

"I am Arnold. I believe that Beatrice and Archie are lovers, that they have been conducting an affair for years, but that I have been too blind to see it before, too unwilling to suspect my own daughter, our daughter of such an indiscretion," and her words caught in her throat causing her to swallow and then to catch her breath.

"Louise I can't think how you have arrived at such a conclusion, and…"

"Because I have seen them!" Louise was aghast at her betrayal.

"Seen them, seen them where?"

"In Tunbridge Wells, last Saturday morning," she admitted. "They were walking together down the street, Beatrice with little Dulcie trotting along and Archie holding her hand."

"Who's hand, Beatrice's?"

"Oh Arnold. No! He was holding Dulcie's hand but they were talking together and laughing. They looked…. together."

"And so that's it. And from that you conclude that our daughter is having a liaison with Archie Minton?"

"No it is not that, but I have for some time thought about Dulcie and wondered what is was that made me so unsure, and it was only then that I finally put two and two together. It was the missing piece of the jigsaw that had evaded me. I just knew. And why were they there, together, like a family? "

"And you seriously believe that Dulcie is Archie Minton's child."

"Yes I do."

Arnold sat back in his chair. He looked back at Louise. "So what do you want me to do? Have it out with him?"

"No Arnold. I just wanted you to know. Perhaps I am wrong. Perhaps it will just finish, but I wanted us to be prepared in case a situation arose that required us to act."

"Act? What kind of situation are you talking about?"

"If Ronald found out, we could be talking about a scandal, even a divorce, dragging through the court. And it may surprise you to know that in my heart I can't condemn her. It is wonderful to see her so at peace with herself. But Archie is a married man with two children of his own, and what they are both doing is wrong, I know that."

Arnold rose from his chair and went over to Louise he folded her into his arms and kissed the top of her head.

"We'll get through this Louise, don't fret now."

Louise felt the burden lift. "I had wanted to tell you but I couldn't bring myself to admit it even to myself. And there's something else."

Arnold held her head between his hands, "You're having twins." And they both laughed, thankful to relieve the tension.

"Well come on what else?"

"I think we need to consider the future for both girls. If Ronald found out one day about Dulcie he could, perhaps leave her out of any will. Ivy Leaf Cottage might be left just to Millie then Dulcie wouldn't have anything. Perhaps we should leave this house to them both. If anything happened to us, and Beatrice inherited our Mote House, could Ronald take it all if they were to be divorced? I'm just trying to think out aloud of what could happen."

Arnold shook his head, "No, goodness no Louise, the law changed that ten or more years ago now, a married woman like Beatrice has the same rights as Ronald, more's the pity when I think that he didn't put penny towards that house of theirs, the pompous scoundrel!"

They looked bleakly at each other across the table. The food on their plates had grown cold, their appetites quite diminished by anxiety.

"But could it come to that Arnold, a divorce? Think of the shame, when you have worked so hard to raise us up. And if Ronald did divorce her, would Archie leave his wife and children? I don't believe that this affair is his first."

Arnold looked at her sharply.

"No, hear me out. I know you like the man, and you don't want to believe ill of him, but I've heard things in the village..... Archie and that barmaid of his."

"Oh stuff and nonsense! Louise this is just village gossip! You're getting worked up about.... well, it all could be just a coincidence and nothing more. You've put two and two together and made five. What have you discovered? A man meeting a neighbour in town and passing the time of day, why Louise, you've let your imagination run riot. And just because the tittle-tattle gossips you believe him to be a philanderer! All this sounds quite innocent to me. Come we are not Victorians my dear. Even our own King is consorting with that American woman Wallis Simpson, and she's been divorced twice so the papers say! Mind I've no idea how that's going to turn out."

But Louise wearily shook her head.

"Don't you think that I would be glad not to believe my own eyes? And it's not about the gossip! I saw the way Beatrice looked up at him. She looked so happy Arnold. I have never seen her so animated. That's why I am so anxious, it catches at my heart, I want her to be happy, but I can only see disaster ahead. It will end badly and then there are the children, innocents in all of this. Dulcie is too young to understand, but Millie, I know she's growing fast and in a couple or more years she will have finished school, but for all that she is a sensitive young girl, close to them both."

Prodding his food aimlessly with his fork Arnold leaned back into the chair.

"There is Archie's family. Edith, well I can't say that I care for her but he is her husband. What would be become of them? Jack seems to be getting on well at Rootes, thanks to you, and I am sure that he can take care of himself but then there is Rosie. I have always had a soft spot for her. She is a strange girl but there's something special about her."

An image of Rosie came into Arnold's mind. He saw her curled up in one of their library chairs, her head deep in a book, quite oblivious of her surroundings; a child who had a wonderful curiosity about the world. Now she too was becoming a young woman, but without the affectations that seemed to be in vogue with so many of the young women these days. She seemed quite indifferent to the fashions of the day unlike Millie, constantly attracted to pretty bits and pieces.

He roused himself and looked at the table.

"Enough. We will go round in circles all evening and there is nothing that we can do now. I'll find a way to speak with Archie. Leave it with me Louise. I don't want anything more said that could muddy the water. Ask the maid to take this away, and bring me a something later. I need some fresh air. I think a walk will give me chance to think."

Louise watched as he rose from the chair and straightened his back.

"Don't fret Louise, you do enough worrying for the both of us and it won't help. Trust me. Just let me work it out in my own way."

Coronation Day 1937
Rosie, Jack, Thomas and Millie

"I wish I could have gone up to London to see it." Millie pouted. "I bet there'll be crowds of people there."

"Well they'll show it on the Pathe News, Thomas tried to pacify her.

"You are too young to travel with us, and you probably would be too short to see anything anyway!" Jack smirked.

"I am not short. I am one of the tallest in my class if you must know." she gasped with indignation. "Really Jack you say such nasty things. Doesn't he?" she turned to Rosie for sympathy.

"There were only two free railway passes that Tom's dad had got anyway," Rosie shrugged, "so we couldn't have gone."

"My father would have paid for me to go."

"No he wouldn't Millie. If they had wanted you to go they would've taken you themselves." Jack peered into the distance to see if the train was approaching.

Lining each side of the station the flower boxes had been planted up. A large group of people stood outside the waiting room, Rosie glanced round at them, and then at the signal box where she could see Sid Fowler by the window watching the line.

"'Spec you'll get a job finding a seat, let alone a carriage to yourself," she offered the opinion to nobody in particular. "The carriages towards the back will be your best bet." She turned to Thomas.

"When you come back meet us up by the pond and tell us all about it. We'll have eaten most of the party food by then," she grinned.

"You're going to have a lovely day, just look at the sky." Millie said.

They all looked up, and watched the fine white horse manes that lazily drifted faintly veiling the blue skies.

Rosie shook her head. "It will be cloudy and trying to rain when you get there, you'll be glad that I suggested an umbrella!" Suddenly a shout went up and as they looked along the line they saw that the front of the train had been decked in red white and blue bunting. It fluttered and danced as the early morning train finally came to a halt with a loud snort of steam and scream of brakes. There was a mad scramble and jostling as doors were flung open and people climbed aboard. Those in the already crowded carriages slammed down the windows and waved their flags in a frenzy of celebration the air.

"Isn't it grand?" Millie's eyes were dancing. "Oh I wish I was going! Did you see the garlands and the banner at the front? " Rosie grinned and nodded; the exuberant mood was exhilarating Thomas and Jack were lost in the mêlée and then suddenly they could see them poking their heads from a window further down the train and waving frantically. Their shouts were lost amongst others, some cheering, others trying to communicate with those in other carriages, calling out last minute instructions, saying their goodbyes.

At last the green flag waved, a whistle blew, and those left behind on the platform stepped away. The train belched a triumphant plume of steam into the air signalling its impatient desire to depart, then it snorted slowly as the wheels took the strain metal on metal, and bursts of steam and water enveloped the moving pistons. Slowly at first and then as it edged its way past the platform it found a rhythm and with power and majesty it pulled away leaving behind it forlorn vacuum of anti-climax and a haze of black smoke.

Rosie and Mille had watched until the train became toy sized and disappeared round the curve of the track. The clouds had thickened and there was a chill in the air.

The two girls trudged back up towards the village.

"I don't know why they built the station so far away," grumbled Millie, "my shoes will be quite worn out by the time we get home."

Rosie looked down at the dainty laced leather shoes with their neat stitching at the front and then back to face Millie. Her beautiful fair curls escaping from the beret, created a perfect frame for her pretty face. The new wool crepe low- belted coat set off her slim figure.

Rosie glanced down at her old brown coat whose pockets were beginning to bulge and sag due to the number of times that she had thrust her hands into them despite warnings to 'take your hands out of your pockets Rosie'! Its astrakhan collar had long since worn thin giving it a weary moth-eaten appearance.

"What are you going to do when you leave school Rosie? My mother said that I should learn some typing and shorthand and then I would have the choice of all kinds of office work. I could become a personal secretary if my speed was really good." Millie contemplated her hands." I do think that it is important to find the right kind of work, don't you Rosie?"

Rosie stared at the road ahead. Already the hops were beginning to climb the tall poles. At the hedges small pink-centred daisies mingled with ochre-yellow dandelions, and thick green-veined cuckoo pints, red-ragged campions and delicate white, lace-fronded cow parsley vied for space. Small gregarious birds cheeped noisily and then quietened as the girls drew level.

"My grandmother said that perhaps I could be enrolled in a secretarial school, she said that qualifications open so many doors. Obviously though I eventually want to get married, have a nice house, children, that sort of thing."

She turned to Rosie to see if she had been listening.

"Do you want to get married Rosie?" She put her head to one side to get a better look at her response.

Rosie pulled at a long stemmed piece of grass and drawing it from its sheath sucked the sap.

"Perhaps one day."

"I think that I would like two or three children.... and a house with a nice sized garden for them to play in and a car...... so that we could go for drives in the country or into town...... or anywhere really. Grandma has been to the Ideal Home Exhibition at Earls Court and said that next time she will take me. You have to be up to date with things."

A startled blackbird flew from the hedge across their path calling of its outrage of being disturbed before plunging into the opposite field.

"I wonder what the queen will be wearing, will they drive in a gold carriage do you s'posese?" Millie squinted up at the gathering clouds.

"Of course they'll be in a coach. There will be thousands watching them." Rosie imagined the long procession stretching along the Mall.

"I wish that Edward was still the King, he's far more handsome than his brother, isn't he?" Millie turned to see Rosie's reaction and seeing that she didn't respond she tried again.

"Well I think it is so very romantic, 'I give up the throne for the woman I love'. But I don't think she is very pretty do you? She looks very old, much older than him."

"Mmm...." Rosie murmured, " I don't think he had much choice in the end."

"Well!" Millie was indignant. "Then he should have jolly well told them that he was going to marry her and make her his queen, he was the king after all."

As they reached the lower cottages they could see in the distance that the preparations for the street party had begun.

"Oh I'm so looking forward to this," Millie strained her eyes trying to see the detail. "Oh look, your dad is bringing out some of your chairs, with Mr Simmons!" She clasped her hands together with delight. "It's going to be so much fun!"

183

Rosie smiled at her enthusiasm and relaxed. "I think it will be lovely."

"Mother has made hundreds of jellies; our kitchen table was covered with them."

The hyperbole made Rosie smile again.

"Mr Ticehurst has made loads of iced buns and Betty said that we are going to have jam sandwiches, ham sandwiches, cheese sandwiches, sausage rolls, and then jelly and cream for afters….mmm….it will be so grand. Oh and I nearly forgot. Mother said that there's going to be a gigantic decorated cake, enough for everyone, just imagine!"

As the two girls drew level with The Papermakers Arms they stopped to watch Mike and Ron Drewe put up the last of the trailing bunting. Mike stood at the top of the ladder and looped the line of little flags through the sign before finally fastening it round the eaves.

At the pond two sturdy tables had been set under the tree and at the crossroads there stretched a thin line of trestle tables arranged end to end. The men were setting the odd mixture of chairs along each of the sides.

"It's a good job that they chose Wednesday for the Coronation seeing as its early closing." Millie offered.

"You are funny sometimes Millie." Rosie laughed. "I don't think that Cranesbury's early closing day was the reason that they chose the date!"

"Well I didn't say that!" Millie sensed faint ridicule in Rosie's laugh.

"All I said was that it is easier for everyone to prepare a party when they haven't got to open their shops that all! Even father isn't working today."

"It's a Public Holiday all day." Rosie shook her head and laughed again as she watched Mike pretending to wobble on the ladder. He opened his eyes as if suddenly startled and his mouth gaped wide as a clown would have done. Robert Drewe looked up to see why the ladder that he was footing had moved.

"Silly sod! You'll have the ladder over, you great chump!"

"Well I knew that of course!" Millie retorted turning away from Rosie towards the lane leading to Ivy leaf Cottage.

"Sorry Mr Drewe thought that I had lost my balance!" Mike shouted down and then looking across at Rosie drew his lips together in a downward clownish crescent.

Rosie felt an uncontrollable bubble of laughter rise in her chest and had to turn away in case Drewe saw her.

Turning into the public house Rosie saw a pile of paper crowns piled onto one table.

Edith looked up and glared. "Wherever have you been? You can start on this lot. I've got sandwiches to make which I haven't even finished yet because you're so late my girl. Now I'm all behind with everything! You really are such a selfish girl Rosemary, why can't you be like that nice little Millie, I'm sure she's a great help to her mother!"

She threw down a paper crown and went behind the bar into the kitchen. Her angular back added an extra rebuke.

Rosie exhaled slowly then sat at the table to begin her task.

∞

It was later in the day when Jack and Thomas toiled back up the hill from the station. Dark rain clouds still stretched across the sky turning the last part of the afternoon into an early twilight. But as they walked along the lane they could just make out the sounds of music and then shouts of laughter and buzzing chatter as they grew closer.

Finally they came upon the scene. By the village pond people had gathered in small groups, whilst the children used up their last vestiges of energy, running in and out in games of tag where normal rules seemed not to apply to their play that afternoon.

Dulcie saw them and came running towards them breathless after all her exertions.

"I won the three-legged race and I came second in the egg and spoon!" she announced proudly.

Thomas caught her up and twirled her around, her legs creating a wider circle as he increased the speed before setting her down again.

"Dulcie, I do believe that you are just too fast for your own good! And how many cakes have you eaten, have you left any for us?"

"Oh there's loads and loads of stuff left. You should have seen the enormous cake though before they cut it. It was terrific, just like the Union Flag all red, white and blue. It was sponge with jam and cream inside, really scrumptious" she smiled at the memory. "I had two pieces."

Thomas saw Millie at the far side of the green and wandered off. Dulcie squinted up at Jack. "Did you see the King and Queen? Were they wearing their crowns? We wore crowns today, but mine got torn up when it got stuck under the chair leg. But do you know the best thing?" she whispered conspiratorially.

Jack grinned at her.

"No tell me!" he whispered back in her ear making her giggle. "Stop it, you're tickling me!" she was delighted.

"I heard mummy telling Betty that all us schoolchildren are to get a special Coronation spoon at school tomorrow. What do you think about that then?" She folded her arms in front of her chest to emphasise the importance of the information. And then she pulled at him to make him bow his head down towards her.

"And nobody else knows but me!" She whispered again, her blue eyes widened and she raised her brows in mock surprise, pressing her lips tight together and nodding before another grin spread across her face.

"But you're not to tell." She frowned, "Cross your heart and hope to die."

"Can't I even tell Tom, he is my best friend?" He asked solemnly.

Dulcie considered his situation carefully, weighing up the worth of her shared secret.

"No." She whispered "If he knows he'll only go and tell Millie 'cos he's sweet on her."

"Is he?" Jack looked at her with renewed interest. "How do you know that?"

"I just know." She said firmly closing down the discussion, and then relenting just a little. "Rosie knows too, but she wouldn't tell!"

She turned, losing sudden interest when she saw her friends in a game and ran off to join them.

Jack looked around to see where Thomas was and then saw Rosie at a table by the oak tree. The remains of the party food had been carefully laid out. The few sandwiches left had been placed under a teacloth to try to keep them moist, some iced buns were encased by glass domes and the sectioned cake was covered in some pieces of greaseproof paper. Jack helped himself, suddenly hungry.

"Did you have a good day?" Rosie asked.

Jack nodded his mouth full of cake."Mmm," He swallowed. "Loads of people there..... thousands! Some had camped out all night to get a good pitch. Couldn't get anywhere near the front of course but we managed to get a space on a step by a lamppost. It was on a bend so they all had to slow up a bit on their way round."

"Had a real bit of luck too. Found this on the way back." He pulled a coin out from his pocket. The small golden coin glinted in his hand. "Finders keepers huh! Saw a sovereign and found one too!"

Rosie picked up two cups of lemonade and wove her way back through the thinning crowds leaving Jack still hovering over the table. She found Thomas still at Millie's side.

"I bet you haven't even had anything to eat or drink yet have you?" and she passed the cup to Thomas.

"Thanks Rosie," he accepted the drink and drained the contents. "I didn't realise that I was that thirsty!"

"If you don't have something to eat soon Jack will have finished the lot," she smiled up at him.

"Come on." And she linked her arm through his leading him away from Millie who was still absorbed in wondering if her coat looked as smart compared with a girl whom she had vaguely seen before standing a little way from her.

"Rosie you always seem to hit the nail on the head!" Thomas grinned. "What would I do without you?"

She smiled up at him and saw a slight frown pass over his face as he watched Mike saunter up to Millie.

Rosie gave him a little shake to bring him back to her. "Iced buns, fresh this morning with oodles of icing. Look Jack has even managed to leave you some!"

Thomas laughed, distracted from his concern, "Rosie Minton you are such a tease! A fellow is not safe when you're around, offering all these delights."

He stuffed an iced bun in his mouth as if ravenous with hunger, biting more chunks off as if his very life depended on it.

Rosie watched his performance.

"Well if you don't choke to death after that, there's no justice in the world." She remarked with a grin, and she shook him again before turning her face up towards him.

Carried away by the moment of playfulness he bent down and pecked her cheek. In a split second of time he saw her face change, his retort stayed on his lips unsaid as her serious eyes held him in a fleeting glance, before she loosened her hold on his sleeve and stepped away.

"Sorry Rosie! Didn't mean to upset you, got carried away!"

The sadness in her smile and her faint denial of any upset caused, left Thomas experiencing a strange sense of emptiness. She was always such a steady companion, such good company. He valued her clever remarks and her ability to enliven each moment. And now he had somehow misjudged it all.

And then it came to him. She was no longer a childhood playmate. She was becoming a woman. He watched her move away and considered her. She wasn't pretty like Millie. Millie who could be so exasperating, so tantalisingly captivating, but Rosie had a special quality, an air about her that he couldn't exactly explain. He couldn't pin it down. She could reach deep inside you and you knew that she cared. For all her ability to mock the world he knew that she was constant. He felt that she deserved more. The world had given her a poor deal. He disliked Ethel; so unlike his own mother. There was no warmth there, and Archie seemed indifferent. No wonder she spent so much time up at Mote House, lost in her books. And now he too had let her down.

"What's up Tom, lost a pound and found a penny?" Jack slapped him on the back. "Thought Rosie was with you, where did she go?"

"Not sure. She was here and then she wandered off." His evasion left a sense of guilt.

Jack scanned the crowd that was starting to disperse. "Nope, can't see her, but there's Millie." And he pointed to the far side of the pond. His eyes darted around before he saw two girls looking pointedly in their direction.

"Get a look at those two Tom. She's interested in you right enough!" and he nudged him in the ribs. "Let's go over and introduce ourselves."

But Thomas turned away. "Think I'll call it a day if it all the same to you. I'll leave you to it." He slapped Jack's back. "Say goodbye to Rosie and Millie for me," he called back over his shoulder.

Jack called after him, "Don't go yet, the night's still young!"

But Thomas continued in his way down the hill towards home.

Ivy Leaf Cottage 2009

Rosie

The war changed so many things for us all. Millie did start her shorthand and typing evening class at the technical school and I got a job first as a waitress at the Lyons Corner House in Maidstone and then as a chambermaid at The George Hotel in Cranbrook as it was closer to home. For a while I would meet up with Thomas on his way home after school, and then when he left to go to University I didn't get to see him so much. But then I am running away with myself.

I left school when I was fifteen gaining my School Leaving Certificate as my one and only qualification, unlike Jack who left when he was fourteen. They had raised the school leaving age the year before much to my mother's displeasure which meant that I was not earning my keep until a year later.

Thomas had gained a special place in Lady Faversham's heart. I think she saw in him the son that she had lost to the barbarous battlefields of France. He was a beautiful youth. At eighteen, at six foot three, he had grown to tower over most of the other lads in the village. He was strong and steady, and intelligent, a prize for any woman. But he had the fatal Othello flaw of so many men; he loved not wisely but too well. His loyalty to, and early affection for, Millie continued. Millie became as pretty as her mother but whereas Beatrice had a natural modesty, Millie was only too well aware of her charms. She flaunted herself and Thomas was cast under her spell. She knew that he was captivated by her but she was dismissive of his attentions. She wanted danger and romance. Thomas offered undying love which was not an attractive proposition for Millie. She wanted intrigue and to experience the heady heights of conquest. She sought out unsuitable boys to tease.

Lady Faversham took Thomas under her wing although by then she was very frail. Sir Richard had passed away two years previously and Kilndown Manor was showing serious signs of neglect. Many of the staff who had served there for so many years were also advancing in years and were not replaced. Young people were turning to the towns for employment and the idea of being subservient, with the strict codes and Victorian rules of large houses was becoming unfashionable. Knowing one's place was deemed to be outdated, for the young people had hungered for freedoms not imagined by their parents. The years of the Great Depression brought with it a demand to change the structure of the classes.

At Kilndown Manor Lady Faversham found herself having to close up some of the rooms as many of them could only be heated by coal fires. The situation irked her; it insulted her perceived right to privilege. Even the plumbing arrangements had conspired against her and were deemed to be lamentable. It was an affront, an irritation that she felt keenly. She found herself at odds with the new world and she railed against it. It proved to her that she and the Empire were lost in a conspiracy and that those who followed would rue the day when they belatedly realised their role in its downfall.

Thankfully there were still areas for her control. As Thomas had proved himself to be a diligent student she arranged for an interview with the head of the school to see what the future could hold for him. When she heard the glowing testimony she arranged for the funds to prepare him for the university entrance exams. As always she had not thought to consult his family or to consider the feelings of Samuel and Alice. She fleetingly presumed her generosity would be appreciated, but had no desire to be thanked or involved in their lives. Her ambition was for Thomas only; the rest was of no consequence to her. She assumed the right to dictate a future for him. During her lifetime her authority had been unfailingly unquestioned and she saw no reason for this to change.

So Thomas took the exams and in passing them, gained a place at Cambridge, taking him further away from me.

I savoured his letters that came spasmodically, feigning a lack of any interest when unexpectedly confronted by the postman. I hid them from prying eyes, especially Jack who was often around at the most inconvenient times.

And I knew that he was writing regularly to Millie. She showed me her letters almost dismissively, having more regard from where they had come, rather than from whom. Cambridge and the romance of a city filled with eligible young men held far more magic than Thomas's serious descriptions of his student life. The idea of the correspondence was more thrilling than the vision of a student not having funds for the theatre, shows, day trips to the capital; in short, the money for a good time. His carefully crafted letters bored her. His modest descriptions of his life and his absorbing studies, the friends that he had made, both irritated and irked her. They seemed to suggest a rebuke, that there was more to life than having fun. The world of work and of having to earn her keep had not yet entered her domain. She had another year or two of school before her secretarial course and work beckoned.

For me the work at the George Hotel was a world away from them both. My day was filled with stiff starched sheets, the detritus of careless travelling salesmen and the unfailing demands of exacting guests who seemed to believe that their key to the room should open a door of unending delights. Their complaints of a lack of constant hot water, lime scale in the bath, a disappointing front view of the busy high street or the quiet back yard, and other guests who had disturbed their sleep, seemed to be something that I had caused or had the power to improve. It was the seemingly timid and unworldly who were

192

able to cause most offence. Their sharp comments penetrated my resolve to remain detached.

By contrast I was often unexpectedly charmed by guests, who had alighted on the hotel by chance, as they made their way south to season in warmer climes. The gaiety of these spontaneous travellers, who seemed to take everything in their stride, delighted me. They saw adversity as just mere inconvenience; as something that they could regale their friends with at their next dinner party. I was entranced by them, by their good humour and unrestrained laughter. I hugged their frank acceptance of the world and its foibles desperately wanting to emulate them. I desired their fulfilment and their ability to be generous with their emotions. They seemed to soar when others merely crawled. But my world and my position in it dictated that I should be careful; that I should remain a watcher and not the watched. In my darkest moments I knew that I had unwittingly aligned myself with those that crawled, and would only sprout wings if I could summon up enough courage to defy my nemesis.

At home Archie and Ethel rubbed along. Roseanne had finally left when she realised that the fortunes of The Papermakers Arms was on a downward spiral and that Ethel was going to assume more of a role in the everyday running of the pub. Archie was more than happy to let her go. Her wages and her manner were proving to be an irritant in Ethel's side, as the tradesmen of the village became more pressing for their bills to be paid. Archie had found himself unwillingly vacillating from one to another trying to establish an awkward truce, placating one, only to find that it enraged the other. His only peace was to be found with Beatrice and yet even she seemed to be becoming more distant. He felt that his hold on life was slipping away. Ethel was unpopular with his locals and had quietly wrestled financial responsibility away from him whilst he was consumed by Beatrice. Her direct confrontation with their suppliers and to those whom they owed money had led to more difficulties.

Ethel then demanded that my earnings at The George contributed to the household budget, but she happily allowed Jack to retain his weekly wage. Jack had to establish himself, to make his way in the world. He needed to look presentable; he was destined for better things. He could do anything once his mind was set on it. A son would have to provide for his own family one day. I heard all her arguments put to Archie. I heard her quietly working out her strategy, silently chewing over her words, making the case for inequality whilst audibly dismissing my initial protests.

And as I raged and seethed against her petty judgements I resolved to outmanoeuvre her. The wage slips from the hotel were kept in the back office, all hand written without printed serial numbers. Once I had acquired a supply I was able to replicate the cursive style annotation to include the amounts and hours that I had supposedly worked. I received one wage slip with my full pay, replacing it with another notification of a smaller amount and pocketed the remaining sum of money, so that slip and money matched. It was a small defiance, a payment of a few hours but it was something of my own to keep, and week by week it grew, my little nest egg of deceit.

Jack's new independence and money to spend for his own enjoyment meant that he quickly acquired a new set of friends. He frequented the dance hall in Maidstone on Saturday night but more importantly had learnt to drive, taking the serviced cars to and from the garage. In a short space of time he had watched and learnt; focussing on the mechanical prowess of the older men, carefully assisting, becoming useful, dependable, and reliable; an esteemed byword for a valued employee. His willingness to learn, to stay and finish a job, his quick humour and his ability to camouflage his failings convinced some of the other men that he had more experience than he actually had. He sought out the skilful mechanics who unwittingly taught him their trade, and listened to their diagnosis, how they handled the tools, appraising each job, learning the tricks of the trade. One man in particular was asked for by name with some of the regular customers who knew his work was sound.

But Jack had his sights set on a higher prize. His work in the garage workshop meant grime, grease and dirty fingernails, oily rags and stained brown overalls. By the end of each day the grease stubbornly resisted his attempts to remove it with a paraffin-soaked rag. He spent his hours endeavouring to reach inaccessible parts of the engine with traitorous tools that could slip from his inexpert grasp just at the wrong moment and fall to the floor declaring his failures with a resentful clang. He watched the dapper salesman in the front of the shop absentmindedly running a polishing cloth over the gleaming bodywork of the latest model, whilst explaining the wonders of the automobile to a beguiled customer.

During the summer his sweat had mingled with the grease and oil, and the air would hold the smell of hot engines whilst in the winter his fingers turned blue and clumsy in the cold workshop. In the spring he had idly watched a pair of swans building a nest in the River Len that ran next to the garage. They had flown in and somehow discovered in mid-stream a small mound, surrounded by straggly thin bushes, just sufficient in size to accommodate and hide their sprawling nest of untidy twigs and weed. He learnt from the other men that this was their preferred site to which they had returned for a number of years. The faithfulness and longevity of their coupling was commented upon by one of the men. It seemed that they all found a virtue in the pairing of the swans. Jack nodded his agreement and felt nothing.

He also had his eye on Diana. She came with her father who wished to purchase a car. They first came into the car showroom just as he had come by to collect a repair card. She had stood a little way apart from her father facing towards the road and the Bishop's Palace, impatiently twirling a soft doeskin dove-grey glove around in her hand. Jack had backed away so that she wouldn't see him in his overalls and the back of his hands still showing traces of black oil that had resisted the paraffin rag. She was tall, elegant but still young though striving to look older than her years, with reddened lips and a hat set at an impossible angle to her head. The ensemble right down to her perfectly polished two-toned shoes spoke of wealth and comfort. He had watched them both and listened to the father, catching the words Tonbridge Wells before slipping away.

Strange how our lives are fashioned by these little uncontrived moments, and how we spend the intervening years endeavouring to direct our destiny, believing that we can change the course of events by our will. I should know, my whole being centred on my perversity to direct and control others.

When Jack came home that night I could see that she had lit a fire in him. He was unusually distracted, trying to work out a long term strategy. A little worry frown centred above his nose as he finished his tea and then sighing he abruptly left the table without explanation. Ethel had sensed his distance and had been upset, suggesting to the room that "a thank you would not have gone amiss!" I took the advantage to leave the room by clearing the dishes as a means of escaping her, as she had a habit of finding some fault in me in these moments of rejection.

Cranesbury Village Winter Snow 1938
Thomas

The snow started silently during the Saturday night of the 18th December and continued throughout the day. By the time that Thomas awoke on Sunday, the railway line, roads, cottages and fields had merged into one white rumpled eiderdown, and each had become indistinguishable from one another. Through the thickly falling snowflakes it was just possible to see that only the telegraph poles were poking uniformly through the blanket, with their thickened wires just managing to hold on to their impossible load. Thomas could just make out that whilst the taller trees still resembled themselves with their encrusted limbs and foreshortened thickened trunks enveloped in the snow, the smaller fruit trees, bushes and hedgerows had developed strange animal shapes. He now saw lumpy polar bears, giant hedgehogs and bedraggled lines of elephants in their place.

A leaden sky held a faintly sulphurous yellow glow as the flakes swirling and scurried after each other in their furious whirling dervish race to descend. His bedroom window had shrunk in size. A thick white sill of snow curved around the bottom half rounding the window and restricting his view.

His room was normally freezing in winter but the unnatural gloom made the cold feel more intense. He shivered and pulled the thin brown blanket closer around his shoulders and then tugged at the reluctant sheet that had ridden and twisted beneath him. His bed had shrunk in length as he had grown in height. These days he had to tuck his knees up to prevent his feet being exposed to the cold air. It was the same back at college. His single bed there was designed to accommodate a far smaller frame.

Downstairs he could hear movement, the kettle whistled on the stove and cups rattled. His mother was usually the first to stir, unable to remain in bed once she had woken. Both his parents were early risers, a force of habit developed over their working lives. They and their neighbours were quick to condemn those who stayed overlong in their morning beds. It would elicit a sharp tut of disapproval unless one could prove some indisputable kind of malaise. There were age-old rules to be followed, or cast aside at your peril. Owing money or defaulting on debt, keeping people waiting, answering back, missing Sunday church, spitting in the street, having dirty windows, hanging washing out on a Sunday, not clearing your plate of food, talking too loudly in public places, pushing in when there was a queue, staring at someone's deformity, interfering in a domestic argument, not remembering to write thank- you notes to aunts and uncles at Christmas, walking with hands in pockets, not polishing the backs of shoes, not knowing your place, entering to a discussion of religion or politics at the table, and so the list went on.

Thomas clasped his hands behind his head. This world of theirs had so quickly become alien to him. The pettiness of it all irked him. He had realised with horror last night that he was struggling to find his place with his parents in their conversation. The frequent silences had rebuked him and he felt disloyal, hoping that they had not recognised his discomfort or seen a change in him.

At Cambridge, amongst the other students on his law course the easy conversations flowed from one to another. They had discussed the rise of fascism, Spain and Mussolini, Chamberlain, eugenics, The National Socialist League, the working man's role in the modern age; and close to his heart the news of Jewish lawyers banned from practising in Germany, there seemed no subject that was taboo. He had found his own ideas wanting and was keen to find his own voice.

He realised that he was already counting the days when the holiday was over and he could return to university. He knew that his parents would not understand and would be desperately hurt by his need to live this other life.

He could not begin to discuss other matters with them such as mixing with a small group of friends who had been talking of working for the government, trying to ascertain the truth behind the headlines. One of his tutors had confided in him there were agencies both in England and abroad who were threatening the stability of a free Europe. He had wondered if Thomas wanted to support their work. He called it intelligence work, just gathering data in London.

He ran his hand over his face and felt the stipples of his unshaven chin. Throwing off his covers he dived to retrieve the clothes from the chair and got dressed quickly.

∞

Millie stirred lazily. She took a while to remember that it was Sunday and then having realised the day, turned over to catch more sleep, but sleep was unusually evasive. She stretched and opened her eyes then felt that something was amiss. Her light room seemed darker than usual. She thought that perhaps she had awoken too early and reached out for the alarm clock. It said eight o'clock. But it was far too gloomy to be that time. Kicking against the constraints of her nightdress that had managed to wrap itself around her legs she pushed back the bedclothes and wriggled into her slippers. Pushing back the curtains she peered out and saw a strange white garden that looked similar to theirs but without any familiar form. The snow was still falling. Thin flakes fluttered past the window as if trying to find their way. She watched them dance until her breath clouded the window pane. A bubble of pleasure surged inside her.

Snow! At last! She still retained the childish delight of the wonder. Snow that re-landscaped the village and placed thick bulky cloaks over roofs and sheds, softened sharp edges, rounded the hedges and provided a white canvas for birds and small animals to mark their early comings and goings across the lawn. She ran across the landing to see the village road. There were no markings in the street, nothing to suggest any human activity. At the doorways the snow had banked up creating small curved slopes. There was no difference between pavements or street, they had merged into one thick road that led away from the village.

"Millie! Is that you up?" her mother's voice called from the kitchen. "I hope you're not running around in bare feet up there."

"No!" Millie turned her head away from the window and then back again to resume her vigil.

Archie Minton had pushed the door of the pub open and had gone back inside. She watched as he returned with a broom and started to sweep the pile of snow away from the entrance. Then making headway he brushed a little pathway parallel to where the road should have been, creating little walls on either side. Once he reached the end of the building he started back at the doorway to begin a fresh pathway towards the village pond. The soft snow was deceptively hard to shift. Millie watched as he stopped to lean against the broom and stretch his back before resuming his task. Behind him, where he uncovered the grey path it was already changing to a lighter shade. The snow was covering his tracks.

∞

By ten o'clock the snow stopped falling. Thomas made slow progress up the hill towards the village from the railway station. Wading through the thick snow, even Thomas, with his advantage of youth and long legs, felt the effort of each raised step. After a while his muscles complained about the unusual gait and his breath became more laboured. He had not been the first to tread his way through. Others had been before him; their

200

tracks had been partially covered but he still tried to use them to lessen the effort of forging a new path. Snippets of a favourite old carol swirled in his brain,

'Mark my footsteps, good my page. Tread thou in them boldly.'
His heavy plodding footsteps marked time with each phrase, heavier on the first syllable, treading with a new found regularity.
'Thou shall find the winters' rage, freeze thy blood less coldly.'
His staccato breath created little clouds as he breathed out and then there was a rush of cold air into his lungs as he sucked it in.
'In his Master's steps he trod, where the snow lay dinted'.
One- two, left- right, the trek turned into a march as he lowered his head and swung his arms to the new rhythm.

As the middle of the village came into view Thomas saw the men were making attempts to clear paths outside each shop and up towards the church.

Ron looked up and saw Thomas.

"Good lad, lend a hand. They say there's more of this on the way!"

Jack was standing by Simmons store, a broom resting on his shoulder. The pond was frozen solid. A small group of ducks huddled together by the stiff weeds, trying to console themselves, waggling their heads as if to disapprove of the sorry state of affairs.

Thomas grinned at Jack. "See you've finished for the day then!"

"Cheeky blighter! I was here at the crack of dawn! What kept you then? Do your uni types know what this is then, huh?" Jack whirled his broom to provoke and then pointed it towards Thomas in a jousting stance.

Thomas grabbed Ron's broom and the two brooms became swords as he engaged Jack. They clashed and thrust each trying to maintain foothold in the snow.

"You daft pair of beggars! You'll be breaking my broom if you don't watch out!" Ron's cheerful reproach caused the others to stop their work and for a few moments the older men stood up to catch their own breath becoming an audience for the ungainly swordsmen.

Being taller Thomas had the advantage of reach but Jack was more nimble, managing to parry each jab.

"Now then that's enough." Ron called out. "You'll be taking an eye out at this rate!"

"You're just worried about your broom!" Jack's voice rasped with the effort of the performance.

As Thomas realised that Jack had been caught off guard he arched his broom and Jack's flew from his grasp. Thomas let go of his own and grabbed Jack in an enveloping bear hug. They whirled round as one as Thomas attempted to bring him to the ground. Finally Thomas's strength defeated Jack's writhing and they fell back into the pile of snow both claiming victory.

"I'll be taking that back before you do any more damage, you pair of great chumps!" Ron grabbed his broom and cuffed Thomas around the head.

Both Jack and Thomas lay back in the snow, grinning at each other, before attempting to set themselves back on their feet. Each one pretended to lend a hand to the other but just kept out of reach which made them both unsteady again. Their coats were coated in snow, Thomas's had lost a button.

"Men, do yer want a cuppa? I'm making a brew!"

They all turned to see Betty standing in the doorway of the bakery.

"Don't you step out woman, it's lethal out here." Ron's sharp warning made her catch hold of the doorjamb then she nodded that she had heard him.

Ron turned to the other men. "I nearly went flying myself! There was a nasty patch of ice. Didn't see it at first!"

He called back up the road to her. "Give us a shout and we'll come up for it."

"Right then... you two as well," he turned back to Jack and Thomas who were brushing themselves down.

"If we get our backs into it we can at least do the paths here this morning, put some sand down, and then do a bit for the Rev up the hill otherwise no one will make it up there. Tom, Jack...you clear in front of Simmons's shop, you big girl's blouses.... the pair of you."

The two lads pointed to each other as if to attribute Ron's insult to the other.

"You!"

"No! You!" And smirking they made sheep's eyes at each other, pouting their lips in mock air kisses.

"What have we done to deserve a pair of idiots like you?" Ron shook his head in amusement at their antics.

"Jack, well we expect that, but you Thomas lad! A scholarship and university, they must be scraping the barrel these days!" Ron grinned at them both. "I don't know, a sight for sore eyes 'n no mistake!"

For the next ten minutes they all became absorbed by their task. Squeaky snow scrunched under their boots as they moved together brushing and shovelling, scraping the excess away to create small hills of dirty snow. Robert Drewe's cheeks took on an alarming crimson blue shade as his body struggled against the unusual exercise.

"Whew.... I think I'm done for!" he announced to no one in particular, blowing out his cheeks and then sucking in more air.

"Tea up!" Betty's shout turned their heads.

"Righto love, we're on our way, c'mon lads."

They set their brushes and brooms to one side and stamped up the hill to stand at Betty's doorway.

Betty handed out the mugs and produced a plate of warm muffins to the loud approval of the men. Hands reached out and emptied the plate of its contents, and grunts of appreciation were interspersed with gulps of hot tea.

"This hits the spot!"

"Lovely grub missis T!"

Archie looked up at the sky and waved his mug in the general direction of his gaze.

"Bet there's more of this stuff tonight!"

The others murmured their assent.

"Wonder if there'll be a white Christmas. Haven't had one for a while have we?"

"Nope, last year was a mild one wasn't it."

"Aye, and the one before that."

"It'll keep the little 'uns amused at any rate!"

"That it will."

"S 'all right for them's that don't 'ave to work!"

"True, true."

Their tea break over, they reluctantly handed the mugs back and set off down the hill and across the road.

"Are we doing the Bank as well? It's pretty bad over there. Bus'll have trouble on that bend no doubt."

"If it snows again tonight like last night, reckon there won't be any bus coming, no way."

They continued to clear a thin path and the grey hillocks grew at intervals along the way marking their slow progress.

"Reckon that's enough for now!"

"My missis will have the dinner on the table and there'll be devil to pay if it spoils!"

"Yep. Me too, I can feel my back going."

Each tried to avoid being the first to turn away, but hunger and the thought of the warmth inside decided them at last.

Thomas shouted his goodbyes and began his journey back down the road. Gradually they all dispersed, calling out to one another before each going their own way, as the snow laden sky of the early afternoon cast its gloom over the village.

Cranesbury Village 1938
Snow and Sledging

Monday morning began quietly still and bright. Overnight there
had been another heavy fall. The villagers agreed that they had
had at least four more inches of snow, but whereas the Sunday
had been miserable, Monday saw the fresh snow glinting and
sparkling in the weak winter light. Multi-coloured crystals shone
on the new surface. Leaning as far out as she could Rosie felt the
cold against her cheek and heard a faint creaking of the tree
limbs as they held their bulky load. A lone crow protested in the
distance and then there was just the silence. Stretching out even
further Rosie could, by sitting on the narrow window sill, just see
the edge of the village pond and the road stretching up the hill.
There were no tracks on the paths of marks in the road, only the
dents of ducks' paddle dabs beneath the chestnut tree where
they had huddled for the night.

She contemplated the Christmas card scene and breathed in
quietly to herself, *'deep and crisp and even'* and in her mind's eye
she saw Thomas, and held his image. And closing her eyes she
saw their small party together standing at the top of the hill
beyond Mote Lake. The race began. She felt Thomas wrapping
his arms around her holding on to the rope, constraining her,
tightly binding her to him. Their toboggan parted clouds of snow
which stung her face half blinding her, and then the speed
exhilarating them both as they bumped and flew down the hill
before they finally spilled from the sledge, rolling together
triumphantly in the banked up snow.

He should be mine. I will make him mine. But even as she willed
it to herself she felt a shudder and the image of them all
scattered.

Downstairs she heard their voices. Archie's low tones in response
to Ethel's argument rumbled words together not making any
sense, but Ethel's sharpness rattled through the house. Rosie

listening to her mother's resentment, the well-rehearsed and worn out recriminations that resounded around the house, wearily tried to blot out her venom.

"When will it be paid....leave me with the clothes on my back....blind fool...... and that wasn't the last time you evil devil!" Archie's muffled reply would have allowed an innocent bystander to believe that it was only Ethel that led the battle, but his inaudible answers were just as inflammatory and wounding as hers.

A door banged and then another.

"Don't you walk away from me...think that you have heard the last of this... glad when I see you in your grave...think yourself so high and mighty!"

They raged at each other, their mutual hatred fuelled the battle of wills.

Rosie turned back into her room. In the past Archie would lash out; her mother's provocation tipping him over the edge. But these days he would walk away, reaching for his hat or coat and walking away from the pub until his anger could be controlled and her voice no longer pounded in his head, and he could become master of himself.

Sitting at her little dressing table Rosie contemplated her reflection. The glass of the mirror distorted the room behind her but one section gave a clear image. She ran her fingers through her short hair. It was a dull dark brown but in a good light, in the summer there was just the slightest a hint of auburn like her grandfather. It never framed her face well. In the summer it would sometimes curl up at the ends, the damp made it stick together in little rat tails and the wind caused it to tangle. Rosie sighed. She held her hair away from her forehead. There was a suspicion of a slight crease between her eyebrows. When had that appeared? Her lips were unremarkable; her skin was pale, annoyingly freckled in the summer and her neck was short. She smoothed her hand upwards stroking the skin up towards her chin. It would never become a swan's neck; she would never become a swan, just a duckling. Her serious eyes held her own hypnotic gaze.

'I know myself. I know how others feel and think, but is this enough?' she thought. 'Do I need to try harder or should I accept things as they are?' She brought her hands and fingers together, as if in prayer, cupping her mouth and nose and breathed in her own scent. Her half-masked face looked at itself impassively. Suddenly she decided. She would take the consequences later.

Downstairs the war had come to a temporary impasse. Archie had tramped down to the cellar; the thick snow had caused him to turn back from the front entrance to the street.

Ethel was still in the kitchen. She needed to direct her anger. The cups and saucers felt her surges of fury as she took them from the cupboard and banged them on the table.

"Rosie! Are you ever getting down here! Jack love… breakfast is waiting."

∞

The villagers had been right to say that the buses wouldn't come. Even the farmer had attempted to bring the milk on his tractor to the villages but his slow progress that morning had forced him to leave the churns by the station telling Samuel that he had to get back to the cows.

" Only bin trying all morning to clear the yard for them to get across for milking, right old mess an' no mistake. And there's more to come!"

He went away shaking his head.

Samuel told Thomas to go up to the village and fetch some men back with him if they wanted to get the milk.

"They could put one of them in that old wheelbarrow that we have round the back. If you strap them down they should be alright, but you'll need two or three to pull it."

When Thomas reached the village he found everything was at a standstill. No cars had reached the village. There were no buses running and the Bank hadn't opened as the manager couldn't get in.

Thomas found Jack at the pub.

"Can't get anywhere at the moment. Had to go and phone the garage to say that I wouldn't be in. That'll cost me a day's pay I shouldn't wonder. Whole place seems to be closed down. No trains either then?"

Thomas shook his head. "Too much snow on the lines at the moment. Think there are the gangs out trying to shift it. Don't know how long that will take though."

Jack squinted at the sky.

"Anyway can you can lend a hand with the milk. Dad's got a wheelbarrow. The farmer left it down at the station... seems he's got a problem with the cows in the yard or something."

Jack nodded. "I just need to get my boots."

Thomas called after him, "Do you know where Mike is? We need three of us I think in case it decides to roll off! Have you got any rope as well? Dad thought that he had some but blowed if I can find it!"

Jack's voice carried from the back.

"Think he's still with Ron. They tried to get some deliveries out just local but I don't think he got very far. Ending up just pushing the bike through drifts, that's what he said. Waste of time in the end."

He reappeared with his boots in one hand and some rope in the other. "That's all we've got here. What about asking Simmons for some to borrow as it's an emergency like, he's bound to have some old stuff hanging around."

They turned back out into the glare of the street. The snow reflected the light and small translucent thin icicles had formed above the porch. Jack reached up and snapped one off, feeling the sharp tip before throwing it into the road where it disappeared leaving a small line trace in the snow.

They tramped up the hill and found Mike leaning against the counter with a fresh mug of tea.

"What's up?" he asked seeing their rope.

"Lend a hand mate." Jack flicked his thumb back at Thomas. "Milk's still down at the station so we're bringing it up here in a wheelbarrow."

"Ron!" he shouted, "Can we borrow your lad?

Ron bustled in from the back wiping his hands on his apron.

"Borrow him? You can keep him!" he smiled at Thomas. "What do you want him for anyway?"

"Milk's at the station. Farmer's got a problem and had to leave it there. I think he only made a few runs in the tractor."

"How're you getting it up here then?"

"Using Mr Fulwood's wheelbarrow!"

"Oh, crikey… a recipe for disaster, you, Mike, and a full milk churn in a wheelbarrow!"

"And Tom!" Jack turned to his friend.

"Aye, and the only one with any sense around here!"

Jack and Mike pulled a face at each other.

"Excuse us Ron…. it was Tom here who came and asked us to help him out."

"Mmm I dare say. Go on then what're you waiting for?"

Jack shouted back over his shoulder, "and if we're not back by sun down send a search party!"

"Silly beggars all of them!" Ron chuckled to himself.

∞

When they finally got the milk to the village and Mike had returned to the bakery, Jack and Thomas went into the pub. Rosie was sitting perched on a bar stool waiting for them.

209

"Staying for some dinner Thomas, there's some stew on the stove?"

"Oh great, thanks."

"Simmons said that we could have his old sledge and we've got one in the shed, fancy going afterwards?" Rosie suggested.

"Yes, why not... haven't done it for years."

Thomas turned to Jack "Bet Millie would like to come too."

Jack shrugged, "Could ask."

Rosie stared into space. "Do you want me to go and ask?"

"Thanks Rosie!"

She went to fetch her coat and returned fastening it up.

"Shan't be long. Enjoy the stew," she called back before wrestling with her old wellingtons that had squashed themselves closed.

She stamped across the road, swung open the gate and walked up the path. She knew that Ronald would be home, the Bank had not been able to open.

Ronald appeared at the door when she knocked.

"Yes? Oh, hello Rosie."

"Oh yes!" Rosie began brightly. "I just wondered if Millie would like to come tobogganing with me and Jack up by Mote Lake. We can't get into work either. Stuck here instead......"

Ronald looked back into the hall as if to summon Millie.

Rosie hurried on. "We got a couple of old sledges. They've seen better days, a bit splintered....haven't used them for years! But they should hold together I'd think!" She laughed distractedly as if she was unsure of being able to convince herself.

Ronald frowned as she knew he would.

"Well Rosie that's very kind of you to think of including Millie..." he faltered.

"We understand if you think she shouldn't," she shrugged.

"Probably they will only last this time out...... but I'm sure that she'd be fine." She bit her lip and carefully watched his discomfort grow.

"Well, I don't think Mrs Latterbridge would be too keen you see."

"No, 'suppose she wouldn't really."

"Pity that your sledges seem to be so… so dilapidated……
otherwise….." He spread his thin hands as if to wave away the
disappointment for her.

Rosie nodded again, "just didn't want to go without saying….."

"Uh huh." He smiled at her, "very kind of you both……. very
considerate."

"Tell Millie I called!" Rosie turned and walked away quickly, "got
to dash! Bye."

She returned to The Papermakers Arms and went into the
kitchen. Thomas was just finishing his bowl wiping out the
remains of the stew with a chunk of bread and looked up
expectantly. "Well?"

Rosie busied herself with the other plates on the table and took
them to the sink.

"Not coming."

"Why not?"

"Not sure, got her dad to come to the door to say that she
couldn't come. Shame really. Would have been far better with
four…even up the races, two against two!"

She turned to Thomas and grimaced, "Pity huh?"

Jack came carrying an old coat. "Found a scarf in the drawer
d'you want one, fetch another if you like?"

Thomas scraped the chair against the floor and as he stood up his
frame dwarfed the room.

"C'mon lets go. He shook off his disappointment and smiled at
Rosie.

A swelling of happiness smothered her, cocooning her in
warmth.

∞

The afternoon had been everything that had it promised to be.
The snow had formed a thick skin which allowed the sledges to
skim effortlessly down the hill. The exhilaration was contagious.

Each time they tried to be more daring, to give the sledge an extra push at the top, pulling it back and forth to form an icy film and then providing it an extra shove which launched them and sent them arching, ricocheting over the humps until they became safely entombed in the soft drift at the foot of the hill. Hearts pounding and breathless with the rollercoaster of movement. Jack had easily won most of the races skimming down the hill as if in flight. His face flushed with his success. Thomas and Jack had become children again; the sport had allowed their innocence enjoyment of the moment to creep back.

Finally the sky began to lose its wintry light. They trailed the sledges behind them, weary now that the excitement of the afternoon had left them. Their legs felt quite leaden and their breathing laboured as they trudged home.

Rosie blew on her fingers protesting that her wet gloves were freezing her hands.

"Take them off then!" Jack's voice was muffled against the scarf that he had wrapped around his face to keep the cold air away.

Thomas stopped and turned back to her, and with brotherly affection caught her hands in his rubbing them together vigorously.

"Brrr lovely!" she grinned up at him and they walked together behind Jack, Thomas still carelessly holding one hand of hers in his, his large warm hand enclosing hers, the other catching fast the rope and pulling the sledge behind them..

"How's university treating you, is it what you expected?"

"Mmm…. difficult to know what I had expected really. The work's not hard, just a different kind of studying I suppose. The reading list goes on and on, some of the fellows say that they don't bother…but I'm not sure…"

"So how do you find them…'spec they're different from us uneducated lot here! Bet they talk about all kinds of interesting things." He looked down at her. "I never think like that of you

Rosie, or the rest of the people here. Roots are important, 'specially at these times"

"Times of change, a changing world... that we might get swept up in?" She murmured.

"You always hit the nail on the head Rosie! The world is becoming a dangerous place and we could be sleepwalking into a disaster."

He shook his head. "And our politicians seem to look the other way when it suits them, trying to appease instead of seeing what's happening. And it's bad. Laws changing, freedom to work, to own property, all kinds of subtle persecution and subversion......".

"Is that what the other students say?"

"Well no.... not all of them of course, but there are a few of us who do talk about things."

"The enlightened few!"

"No! Now you're laughing at me!"

She looked up at him her "You must do what you think is right but be careful. There are those who like to lead and others who follow."

"Quite right little Miss. And what are you then?"

Oh I just watch and listen. I'm not important like you."

"But you are Rosie.... and you are a good listener!"

"Well that will take me far won't it, changing beds, cleaning rooms my, my, I have such an important life." She tried to laugh off the anger that she felt, railing against her future.

"I'm sorry, I've upset you now...."

"No.... it's not you... I just wish that... oh I don't know.... forget what I said, I don't know what I'm saying sometimes."

"You're one of the most intuitive people that I know Rosie Minton.... you see things that others miss...I wish that I had half the ..."

"No don't wish that!" She twisted her hand away from his.

"Well we did have a good day didn't we?" Her sudden change of humour caught him off balance.

"Time for a nice cup of tea, and a roaring fire to toast a crumpet or two!" She grinned. "I'm starving aren't you?"

"Wonder what tomorrow will bring…what do you think Jack?" he shouted at Jack's back.

"Dunno mate. Be glad to get back to normal though. Time is money!"

"Bet Parsons will make sure that this lane is cleared and 'spec that the tractors will do the main roads then we should be able to get through tomorrow."

"Pity that Millie missed this afternoon though wasn't it." Thomas breath clouded in front of him, and the temperature suddenly seemed to lower.

"There's always another time." Rosie dug her hands into her pockets and burst into song

"In the meadow we can build a snowman. Then pretend that he is Parson Brown."

Thomas and Jack joined in.

*"He'll say are you married? We'll say No Man! But you can do the job when you're in town…*how does the rest go Rosie?"

Rosie played the words silently in her head.

Later on we'll conspire, as we dream by the fire, to face unafraid the plans that we've made………

She sang, *"In the meadow we can build a snowman, and pretend that he's a circus clown…"*

"Think we missed a bit out somewhere Rosie Lee!" laughed Thomas.

"She never knows all the words to anything!" Jack turned back to him, "always fluffing the words….. never make the music hall!"

"Oh and you're such an impresario Jack." She retorted. "Missed your vocation!"

"Now then children, children…… now, now! We come together on this day in harmony and reconciliation!" Thomas intoned. His accurate mimicry of Reverent Martin, caused them both to draw back from hostilities and smile in spite of themselves.

"Thomas Fulwood! I am shocked, d'you hear man! Shocked, at such sacrilege! And our dear Rev, a man of the cloth; a shepherd to his undeserving sheep!" Jack drew himself up and crossed himself awkwardly, whilst still holding the frayed rope of the sledge.

Suddenly Rosie drew in her breath; in her mind's eye she could see Thomas talking quietly on the telephone, but she couldn't understand his whispered words. Then it came to her, French, he was speaking French; his accent perfect as it would be. He was a mimic; of course he had a good ear. A chill of fear entered her and she shivered.

"What's up Rosie feeling the cold?" He looked down at her smiling.

The thick falls of snow lasted right through to the Boxing Day with the thaw not starting until well into the New Year. It was a white Christmas to remember, one that I have treasured over the years. We spent the time, in between struggling to get back and forth to work, enjoying our time together. There were snowball fights and walks across the lanes where our familiar landscape had been magically transformed by Jack Frost.

I became so close to Thomas then. For that precious time he almost became mine. When his mind was not caught up in the political maelstrom he confided in me. He spoke of his earnest hopes for a better future, whilst I played the part of his confidante. For him I was still the little sister that he had never had, his brotherly affection was innocent and kind. But then his kindness always was the biggest part of him. Where he was generous with his affection I rationed mine. Mine was a jealous kind of need. My love diminished me whereas his, well, his was just a superior kind in every way. His capacity to forgive and to accept the failings of Millie, Jack and me was something that I could never have done. Even now, after all these passing years I have not learnt to develop that largesse of spirit.

His friendship with Jack was unfathomable to me, knowing how Jack could be so disloyal and greedy, and Millie's childish superficiality simply drove me to distraction, but Thomas would just shrug, shake his head and smile. She simply dazzled him as immature as she was. He could not, did not, talk to her in the way he did to me. He just felt such a need to protect her, as if she was made of some special kind of delicate material and this overcame any sense that he had, as clever as he was. And the most frustrating part of it was that whilst she still accepted his devotion she really cared little for him.

Her favourite pastime was being taken to the picture houses in Maidstone and watching the big movie stars. Her screen idols were Cary Grant romancing Katherine Hepburn, Gregory Peck, or William Powell with Myrna Loy in The Great Ziegfeld or his fellow star Carole Lombard. She was captivated by their on screen liaisons and their tall, dark, dangerous and impossibly manufactured good looks. The fantasy of the films entranced her. She wanted to imitate their style and fashion and with the indulgence of family money she was able to do both. She had her hair crimped and wore the latest fashion that Tunbridge Wells could bring to the town and that her mother would allow.

I never completely mastered our sewing machine that would wilfully break cottons and need re-threading at the most inconvenient moments, or I'd find that the lower bobbin had subversively become entangled, leading to a time-consuming task of cutting away the spidery balls of thread.

I affected an air of unconcern with the fripperies of fashion but in fact I was painfully aware of my inadequacies in the looks department and Ethel did nothing to dissuade me otherwise. Jack however, as he matured, began to emulate the matinee idols. He started to wear a moustache which added extra years affect a certain caddish air that Millie so admired. But Jack has set his bar for success much higher than Millie. He was quite determined and driven by his ambition which Ethel encouraged. She ensured that Archie heard of her hopes for Jack, to make a far better future for himself that she had had to endure. She knew how to turn the screw even though Archie believed that he had acquired more self-control. His exasperation of her constant nagging still managed to penetrate his defences.

He fumbled around as a mole caught in the sudden glare of daylight wanting to find some shelter, some respite, but a future that he craved with Beatrice was not possible. He had to suffice with their illicit meetings which were always too short and left him wanting more as his love for Beatrice deepened. Archie had constructed an ideal of her. He had set her up as the love of his life, his soul mate. Unhappily as time went on Beatrice found the strain of their encounters had the opposite effect. She felt herself slowly withdrawing from him. His desperation unsettled her as did her concern for any possibility that their liaison would become known with the exposure of her situation and the ensuing judgement by their community. She grew afraid, and her fear began to worm away at her confidence, that she would become faintly ridiculous, a figure of fun. Beatrice and her middle-aged publican, it was the stuff of music halls and bawdy jokes.

Then there was Dulcie. She feared for her too. The child already showed such promise. She felt such pride in her quickness and aptitude for learning, but at the same time her heart sank when it was apparent to her how she took after Archie in looks and mannerisms. There was no mistaking that the child was his, and if she saw it, how soon would it be noticed by others who had little to do but idly gossip. Once their tongues wagged how would she protect both girls? They would all become tainted by her indiscretions. Worst of all Ronald would be triumphant at her downfall and be the first to hold the higher moral ground. All his disappointments and failures would be shown to be caused by her depravity. She would be the scapegoat for his unsatisfactory life. Even worst he could set himself as a martyr, to prove his magnanimity, able to forgive the unforgivable and the thought sickened her.

She did not even confide in Archie, perhaps she realised, as I knew, that when he finally lost her that he would become lost. Archie did not die of a broken heart but he lost heart in life when he found himself cast adrift. In saving herself from drowning it caused him to sink. In another life they could have found so much happiness. Perhaps if she had had more courage her bravery would have saved them both. Ironically during her early married life she had made judgements about Ronald's parents and had never thought to question how she arrived at her own conclusions. Their indulgence towards Ronald made them appear to be superficial in her eyes. Had she looked closer she would have seen how a partnership forged in love had provided them with strength and fortitude. She would have seen that they had not led a charmed existence. They had battled against family rejection, Sylvia's aristocratic status had been purged, and there had been serious financial concerns throughout their marriage. Finally there had been Roland's sacrifice of his art to please the tastes of his fickle clients, knowing that he had wasted his talent to produce mediocre pictures for a prescribed interior; pretty pictures to fit in with the décor.

Roland had put Sylvia before his life's work and had never shown any bitterness that, without her, he could have become renowned. Beatrice just saw their shambolic house with the dog's hairs and chipped china and Roland unable to make a success of his work.

Then there were her parents.

Mote House 1938
Beatrice and Louise

It had been such a difficult afternoon that day when she had gone to the house. Louise had sent out Dulcie to play in the garden; had almost ordered her out. Then there had been a look about her mother that she had not seen before, an air of distance, embarrassment, she couldn't be sure just how to describe it. It was uncomfortable.

At first Beatrice had imagined that it was going to be about money and Ronald. Her mother had never taken to him and had never been able to conceal her feelings as well as her father had done. Not that she blamed either of them for their dislike; it just deepened the guilt and sadness of the hurt that she had caused to both of them.

But that afternoon she sensed a completely different atmosphere. Her mother was nervous, plucking at cushions to shake, straightening the drapes at the window unable to settle. She had rung for tea to be served and when it had come she had been uncharacteristically curt.

 "I am glad that you have come today Beatrice," she began, "especially this afternoon as your father is not here with us."
 Louise rearranged the cups on the tray without pouring the tea. "There was something...there is something that I need to ask...or rather to tell you." Louise's rehearsed speech faltered as she picked at her words one at a time.

"Your father and I....we both .....he and I have been worried."
"Worried?" Beatrice stared blankly at her mother, "Worried about...?"

Louise started again. "Your father and I have noticed.... we have known for some time how unhappy Ronald has made you."
Beatrice realised that she had been holding her breath and let it out slowly, reassured now that she knew that cause of her mother's anxiety.

"Mother I made a mistake but that's in the past now, there's really no need for you to worry. We rub along in our own way. I get by."

"No but that is not it Beatrice! It's not in the past is it! The mistake I am talking about is……is the one that you are making now." Her mother flushed.

Beatrice stared at her, and she felt her chest contract.

"No indeed Beatrice! The past is one thing but we are talking about now…you…Dulcie…and…" she faltered, not being able to put his name in the same sentence.

Beatrice felt the sense of her mother's humiliation but at the mention of her child's name she became confused and then fearful.

"Dulcie…what do you mean?"

"Oh Beatrice do I have to spell it out! In God's name you and Archie!"

Beatrice felt the words sting their reproach.

Louise held the teapot and poured unsteadily, slopping the tea into each cup, before setting it down hard against the tray.

Beatrice did not know how to respond, suddenly weary of the charade that she had played for so long. She slumped back into her chair. Her body refused to provide her with support.

The silence between them opened a chasm making them both fearful to make the leap across.

Beatrice thought, 'how do I begin…what can I say?' And as she tried to gather her thoughts her mother began again but this time her voice became hard.

"When you wanted to marry Ronald we tried to warn you, but no, you went ahead despite everything."

"Oh .. not this again Mother!" Beatrice bit her lip.

"No Beatrice, it is not that again. Will you hear me out? You have no idea how painful this is for me to say. Your father would not hear a word against you. But I have a duty to… to Millie, and little Dulcie. They are the innocents in all of this Beatrice. But they will

221

suffer from your… well… your dalliance with Archie Minton. There! You have made me say it."

"Dalliance? What a strange thing to say." Her voice was almost inaudible.

"Well what would you have me call it Beatrice?" Louise pressed her hands to the arms of the chair holding on to them to steady her nerve.

"A grand passion….or shall I give it a name that the village would use? That you and Archie have been having a common affair? That you and he have committed adultery and then thought that no one would see! Why could you have not been more discreet? At least not to have… not to have had a….. "And she spread her hands out in supplication pleading with her not to have to name the child.

"This has to end Beatrice before we are all dragged down. Think of the children at least. Surely this time….for their sake you will give him up."

Beatrice stood up. "For the sake of the children, for the sake of what our neighbours would say, for your sake…what about me…what about my happiness!"

"Oh Beatrice. Don't be so melodramatic. That is unfair of you! We have only ever wanted your happiness!"

"And this is how I will be happy? Giving up that one person who has made my life bearable!"

"But a publican Beatrice! His reputation… consider that?"

"What do you mean…what are you trying to say now?"

Louise breathed deeply, "Archie Minton. A married man…..known to raise his fists to his wife and has been carrying on for years with his barmaid. Is this the man that you are willing to risk your reputation on?"

"He loves me!"

"Oh Beatrice, how could you believe a man like that would ever be faithful? You will become ridiculous, a laughing stock. He plays the field. You are just another one to him."

"Don't mother. You go too far." Beatrice raised her voice.

"Too far? I go too far? So you want me stay quiet when you have gone too far?"

"How so?"

"You have driven me to it Beatrice. I wasn't going to say but you will not heed me. I know that Dulcie is Archie's!"

Beatrice lowered her head. In one way, the words that had stung her, half expected, released something in her. The weight of secrecy had become wearisome. But then a new feeling of horror took hold, taking its place. She saw herself and Archie through the eyes of her mother. Their love affair suddenly made tawdry, she, a figure of fun, and he, a shallow philanderer. Her mother had judged them. She thought it sordid. Something shrivelled in her. There was an overpowering sense of loss and pain.

Beatrice crumpled and sat down heavily. A lump in her throat constricted her breath. She felt lightheaded, cast adrift in a bubble of despair.

Neither woman dared to break the silence that engulfed them as they both tried to recover their composure. Faintly there was the rhythmic sound of the lawn mower outside but inside it was if the room shrank at the catastrophe; it seemed to oppress them as they sat within easy reach of the tea table, their cups still full with the untouched tea.

Finally Louise drew herself up and steadying herself reached for her cup carefully holding fast to the delicate cup and saucer and tasting the chilled tea. She willed herself not to break the silence but the sight of her daughter's face undid her resolve. Her daughter was still beautiful. The intervening years had filled her frame but she had acquired elegance in her maturity. She and Arnold had always been so proud of her. She had been the apple of her father's eye despite Ronald. What a catch she would have been for any man, and then to have wasted herself on that silly man!

And it had led her to this.

223

Uneasily she recalled Arnold's last conversation with her on the subject of Archie. For some reason he would not condemn him. He actually liked the man! Would not hear out her argument, had actually walked away! But men are sometimes so blind to the world's condemnation. They seem to think that by not admitting it that it will just vanish. Such children at times! Then it leaves the women to pick up the pieces and try to mend them. She pressed her lips together trying to think of a way to begin again.

"Perhaps if you made more of an effort.... to be seen with Ronald...... at the very least?" She stumbled around blindly. Even to herself she sounded ridiculous.

Beatrice turned towards her frowning and shaking her head in disbelief. "Be seen with Ronald...whatever can you mean!"

"Make more of a show of being man and wife...together...." Her mother looked alarmed hearing the harshness in Beatrice's tone and faltered.

"So you want Ronald and I to promenade, walk around the village arm in arm, is that what you are saying!"

"Beatrice don't be so... so silly! Of course I didn't say that. I simply mean that whether you like it or not this affair needs to end, once and for all, for all your sakes."

"It is not an affair!"

"Well what would you have me call it!"

"And I can't just end it."

"Can't or won't?"

"We mean so much to each other."

"So it's worth the risk?"

"Risk?"

"Risk of exposure... breaking up a marriage.... exposing the girls to it all. Think of them Beatrice!"

"I have never asked him to leave his wife."

"So that's right is it? And what happens when others find out, start gossiping and pointing fingers at you all? And you keep deliberately ignoring the point Beatrice. Poor little Dulcie and Millie...don't they have a right not to be dragged down in all of this? Dulcie is too young at the moment but Millie is a sensitive girl."

"Leave the girls out of this!"

"How can I leave them out as you put it? Even your father has realised that Dulcie is not Ronald's."

"When?"

"I'm not prepared to discuss that."

"So only when you told him you mean?"

"So no denial now...you finally admit it? I just hope for your sake that others don't have my... intuition."

Beatrice stood up. "I think enough has been said." And she moved swiftly towards the door.

"Beatrice!"

"No mother. No more."

"Don't part from me like this. Beatrice please!" she implored. But Beatrice could not turn back. An awful confusion drove her from the house. Two parts of her waged an internal battle. One voice fiercely denied her mother's entreaty whilst the other ashamedly raged at her own unkindness. But she could not admit her fault even to herself.

They had agreed to meet at the windmill end of town towards
Bakers Cross that afternoon. When Archie saw Beatrice walking
towards him he automatically raised his hat hardly noticing that
she did not give him her customary wave. Neither, as she drew
level with him, did she meet his eye.
"I can't stay long."
"Well hello to you too!" he smiled down at her and went to take
her hand and peck her cheek.
But she shook her head and shrugged him away.
"What's the matter Beatrice, something I said?" But he was still
unaware of her tension, still so pleased to see her, not
considering that there was anything untoward.
The day had started so well. The rain that they had expected had
not occurred. Along the lanes the first stirrings of spring were
apparent. At the bases of the hedgerows clumps of dainty
snowdrops mingled with their sturdier neighbours of wood
sorrel. Closer to the road were some small buttery celandines,
early daises, and the long pale leaves of the delicate primrose
still not quite ready to flower.
Archie had noticed their arrival with pleasure. The severe winter
had been hard and it had taken its toll both on his takings and on
his health. He had had a heavy cold that had been difficult to
shake off leaving him with a hacking cough that still left him
fighting for breath some mornings. The linctus that he had taken
seemed to have had little effect, but the warm sunshine and the
clear sky of the morning had given him a renewed vigour. He felt
that he was on the road to recovery.
He had been pleased with himself. Good things come in threes
he had thought. My chest seems to be getting better, it's a lovely
day and soon I will be with Beatrice. He had been worried about
her for some months. He had taken the bus and got off at the

earlier stop. By the time he had reached Stone Street he could feel the heat of afternoon sun warming the air. The florist had placed a bucket of early daffodils and narcissus outside her shop. They were still in tight bud each bud wrapped in its sheath of light green.

Archie looked down at her realising that she had still not spoken, and suddenly concerned at seeing her pale face turned away from him.

"Are you not feeling well?"

She seemed to consider the question screwing up her eyes to look back down at the town centre.

"Am I not well?" she murmured.

"Has something happened to upset you my dear?" Archie once again tried to catch her hand but she stepped away from him.

"I can't go on Archie." She spoke so quietly.

"Pardon?" Archie could not be sure that he had heard her correctly. "Go on where… why….what has happened. Is it Ronald?"

"No, no." She looked pained by his interruption, almost as if wanting to dismiss his questioning.

Archie followed her gaze down the street. The iron railings glinted in the sunshine.

"We can't go on like this Archie…meeting here."

Relief flooded through him. It had been silly of him to have arranged for them to see each other here, so close to home. But then he had seen so little of her. The winter months had dragged on and it had seemed as if it was dragging them both down. She had, come to think of it, been quite unlike herself when they had last met. His chest cold hadn't helped either, he had felt so wretched. The pain had gripped his chest so hard at night, and lying awake everything became magnified. He had imagined all kinds of things as his jumbled thoughts became entangled.

"Of course, I haven't been thinking straight these days!" He turned to see if she had heard him. But her head was still averted as if something was holding her attention. She was unusually distracted. Something must have upset her at home. She often took a while before she could tell him what was on her mind. Perhaps it was one of the girls.

"I have to go Archie." She suddenly announced.

"Go where, you've only just got here!" He tried to bring her round to face him, but she twisted away sharply.

"I really need to go." And she stepped away and started back down the hill.

Archie watched her leave, unable to believe that she was actually going.

"Beatrice!" He called after her, "what has happened where you are going?"

But his entreaty merely disappeared into the space that increased between them.

∞

Archie heard them arguing in the kitchen, raised voices, Ethel's thin high voice and Rosie's lower, quieter tone.

"It's not fair mother. I only ask for what is mine."

"Oh no not this all over again, just like your father, never satisfied."

"There's only so many times that it can be mended!"

"I've had to make things last my girl."

"And so have I!"

"Don't you use that tone with me! Always have to have the last word, just like him."

"Stop dragging father into everything. I haven't had a new blouse since I don't know when. The last one was a hand- me-down that Mrs Parsons gave me, and I've had to sew the shoulder seam on that twice."

"You are just so hard wearing on clothes......that's your problem."

"You want to let me look shabby all the time!"

"Some people wear clothes better that's all, there's nothing wrong with the things you have. If you'd have kept one or two bits and pieces for Sunday best we won't be having this discussion."

"Sunday best! Which one do you think I should keep then? I only have the grey one and that caught in the wringer and the buttons tore off."

"Well you've just proved my point. You should have wrung it out by hand. A delicate blouse like that!"

"It's not delicate it's worn out!"

"Stop shouting!"

"I'm not shouting!"

Rosie stormed from the room and turned to stomp up the stairs. "And Millie's mum is going into Tunbridge Wells this morning to get Millie another new dress and I haven't even got a decent old one!" she yelled down before banging her bedroom door to close off her mother's reply.

Archie finished putting the chairs back on the floor and considered his options. He looked around the bar and saw Ethel wiping the kitchen table down.

"I'm going out. Need some supplies." He called and taking his coat from the kitchen door he went out into the street without a backward glance.

Rosie watched him stride down the road. 'He's going towards the station' she thought. And she felt uneasy, trying to ignore the niggling guilt that stirred reproachfully in her stomach.

∞

Already the train was pulling into the station when Archie had hurriedly purchased his return ticket. Just a handful of people were waiting their turn to board. He looked down the platform to see if he could see her but an escape of steam obscured his view. Doors were clanging closed. Fulwood was waiting with his red flag draping down at his side. Archie chose the carriage closest to him, twisting the metal handle down, and then stepping up before banging it shut behind him. Two other people were occupying the window seats of the carriage, sitting opposite to one another immersed in their newspapers. One glanced up briefly and nodded before going back to his paper. He chose a seat as the train pulled away, his body swayed to the first urgent tugs of the engine as it began its onward journey. As they settled into a smoother rhythm Archie opened the door into the corridor and, slightly lurching, began his drunken styled walk down the corridor peering into every small curtained window as he passed each compartment. After a few he began to doubt that she was on the train, and then just as he had decided that he had made a mistake he saw her.

He slid open the door and stepped inside. She looked up not aware for the first fleeting second who had come in and then her hand flew to her mouth when realising that it was him.

He had entered the carriage pleased with himself, but when he saw her defensive gesture he, like her, was caught off balance. They stared at each other not quite knowing at first how to begin.

"Archie!" and she faltered and her hands gasped her handbag tightly to her as if the contents would be spirited away.

"Well Beatrice, thought that I would surprise you!" He sat down heavily beside her as the train gave a jolt.

"Oops a-daisy!" He grinned at her and then his smile faded as she sat frozen, her eyes wide as if in a trance.

"What on earth's the matter my dear?" He kissed her slightly parted lips and then drew back as she had made no attempt to respond.

"Beatrice!" he was perplexed.

"What are you doing here Archie?" She almost hissed her question. "How did you know that I was here, where I was going?"

"A little bird told me." He still tried to bring her round, and catching hold of her hand he pressed it to his chest.

"No don't!"

"Who's to see us here, we are quite safe Beatrice."

"Safe! Safe! Huh? You have no idea Archie." Her hard tone was offensive.

"Now enough Beatrice, stop this! I don't know what has got into you these last few months. I hardly been able to see you and when I do you have been... well I don't know how to say it. If there is something troubling you for Pete's sake spill it out. Anyone would think that you didn't care for me!"

"That's just it Archie what would anyone think."

He shook his head. "Has someone said something? Has Ronald said something to you?"

"No," she looked scornful. "He wouldn't see anything unless it hit him in the face. No, not Ronald."

"Who then?"

"It's not who."

"Really you are making no sense at all. First you say that you are worried about who knows about us and then you won't say who it is!"

She looked at him and turned her head to stare out of the window. Her betrayal of him, seeing such sadness creep into his face threatened her ability to continue.

"These past few months I have felt.....don't make me say things....I can't."

Archie felt a bleak darkness descend. His bright world with her, his love of her was in awful conflict with his sudden realisation that he was in danger of losing her. Then he felt a surge of anger she could not explain, to tell him what had happened to bring her to that state.

Since Christmas things were not right but he had dismissed his worries believing that it was just the illness; that he was still feeling under the weather. Then there had been the times when they had arranged to be together and again she had been distant. Their love making had been perfunctory, as if going through a ritual. And then there had been their meeting in Cranbrook earlier when she had just hurried away without a word. He had not questioned her, believing that in her own good time she would explain.

They sat together surrounded by their own misery swaying to the rattle and pull of the train. Apple orchards flew past, then cherry orchards with just a hint of tight blossom at the tips on the trees, ditches and hedges, oast houses, more orchards, and so the pattern of the landscape went on. Two horses galloped around a small field as if suddenly galvanised into action by the snorting beast of the train. As the train passed they slowed, settled, and shook their heads lowering them to catch once again at the long grass.

Disused small ploughs and other rusting farm implements cluttered some disorganised yards. Other farms had a pleasing order; their yards swept clean, their cows moving slowly in a single line towards the sheds.

Small fleecy clouds flitted across the otherwise blue sky. A flock of birds turned together in an aerial pirouette, appearing black at first and then seeming to momentarily disappear as they danced before the sunlight.

But now he couldn't ignore it any longer. If she was giving him up he had to know why. Was it something that he had said or done? "I think we need to have this out Beatrice. What's happened to us?"

"There can't be us any more now." Her large eyes became wet but tears did not fall.

"I think we were always fooling ourselves Archie. Making this out to be more than it was."

"Beatrice!" His reproach at her deceit almost weakened her resolve. She was frightened that he would be able to find her out, but the fear of public ridicule buried her doubts. She needed to be strong for both of them.

"Beatrice!" he entreated her. "I'll always love you. You know that... and you've felt the same. I know you have. You can't go back on all that. When have I ever given you any reason to doubt?"

The change of rhythm made them both look out of the window. Larger buildings of the town were coming into view. As the train began to slow down they drew alongside the platform and the white name plate of the town flashed past them. The brakes of the train eased them forwards and then backwards against the seats. Then there was the hiss of steam as the train, released from its labour came to rest.

For a moment they sat immobile neither willing to make the first move. Then Beatrice rose from her seat and automatically Archie leaned forward to open the door for her. His body asserted itself, a reflex action that his mind had not controlled.

She stepped carefully down first on the small metal plate and then alighted safely onto the platform. Archie followed her and they walked together towards the exit as others milled around them oblivious to their turmoil. They turned out into the bright spring sunshine.

"Let me go on Archie, I just need some time to think." She looked up at him and when he nodded back a faint smile flitted across her face for the first time since their meeting.

He watched her quickly walk away towards the Pantiles. Her heels clicked sharply against the pavement. Then the sound of the traffic drowned them out and she disappeared in the mêlée of shoppers.

He stood unsure whether to continue along the path that she was following or to turn in a new direction. He had no idea where to go, or what to do. He had lost his moorings. He felt drained, stupefied by her words.

He stepped quickly off the pavement. There was a sudden squeal of brakes and a deafening roar in his ears.

"I didn't see him. He just stepped out in front of me! I couldn't stop!" The lorry driver shook, anxiously wringing his hands, pleading for forgiveness from the surrounding crowd, but they were looking down at the road where Archie's body lay unmoving. Someone bent over him.

"I think the poor chap's gone." He sighed as he straightened up and the crowd clicked their tongues and tutted their sympathy, unwilling to leave him lying crumpled in the gutter.

Beatrice took the train home unaware of the turn of events. It wasn't until the next day when they all heard the news.

A Funeral 1939
Ethel

Ethel had not expected so many mourners at the church. She was pleased to find them seeking her out, murmuring their sympathy; giving her due attention. There had been an old black dress hanging at the back of the wardrobe that she had found when looking for something suitable to wear and when she had tried it on she realised with some satisfaction that not only did it still fit her but she looked well in it.

They were going to have the wake back at The Papermakers Arms. Betty and Ron said that they would do the catering, just a few sandwiches and tea she had told them, that was all that was required. But they had batted away her protests and had come that morning each carrying two trays of sandwiches and then Betty went back for some fancies and returned with more laden platters.

They had set up the area at the side of the bar for the plates and food and reserved the table at the window for teacups and saucers. There was a strange array of assorted china that had been tucked away in the cupboards, and some that she couldn't actually remember ever having used. She fingered a gold-rimmed teacup with small forget-me-nots painted around the sides not remembering its provenance: a full tea set, together with a dainty milk jug and sugar bowl. Why have I never seen them before? The thought of not knowing niggled at her. Rosie must have found them she thought. Had they been a wedding present?

She could hear Rosie upstairs the floorboards creaked betraying her presence.

Ethel was suddenly irritated. 'Why does that girl never help when it is needed? What is she up to now?' She breathed deeply and squared her shoulders feeling a tension between her shoulder blades. She glanced at the old wall clock, its hands had hardly moved since she last looked at it. The church service was due to begin at ten thirty and the undertakers would be coming at ten. His body was laid out in the back kitchen; there had been nowhere else to put him. At least the lid had been screwed down.

Poor Jack had had to identify the body and then there had to be an inquest. The coroner had given the verdict of accidental death and the driver was not prosecuted. Too many witnesses had vouched that Archie had simply stepped into his path. They said that the driver couldn't have avoided him. All the statements for the cause of the accident were clear, but Ethel could not settle. As she had listened to the case she felt a growing anger against him, and that she could no longer rail at him increased her resentment. Why had he been there? What had he intended to do that day? They had found a return railway ticket in his pocket but nothing to tell her of the reasons for his visit.

He had hidden his secret life from her and now he had hidden the reasons for his death. It outraged her that he could defeat her in such a way; that his death had snatched away her last chance to continue to wage a war against him that had sustained her over the years. He had been the cause of her blighted life. That she had not made anything of herself had been due to him. Her grievances had been laid at his door. He was the fault line of her existence.

Her interfering mother had set herself against Archie when they had first courted. Her parents had set their designs on Ethel marrying her cousin William. But even although Ethel never warmed to him she had felt a strange sense of betrayal when she learnt that he had fallen in the first month of the war. It was almost a reproach that she had not cared enough to bring him back safely. Such a silly thought, but she had been such a superstitious little thing back then, counting cracks in the pavements, not putting shoes on a table, not walking under ladders, afraid when a mirror cracked, almost afraid of her own shadow.

William's death had shaken her and for a while she did not dare seek out the companionship of men. But after the war, when such a few soldiers had returned to their village and surrounding ones, they began to realise an awful truth; that the country had lost the best of their men, so many had perished in the trenches and muddy fields of France.

Women began to throw themselves, as driven lemmings, into unsuitable marriages when they realised the alternative was a lifetime of childless spinsterhood. And then she met Archie. He was the complete opposite of William. She wasn't sure whether she liked him or not but a kind of desperation, driven by her mother's vocal opposition, drove her on. She was determined to have her own way for once, despite her own secret misgivings. He attracted her with his easy charm but his physical courtship which at first she had found exciting soon lost its allure. She had enjoyed tantalising him, seeing the desire in his eyes; she enjoyed the acquisition of romantic power. It had been an unexpected sensation, an aphrodisiac. Drawing him on and then casting him aside, it was wonderful to be his quarry, but still be in control of the chase.

After the wedding she found to her disappointment that there was no longer a chase. He had caught her. Most shocking were final demands made of her in their marriage bed which had utterly disgusted her. She thought that she had understood the rudiments of procreation and believed that she was prepared for her necessary part that she must play in the process. Wives became mothers; it was the pattern of marriage that she had accepted, taking her vows promising to obey.

She had no idea that she would suffer such exposure, that he would remove her nightdress and see her naked. It had been quite dreadful. She had imagined some kind of quick manly caress in the darkness under the modesty of their bed coverings.

237

That her whole body would be subjected to such indecent indignities before he finally violated her was abhorrent. That, and then the knowledge that this was a pattern that would be repeated and expected of her, she felt humiliated and betrayed. Then there had been her time of confinement when her body had become horribly distorted and an awful lethargy had followed her bouts of sickness.

When she finally delivered Jack, her precious son, she vowed to herself that she would never undergo such tearing agony again. Archie had been provided with a son; she had done her duty. Her marriage vows had been kept and that should have been an end to it. Archie had agreed when she had said that she wanted no more children, when he saw how draining it was for her to nurse Jack. He had agreed to her demands that they keep separate rooms, but of course he had not been a man of his word.

He had plagued her throughout his marriage. She was glad at last that she was free of him, his brutality and his awful needs. People had no idea of the life that she had had to lead. They saw only the side that he liked to present. But she knew that real Archie Minton, the devil that he really was. There was only one saving grace in their marriage. Jack was a son that any mother would have been proud to have had. He showed promise even as a youngster and now he showed that he had ambition and determination to better himself. Had they had the money he would have easily outstripped young Thomas. Not that she held that against Thom. He was a nice enough lad. He and Jack had been friends from the very first; thick as thieves. But there was one part of her that resented the unfairness of it all. She had accepted her lot for the most part, and had put up with far more than most would have done. But Jack deserved better. If Archie had had anything about him he could have put in a good word with the Parsons. They had money to spare right enough, but Archie would not hear of it. Set his face against her suggestion to plead Jack's case just to spite her.

There was a knock at the door. The undertakers had arrived. Ethel glanced around the room to see that all was as it should be and went to let them in.

∞

The vases of lilies at the base of the pulpit gave off a pungent sweetness when they entered the church, cloying the air with their perfume. Light filtered through the stained glass windows, draping the black suits, coats and hats of the mourners sitting in the pews with dappled shades of yellow, red and blue. The burnished brass eagle sitting astride the lectern balefully glared down at them as if to resent their intrusion. He looked ready to take flight with his glorious outstretched wings.

Edith followed the coffin held by two pallbearers assisted by Thomas and Ron. Jack walked with her and Rosemary followed behind them. She was aware of the congregation rising as one wave, as they entered the church, suddenly making the aisle of the nave appear smaller as their slow procession swayed their way to the front, stopping just short of the transept. The funeral director turned to her sorrowfully indicting the pew that she might like to occupy. Jack stood back for her to sit first and then placed himself beside her. They both turned with a slight annoyance to find that Rosie had also been shown to their pew and still needed to be accommodated. They had had to stand again and then shuffle unceremoniously up to provide her with enough room. Ethel's mouth closed in a thin line at the indignity of the movement, 'why was she always so awkward even on a day like today!'

Reverent Martin swept back his vestments with a flourish to allow himself to ascend the pulpit without catching his feet on the hem. He smiled down benignly at the little group on the front bench to encourage their fortitude. The choir boys fidgeted in the choir stalls, adjusting their ruffs which caught at their throat and tugging at their surplices.

As Ethel half listened to the eulogy encapsulating Archie's life she found her mind wandering to the future. This had more relevance to her now than the history of his past. She considered her position. To have come to widowhood so soon had been both unexpected and liberating but then she was frightened by the certainty of financial crisis. The pub was not paying its way; there were unsettled bills some had been outstanding for some time. As usual Archie had left his family without any means. He had made no will but then he had nothing to leave. There were no savings or investments except the freehold of The Papermakers Arms which he had bought just before they met. She considered the options, hold on to the pub and to put her name down as the licensee or sell up. The brewery, Fremlin Brothers of Maidstone, was buying up pubs around and about. She could perhaps approach them and then carry on as the tenant; at least then some of the debt could be settled.
She stood mechanically as the organ puffed and groaned summoning the congregation to join the choir in yet another hymn, and considered whether she was *'to blossom and flourish'* or whether they would *'wither and perish'* according to the words of the verse that grandly reverberated around the church.

∞

By the early afternoon the wake was almost at an end. She had been pleased by the turn out and the number who came back to offer their condolences. Some who had previously hardly given her the time of day gently deferred to her and she was buoyed up by her central role. Surprisingly both Arnold and Louise Parsons had been at the church and she had certainly not expected them to attend the wake. Arnold stood at her elbow, and after he had again voiced his sympathy he lowering his head to speak quietly to her.

"I would like you to come to Mote House at your earliest convenience Mrs Minton. My wife and I have something of importance to discuss."

She looked up and her mouth gaped open. She was quite uncertain as to the meaning of his words and suddenly embarrassed by her gauche reaction. What must she have looked like! It piqued her that he had made something of a mystery of his invitation. Was it an invitation or a request? Her mind whirled. Was he offering her employment? Could it be something to do with Jack? It was annoyingly unsettling just when she was coming to terms with her loss. He had quite spoilt the moment.

∞

Two days later she walked up the avenue of trees towards Mote House. Jack was not with her, although obviously he had wanted to come, but as he said that morning, he just couldn't afford the time away. Rosie was at The George. Ethel hadn't seen the need to involve her.

The maid had shown her into the drawing room. She looked around. It was not to her taste.

"Ah there you are!" Arnold came forward stretching out his hand in welcome. Louise followed him into the room.

"Please take a chair..." and she waved towards the three chairs set deliberately by the window.

"Tea?" she offered as Ethel sat down.

They exchanged stiff pleasantries about the mild spring weather, the length of that winter, but they struggled to maintain the conversation as they sat waiting for the tea to arrive. Both seemed to be on edge, as if it were they who were in a strange house not the other way around. Ethel did not intend to put them at their ease, she felt awkward enough just to murmur a response to their disjointed bursts of small talk.

When the tea had been served and they had all taken time to adjust Arnold leaned forward on his chair and cleared his throat. "Louise and I know that you and your family have suffered a tremendous blow. Terrible for you all." He turned to Louise for her to agree.

"We can't begin to understand how you're feeling and we certainly wouldn't want to intrude into your grief." Again he turned to back to Louise. This time she seemed to draw into herself and just stared blankly.

"My wife and I believe that…." He began and then interrupted himself.

"We'd like to offer…" and again he stopped to take a sip of tea. *He's going to offer me some kind of employment here at the house!* her indignation at the thought made her draw herself up, *to become one of their servants!*

"Times are hard Mrs Minton, I know that it can't be easy making a living in a small village like ours. Businesses are struggling, have been for a number of years now. I think that we've seen the worst of this damned depression but it'll take time for all of us to recover. Isn't that so Louise?" Louise looked expressionless. He weighed in again.

"So, as one neighbour to another, we felt that we could… should…. extend a helping hand just until you are back on your feet so to speak."

He looked at her expecting a response and was slightly taken aback to see her calmly weighing him up. There was a stillness in her that shook him and he shuddered involuntarily.

My goodness she's a cold fish! he thought. *Whatever did Archie see in her?*

"Your husband has been a good friend to our family over the years. We have had cause to be thankful for his…. how can I put it….for his interventions? There was a time when we were all facing some business difficulties and I was personally able to rely on Archie for his.. …for his discretion. Yes, he was discrete…and for that we, my family, well to put it very simply he provided a valuable service when I most needed it. Yes indeed!" Arnold took a breath, smiled and nodded at her to signify that he had satisfactorily concluded his speech.

Ethel was stupefied. She couldn't imagine what he meant, *he and Archie....a valuable service.* The words run ran in her head. *Interventions, discretion, whatever was he saying, when did this happen, why did she not know!*

"Mr Parsons I'm sorry I have no idea what you are saying." Arnold frowned, and cleared his throat. "Well of course we are talking about the past here, quite a number of years now." And he nodded as if to say that perhaps she had forgotten.

"Shall I ring for more tea perhaps? Mrs Minton? Arnold?" Ethel looked at Louise. *Why she's almost more unsettled than I am!* she thought, *something has upset her, why does she look so glum, could it be that she didn't know any of this, did he keep her in the dark too?*

"Capital Louise! Yes of course we should have more tea!" His sudden joviality was odds with the strained look that passed between them. He stood up as if there was an overriding need to stretch his legs.

The two women watched as he took a turn around the room. Louise fidgeted, first straightening the cushion placed behind her, and then smoothing her hand across her skirt, ironing out the imagined creases, before realising that he was not about to break the awkward silence that had ensued since she rang the bell.

"How are Jack and Rosie since the accident? I expect that it will take some time for them to adjust." She said answering her own question, annoyed at how trite her question sounded once said out loud.

Ethel merely shook her head.

"Such a tragedy for you all and with him being so ..... still in his prime.... what was he... forty thereabouts.....?"

Ethel narrowed her eyes, "forty three."

"And young Jack..?"

"Nineteen."

My, my, you have a sharp tongue and no mistake Mrs Minton, she thought, and then an unwonted image of Beatrice and Archie came suddenly into her mind. *No wonder he....* but her mind would not let her finish. It was too painful to admit even to herself of the awful part that she had played.

There was almost an audible sigh of relief when the maid entered bearing another laden tray of fresh cups and a teapot. They watched as she placed the used cups and empty teapot back onto the tray and left the room.

Arnold came back to his chair. There was a decided air about him.

"It's my understanding that The Papermakers Arms has not been a viable business for some time now am I correct?" He paused momentarily not really expecting a reply before ploughing on. "When I last spoke to Archie, a couple of months ago he indicated that he had been thinking of selling off the freehold to Fremlins and to take up a tenancy instead."

Ethel drew in her breath. This was the first that she had heard it and it angered her that they should know more about her business than she did of her own.

"At the time I thought that it was a sensible decision, and I told him so. I am not sure how far these negotiations have gone." He looked at her sharply. She flinched as if his words had reached out and touched her.

"If you propose to see this arrangement through then so be it but we perhaps could look at another..."

"No!" Ethel interrupted. "I have not yet concluded my business with the brewery. I have wanted to consider Jack's wishes in all of this."

"Of course, of course and Rosie's wishes....."

"She's far too young to be party to this." Ethel's hackles rose but she attempted to quieten her rage. "But you wished to make an offer to me. What exactly was that.....a position of employment perhaps?"

They both looked momentarily stunned at her outburst.

"No, no! Mrs Minton whatever led you to think that. No indeed not."

Arnold was appalled at the way things were going. He felt as if he were losing control.

"We seem to be at odds Mrs Minton. Our intentions were certainly not to demean you in any way. Indeed not. We merely felt that now was an opportunity to repay our debt to Archie, and his memory in a more practical form. Something to assist you, to get back on your feet so as to speak."

"Money?"

"Well yes a sum of money, a small gift as a way of thanks."

"Charity!"

"Far from it! We were in your debt. It is something that was long overdue."

"And you had discussed this with Archie."

Arnold faltered, "well.... we had not actually..."

"So he knew nothing of this?"

"Well no." he admitted.

"So why now. Why have you waited until his death to make this offer when he could have had the benefit of your generosity? Was it because you knew that he would not accept it? That his pride would not allow him to....and you think that I am that desperate...that I will take your charity because?"

"Please, please! Mrs Minton, do not upset yourself." Louise looked from one to the other. "We had the best of intentions, my husband and I. We didn't think that it would ever end in this way!"

She seemed to be asking for some kind of forgiveness. They exchanged a sad look of guilt that Ethel saw.

"There is more to this than you are saying." Ethel stood holding her bag protectively in front of her. "I don't know what it is, but I have the feeling that it will come out someday. I will consider your offer once I have spoken to my son. What exactly is the amount that you propose?

"Five hundred pounds."

Ethel snapped round. "Five hundred pounds! Did you say five hundred pounds?" It was unbelievable, she realised that she was holding her breath.

"A chance to start again Mrs Minton, anywhere, a new life even."

"Indeed it is."

Arnold stepped forward and stretched out his hand. "Thank you for coming. Perhaps when you've had time to consider..?"

She looked at his hand and took it briefly nodding her head.

"Thank you for the tea Mrs Parsons. Very kind."

Her formal thanks discomforted Louise; it sounded more of a rebuke than a statement of appreciation to her ears. *Why she is able to say one thing and mean quite another! What a sad household she must control.* And as she thought of Rosie, who had become so dear to them over the years, and their own Dulcie, her hand went to her chest to massage away the weight that seemed to bind her.

Mote House 1939
Beatrice

When Beatrice had risen that morning and made her way to the
bakers she had noticed that there was a small notice that had
been pinned to The Papermakers Arms door fluttering in the
slight breeze.

She opened the door of the shop and felt a strange sensation; it
was as if everything was happening in slow motion. Ron looked
up her and his customary welcome hello was absent. He looked
quite grave. Then just as she was about to ask for a loaf, Betty
appeared from the back room.

Oh dear they do look glum, she thought. But then Betty's hand
went to her mouth, looked at her, shook her head and turned
back from where she had just come.

Beatrice felt a flutter of unease. Ron stood silent before her,
before shaking himself out of his stupor.

"Whatever's the matter Ron?"

He frowned at her as if not understanding her question.

"You haven't heard then!" he seemed unable to believe what she
had just said.

"Heard what?" She stared at him.

"About Archie Minton."

"Pardon?"

"About the accident!" he shook his head, "you didn't know?"

"What accident? What's happened to him?" She imagined him
falling down the cellar stairs.

"Is he badly hurt?"

Ron passed his hand across his face.

"Was it at the pub….the accident?"

"No, no, over in Tunbridge Wells, sometime yesterday
afternoon."

"Tunbridge Wells!" She felt the heat rise at her throat, flushing
her neck.

"How is he?"

Ron shook his head. "Gone. He's dead!"

"Oh my God..! No!" she gasped involuntarily. Her knees buckled and she gripped the counter to stop herself from sliding. For a few terrifying minutes she thought that she was going to sink to the floor. *I can't breathe!* she thought. And she fought against the bounding waves of giddiness, before they subsided and she was finally able to let go of the counter. *I must not make a show!* she thought. *Please God do not let me make a show of myself!* She became aware of Ron's look of concern and composed herself.

"What happened?" she wanted time to come to herself.

"Run over...seems he stepped off the kerb, no chance for the driver, quick as that. From what we've heard he was walking into town from the station and just turned to cross the road. Wasn't looking you see."

He passed to provide the next instalment.

"Straight into the path of the lorry....poor chap had no time to stop at all. Terrible thing to happen. There'll have to be an inquest though, so they say, being as it's a street accident. Can't think what he was doing over there though, that's the strange thing. One moment he was here and then the next thing he went tearing off down to the train station. Only just caught it too by the sound of things."

He shook his head at the tale that he was repeating.

"And Samuel Fuller said that he looked right though him when he got there, standing on the platform.....just ignored him so to speak...he thought that he seemed to be looking out for someone. I reckon there must have been something playing on his mind poor devil. The business was struggling mind, one way and another, but there must have been something else. My Betty had said that he seemed down at the mouth for some time now, not his usual self. Preoccupied... likewise that's what Samuel said too."

Beatrice listened to the words as they cascaded from him.
"Don't know what Ethel'll do now....can't think that she will want
to carry on the business on her own. They owe me a few bob, not
that I'll speak ill of the dead...but there's always some that will..."
He huffed, resigned to the inevitability of gossips, staring out
towards the street, imagining them to be already there.
"But me, well I always got on with Archie. He had time for
everyone. No side to him. I liked the man God rest his soul."
Beatrice could stand it no longer. The need to escape from his
platitudes and his pomposity overcame her, that and a dreadful
sense that she had a part to play. That she had not only lost him
but part of herself too.
"I need to get on Ron." She left him quickly without the bread
that she had intended to buy. The banality of everyday life shook
her. As she walked with quickened steps she felt such a fierce
rage course through her. It consumed her. The anger drove her
down towards Mote House. Anger and guilt and the need to
exact some kind of revenge overtook her. Someone was to blame
for her loss, someone needed to pay. She would not bear it on
her own, it was too unfair.

∞

The maid was startled when she pushed passed her and strode
into the drawing room.
"Why Beatrice! We weren't expecting you." Her mother look
flustered as she rode from her chair to greet her.
Beatrice narrowed her eyes "No I don't imagine you were. I
suppose you've heard the news?"
Louise shook her head her lips parted in surprise at the tone.
"Goodness dear you don't look well. What has happened to
upset you."

"Upset me! Oh it's gone further than that mother! Upset does not describe the half of it!" She attempted to keep a check on herself.

"Beatrice!"

"You would have to meddle wouldn't you! If only I hadn't listened to you this would never had happened."

Mother and daughter faced each other. Beatrice was angry, hot and flushed, whilst her mother's cheeks took on a tinge of pink.

"Beatrice you will have to explain yourself I have no idea what is making you so....so unlike yourself!"

They turned as Arnold came into the room.

"What on earth is happening here?" Concerned he looked from one to another.

"Beatrice why are you upsetting your mother in this way?" He went to comfort his wife.

"Archie's dead!" she shouted at them, "and it's all my fault!"

"Oh my goodness." Louise sank into her chair.

"Think of what people might say you said... think of your reputation. Well there's no need for you to worry now is there! He's gone!"

"I don't understand Beatrice." Arnold spoke quietly. "What are you accusing your mother of exactly?"

Beatrice felt suddenly very tired. "Mother told me to give Archie up..... to think of Millie and Dulcie. She said that he was a philanderer and that I was making myself a laughing stock." She spoke the words wearily as if reciting the plot of some old theatre play.

"So I did. I tried to stop seeing him. I tried to tell him that it was over. That I didn't care for him anymore."

"But how..."

"I took the train. I was going to buy something for Millie." The details seemed cumbersome; the effort to explain was draining her.

"He was on the same train. He tried to ..."

"You met on the train?"

"Yes! No… not that way, we hadn't arranged to meet. I didn't know that he would be on it too. I didn't see him at the station. I would have seen him." She closed her eyes to recall the day.

"A coincidence then?"

"I said I don't know! He just seemed to be there. One moment I was sitting on my own and the next he was there, opened the door and was there."

"What did you say?"

"I…. we talked…. I told him again that things had changed… and when we left the station we parted. I walked into town." There was a look of sad bewilderment in their faces as they tried to piece the story together; to make sense of it all.

"They said there was an accident…he stepped into the road… a lorry came…. it couldn't stop!" She could not continue, waiting for the pounding in her head to stop.

"Oh no!" Her mother gasped and turned to Arnold.

"So you see."

Finally it had been said.

"We are to blame. It was my fault that he was there that day. It was my fault that he followed me. And there was an accident. What if it wasn't an accident…. that he meant to do it! If it wasn't for me he would still be alive!" Her voice rose in a sob.

Arnold went over to comfort her but she twisted away.

"No it's all too late now! We killed him!"

"Beatrice you cannot say such things. You cannot imagine that we are to blame for all of this. The man had an accident. These things happen."

"But it shouldn't have happened!"

"It shouldn't but it has. We can't stop the unexpected. We don't know what is round each corner. Come now be sensible Beatrice!" He looked at Louise anxiously, she seemed unable to focus.

251

"And it was being sensible, as you put it, which has led to this!" Beatrice glared at them both.

"Now that's enough Beatrice. I will not let you speak to your mother like this. This is unkind of you, just look at your poor mother. This is shocking behaviour, unworthy of you…. implying some kind of culpability on our part."

Louise finally stirred herself. "Leave this Arnold, I can speak for myself." She turned to face Beatrice.

"You are distraught. You don't know what you are saying. But as far as we are concerned, whatever your father and I had done or said, now or in the past, you have always gone your own way. First Ronald then Archie. Despite that we have tried to support you. But you ended your affair with Archie. It was your decision, don't pretend otherwise. If you had wanted to continue your liaison you would have done so. Nothing that we could have said or done would have made the slightest difference. So if you feel some guilt in his death, it's your guilt not ours. "

Beatrice went to speak but Louise held up her hand.

"No Beatrice. It pains me to say I told you so, but it was bound to end badly one way or another. That it came to this is very bad, very bad indeed. But it's not you that is the victim here. He has left a family without support so they are the innocents in all of this. Give a thought to them instead of yourself for a change."

"You mother is right. Archie has been a good friend to this family. I am shocked at your deception Beatrice…..we didn't bring you up this way. Still what is done is done and we have to look to the future, to discuss what's to be done."

∞

Her kitchen was as she left it, tidy, clean. All the surfaces had been wiped. Breakfast things washed up and put away. The quiet of the house seemed to soothe her nerves, it understood her, and it defined who she was. Dulcie was at school, Millie at college, Ronald at work, there was nobody here but herself. Here she could be her own mistress, finally she was in control. Sitting at the table she could feel her strength returning, flowing slowly back into her, washing over her. She closed her eyes. 'I have survived worse than this'. A tide that had threatened to overwhelm her, and drag her under, had instead released her. She spread her arms across the table feeling the silk of the scrubbed surface, running her hands over the slight ripples of the grain worn smooth by her administrations. They caressed her.

As she had marched away from Mote House, the words of her parents still echoing and swirling in her brain, she had railed against the bright blue of the sky, the insistent chirping of the nest-building sparrows, the warm scent of the new growth in the hedgerows. It was as they were all mocking her. A moment that Icarus fell and the world kept turning, oblivious to the catastrophe.

She had almost been fearful as she turned by the duck pond towards the main road of meeting anyone. Fearful of what they may see in her eyes, that by word or deed she would be exposed. Her steps quickened; she needed time to gather herself, to seek shelter as a hunted animal would need; to go to ground. Her sanctuary was her home.

A movement at the window caught her eye. A magpie had hopped heavily onto the window sill was peering in. Its head tilted from one side to another as it considered her with its glinting eye, then it shuffled awkwardly along the sill stabbing at the putty and then glancing back at her boldly defying her to move, to shoo him away. Finally, bored with its own vandalism it cocked its head skyward as if listening for a sign before crouching low then upwardly stretching to take flight.

'One for sorrow, two for joy' she smiled grimly to herself. *Well sorrow has taken flight now.* Leaving the kitchen she opened the back door and squinted up at the sky as he joined another, and

253

she watched as the two flew over the garden, before soaring higher and vanishing over the tree tops.

∞

When the date for the funeral was announced it flew her into a sudden panic. A myriad of emotions surged in her. To quieten them she tried to order her thoughts. There was no question that she and Ronald would be attending, whether she wanted to or not, this could not be avoided. Somehow she would have to find the courage but the image of a cold winter's day and her earlier loss bleakly reclaimed her before it reluctantly ebbed away. Standing in the bedroom she surveyed the clothes that were strewn on the bed: a sleeved grey silk blouse with pearl buttons, a black skirt, her winter coat with its curly astrakhan collar and long lapels. She shuddered when she saw them. She could not wear them and put them back on their wooden hangers pushing them back into the wardrobe. Delving there she found a pale violet tailored panelled dress with a front bow at the neck, an old fawn dress with a dropped satin waistband that she had forgotten that she still had, a peacock blue tea dance dress with a thin belt and a handkerchief hemline, worn just once, a beige and chocolate brown dress with gored skirt bought last autumn, with wide overlapping panels in the bodice. She pushed them to one side.

Then she found it; a calf length crepe black dress with a skirt flounce and a demure scarf tie at the neck and long sleeves. It would be too warm with a long coat but she had a three-quarter black flared jacket with a fur trimmed collar, cuffs and pockets that she had bought three years or fours ago. She placed them side by side on the bed.

Now a hat: her hat boxes were neatly stacked on top of the wardrobe and on the top shelf. She decided to look at the ones on the shelf first. It was in the first box that she opened. A demure sailor-style small peaked black wool felt hat nestled inside, with a wide brim that dipped at the front, the rayon satin bow holding in place a small net veil, and a small band around the back to hold the hat in place. It was a triumph. They would ensure that whatever the day threw at her that she would feel appropriate for the occasion. Smart but not showy, dressed for the part she had to play.

As the day approached her nerves began to jangle. Thankfully the inquest that had been held in Maidstone was over. Accidental death; a tragic accident. He had died instantly. There was no one to blame. The driver had been exonerated with no case to answer. But a small voice wormed its way into her head. What if..... was it because of you? Were you the reason? Why wasn't he looking where he was going? Was he thinking of you as he lay there dying? Did he die because of you!

That week she had decided that Dulcie was far too young to be at a funeral. It would upset her. She would not have her there. Anyway when she had spoken to Ronald he had agreed with her. As for Millie, well she could make up her own mind. But Millie announced that she didn't want to go, it would be too horrible, too gloomy.

They walked up to the church together. At the top of the hill there were still a few black coated figures chatting together with quietened voices, milling around the lych-gate, whilst others ahead of them were entering the church, the men respectfully taking off their hats. It was a beautiful day. Orchards had transformed themselves in clustered profusion of white blossom and the warm spring air mingled with the scent of new mown grass.

As Beatrice and Ronald went inside the air cooled, and their steps echoed as they walked up to take their place in a pew. Ronald lowered himself awkwardly onto the hassock. Irritably she watched him sink to his knees. *Why does he make such a show of piety! He is probably just counting to ten!* She leaned her head forward. No image of Archie came to her. She just felt smelt the old smell of mothballs wafting back to her.

Then there was rippling wave of movement from the back of the church as people rose together each taking their cue from their neighbour. The organ groaned and wheezed before heralding the solemn cords of Handel's Death March.

Out of the corner of her eye Beatrice saw the top of the coffin as it passed her held aloft by the bare headed pallbearers. Edith followed holding Jack's arm for support and behind them trailed Rosie. As she watched mother and son proceed down the aisle Beatrice had the distinct impression that she was being closely observed. A faint sense of apprehension overcame her. She glanced to her left. Rosie had just walked passed. A shudder went through her and Ronald noticing her tremor frowned down at her, his lips thinning in disapproval.

She did not attend the wake pleading a bad head. Ronald went on alone as she returned to the sanctuary of her house.

Kilndown Woods 1939
Rosie

In a strange way my father's death released me. I no longer felt trapped by their violent rows and strained silences and their bitter struggles to usurp the other. Jack had happily accepted that his name be placed over the door as licensee. Ethel would run the pub and I would be called upon to act as fulltime barmaid. My days at The George were suddenly at an end.

The money from Parsons did not propel us out into the unknown and buy a house away from the village as they had intended. Perversely Ethel felt that her continuing presence in the village served as a reminder to the Parsons that the debt had not been fully settled. Jack soon reassured her that it was not charity that they had offered, but a payment for the service that Archie had rendered to them, long overdue. If they played their cards right it would be the first payment of many. Ethel settled the outstanding debts, sold the freehold to Fremlins and we became their tenants.

After putting some of the money away as her savings for a rainy day Ethel showered the rest on Jack. He drove around the countryside showing off his new acquisition, its chrome highly polished and gleaming. You would have thought that this would have galvanised my wrath, seeing the money so carelessly spent, but it played into my hands. I knew exactly how Millie would react. The effect that I had hoped for even exceeded my expectations. I delighted in their careless artificiality, their lack of control and blinkered aspirations. She was entranced by the gleaming motor and pleaded to be taken out for rides, as he recklessly drove round the narrow lanes, demonstrating his prowess, master of machine and maid. As they spent more time together that Easter in their superficial dalliance, so Thomas and I grew closer, our mutual affection becoming stronger. But I am going ahead of myself.

Jack's new mobility gave him some of the movie star allure that captivated Millie during her frequent visits to the cinema, that and his increasingly smooth good looks. They both turned heads; Millie, the epitome of the air-headed blond bombshell and he with the suave dark danger of Clark Gable. I was their director and they danced to my tune and took their lines from my script. They were light and shade, day and night, thrilled with the idea of each other, bathing in each other's glow, dazzling in the limelight of the set, although Jack would never have admitted it. He still had his mind set on a far more prosperous liaison that would set him up for life.

Jack saw her merely as his plaything. Millie was not yet seventeen, he was nearly twenty, but their mutual attraction had narrowed the small gap into an insignificant irrelevance.

In his eyes she had morphed from an irritating child into something far more interesting but he had no plans for her to be a permanent fixture in his life. Millie hadn't thought any further than the romance of the moment. She had no idea where she was heading. But I knew the end and I encouraged it. It was just the beginning. I ensured that the timings and the opportunities would be available to them both. It was easy to hide the coming and goings from Ethel. Jack was unwittingly complicit in the deception. I hinted at Jack's ambition and his rising star to Millie, and then led Jack to believe that it Millie would soon be a willing conquest. In truth she was, but it was me that edged it forward. Their days out driving around the lanes of Kent meant that they increasingly discovered delightfully secluded woods and remote fields to explore. Jack was still careful, enjoying the chase; Millie was sixteen and had been entranced at his first kiss where he had tenderly brushed his lips to hers. She had been dizzy with excitement that she had only been able to previously witness on the screen. Her new role enchanted her. In their second kiss his hard lips had crushed hers and he had held her tightly to him. It had taken her breath away. She assumed that his love for her had overwhelmed him. His whispered assertions that he was losing control, that she was unleashing a passion in him that he could barely contain, cleverly created the illusion that it was her that was setting the pace of their romance and that he was just caught up by her allure and beauty. It was a pattern that he repeated during the warm spring days as he stealthily assumed control. He could see that she was giddy by the promise of such romantic passion but led her on slowly. He would tantalise her. It amused him to toy with her.

So far but no more, she was only sixteen, he did not want to burn his fingers, his risks with her were calculated, to provide maximum pleasure with no consequences. His power delighted him; he allowed himself, under a guise of love, to take extra liberties with her, and then to feign disappointment when she stayed his advances, as if cruelly crushed by her rejection. He led her to accept his intimate caresses as if he had, in the innocence of their love, needed to express his devotion to her, and all the while he gave nothing of himself to her. Her eyes remained steadfastly closed, still believing in the love story, whilst he became more watchful, calculating his chances with each encounter. He convinced her that her modesty was unjust and unnatural; that if she really cared for him as he did her, then their extraordinary love could not be contained by the normal conventions. Theirs was a love affair like no other.

Finally as the summer progressed he grew tired of the game, it had monopolised too much of his time. He had taken what he needed from her and the charade of play acting began to become tiresome he wanted new diversions. Millie was making too many demands, assurances of his devotion.

Finally even she sensed that she was just a phase for him and feeling less than adored she too became bored by repetitive pattern of the monogamous romance and then resentful first of his demands and then of his indifference. She discovered with annoyance that he would made promises of a gloriously exciting future together one day and then choose to ignore her. He had beguiled her and she had stupidly allowed herself to be used when there had been others who, given half a chance would have adored her. She wanted nothing short of that. She had seen some who had showed a keen interest in her but had shrugged them off. She was irritated that she had been so foolish as to believe half the things that he had said. Her pride had been crushed and she needed to reassert herself and to find new suitors who would be suitably excited and enslaved by her. Her time with him had given her some experience and it was time to play the field.

∞

I knew that Jack would drop her just as quickly as he had taken her up. His ability to sustain any serious role had always been limited. But their brief dalliance had given me more time with Thomas that spring and my delight in spending days in his company made me lose sight of how they could endanger my future happiness with their promiscuous liaisons.

Thomas and I talked of the worrying news in Europe that his friends alluded to and whether it was inevitable that we would be drawn into the conflicts. Thomas was able to make more informed judgements than I had been able to glean from the newspapers that I had read. One of his friends had anecdotal evidence from a family whom they knew who were talking about the situation in Austria. They had already made plans to travel but were finding it difficult to get the necessary papers to leave the country.

"It is getting worse Rosie; these people could lose everything, their businesses, and their homes. There is no guarantee about anything."

I wanted to trace my fingers over the lines on his forehead, to smooth them away. I had no knowledge of the people, of the friends and families who he spoke of but my heart sank. I could sense the horror that was to come. His time with me was slipping away. I knew that this was our special moment.

"And how is your French progressing...a useful language to have at this time?"

He looked down at me quickly, his frown deepening, and then he smiled and shrugged, "oh you know still just schoolboy standard I'm afraid to say!"

"Surely not."

"Mais oui...mon cheri." His exaggerated English accent made a mockery of the words and he spread his hands wide in exasperation, "I know I know...I should have paid more attention in my lessons!"

"Thomas Fulwood, your attempts to lie to me are as ridiculous as your accent. Don't treat me like a fool, it's not fair."

"I would never do that Rosie!"

"Then don't do it now. When have I ever betrayed your confidence, am I not to be trusted?"

"There are things that are best left unsaid, that's all Rosie, if times were different then I would..." and he shook his head and took hold of my hand.

"At times I understand the agony of Cassandra, but for me, well; I can't speak of things that I see ...so at least there is no likelihood of not being believed huh!"

He saw my hurt, my desperation to expunge the weight of my gifted curse, but there was also bewilderment in him and I knew then that I could not unburden myself, even to him, especially to him. But I had to warn him.

"Be careful Thom...that's all I'm saying. Don't be persuaded by those who you barely know...whatever they might say to convince you. It will be your risk, not theirs, at the end of the day."

"Rosie you sometimes talk in riddles!"

"No, you know what I am saying.... but I sometimes wonder if you know me at all."

"Of course I do! We have known each other since we were children."

"For a clever man you can be very stupid. We are no longer children; I am no longer a child."

And I watched as his eyes widened and look deep into me. He let go of my hand and drew me to him crushing me against him. I buried my head against his chest and could feel his heart pound against my ear.

"I'm so sorry Rosie."

And then he let me go and sighed. "You are the best part of me Rosie, I'm sorry that I never seem to give...that I am so... careless. I don't deserve such a friend as you."

And there it was, I was special but in friendship and nothing more. I had to risk more.

"In time you may come to see how much you mean to me too." And I reached up to him and drew his face to mine and kissed him. It was just the shortest of moments and I held my breath waiting, listening to his thoughts. He was confused. I had suddenly turned his world upside down. He didn't know how to respond. He had never considered me in this way and yet he felt a huge unexpected surge of affection and warmth, a strange almost guilty desire, and then a rush of longing and belonging.

"Rosie I don't know what to say." He pleaded with me unsettled by a plethora of new emotions which he had never felt before. There was Millie, his dream of a certain future, an ideal; his beautiful simple childhood sweetheart whom he had unwaveringly worshipped, and then the complicated reality of me.

"Then don't say it." I whispered as he drew me to him again and this time he kissed me, silently folding me in his arms as if we were just one.

That early summer, with Thomas on his University break, allowed us just enough time to develop our brief love affair. Every day and each encounter was a bonus for me knowing that September would soon come and steal him away from us all. He somehow discovered that Jack and Millie had been seeing each other, but was too loyal and forgiving to confront them. I may have inadvertently said something. He was hurt but reasoned that as he did not have a claim on her there was nothing to be done. I was deliriously happy. We spent so much time enjoying each other's company, and as we grew together so he began to believe in our love. I think that he realised that we were in tune, that in body and mind we blended together. There was a point when he slowly began to realise that his infatuation with Millie had been superficial, but despite this it did not prevent him from feeling somehow guilty that he had transferred his affections to me.

We walked to Kilndown Woods one afternoon.

"I didn't know that it was possible to feel like this" he said as we sat on the bank and dangled our feet in the stream.

"You have changed me Rosie, I don't know how you do it but I feel a different person. It's as if things are so much clearer, I can make sense of my life."

I grunted my approval and lay back on the grassy bank looking up at the wispy clouds scudding across the blue sky, "Well that's because I am so extraordinary."

He turned and leaned over me, his face hovered over mine and his breath brushed my cheek. "No I really mean it Rosie. When I'm with you I feel...contentment..... no, that's not it.... I feel that I have a special strength to meet any adversity, that your support gives me knowledge about myself. That I can be myself and there is no pretence or need to explain. "

"Well that's good because you're being quite obtuse at the moment!"

"Stop it you insensitive little vixen....I shall have to tickle you to death now!" He dug his fingers on my rib cage and then as I gasped for air and cried for him to stop he smothered me in loud sloppy kisses before finally becoming quite serious. He carefully brushed my hair away from my forehead where he planted the lightest of kisses; his voice so quiet that I almost thought that I had dreamt it. "I think I'm falling for you Rosie."

Perhaps I did dream it. He never said it again.

We snatched times, when I was not working at the pub to meet and talk. It became a pattern. I would walk down to the station where he would be waiting for me and then we would continue past the old Kilndown Manor lodge house and up through the grounds of the manor. He pointed out some of the work that he has been asked to do by Lady Faversham. Minor repairs to the outhouses, some coppicing along the main avenue, but the estate still looked woefully neglected. Here and there the grandeur of the place was still in evidence. Grecian statues that had been strategically placed at the ends of yew hedges had started to become entwined in wayward branches, some of the vast plaster urns had cracked and crumbled, manicured lawns had given way to wild flower pastures. Tall thistles mingled with nettles at the outer edges whilst clumps of clover, buttercups, dandelion clock heads, white daises and yellow birdsfoot trefoil prospered amongst straggly tangled long couch grasses.

"It's amazing how quickly nature reclaims her own."

"Mmm, but beautiful in its own way," I pulled at a long tube of grass that came away from its shiny protective sheath and munched its sweetness.

"Yes of course, but when you think of the years of work men put in to create these gardens." Thomas squinted at the house.

"Those orchards...last year the apples were just left to rot. Such a waste."

"What's she like?"

"Who?"

"The lady of the manor."

"Oh, she's a game old bird."

"Do you like her?"

He considered my question. "She's seen some bad times. Bound to affect someone...."

"That's not an answer."

"Well, no....it's not, not that straightforward."

"You feel compromised because you know that she likes you?"

"Don't know about that," he blew down his nose.

"But you do know. She sees in you something that she thought was lost."

"Really Rosie. You get too deep at times!"

"You know that she has affection for you, she has helped you in the past and she will continue to reward you in the future."

"Oh really! Gosh. You seem to know a lot when you've never even met her! So oh worldly one, why would she do that?"

"Because you're all she's got."

"Oh Rosie, don't be ridiculous! Her family go back generations, and then there's her daughter, Mrs Latterbridge..."

"Who she never sees."

"Okay, well yes, but there's her grandson and even her great grandchildren."

"Ronald... yes well, but sometimes generous gifts mask another motive altogether."

He peered down shaking his head, about to laugh at me and then stopped short when he saw my expression.

"Is this another of your Cassandra moments?"

I stared back at him glumly. "You may never know of her legacy."

He shivered in spite of the warmth of the day.

"Rosie?"

And I pulled him to me and buried myself in his chest. Such a sadness overwhelmed me and I didn't want him to see it, to look into my face and see what I knew.

A sudden shout broke us apart and we turned to see old Bert waving from the orchard walk.

"Hello young Thomas! Who have you brought with you.... your young lady is it?"

"Hello Bert." Thomas turned back to me and winked. "Nothing passes your eagle eye does it!"

"You're right there young un, 'specially when the sap is rising heh?"

Thomas smiled ruefully at me. "I had better introduce you otherwise he'll be making up his own stories!"

"Stay there...we're coming over."

We picked our way across the pasture avoiding the clumps of waving nettles.

"You know Rosie..... daughter of Mrs Minton at the Papermakers Arms in the village."

"Why of course I known 'er. Just didn't recognise her at first!"

"How are you m'dear?" and he doffed an imaginary cap in my direction.

"My you're looking very grown up these days. Don't get up to the village as much these days, it's me knees you see, such a haul up that old hill!" His gnarled hands rubbed up and down his thighs to emphasis his point. "A touch of the rheumatics now 'n then....need a bit of horse liniment to rub in!"

His rasping laugh displayed a depleted row of headstone teeth and his red rimmed blue eyes narrowed, the lids lowered imperceptibly, as he searched my face.

"Heard about your dad.....bad business together... an 'e were a good man, no doubt about it. Always had the time of the day for us old 'uns. Speak as you find that what I always say." And he nodded up to Thomas and then back down at me.

"Now this fine lad, well what can I say? Not many round here to beat the likes of him!"

Thomas reddened and shook his head at me raising his eyebrows in a query of embarrassment.

"Isn't that so Miss Rosie...isn't your beau a good 'un?"

I smiled at them both. "I think so...but he's not my beau.....we're just old school chums."

"Hum you don't say...could 'ave fooled me! Anyways are you up to the house today to see her ladyship? You knows she likes to see yon self."

"Oh I'm not sure she would like that Bert....not without an invitation anyway."

"Suit yourself...just that she don't see many folk these days. Keeps herself to herself like. Well I'll bid you good day then, and to you young miss."

And he turned back to the wheel barrow where he had been working.

We walked back across towards the yew tree hedge.

"Perhaps we should call." I said "She'll have known that you were here."

"Ah I know what you want....your curiosity is getting the better of you, nothing to do with feeling sorry for the old lady, admit it!"

"Perhaps so, what's wrong in that?" It was true my curiosity had been piqued.

Thomas linked his arm in mine and turned us round to face the house. "In all probability we'll be turned away. You don't just turn up at places like this! There's such a thing as etiquette. She is not your common or garden neighbour!"

"You never know, this could be the day." And I pulled him to begin our walk up the drive.

"Rosie Minton you are just impossible at times."

"And that's why you love being with me!"

"Mmm is that so? Well don't say I didn't say so when we get turned away."

The heavy panelled door stood solidly set in its stone frame. Four pillars supported the porch canopy. With no sun it was quite chilly as we stood there. Thomas pulled the rope bell at one side of the frame. I couldn't hear a sound.

"Does it work?"

"Well it did that last time I was here."

The front mullion sash windows to either side of the door were heavily shaded: three to each side, their sills and heads were cracked.

"Try again."

The door opened slowly and the maid stood waiting for us to speak.

"I wondered if her ladyship is at home?"

"Is she expecting you Thomas?"

"Er, not today, no."

"Mmm, well as you know, I'm afraid she does not receive visitors without an appointment."

"No, no of course not, it's just that we saw old Bert and he, well he put it to us that she might like to see..." Thomas tailed off.

She tutted. "What's got into the man? Getting quite feather brained in his old age."

"Well we best be going." And Thomas turned away leaving me staring into the hallway, before the door slowly closed.

"Come on Miss Know it all." He gave me a dig in the ribs, "What did I say?"

"Alright have it your own way." But instead of continuing down the drive I turned back towards a little side gate.

"Is this the way to the walled garden?"

"Yes...but we are not going that way...come back Rosie!"

I lifted the latch and found myself in a tranquil setting. On one side the beds had been freshly dug. Dark soil set off the lightness of the

Delphinium leaves, their deep blue blooms not yet fully developed. Apple and pear trees had been cordoned against the wall and some papery clematis had wound themselves tenaciously round the lower trunks.

"I love walled gardens; they are so secret, so private."

Thomas smiled at me in spite of himself.

"Now can we go?"

"In a moment.....just a few more minutes!"

268

At the front of the bed some pale lilac Asters and white Astilbe swayed together with purple foxgloves whilst some newly planted Lobelia sat at the edge.

"Look how the colours blend together, such clever planting. I turned to Thomas but he was looking the other way towards the gate. A frail lady stood leaning on a stick.

"Lady Faversham, forgive our intrusion, we were just passing…" She waved away his apology with her stick.

"Thomas, come here. Who have you brought with you? Who is this young girl?"

"This is my friend Rosie."

She looked at me. "The publican's daughter? A funny looking thing aren't you?" She dismissed me.

"And how are you Thomas. How are your studies? Are you enjoying University life? Is it challenging? Is it what you expected?"

Her questions rattled on so fast as if she was not expecting a reply to them.

"Sebastian said that they were the best of days you know."

"Yes it is certainly a very different world for me." He smiled at her and she nodded as if content with his response.

"Good, good." Have you had tea? Come we will have some tea." Her invitation turned itself into a command and we found ourselves trailing in her wake.

I couldn't resist the urge to make him acknowledge my victory. And though he attempted not to meet my eye, and continued to look straight ahead, I could see his mouth twitching, threatening to undo his composure.

As we neared the French doors he turned to me and hissed.

"I'm warning you…best behaviour Miss Know it all!"

"Glad you have finally realised it…" I whispered back, and sticking my nose in the air I graciously sailed past him, inclining my head in thanks, as he stood aside to let me pass.

The air was still in the room. I felt it oppressive. The gloom dispersed as our eyes became accustomed to the dull light after the brightness of the day outside.

Lady Faversham found her chair and indicated for Thomas to sit by her. I was left to find a seat further away. I knew that she had not long in the world. I could feel her weariness and her sadness and for a brief second in that moment I pitied her. She was alone and afraid.

She rang a little bell on the small fluted table beside her and turned back to Thomas.

They talked of his studies at the university, of the city, she asked about his rooms and the food, his friends, had he been to the theatre, what he thought of the political situation. And as they talked I allowed myself to study her and take in the surroundings. I saw the clock and the French bronzes that Thomas had admired. I saw those things that she would bequeath to him. So much would be sold off piecemeal but he would have the best of them. She needed to make some amends for those she had cast off and through him would be her salvation. She could be at peace with herself.

When the maid appeared with the tea set on a tray with just one cup she started when she saw the three of us together.

"Oh I didn't realise that you had company my lady, I will fetch some extra cups." And she frowned at me before leaving the room.

I was impervious to her disapproval or that Lady Faversham seemed fit not to acknowledge me. It was enough that she liked Thomas. I tried to quell the warning that it would all be to no avail.

On the way back through the woods Thomas was quiet. He had been sad to see such a change in her; to see her frailty. He wondered about the rift between her and her daughter Mrs Latterbridge. What had caused them to live so apart?

"She married an artist, disreputable in her eyes." I murmured half to myself.

Thomas stopped and turned to me. "What did you say?"

"Oh just thinking aloud, you know ....you were talking about Mrs Latterbridge."

He shook his head, "No I wasn't talking about her! I didn't say a word...so how did you know I was thinking about her just at that very moment."

I shrugged, "it's just a coincidence that's all, we were talking about Lady Faversham I suppose, nothing more than that."

"No it's not that Rosie sometimes I have the strangest notion that you can get inside my head and read me like a book."

I smiled lightly, "Oh really? Not much of a book then!"

But he was determined not to let the moment pass. "Oh no not this time.....you do it too many times. You did it even when we were just kids. It's not just me... you seem to know things before they happen, to all of us. Me, Jack, Millie, it's the same with all of us, you watch and you listen like we all do, but you know things that we, well we just don't seem to get. All this time I have put it down to just sheer coincidence, ignored all these signs, but it happens when even I don't know what I am about to say, and then you just come out with something that has only just popped into my head."

"That's because we share things, we talk about things."

"No it's not that. You have a sort of gift, it's uncanny. A special sort of knowing, I don't know what to call it. A kind of sixth sense, telepathy, more than intuition.... Dulcie's a bit like you quite intuitive, she picks up on things too but with you it's on a different level."

"Familiarity that's all it is. It happens with family and friends. Close knit communities. When you do things together it's a kind of shorthand....just ordinary routines. Oh Thomas don't look so serious!"

"No Rosie you are special. It's taken me all this time to see it."

271

"Well of course I'm special, I'm not denying that!"
I twirled around to demonstrate. "And what an extraordinarily developed personality ...mad, bad and dangerous to know!"
"Nice epitaph Miss Lamb!"
 "But you need to recognise those types Thomas... they will drag you in.... just be careful of the company you keep." I looked up squinting as the sun's glare between the trees momentarily blinded me.
Thomas sighed. "Now you're really being obtuse.... I wish I knew the half of it. What the future holds for any of us." He caught hold of my hand and we walked the familiar path together as the station finally came into view.

Ivy Leaf Cottage 2009
Rosie

In that glorious summer of 1939 it was all too brief for me. Millie and Jack bickered and made up and bickered again before it all fizzled out, but I cherished every day that I had with Thomas. It even made the demands of mother more bearable. We were just about keeping our heads above water in the pub and Ethel actually allowed me to take over some of the business accounting which we sent to Fremlins on a monthly basis. It was straightforward book keeping, just a matter of filing accounts of orders, expenditure and creditors.

Due to the size of the bar we had never had the space to develop a separate lounge or snug as some of the town public houses had done. But I did a deal with Ron to supply a modest amount of meat and potato pies on a Saturday lunchtime which went down very well and gave us a modest amount of profit.

Of course it couldn't last. Thomas went away in September and then the grim reality of war and petrol rationing began. Our customer base grew ever smaller and some days we hardly saw any trade at all during the few hours of lunchtimes and evenings that were available for us to open.

Thomas had started writing to me again once he returned to Cambridge and, since Millie and Jack were no longer an item, he felt it only proper to write to her as well. This time however she wanted to prove to Jack that she had a bevy of admirers so I heard more about his correspondence to her whenever she came across to see us.

Was I was jealous? Of course I was. She was blossoming into a beautiful woman. It was becoming the rage for young girls to have photo plates taken in town studios in Maidstone, Cranbrook and Tunbridge Wells. The young men who had been called up were asking newly-found sweethearts to write to them and include a picture with the letter.

I only thought of Thomas but then, after the initial flurry of letters from Cambridge, those later, mysteriously postmarked from Oxford, came spasmodically and then dwindled just to a tantalising one or two. He said less and less about himself. My days turned slowly and I suffocated in that warm autumn. The blues skies mocked my dark thoughts. Thomas had succumbed to intelligence work. I knew he would. His world had become full of dark shadows and whispers, concealment and secrets.

I felt strangely betrayed by his dealings with treachery. I did not trust the motives or the politics of those whom he was serving. Their cloak and dagger games seem to put only others in danger as they plotted to outmanoeuvre their enemies and plan secret deals reneging on promises made. It appeared to me that subversive ideologies had taken hold. That the lives of men and woman would be taken to shape those visions and that unnatural alliances would be forged.

Some days I would find myself remembering the last halcyon days I spent with Thomas when he had been more demonstrative in his affection knowing that the days were racing by. He would frequently hold me in his arms, stroke my cheek, and trace his fingers over my lips. He would hold my gaze and smile.

We went to the pictures, to the Palace Theatre in Gabriel's Hill or dance in The Star ballroom in Maidstone whenever Jack could get hold of a car for Thomas and I could get away from the pub. Sometimes we would even go as a foursome when Milly had decided to make a convenient truce with Jack to enable her to flaunt a new dress, or when Jack decided that he wanted to show that he was a man about town with a blonde on his arm. They were well used to performing dramas sometimes for show and other times for their own secret amusement. Moths and flames not concerned of whose fingers they burnt.

All the while I was with Thomas it was fine but if he thought that Millie had been left without a partner he would ask for a dance, my heart would turn somersaults. His kindness and consideration caused a riot of confusion in me. She looked so lovely in his arms and I knew that I was just a hair's breath away from losing him. I had to check my tongue, to hold my fire, and continually plan diversions.

Once Thomas had left I felt moribund, fettered by the enclosure of village life. It stifled me. I read of a land army of women set up by Lady Denman that June. The glamorous posters had shown carefree strong young women in dungarees framed against sunny skies. When Thomas was at home I had never given it much thought but the slow autumn days in the pub made me yearn for action to be anywhere but home. And then I wondered if I could be placed nearer to Thomas but the age restriction was against me. They were only taking girls aged twenty and over but I had heard that some had lied about their age and said that they were older, even some who were just seventeen had been able to fool the authorities. The idea wormed inside me.

Jack had hoped to avoid any confrontation but in the October of that autumn he had to register with the military authorities and by early 1940 aged twenty he found himself in uniform and marching orders to attend an army camp in East Kent very much to his annoyance. He had been initially interviewed at Chatham but it seemed that the Royal Navy had other ideas about his talents. His work at the garage made him more than suitable for the army mechanical division. "Just a damn grease monkey!" he complained to an anxious Edith.

I had been given no promises by Thomas of a future together. Our romance had been quite chaste that first summer. We had delighted in our exchange of ideas and long ranging conversations. It was much later when everything became hopeless, when he realised what he had lost and by then it was too late, even for me, to change the course of our lives.

Ronald of course was delighted by the outbreak of war. It suddenly gave his life a new purpose. By the late spring of 1940 he found that he could join a newly formed Local Defence League. Suddenly his experience of military life could be put into practice in a safe environment. He excitedly told Beatrice of his plans. Working in the bank gave him some status and by July of that summer he was a fully-fledged member of the Home Guard energised by the work to confound Hitler by renaming all the streets in Cranbrook and taking down direction signs to the local villages and towns. He congratulated himself on the fight that he was valiantly waging against the tyranny of Hitler.

But the outbreak of war did something more special for Beatrice; apart from giving her more time away from Ronald, it finally forged a bond with her mother that had been lost for so many years. Paradoxically it took international hostilities to bring about an end to the women's own hostility to each another. Beatrice decided to become a VAD and sometime later Mote House was deemed suitable to be requisitioned as a convalescence home for officers. Mother and daughter came together working as one. They had always been practical and diligently assisted the transformation of their home into an auxiliary convalescence home. They began to find a new comradeship in each other; recognising strengths and virtues that they had previously ignored.

Poor Arnold found himself displaced and overcome with worry over the impact that the war would have on his businesses. All that he had diligently worked for was at stake once again but there was another complication for this time his age was against him. He grew tired more quickly, found himself with less energy at the end of each day and alarmingly Louise seemed preoccupied with other matters. He had always counted on her to be there. Not that he had, of course, ever discussed business with her but she had always been a sympathetic ear, someone to turn to when he felt the pressure too great.

Yes indeed the war changed the people in our village and for some it turned their lives upside down.

It even had an effect on Ethel for a while. Once Jack left home she became almost subdued. She began to rely on me as if she was almost afraid of the future; she feared the awful prospect that I could be all that she had left in the world.

Then as the months went by she learnt of my plans to join the Land Army and panic set in. I could not and would not be spared to go.... 'haring around the country wielding a pitch fork!' Whatever had I been thinking!

"Your place is here at home with me my girl. How do you think I could manage this on my own? You always have had a selfish streak! If your father knew what you were thinking of he would have turned in his grave!" Her face grew pink with fury.

"Think it's all glamour do you? Mucking out cowsheds? No I don't think so. You have never done a day's hard work....getting your hands dirty...you with your head always in a book! Closest thing you've ever got to farm life is scrumping a few apples from the Parsons orchards!"

She threw down the tea towel and stormed up the stairs giving me no chance to retaliate. And in all honesty what she had said was very true. I had no idea of keeping poultry, milking or lambing, hedging and ditching, let alone driving any kind of machinery. The nearest experience I had of catching rats was having found one in skeletal form in a rusty old trap in the cellar when clearing up.

In the end I stayed put. Once Ron's assistant Mike had been called up I lent a hand with deliveries, mastering the cumbersome bike with varying degrees of competence depending on the terrain. More than often I resorted to walking alongside the contraption judging that the bread would have a better chance of staying in the basket rather than being jolted out.

And because I became familiar face to some of the older folk on the outskirts of the village I found myself becoming a kind of odd job girl; running errands, delivering parcels or the odd bit of

277

shopping, taking messages, or posting letters. Those days I hardly saw Millie as she was taking a commercial secretarial course in Tunbridge Wells, and at the weekends she was invariably out with one of her special friends whom she had met in town. We had never been that close but we seemed to go our separate ways unless she had something to brag about and then she would search me out.

My days were spent frustratingly waiting in queues as rationing took effect, first butter and sugar, bacon and ham, then tea and jam and cheese. Little by little our lives were overshadowed by the want of things. Our village shops became depleted of goods, material possessions suddenly gained status and importance. We watched the scales to ensure our full measure, becoming ever more petty in the tyranny of want, hungry for our fair share. Sadly we were quick to judge another's need and it diminished us. Those who look back to that time with a sense of nostalgia must have decided to brush out some inconvenient truths.

I only came alive when Thomas made a rare appearance back home. I worried how he would find me, dulled by a life centred on the mundane. Need now drove my creativity, how to make food stretch, shorten a hem; make the best of a bad job. Beatrice showed the way. She seemed to have the knack of finding a way to produce preserves, bottling and pickling, 'making meals from nothing' as Ethel sneered. Her house even retained a sense of glamour. She would find wild flowers if there was nothing in the garden to brighten up the rooms. Grudgingly I came to respect her resilience and her devotion to Dulcie. The child was a delight, always interested and curious, quick to learn. I saw in her a kindred spirit; it was as if I was watching myself grow up. Whereas I was tainted by Edith's malevolence she had benefited from Beatrice's gentle nurturing. She was a better version of me and I knew that she shared my sight; so much safer in such a vessel. Through her the gift would survive in a purer form. Archie would have been so delighted; she had the best of their characters, although physically she took after Archie, her easy manner and generosity charmed us all. She saw the goodness in others where I had been quick to judge.

∞

It was at the pictures on Pathe News that we learnt about the Piped Piper evacuation of city children to the country but it was only when a gaggle of children turned up at the railway station that we began to understand the enormity of the operation. Ron and Betty took in a funny little scrap from the East End. He thought all his Christmases had come at once when he realised that he was to live with a baker. But he was only with them for a short time as his mother sent for him to come back home. Poor Betty was so sad to see the little chap go. He was as sharp as a new pin.

Then when we learnt of the Dunkirk evacuation it was with a sense of profound shock. Bombing had been one thing but suddenly a retreat sounded quite ominous. People wondered if it was the shape of things to come.

Ronald spent more time pompously assessing how he would lead the best defence of the realm, but irritatingly could not exactly provide even a vague sketch of his plans in case spies could use the information. Even Ethel was unusually scathing about him. She had previously extolled his virtues of having a respectable occupation and providing such a lovely home for his wife and children. It had been a well-rehearsed mantra and ammunition that she had used against Archie in the past, but seeing him lording over the regulars irked her.

"What a fool he is prattling on about spies and his grand schemes. Couldn't defend himself from a mouse that one."

He became a regular visitor to the pub once he had a band of men to marshal whilst his promotion to Sergeant gave him three visible stripes to parade. But for Edith his showy manner had irritated her; he committed the cardinal sin of not giving her due deference in her own establishment. He had ignored her. Once Ethel had made up her mind to condemn it was a lasting sentence. She even found herself putting aside her antipathy and having some sympathy towards Beatrice.

"Don't know how she puts up with him, going on like that all the time!" she sniffed. "Still you make your own bed so you have to lie in it."

She had already been waging a war with Robert Drew over his insistence that she had not successfully curtailed the amount of light which he had discovered escaping from an upstairs window despite the blackout curtain. Having always prided herself in being meticulous it outraged her sense of pride.

"For two pins I'd go elsewhere for my meat. Mind his sausages seem to have more of the sawdust that he spreads on the floor than having any pork in them. Useless to fry: just gristle and bone."

It was Betty that listened to her tales of woe. Betty managed to soothe her when all else failed. She had the skill to apply the necessary balm without taking sides, it was a natural quality that perhaps we all had taken for granted at one time or another. Where others divided Betty brought them together. It was more apparent because the numbers in the village had dwindled so alarmingly. The young men had gone and so we had been left with just a small band, mostly the elderly folk who had previously relied upon their own children for support.

Ethel had always kept herself to herself but increasingly she sought out Betty and when she returned home it was as if a load had shifted from her shoulders. I saw glimpses of the young woman that she had once been, the better side of her nature that had been missing throughout her marriage and our childhood.

In the end when it was decreed that all women had to undertake some kind of national service I trained with the Red Cross and St

Johns to become a VAD, and actually ending up working up at Mote House. I had no natural vocation to nursing at first but learnt fast and under the guidance of Louise and Beatrice I began to develop a pragmatic approach to the everyday duties and even began to enjoy it. Edith actually approved of my involvement, even the time spent away from home whilst training, when she had been so vehemently opposed it before. It had some respectability and besides she could boast that her daughter was working with officers and gentlemen.

Millie decide to join the WRENS although she spent most of her time doing clerical work in Chatham, after her initial training in Windsor, when she had hoped for a far more exotic posting with dashing young sailors, although she always managed to find a willing companion to drive her down to Cranesbury whenever she had leave, despite the petrol rationing that curtailed the rest of us from travelling by car. She wore her tailored uniform well, looking trim and glamourous as usual with her bright curls escaping from under her cap. It was around this time that I started to see a resemblance to her grandmother Sylvia Latterbridge. It was in the way she held herself and her pale skin had the same translucent quality.

Jack had very limited periods of leave and much to Ethel's anguish he wrote very little in his infrequent letters home or told her where he was stationed. We were never prepared for his visits; he just turned up, often surreptitiously thrusting a small gift into her hands with an 'ask no questions' wink, and then once he had gone Ethel was left unable to settle.

We hardly ever saw Thomas during the first two years. When he did come back for a brief visit he too had changed. He looked not just older but thinner and there was a grey look about him. It was as if he had retreated into himself. He remained affable to Ethel and was still as affectionate with me. However one year later I saw that the boy had gone and a man had taken his place. A quiet authority settled on him, and that's when Millie became ill, and everything turned upside down.

Ivy leaf Cottage 1941
Beatrice, Ronald & Rosie

It was early afternoon on Saturday when there was a knock on the door. Ronald went to answer it and found himself face to face with the telegram boy holding a small brown envelope in his hand.

Ronald took it from him with a grim sense of unease. Before he had a chance to open it properly to read the contents the lad spoke.

"Will there be an answer Sir?"

Ronald answered with a glare, transfixing the lad to the spot.

Millie Latterbridge at Chatham General 11.30hrs today. Stop. Investigation proceeding. Stop. Operation may be required. Stop Please attend. Stop. Chief Officer N. Roberts'

"No, no reply." The unexpected nature of the staccato message mesmerised him. He took a moment to take in the news and then re-read it as if the strips of wording would suddenly start explaining themselves to him. He glanced up at the retreating figure of the boy as he cycled away.

His stomach contracted and he took a deep breath. Whatever had happened? Had she had an accident? Was she ill? What an earth was wrong?

He glanced around him uncertain at what to do. Beatrice! He needed to let Beatrice know. Grabbing his hat and coat from the hook by the door he went to go out and then stepped back.

What if she wasn't at Mote House? What if she was already coming home and he missed her. He realised that he couldn't remember what she had said to him that morning when she had gone out.

He went back into the kitchen and started to pull open drawers. I need to write a note!

He looked at the telegram that he had crushed in his haste to snatch his coat. The words started to swim before him and he

283

held on to the table. Going into the dining room he went to the bureau and there he found a pencil and note pad neatly placed inside a pigeon hole.

'Gone to Mote House to find you. Millie ill at Chatham General. Need to catch train. Meet me at station. ~~I will try to telephone hospital from there.~~ I will use phone box here see if I can get through. Ronald'

He stared down at the note. Was it clear? Would she realise that he was going straight to the station after Mote House. Yes of course it was! He noticed that his hand was shaking. Money, he needed money, coins for the phone box. Back to the kitchen he tipped the loose coins from the little bowl on the shelf, patted his pocket to check for his wallet, placed the note on the table with the bowl on it to keep it from moving, checked that the back door was locked and rushed once again into the hall.

As he pulled it open Beatrice stepped back.

"Goodness me Ronald wherever are you going in such a hurry?" She laughed and then caught sight of his face and her heart jumped.

"What is it Ronald!"

He pulled the door closed behind him and propelled her before him.

"It's Millie, she's in hospital. We've had a telegram. It's just come!" He pulled the envelope from his pocket and waved it in front of her and caught hold of her arm.

"We need to go, it says for us to attend."

"Let go." Beatrice tried to extradite herself from his grasp. "Calm down Ronald. I haven't had a chance to look at it yet. Wait a moment please!" She shook her sleeve free.

Her tone caused him to take stock of the figure that he had presented to her and he waited impatiently as she read the telegram.

"Right!" He puffed. "We need to get down to the station. We could get the ..."

"No!" Beatrice protest was impatient. "We'll go back to Mote

House and get one of the men to drive father's car if Maynard is not there."

She turned on her heel, "and we can phone from there first."

Her lucid plan irritated him. "There may not be enough petrol in it."

"Well we'll see when we get there, there's always the staff car in any case."

He followed her across the road catching up with her before she turned down by the pond. He had recovered his composure and glanced down at Beatrice. Her face was set, inscrutable; she looked straight ahead driven by the need to know, her outward calm disguised the thudding of her heart.

I was on duty that afternoon and saw them come into the hall. They turned towards Arnold's old study, before I could reach to speak to them. I knew it was Millie. I could feel their tension and their fear. They were frightened of losing her. Her image came into my head and then faded, and I realised with some horror that it did not cause me the same concern. For a moment I put my happiness above any anxiety for her. And then I realised that this was the catalyst, this was to be my undoing. Her emotional or physical fragility would reawaken Thomas's old loyalty, his boyhood protectiveness and his generous capacity to love. She had to get well, to regain her strength, so that I could then diminish her power over him. I could only trust that time would be on my side. If he knew that she was in any trouble it would be the same. I needed her to dismiss him as she done when we were children and for that she needed to be well again. A nagging sense of not quite being able to see with my usual clarity disturbed me. I needed to ascertain the facts to work out a strategy.

I walked towards the study and listened. Beatrice was on the telephone.

"Yes Millie Latterbridge...she is....yes, yes I'll hold."

"They are going to speak to the ward sister now." She turned to Ronald covering the mouthpiece with her hand.

"Hello? Yes. Mrs Latterbridge here… is she…no, no I understand….I see yes, oh my goodness…oh dear….thank goodness….yes…. and visiting hours are..? Oh fine, yes, thank you sister. Four o'clock until six. " She replaced the receiver on the cradle.

"It was her appendix. It had nearly burst. It all happened so fast!" Her voice wavered and I heard her sink into the chair.

"She thought that it was something she had eaten and had gone to bed last night with an aspirin. Then this morning it had got worse!"

Ronald attempted to assume control. "Right, well we need to find a car to take us to Chatham straight away. Did you say that there are staff cars available?"

"No Ronald, goodness you can't just commandeer cars like that! I'll see where father is here and you go and have a word with matron. See if she can suggest something."

Beatrice came out into the hall and saw me as I was passing by. "Rosie, I'm glad I caught you. Millie is in the hospital and her father and I are going up to see her. Do you think you could you do me an enormous favour?"

"Yes of course. It's Dulcie; you want me to meet her from school? My shift finishes at four but I can ask matron if she can let me go earlier and then bring her back here with me."

"Goodness Rosie, "Beatrice shook her head, " you know what I'm going to say before I thought of it myself, yes if she could stay here with mother, I'm not sure what time we will be able to get back."

I smiled at her, "I'll ask straight away." And I turned to go.

She called after me, "I don't know if we will be able to ring from the hospital either, we'll find a phone box and call mother when we know anything."

I nodded and left them.

Later that day we learnt that had Millie not been admitted, and the appendix ruptured, she could have contracted peritonitis. I felt a swirl of guilt as I saw the image of her lying in hospital. Dulcie turned from her book and glanced up at me.

"She will get better won't she Rosie?"

"Of course she will." My heart turned over. What had I been thinking!

"She'll be up and about before you know it."

Dulcie screwed up her face. "She'll be coming back here then won't she until she gets better?"

"Yes once she's been given the all clear, and they discharge her she'll have to have some time to get strong again. Until it all mends."

"Do you think that Thomas will come to see her?" Her wide eyes met mine.

"Well I'm not sure that he would be able to just come like that. He has important war work to do you know!" I smiled as if we had shared some kind of joke.

"I know that but he'll still come won't he." It was a statement and we looked at each other again. I felt my smile fade. The child knows my heart too, I thought, and then shook off my sense of foreboding.

"You'll write and tell him won't you Rosie. Promise?"

"Of course I will." And my heart thudded against my ribs and I added treacherously, "We're all old friends."

But I didn't write, well, of course I wrote to Thomas as usual, but just neglected to add all the details of village life at that time. He had enough to worry about with his important work. Besides what could he have done? He could hardly drop everything and come down to Cranesbury. He might not have even been in the country at that time.

Anyway Millie more or less made a full recovery so I did write to him later to say that she had spent a short spell in hospital but was back to being her old self, which she was all things considered. Perhaps she had seemed a little subdued for a while. I've always found that it is always a shock to those who are young and think themselves invincible to find that an illness can be so debilitating. The young are so reckless and unthinking about their good health and the energy that they possess. It is when one comes to my time of life when the ability to get through each day without any mishap is treated as a bonus.

So it was left to Beatrice, who had finally written to Thomas, to fill him in the details that I had omitted to include in my correspondence, to tell him that Millie had been dangerously ill and that she had been lucky to have survived the post-operative complications. Something about suffering from some trauma, from an infection at the wound site that had not responded to treatment, after the removal of the appendix.

I saw an envelope with his distinctive handwriting addressed them on their kitchen table. Curiously on examination I saw that the postmark was from London. I had gone over to see them to find how things were progressing and found that Millie was still at home making a slow recovery. I then knew for certain that Thomas was one of the Baker Street Irregulars. His dangerous life of subterfuge had begun in earnest. But it still wasn't until the very beginning of December that Thomas was able to come back.

After a depressing cold spell we had had a particularly thick fog that settled and surrounded the area in a ghastly green tinge. The miserable gloom of the day was replaced by the impenetrable blackness of night. With no light showing from any window and no guiding light from stars or moon we had been marooned by it; kept inside to wait out the removal of the malevolent cloak that kept us by our firesides. The relentless deletion of everyday items from the shops made us resentful, there had seemed no relief from the difficulties of coping without even the basic provision of soap, shampoos or washing powder. Wash days turned into feats of endurance as we turned collars and brushed out the dust from our clothes. Even dirt had become the enemy by then to harassed mothers. Looking well turned out caused us to scrimp and save every bar of soap as we tried to spit and polish our way to respectability.

∞

Thomas arrived unannounced that Sunday evening and the knock at the door startled Ethel who had been sitting mending a hem on her skirt by the oven. I had been brooding and fidgety all day. When he stooped inside, drawing aside the curtain at the kitchen door, I could see such a change in him. His mackintosh held the sulphur of the night air. He patted Ethel shoulder in welcome as she had made to rise from her chair indicating to her to remain seated
 "Don't get up on my account. Stay by the fire." He brushed my cheek briefly with his cold lips.
Ethel put aside her sewing and despite his protests stood and went over to the sink to fill the kettle.
"Well Thomas I hope that you will at least stay for some tea. We haven't seen you for such an age. Your parents must be so pleased to have you home. How long is your leave?"

Thomas grinned down at her and sighed, "Always the way, no sooner do I arrive and you're asking when I'll go."

"Stop teasing Thomas my lad, you're not too old to get a clip round the ear!"

Ethel smiled indulgently at him as he sank into the spare chair by the window. It never ceased to amaze me how he could coax out the softer side of mother. She became almost coquettish with him. The kettle came to the boil announcing itself with a shrill whistle, and then grumpily wheezed and whined as Ethel filled the teapot.

"I afraid we're out of sugar."

"No! Is there a war on then?" Thomas shook his head, "it's a long time since I took sugar, I think I've probably solved my sweet tooth addiction by now......except if there any biscuits going?"

"There may be some left in the barrel." She glanced at me and I rose to check the cupboard.

"You're in luck...the mice must have spared us these." I opened the lid and showed him the contents.

"Dead fly biscuits! Now there's a treat!" He took a bite and smiled.

"How are things with you then Thomas or shouldn't I ask? Rosie never seems to remember to share any news from you. I think she forgets that our generation fought a war too." Her short laugh belied her intended malice.

"Oh I can't grumble Mrs M. A desk job is not what I planned but they were short of interpreters and so there we are. Monotonous stuff for the most part. Anyway more to the point have you heard from Jack?"

"Funny you should say that but I did get one yesterday. Short as usual, hardly more than a few lines…. but he did say that he had been very sorry to hear about Millie. Of course he has been in the thick of it from almost day one poor boy. France first and now…" She waved her hand at me.

290

"Go and get Jack's letter from the sideboard." But I had risen before she had completed her request and put the letter into her hands. She took it carefully and delicately opened the contents. "Shall I read it?" she was delighted to have an appreciative audience and to share Jack's words with Thomas.

"Yes Millie…. how is she?" he glanced sideways at me before turning back to Ethel.

Ethel put down the letter. "Well of course it was a very bad do. You know it was touch and go for a while!"

"Well not quite!" I murmured.

"Really? So now you're an authority on all medical matters are you since working over at Mote House?" she turned indignantly back to Thomas.

"A bit of Red Cross training and now suddenly thinks she's a doctor! Yes indeed… despite what Rosie would have you believe, Millie was very poorly indeed. I'm not sure of all the medical terms but she was very lucky to receive excellent care over in Chatham. They did think that they might have to transfer her to a London hospital but in the end they contained the spread of infection and, I'm happy to report, the poor girl is now on the mend. It's been a difficult time for them."

Thomas nodded to her keeping his face away from mine. "Mrs Latterbridge did write but it was a while before I received it… it probably got caught up in the internal mail, such a busy place where I am….paperwork all over the shop. Anyway let's hear what Jack has to say."

I sat apart gazing at the back of his head as Ethel's reading of the letter absorbed them both. He knows! He came here to challenge me; to have it out with me before he sees Millie. And as I sat there quietly a thought took hold. Yes there had been the appendicitis; but something else, a niggling doubt started to grow. There had been an infection it was said, but there was something else. A complication, caused by what… Millie's careless life style, the company she was keeping, the wild young men who were dancing attendance; had they been the cause…one that had to be kept hidden? Why had I not thought of that before?

I was aware of the silence. They had finished reading the letter.

"Oh yes Jack has had a bad time of it, but then he wouldn't let me know the half of it, not the kind of son to ever complain you see. He has always been such a thoughtful son…tried to protect me….it was always his way, cheerful in adversity. Well you know that Thom. There's not many who can pick themselves up and bounce back again. But you could see that in him even as a little lad, he was always on the go." She smiled and sighed contentedly at the recollection.

"The best of them my Jack."

Thomas nodded and placed a reassuring hand on her arm before turning to me.

"Are they keeping you busy there at Mote House or have you managed to see young Millie then?"

"No of course they do let me have time off now and then!" I joked but the words stuck in my throat and I turned away to avoid the penetration of his subtle glance.

"Well I can't stay long Mrs Minton. And now that I've eaten you out of house and home I'd best be going. I might just nip over the road on my way back to see how things are over there." His frame as he rose filled the room.

"No don't get up. I'll try and pop in before I leave. Can't promise anything though. Keep your spirits up Mrs Minton, no, don't get up I'll see myself out."

"Such a good lad that one! He and Jack were always inseparable even as youngsters." She bent over the table to clear the cups as I came back into the room.

"He and Millie were close too. I wouldn't wonder that after all this is over that we hear wedding bells with those two. They would make such a handsome couple. I did think at one time that she and Jack…"she shook her head.

"Mind, I think he wants to take his time to find the right one, set his sights a little higher, not that I'm saying that Millie's not a good catch but she's always been a bit too flighty for my liking. I think Jack felt the same. Jack could take his pick but he's too young to be tied down yet. A young man like him needs to be able to spread his wings."

I listened as her cheerful ramblings wore on. In his brief visit Thomas had cast his magic, had indeed lifted her spirits, Ethel was glowing.

In my mind's eye I saw him enter Ivy Leaf Cottage. Millie, with Beatrice's encouragement, would see him as a saviour who could rescue her from the predicament that had almost threatened to undo them, and in securing her own release she would capture him.

My fear for the consequences I perceived for once played badly with my ability to see things clearly. I panicked, jumped to the wrong conclusion in my desperation to avert a disaster and in doing so created another one. I had foreseen the future but hadn't realised that I would be the cause of it. The next morning I went down to the station, desperate to see Thomas and found him waiting on the platform for the next train to London.

"Goodness you didn't say that you were leaving so early! And with not even a goodbye." I tried to adopt a flippant tone.

"I hadn't known myself before this morning. Something came up." He looked down the platform squinting. The remains of the previous day's fog still lingered making the platform and track disappear into the swirl of grey cloud.

"Thom...please don't..."I didn't know how to plead my case.

"It was pretty low of you Rosie. I didn't expect that of you." He still would not look at me but frowned at the forlorn sky.

"I don't know what you mean. What are you trying to say?"

He slowly turned to face me. ! I don't think I need to explain, do you?"

"Millie...you mean?"

"Oh Rosie, what else, don't be obtuse." He sighed. "It's...it's....I just didn't think that you of all people..."he faltered not wanting to go on.

"But I haven't done anything wrong!"

"Really? You astonish me, you really do." He pulled open the lapel of his coat and took out a packet of cigarettes, withdrew one, and lit it exhaling slowly as if in deep contemplation.

"I just didn't want you to do something that you would regret."

"And what was it that I would regret Rosie?"

"To get tangled up, well, to promise something....."

"So let's get this straight. You didn't think to write to say how ill Millie was, your friend and mine since we were kids Rosie, in all your letters, not one word. And you did that because you were concerned for me. Well I think that's pretty bizarre Rosie even for you."

"What do you mean even for me!"

"You've always have been a strange one; had to fight your own battles along the way, but I liked to think that you were the best of us. I never imagined that you could be so...indifferent, no that's not what I meant, so callous Rosie. It has been a shock."

His words sliced through the air and I recoiled as if to repel a sword. I found that I was holding my breath. My brain seemed to shrivel into one core of intense white, blotting out all other senses until I became conscious of a relentless pulse pounding through my head.

I stepped back, horrified. I knew then that he was lost to me and that when he came to recognise his mistake it would be too late and by then we would all share his loss.

"I shouldn't have come." I managed to say. "Whatever was I thinking of. What a hopeless mess!"

I turned away from him and walked away. The shame of his words clung to me refusing to be shaken off.

I didn't write to him or see him again until the following spring. It was a long winter although it lasted no longer the ones that came later or the ones that we had had before. Perhaps it was because sleep was reluctant to visit me each night, and when it did come it bought with it dreams that tormented me so that I almost began to welcome the weariness of insomnia. At least then I could control my thoughts. Even Ethel remarked on the dark shadows that underlined my eyes.

"Goodness Rosie. You really ought to go to bed earlier. And you need every bit of beauty sleep that you can get!"

I could lose myself at Mote House. The everyday trivia of mundane tasks employed my energy. It stopped me from feeling. I became an empty vessel; stopping up my voices.

One day Beatrice stopped me as I was about to take my coat from the hanger and I turned to her thinking that she had one last request to make before I left.

"Rosie. Could I have a word?"

I nodded and followed her as she led the way to what had been the dining room and was now recreational room.

She closed the door behind us.

"I haven't said anything to you until it was confirmed but Millie is a little embarrassed to ask so I said that I would have a word to you first." She began brightly.

My smile faded I knew what she would request.

"Thomas proposed to her when he was last here and she has accepted. They hope to get married sometime in March or April if Thomas can get leave. Millie is still hoping for a spring wedding. There should at least be some flowers available then. There's nothing in the shops these days." She laughed happily.

I gazed at her wiling myself to say the right thing. My dry mouth set itself in a smile.

"How lovely, you must be delighted Please pass on my congratulations to them both."

"Well of course I will but we want you to come over to us tonight so that Millie can ask you herself if you would be her bridesmaid along with Dulcie. She got it into her head that you might not like the idea but I told her not to be so silly. I said to her, goodness Rosie is your oldest friend; she would be so hurt if you didn't ask her. And of course I was right wasn't I!"

"Yes of course!" my response was mechanical. I had adopted the right tone and she was satisfied.

"What a day it will be. They will make such a handsome couple won't they?"

I nodded again.

"And to think that it was only a little while ago that, well...we've weathered a storm so to speak." And she passed her hand over her brow as if to erase the thought that lingered there.

"Her father is still getting used to the idea. I believe that men don't like to think that their little girls grow up." She laughed again but this time there was brittle edge to her voice.

"Anyway perhaps you could come and stay for some tea as well?"

I nodded again,

"Oh there is so much to arrange. It's just so difficult to know how we are going to manage. Of course her father and I would have liked to have made a proper day of it, but this blessed war has put paid to that. Just trying to locate some suitable material has been a nightmare.... and I don't know how we'll manage the wedding breakfast. I had always imaged when the day came that we could have had the reception here in Mote House but now, well that's totally out of the question. Still at least we have the church booked."

I could see that she had been given a new purpose. She was an unstoppable force.

I realised that she was waiting for me to make some kind of response.

"Lovely....yes!" I murmured inadequately aware of not having listened to her properly

Her eyes narrowed and she pressed her lips together as if slightly puzzled.

"Well let's hope so Rosie. We will certainly make sure that Millie and Thomas have the very best for their special day no matter what is thrown at us! I had just hoped that she would have been able to enjoy a different type of wedding with all her friends and family but it seems that we will have to make do with a smaller gathering. Well I mustn't keep you. We will see you later?"
As I walked down the drive the peeping snowdrops clustered under the trees bent their green fringed heads away from me as I passed.

The Wedding March 1942
Millie, Rosie and Thomas

On the day my dress didn't fit. The darts of the bodice hung in loose folds. Beatrice frowned and tutted when she came over to look at me. She pulled at the sagging fabric.

"I can't understand it, you only had a fitting a week ago. We'll just have to put some in pins…. to take it in somehow." Her irritation made her clumsy.

Millie looked breath-taking. A small floral coronet encircled the delicate waist length laced-fringed tulle veil. The ivory satin of the long sleeved dress fell into a full shirt from her waist to the ground, and delicate folds of box pleats at the shoulder, crossing at the bodice, emphasised her long neck. She wore a single drop pearl necklace and was just fitting on a matching earring as she turned to look at me.

"You've lost more weight haven't you!" she threw an accusing glance at me before turning back to the mirror. The line of covered buttons at the back strained against the fabric as she drew herself in. Stepping back from the mirror she pressed her hands over the front of the bodice and sighed.

I saw her glance over towards Beatrice who saw the action and immediately went over to fetch the arum lilies from the box. She handed the bouquet to her and nodded as they stood together before the mirror as Millie carefully held the long cascading bouquet before her; mother and daughter in silent conspiracy.

They both turned as Dulcie and Louise came in carrying a fur cape. Dulcie tugged to straighten her little Dutch style cap. Her puffed sleeves were short and the hem of the skirt was caught up in looped intervals with little yellow rosebuds.

"I do hope she'll be warm enough." She remarked to the room. "Come here child and put this on again."

Dulcie looked over at me with a grin of resignation and then stood patiently as Louise fussed over her, draping the cape over her shoulders before bringing together the little wire fastening at the neck.

"I don't know what's the matter with this. I think the fastening is too wide... as soon as the child moves it unfastens itself again." Beatrice turned to her but I went over.

"Let me look." I could see that the hook had opened out and bent it back. "There."

"I said that Rosie would fix it." Dulcie smiled at me. "You look nice."

"Thank you." We both looked over to Millie who was twisting in front of the mirror trying to catch the sight of her train.

"She always looks lovely doesn't she?" Dulcie wriggled her nose and then rubbed it.

We all contemplated the vision before us; it was true she presented a faultless picture.

"Now are we all ready?" Beatrice marshalled us.

"Dulcie, here is your posy basket and remember, be careful do not scuff your shoes." She turned back to me, realising that she had not made any changes and then looked at her wrist watch.

"Goodness just look at the time! Rosie there is no time now, you'll just have to do as you are. Now have we got everything? I'll see you in the church darling. I'll go down and tell your father that you're ready."

Louise turned to leave but a sudden thought made Beatrice turn. "Rosie, make sure that Ronald doesn't stand on her train. Don't spread it out until he is standing beside her and make sure that Dulcie has a handkerchief in the little pocket, there's one in the dressing table," and with a slight hesitation she finally allowed Louise to lead her away.

"Darling I'm sure that they can cope now, Rosie's more than capable...."

I could hear her protestations as they descended the stairs and then the front door finally closed and a brief silence enveloped the waiting house.

Millie stood away from the mirror. "Do you think he's already there?"

"Of course he will be there." I surveyed the jumbled room to ensure that she had not missed anything.

"And Jack?"

"He came back late last night, but he's got to leave first thing tomorrow."

"I'm glad that he'll be there to see me." She looked straight at me before picking up the lucky horseshoe on the dressing table.

"And I'm sure that Thomas will be pleased to have his best man with him" I replied offering her a glass of water.

Millie shook her head. "No goodness take it away, I don't want to get a water mark on this."

We walked downstairs to where Ronald was waiting at the foot of the steps.

"You look wonderful." He went to hold her arm but she shrugged him away

"Be careful! Just hold my train for me," and she picked up the hem of her dress carefully before they went from the house.

∞

The small congregation stood expectantly as Millie entered the church and she noted with delight the small gasps of approval that swept through the rows.

"Slowly!" she hissed to Ronald and tugged his arm back in warning as he threatened to break into a stride. She wanted to savour each exhilarating moment. She straightened her back and repositioned the large bouquet a little higher at her waist, and then at each passing pew she inclined her head to acknowledge their adulation. As they continued their slow possession down the aisle she saw Thomas turn his head and then, as if hooked on the same line, Jack turned back too. The two men gazed at her. Thomas's eyes held a look of awed adoration and pride but it was with triumph that she caught Jack's startled expression of greedy desire before he was able to turn back. She breathed in deeply, her lip curled, satisfied with her performance.

At the altar she turned, ceremoniously handing her bouquet back to me before rewarding Thomas with a wistful chaste smile.

"You look wonderful darling!" he scarcely dared to breath as he looked down at her.

She heard the catch in his throat and knew that her secret was safe. But I saw the look the passed between her and Jack. I understood the charade that was being played out. My longing to keep Thomas close to me had clouded my judgement and had allowed far greater hurt to be visited upon him. My meddling had bought about the very conclusion that I had sought to avoid. As I glanced to my left I saw Beatrice drawing herself up and then look towards the alter as if to offer up her thanks before she smiled as if a great burden had been lifted from her. She looked at me and an almost imperceptible frown flitted across her face before she turned away.

She knows! I thought. Of course she knows and now she is not sure whether I have found them out!

The service passed and I took no notice of the vows or the sermon that followed. The words droned, voices took up the lyrics for each hymn but I remained numb, stupefied by the treachery but rooted to the spot. I had become as lifeless as Lot's wife. The heaviness in my heart grew, enveloping me until I felt like a pillar of unyielding salt stone. I had not heeded the warnings. I had observed but not seen the consequences. I had focused on the detail and missed the bigger picture. Destiny had a way of proving herself to be beyond my petty interference. I had dammed the path of one small stream only to allow the river to flow. It had found another course to follow.

I hated Jack with a vengeance then. His careless dishonesty that I had actually used to further my ambition had caused me, and the one whom I loved more than life itself, to lose everything.

301

The organ rose into a triumph crescendo. Millie, holding Thomas close, began to move back down the aisle, accepting back her bouquet and receiving congratulations with a dignified smile. I turned to follow keeping in step with Dulcie. At the porch door I stepped alongside Thomas with Dulcie, as flower girl, standing next to Millie to balance the group. We waited for the photographer to capture the moment and then suddenly they moved forward as light swirls of petals rose and, caught by the wind, fluttered about their heads.

At the village hall trestle tables lined the two sides of the room. The three tiered cake set upon a stand took centre stage. Two tiny figures adorned the top tier. Speeches were made, the couple's good health toasted, the assembled crowd delighted in the chance to celebrate and momentarily forget the world beyond. Finally a gramophone was wound up and people waited for the bride and groom to take their place in the centre of the room and begin their dance. They moved to the music. Thomas held her lightly against him as if she were a delicate bloom that could be crushed.

"Now the best man with the bride and the groom and bridesmaid please."

The announcement had only just finished as Jack swept Millie to the floor. I looked up as Thomas dutifully held out his hand. We moved awkwardly around the room attempting to keep away from the swirling merriment of Millie and Jack. The strained silence between us added to our discomfort.

"I'm no good at this, sorry." My apology seemed pathetic. Thomas looked down and frowned. "Well it won't last long, it's only one dance that's required of us."

His cool words stung, my eyes blurred and smarted at the rebuke. I went to take my hand away but he held it firmly against his chest.

"You owe it to us both."

As the waltz finished so another started and suddenly we became caught up in the happy multitude of fellow guests determined to enjoy the dance. Thomas had let go of me but then I found that I could not escape the throng of people as they closed around us. Impatiently Thomas saw that I was being propelled against the tide of excited dancers. He looked about for Millie and saw that she and Jack were still dancing together and reluctantly drew me to him again.

"For once in your life Rosie just let me steer." He grimly kept pace with the movements of others so that we moved with them rather than against them.

"You could make more of a show you know. Offer some congratulations; say that you hope we will be very happy, that kind of thing. Or does that offend your sense of propriety?" His anger made his grip tighter, his hand on my back held me rigid so that my steps had to follow his.

I looked up at him. "I have only ever wanted the best for you."

"Well you've a funny way of showing it. Is it guilt or are you jealous?"

"Jealous? Why would you think that?"

"At the way you behaved to poor Millie, to us both, that and what we once were to each other, before you, well before I ceased to recognise the person you once were."

"Did I change then? How did I change?"

"Do you really need me to tell you that?" He spoke to the space above my head.

"To think that I once thought that we were, well, that we could have been close. I must have been deluded, caught up in a web of...!" He looked down angrily unable to finish.

"Deceit? Is that what you think? How so...by default? When have I ever betrayed you...is it wrong if I thought, if I believed that you were making a mistake?"

"Oh thank you Rosie. Saving me from a mistake! Why even God gave man free choice. But you Rosie, you would manipulate me and other poor devils like me because Miss Rosie Minton knows best. Is that it? I'm not yet married for an hour and already you have decided to call into question my choice of a wife and my marriage!"

I attempted to squirm away.

"Next time you look into that crystal ball of yours leave me out do you hear?" The music came to an end and he released me and turned away.

I watched as he pushed his way through the crowd and on finding Jack slapped him on the back before slipping his arm around Millie's waist reclaiming his bride.

I turned to go and found a small hand in mine. Dulcie looked up and smiled and her eyes held my gaze.

"Well little flower girl don't you just look wonderful, have you had something to eat? Shall we find something?"

I held her hand as a drowning man holds on to a raft and together we walked over to the trestle tables.

∞

There was to be no honeymoon. Thomas had just twenty four hours leave and was due to return to London on the early morning train but how Jack had managed to negotiate his leave was a mystery. He didn't appear to have any papers and remained unusually tight-lipped about the whereabouts of his unit.

Thomas and Millie spent their marriage night in the largest room at The Kings' Head next to the church where earlier that day they had exchanged their vows. Cherry trees behind the church yard had provided their own delicate pink confetti for the happy couple and it had swirled around the wide stone steps leading to the hotel leaving a carpet of petals for the day ahead. The early morning air was sweet and fresh. The village was still sleeping. Thomas opened the window quietly and leaned out. Like the village Millie was still sleeping. He looked back at her lying on the bed but hadn't the heart to wake her. The day had proved to be quite exhausting for her. At the reception she had been gay and lively but once they had left their guests and settled into their room he could see that it had tired her out. She had hardly touched the little supper of sandwiches and chilled wine that the hotel had provided for them. He had realised then that she was probably quite unsure of the nature of the marriage night. Even in these enlightened times he could see that he needed to reassure her and be careful.

She had not wished to undress in front of him: her natural modesty had made her shy. He had been disappointed. She had turned her head away and made no sound when he had made love to her so that he was unsure whether she too had been disappointed in him. He did not believe that he had hurt her although he was aware that for some women the first time could be difficult. As soon as he had reached his climax she had turned and moved away. He had hoped that they would talk for a while but she remained unresponsive when he attempted to caress her back; she had shaken away his hand and turned her face to the wall. His inexperience must have been to blame. He had failed her. Their marriage night had been a disaster and he was to blame. His stomach contracted and he found it difficult to breathe. He had dreamed of such a moment as this. He had imaged such joy. His delight in her would have been matched by her radiance. He had waited and longed for this time, it was to have been the zenith.

He tiptoed back to the bed and eased himself back onto the covers and lay looking up at the ceiling and the fringed lightshade of the central light. The quietness of the room unnerved him and he felt constrained by the stillness and for some inexplicable reason felt that he should not move. He couldn't even hear if Millie was breathing. They were lying side by side next to each other, man and wife and yet there was a wide gulf of confusion that separated them. He was conscious that he was holding his breath as if even the sound was an intrusion.

He tried to quell his fears and closed his eyes, willing the joyful events of the day to buoy him up. He saw in his mind's eye the church, remembering his pride as Millie had walked up the aisle toward him smiling to those at each side and then finally looking towards him. His heart fluttered. She had looked towards them both; Jack and he standing together waiting for her to arrive at his side. He and Jack. But when he tried to bring her into focus it seemed as if her eyes had slid away from him. She and Jack. His heart seemed to lurch. It had been a trick of the light. She had come to his side and had smiled up at him. Her beauty seemed to radiate everything around her, bathing them all in a glow. He had not imagined that. The occasion had made her serious from then. She had looked straight ahead only acknowledging him when he had slipped the ring on her finger.

He thought of his mother and father so proudly standing for the family photograph. His father somewhat overwhelmed by the occasion had awkwardly slipped an envelope into this hand at the reception murmuring that it was just a little something 'from mother and me'. The unexpected wedding gift from Kilndown Manor had surprised them all, but he had, with a sense of guilt, felt their particular shame once the beautiful ormolu clock held by two golden angles had been unwrapped, and seen the look that had passed between them both as if it had, by its magnificence, diminished them and their little offering.

Millie had wrinkled her nose, until Arnold Parsons had gone over to inspect the clock and drew Thomas to one side, shook his head, blew through his teeth and whispered.

"My word Thomas, what a specimen, that's worth a bob or two young man you know. It's an original French piece, worth a fortune. Hankered after one myself you know. Whew didn't expect to see one of those here today!"

And he went back to Louise's side still shaking his head in disbelief.

"What did he say to you?" Millie had asked when she saw Arnold walking away.

"He was just admiring the clock, said that he had always wanted one."

"Oh did he?" she smirked delightedly, "oh well, tell him we'll sell it if the price is right!"

He had looked down at her not knowing if she had been joking. And then when he had swept her to him for their first dance she had said crossly, "not so tight Thomas, you're squeezing me, I can't breathe." And as he loosened his hold he realised that he found himself out of the moment, as if an onlooker judging his own performance, and in judging found it wanting.

As soon as the dance ended Jack had come up to them.

"Congratulations mate, my turn I believe Mrs Fulwood. Your best man at your service."

He had slapped Thomas on the back and with a smirk indicated with his thumb towards the back of the room.

"Believe the bridesmaid awaits you....do your duty now!"

And with irritation, as if wrong footed, Thomas had found himself walking towards Rosie who had also looked none too pleased to be presented with a dancing partner.

His strange anger had risen in him as they came together. He wanted to absolve himself of the emotions that were threatening to unsettle his special day. She became a target to vent his hurt and disquiet upon. Her white face became tinged with pink as he confronted her. He had hardly heard her quietly spoken replies. He had not wanted to hear them. And then when he finally turned to go back to Millie he had seen her and Jack still together and watched as Jack held her in a tight embrace. He must have said something to make her laugh as she suddenly threw back her head and laughed delightedly before placing her cheek against his. Then he watched them come together to dance as one; one blonde head resting against the raven black.

Now in the light of the new day he felt ashamed of himself. It had been little Dulcie, such a sweet little thing, who had stood before him as he was gathering up the cards and said softly.

"It wasn't her fault y'know." Before quickly turning and running off before he had chance to question her enigmatic statement.

But of course he knew what she had meant. She wasn't speaking of Millie, it was Rosie. She must have seen Rosie. They had always been close, more like sisters than she and Millie.

He tucked his hands under his head. Rosie and Dulcie. They even looked alike. Had the same gift of knowing. And that was why he had been so cut up. That Rosie had done something so out of character. If Beatrice hadn't written he would have never come home and then it could have been too late. Millie had been so magnanimous and brave. She had said that she couldn't blame Rosie for not realising the danger that she had been in. What a contrast he had seen then; Rosie so secretive and Millie so open and forgiving. It had made him realise that Millie had always needed him. She had said that it was only when she had been so ill that she knew for certain that they were meant to be together. She had admitted that she had always been a little in love with him even when they were just children but didn't know if he felt the same way. It had been so difficult for her to put this into words. She said that she feared that if she had been too open it might have frightened him off.

He had been such a fool worrying and imagining things. It was just marriage jitters. Nothing more. To think that he had put two and two together making five and even questioned the motives of his oldest friend and of his own wife. It was pretty low of him. The room was getting brighter and he knew that his time with her was limited. He had to make the early train and yet he was reluctant to wake her. She seemed so peaceful. Her golden hair splayed about her. He held the strands gently between his

308

fingers. He still could not believe that she was his. *'For better for worse in sickness and in health.'* His to protect and care for, *'for ever and ever Amen.'*

She stirred and murmured. Silently he moved towards the outside of the bed so that she would not be disturbed and rose to dress.

The church clock struck six and he knew that he would have to wake her. Time was running away with him. He knelt by the bed and stroked her head.

"Darling, my dearest, its time."

Her eyes fluttered open not focussing at first, and then settling on him she frowned.

"What time is it?" Her voice was drowsy with sleep.

"Six. I have to make the London train darling."

"Mmm." She licked her lips trying to fashion them for speech. "Oh God!" she muttered "it's the middle of the night." Did you have to wake me. It's still dark!"

"But I have to get going darling. I'm not sure when I'll next be on leave. Things are beginning to hot up."

"And you have to go back to play desk war games up there?"

"Something like that...yes." He stood and smiled down at her. "Nothing for you to worry about anyway."

"Who said that I was worried?" She propped her head up against the pillow. "It's not as if you're on the front line or anything is it."

"No, no nothing like that; snug and safe up there."

"Mmm well you better get off then. Ring me or leave a message or something when you get there."

"Sorry that it's been such a short time for us to be together. No honeymoon or anything I promise that I'll try and make it up to you."

Her eyes narrowed. "Well I'm sure I'll muddle through until then."

"That's the ticket. Chin up old girl."

He bent down to kiss her. She closed her eyes.

"Okay lover boy. On your way now. Need to catch up on my beauty sleep."

She looked up at him waiting for him to speak again.

"I love you my darling. You have made me the happiest of men."

"Of course I have." She smiled, and as he lingered by the door and turned to blow her a kiss, she too raised her hand to her lips before turning to settle down to sleep. As he closed the door gently behind him he thought he heard the quietest sigh.

∞

He had meant to leave much earlier and take his leave of Ron and Betty to thank them properly for their contribution to the reception. The cake had been much admired. As it was he just popped his head around at the back of the bakery and shouted his thanks before continuing his walk to the station. He set himself a good pace and by the time he had reached the pond he knew that he could afford to shorten his stride.

He glanced briefly along the road towards Mote House, heard the ducks muffled squabbles as they moved away at his approach and then looking up realised that Rosie was just coming from the pub. She shut the door and wrapped her coat around her and started to walk towards him. With her head down fumbling with the buttons she didn't look up until they were almost level. She stopped and stood aside to let him pass turning her head towards the wall.

He felt a lurch of regret. "Rosie. I feel I need to apologise. I said some....well...I didn't exactly cover myself in glory."

She looked up at him quickly before she lowered her head. Her eyes seemed bigger than he had remembered. She seemed to have shrunk. Her worn coat hung loosely around her frame.

"No need." She mumbled and went to move past him.

"No, wait." He caught her sleeve.

His action surprised her and she started back.

310

"Rosie!"

She twisted her sleeve from his grasp.

"Rosie! No stop!" He caught hold of her again. "We can't part like this."

"What's done is done." She shook herself free again. "Goodbye Thomas."

She ducked beneath his arm and strode off towards the pond skirting the mallards that were newly irritated by yet another intrusion. They ungainly waddled away from her pecking out at each other in their disgust.

He watched her quickly walk away from him. Her little figure seemed hunched and weary as she rounded the trees before disappearing along the road towards Mote House..

A great sadness settled on him. The happiness of the morning evaporated. As he continued on his walk to the station a perverse mantra started up and peevishly kept step with his stride, one that he could not shake off, *'you've gained a wife but lost your soul'*. The repetition irked him and he struggled to throw it off but it petulantly changed its words, *'marry in haste, repent at leisure.'* Over and over in his head, *'I'm going mad'* he thought.

It wasn't until he reached the station that the words finally died. The platform appeared to be deserted. He felt utterly alone. He glanced along the glistening grey track and in the stillness could only hear his heart pounding. The beat of his blood boomed rhythmically. A few fellow travellers joined him from the waiting room. He acknowledged their presence with a brief nod of his head. The pounding in his head grew louder until he realised that it was the sound of the train nearing the station. It drew itself to a halt signalling its great satisfaction of having arrived so triumphantly before the escape of billowing steam drowned out the clatter of doors banging open.

Thomas found an empty carriage and settled back into his seat. He closed his eyes and attempted to shut out the prying

311

attention and judgements of the day. Eventually the rhythm of the train lulled him into an uneasy sleep.

Millie didn't return to Chatham after her wedding. She had first kept close to home at Ivy Leaf Cottage with Beatrice and Ronald. They convinced Thomas that Millie would be better off staying with them until he was able to make plans for a home of their own, especially as he had been unable to obtain any leave since their spring wedding or make any other plans for their future.

In early May Beatrice had announced that Millie had been invited to stay with an aunt of Ronald's in the Cotswolds who had been recently widowed. Millie was to remain with her aunt throughout that summer. Then in June Beatrice excitedly announced the good news that Millie and Thomas were happy to find that Millie was expecting a baby.

"Imagine! A honeymoon baby!" she told Betty and Ron. "Ronald and I are so happy for them both. I wish that she would come home but she insists that poor Ronald's aunty is on her own and struggling to pick up the pieces. Her husband did everything for them you see. And our Millie is such a comfort to her."

The hot summer cast a languid pall over the village before the tall cerise spikes of the rosebay willow herb swaying in the hedges announced the arrival of July.

Rosie received no letters from Thomas. She carried on at Mote House.

Then in August Beatrice excitedly pronounced the arrival of their granddaughter. It was a girl and Thomas and Millie had decided to call her Katharine, after the actress Katharine Hepburn.

"And there we were thinking it had been a honeymoon baby!" She laughed incredulously.

"These young people, you can't blame them in these precarious days. So many young men risking their lives for us."

313

It was accepted. Thomas and Millie had been a little reckless. It explained why the wedding had been such a rushed affair. The villagers nodded their heads. Well there was a war on after all. Rosie sat listlessly on a chair in the kitchen and listened to Ethel. "Well I didn't expect to hear that! Always thought that Thomas had a sensible head on his shoulders. No wonder the wedding was arranged so quickly. One moment announcing their engagement, and then the next thing, the wedding."
She counted back on her fingers.
"When did Thomas come home to see her? Why it must have been the end of November or was it December? We had that nasty smog when he turned up unannounced, do you remember? And she had had been so ill that previous month when she'd had that do with her appendix."
She counted again ticking off the months, "He came back in December so…. January, February, March, …goodness she was three months or more gone on her wedding day…..who would have thought it! And a white wedding in the church!"
She sat back in the chair. Her eyes narrowed. "Scheming little minx, for all her airs and graces with that mother of hers so high and mighty well, well and she had her designs on our Jack too if I'm not mistaken!"
Ethel looked sharply across at Rosie. "And you've nothing to say for yourself. I thought you were supposed to be close. Didn't you know about all these carrying on?"
She sighed crossly. "No, for once 'Miss Know- it- all' didn't know it all did you!"
"Well I'm disappointed in him. I always had a soft spot for him. But that's men….can't help themselves. Disgusting creatures all of them…. I hope you realise how lucky you are not to attract their attention."
Rosie met her eye. "Yes thank you for pointing that out. I would have never have known had you not constantly told me how inadequate I have been, and what a disappointment to you."

314

"Now don't you take that tone with me...."

But Ethel spoke to the closed door that Rosie banged behind her on her way out.

She strode across the empty bar pulled at the front door and stepped outside. The heat and the glare of the sun took her by surprise. She held up her hand to shield her eyes. The road was empty. The villagers had returned from Sunday church and were preparing the Sunday lunch, scrag end of lamb or Woolton Pie replacing their pre-war roasts of beef.

Rosie turned up the road towards the pond and then headed down the lane towards Mote House before suddenly doubling back and striding back down the hill towards the station. Her anger dictated the pace until her calf muscles protested at the urgency of her stride. The heat of the day had caused a haze to settle on the landscape below her. A skylark wheeled and called above her, whilst at the hedgerow the bees crawled inside the fat heads of purple clover. Reaching the station she turned left and followed the lane past the lodge to Kilndown Manor.

Lime trees in full languid leaf cooled and shaded the long drive. She slowed her pace to an amble, uneasy at the thought of the sad interview ahead, conscious of the untidy picture that she presented and of the perceived intrusion. The old lady was frail; she knew already that she would not see out the month. This would be the only chance before her time came. She was annoyed to think that she had not come sooner and was now afraid of how much she could accomplish without tiring her; how to finally provide some peace and secure some resolution before her end came. And it was a way to salve her own conscience, it would make amends.

In the darkened drawing room the air was stale. Lady Faversham lay on the chaise lounge wrapped in a shawl despite the heat. Strands of thin hair clung to her scalp as a worn cap. Her cheeks were sunken and her white skin had a yellow pallor. Rosie was conscious of her laboured breath and yet her pink rimmed eyes were sharp as she motioned for her to sit nearer, beckoning with her thin arm to draw the chair close by.

"You've come alone this time. No Thomas I see," she pursed her lips in disappointment and sighed.

"No he can't come…"

"I know, I know! The war. Always a war to take them away." She shook her head slowly.

"It took my dear boy you know. Did you know that?"

Rosie nodded.

"Such a beautiful boy he was. My only son you know. It took the best. Stole them away." Her voice became harsh with the effort of speech and remembrance of her heartache.

"And now there's no one left. I am the last you see. The last one."

"A mother can never get over the loss of a child. Unnatural….not the order of things d'you see?"

She reached out her hand to Rosie. "And is he safe? Will we lose him too?"

Rosie took her hand gently. "Well he's in London at the moment. They need him for some intelligence stuff. We don't really know much about it. He can't tell us really."

"Always was a clever boy that one. Always saw it all those years ago. So much like my own dear boy." And she shook her head again and withdrew her hand.

"Well I have brought some good news for you." Rosie slowly began.

"Thomas and his wife have a child. She was born this summer, a little girl. You have a great, great, granddaughter."

Lady Faversham stared at Rosie waiting for her to continue.

Rosie shifted on her chair, "Ronald's daughter Millie. She's had a little girl. They've named her Katharine." She waited to see if she had understood as her expression remained immobile.

"Your grandson Ronald has a granddaughter.

316

"I understand lineage! She said sharply. You don't need to spell it out for me girl."

"No of course. I beg your pardon."

"Mmm." She was still piqued. "I'm not senile you know. Not in my grave, just yet."

A silence hung between them. Rosie felt compelled to seize the moment before an impasse was reached.

"Yes , I'm sorry to have appeared to be so rude. It's just that I hadn't realised until today that of course your family goes on doesn't it, through Thomas and Millie's daughter and then perhaps a son for them in the future. Your line continues." She ploughed on, "knowing how much Thomas has meant to you….. I was worried that the news might not have reached you….bad news travels fast but good news…well perhaps a little slower than it should."

"You meant that I might be dead before the news came to Kilndown, is that it!" Rosie saw the slightest curl of her lip before she drew draw herself up and considered Rosie.

"Ring the bell for me." She waved over to the table.

They sat and waited. The door was knocked softly and the maid came in.

"Fetch my writing things."

The maid bobbed and went out closing the door behind her.

"When you came here with Thomas I thought that you and he had some kind of understanding. Mind I thought then that it was strange choice for him to make. Then the next thing I hear is him and that silly girl of Ronald's. Mind I've heard that she is a pretty thing. Takes after her mother they say. Parson's daughter….."

She stopped to catch her breath, and Rosie leant forward.

"I'm fine, don't fuss. Just too much talking."

She sighed and lay back closing her eyes.

"I need a moment."

The door was knocked again and the maid came forward with a tray with paper and pen. She placed it on the table by the chaise lounge and then withdrew staring at Rosie before turning towards the door.

After a few minutes Lady Faversham roused herself and sat up wearily.

"Write this down." She waved at the tray and back at Rosie. Rosie took up the pen.

"I am appointing you as my executor to my will." She waved with irritation. "No don't write that, I'll tell you what to write in a moment. You are to inform my solicitor that I wish to amend my will. This is to be my last will and testament. I want you to write it down now and I will sign it before you and Nancy. And then when Hawkins comes he can be put into his incomprehensible legalistic jargon that he is so fond of, pompous little man." She allowed herself to smile.

"And all I ask of you… is your complete discretion, is that understood?"

"Well, let us begin."

∞

Two weeks later the village heard the news that Lady Faversham had passed away.

"It was a good age though," Betty twirled the paper bag to seal in the scones. "Ninety- three or four or thereabouts I heard. "Still even with all that money I shouldn't have liked to have been down there in that old mausoleum of a place all on her own. Can't have seen a soul from one day to another." She shuddered at the thought. ""Poor old soul."

Ron came into the shop perspiring from the heat of the day and his still hot ovens.

"What do they say…life is such hard work it kills you in the end!" He rubbed his handkerchief across his forehead.

"Ron Ticehurst! You should be ashamed of yourself making jokes like that!" but she grinned in spite of herself.

"Mind I shouldn't think that she ever did a day's work in her life. What say you Mrs Simmons?"

Phyllis shook her head shyly and reached across to take the bag, and being encouraged by them both then tentatively offered her own piece of conversation.

"My Joseph once went down there years ago when Lord Faversham was still alive. They were having problems with some vermin in the outhouses. Wanted to know if there was anything stronger that they could use. My Joseph said, 'Well Sir you could always try a cat!'"

Betty and Ron looked at each other and burst out laughing and Phyllis encouraged by their laughter allowed herself to smile at the memory.

"What do you think will come of the old place now....it's seen better days? The upkeep must be tremendous and the repairs alone would cost a small fortune...that's if you could find anyone around here to do it!"

Ron looked towards Betty as she leaned forward on the counter. "Wonder if them at Rosemount will see anything of it. I heard that she never had anything to do with her own mother after she ran away with that artist husband of hers and threw in her lot with him. Met him in Paris at an exhibition when she was doing the Grand Tour bit... so I heard."

"Who told you that, you've never said that before? No you've got that wrong Betty love. He came from Paris, quite a leading light in that circle. Had made his mark in London Arnold Parsons told me, said he'd once seen some of his early work up there in some fancy gallery, and very good it was too. Fetched a good price according to him."

"So why do they live so down at heel now then!" Betty turned back." Act as if they haven't two pennies to rub together."

"Fashions change I reckon and don't forget I'm talking about years ago, before the last bad show, turn of the century stuff.....all classical romantic stuff, nude woman and whatnot."

319

"Oh really Ron and what do you know about that! Sorry Mrs Simmons!"

"Ron grinned, "I've got my sources," and he winked at Phyllis who had tried to avoid his eye and was busying herself by putting the scones into her shopping bag.

"Reckon it will be another big do though like the last time", he said to the two women who were shaking their heads. Betty tutted.

"Well of course it will be a big affair, she's hardly going to a pauper's grave is she!"

"And she's never had anything to do with Beatrice and Ronald either, and he's her grandson." Betty looked out at the road squinting against the light as if she could imagine the funeral cortege passing by, "...and to think" she mused, "that she would have been a great great, grandmother to Millie's little one."

"Not she would have been.... she was, Betty. Though I don't think Millie went down to see her, so she would never have seen the baby."

"I've heard that she's a bonny little thing, got a full head of hair already, really dark...must take after Ronald's side of the family."

"And coming so soon after the wedding." Phyllis ventured, "quite a shock for Beatrice and Ronald I would think."

"Can't blame these young folk these days. Never know what is lurking round the corner. Many of the men not coming back just like the last time. And she hasn't seen him since they were wed. Hard on these young ones I reckon." Betty mused,

"Who's to know when we'll see any of them. Parsons have taken it hard. First Mote House turned upside down, hardly anywhere to call their own, and then losing those three young men that he took on. Only poor Forrester left to see to everything, the hedges and lawns alone take a good week to trim and then there's that Palm House."

"Don't think he has been able to keep that up, Betty, had to let that go. Don't think he could get the coal for the heating."

320

"Wonder how they've taken the news about Millie and little Katharine. Can't think that Louise would have been too pleased."
"I thought that she and Jack Minton were sweet on each other a while back. You always saw them together in the swanky car of his gallivanting here and there." Phyllis offered.
"Huh, I expect Beatrice was pleased that that didn't last. Jack was always a fast one. Such a handsome devil though just like his poor father. Ethel must find it hard without a man at home."
The thought of Jack and Archie cast a sudden gloom about them.
"Aye, a real tragedy that was. Always liked the man, had time for everyone despite what the gossips would have you believe."
Ron spoke firmly and Phyllis opened her mouth and closed it suddenly.
Ron shrugged sadly and turned to the back door, "Time waits for no man."
Betty and Phyllis watched him retreat.
"I know he was a man's man as they say...."Phyllis spoke quietly, gaining confidence now that it was just the two of them, "But they do say that he led Ethel a merry dance. I think she had to put up with a lot from him."
Betty breathed in deeply, "who can say what happens behind closed doors."
"I suppose I've been so lucky with Joseph." Phyllis struggled to regain some sympathy for her argument. "Such an even temper, never complains, just gets on with things. I don't know what I'd do without him."
Betty compared the two of them and waited for Phyllis to continue.
"Of course I only speak as I find. Archie was always civil with me and Joseph, we had no cause to complain, but there are always those that say.....well... there's no smoke without fire!"
Betty smiled benignly.
"Will that be all then Phyllis? Can I get you anything else?"

Phyllis realised the shared confidences were over and her shyness suddenly returned. "No, no, that's all! Thank you Betty." And she tugged at the door and stepped out quickly, the bell signalled her departure.

Betty turned and considered the cat who was sitting by the door of the back room. It had been washing its back, one leg stretched out to balance its position but seeing Betty watching him he stopped and sat up, staring at her with green eyes.

"What say you? What do you think then? There's something not quite right here isn't there?"

He blinked his affirmation and then stood, his tail pointing straight as he glided his way through the shop before standing patiently at the door asking her to release him to the outdoor world.

"Yes you go and find out what's what." She bent down to stroke his head, opened the door, and watched him as he made his way purposefully down the road.

In the distance she saw Rosie coming from the lane from Mote House and called out to her.

Rosie looked round to see who was calling her before she glanced back up the road.

"Come here Rosie."

Rosie nodded, stopped by the cat that had waited to be admired and stroked, and then carried on up towards the bakery.

"Kept you a loaf Rosie. Your mother hasn't been out for it today. Is everything alright?"

"Yes fine. We were going over the accounts last night. It was late before we finished that's all."

"And now you've had a busy day down at the house before this evening's work." She was concerned. Rosie looked so worn out.

Rosie squinted and screwed up her nose and took the small loaf.

"Has your mother heard from Jack?"

Rosie shook her head "No nothing at all. Mind he doesn't write much even when we do get a letter. Never one for putting pen to paper." she grinned ruefully and raised her eyebrows.

"And Thomas?"

"No." She pursed her lips and pressed them into a thin line as if to stop her words.

Betty tried another approach.

"How's Millie keeping and the baby?" She began brightly.

"They're both fine I think."

"Well perhaps you could do me a little favour. I have some little baby things here. Could you sound her out see if she would like them? I don't like to go unannounced and she hasn't been here for me to speak to her. I would have spoken to her mother but, well, it's not always that easy with Beatrice."

"Yes of course."

She turned to go but Betty held out her hand and touched her sleeve.

"No don't go. I wanted to ask you if you knew anything about the funeral."

Rosie stared into the distance. "Its next week. Thursday. All the Latterbridges will be there." And she shook herself. "Bye Betty thanks for the bread."

Betty observed her retreating figure; *she's a strange one and such a sad little thing these days. No spark like she used to have* and she shook her head. *No life for these young ones.*

Mote House 1942 Christmas
Thomas and Rosie

They had made a big effort to cheer the men up. A large fir tree stood in the dining room and brown paper wrapped presents had been clustered around the base.

Louise was arranging some springs of holly and pine cones along the mantelpiece. She had made some red bows and placed tall white candles at intervals in between the foliage.

"How does it look?"

"Splendid as usual dear." Arnold turned to go, the newspaper in his hand.

"I don't think you even looked Arnold! Well it's the best that I can do with so little at hand. When I think how is used to look in the old days!" she sighed.

Arnold looked back at her, *it's hard on the old girl,* he thought. *Place not our own and no end in sight, blasted war. Churchill and his not the end but the end of the beginning twaddle! Our chaps sent out on bombing Berlin and the French scuttling ships left, right and centre!* He despaired at the carnage, *and this blasted government squeezing us every which way, what with the national defence contributions and excess profits tax; we'll all go down the pan at this rate. Businesses can't take much more.* He rubbed his hand over his face.

The loud cheerful strains of 'Don't sit under the apple tree' played from the recesses of the library. *Blast!* He had wanted a quiet few moments to himself. *Damned American tripe!* And he walked slowly up the stairs.

Outside the light rain turned icy and the paths glistened. Rosie looked out into the dark, shining her torch before her. She stepped tentatively on the path testing the grip of her shoes against the ice. Her foot slid across the surface. Leaving the path she walked on the whitened verge where she could feel a slight crunch of the frosted grass. Trudging down the drive she

324

concentrated on her progress before stopping with a jolt. She knew he was waiting. She turned and left the verge and walked back over to the summer house.

Inside the house the lighted tip of his cigarette gave away his position and the smell of smoke lingered on the air.

"You knew didn't you." his low voice came to from the darkened room within.

She shone her torch and he turned away the sudden glare of light in his eyes. He was sitting on one of the wicker chairs his foot resting on an upturned pot. He made no attempt to move. Training her torch around she located the second chair and sat down waiting for him to speak again, wrapping her coat closer around her as the cold crept in.

"I was waiting for you. They said that you were here. I said that I would come over and walk you home."

"Thank you." She acknowledged his presence, still waiting for him to continue.

"How did they think that...how did I get played.... for being such a fool?" His anger and his misery had made him inarticulate.

"They took advantage Thomas. They didn't have much time to think. It was the only way they could deal with it. She was desperate. They hoped that you could come to accept it. Given enough time. Besides you were always half in love with her, from the very beginning admit it Thomas."

"So I was the willing bait!"

"It was a solution. They didn't act with malice. They thought that you could be happy, that she could make you happy and they encouraged you. A scandal would be avoided, they were at their wits end until you came back and seemed so taken up with her. What did you expect them to do? Ignore the very answer that was staring in their face....when you were so determined to be with her...and you had wanted her! Remember you asked her to marry you."

Thomas drew on his cigarette the tip glowed red.

"And do you think that I am happy, happy to accept another man's child?"

"It's not the child that is the question. It's another that you should be asking."

"What... who's child is it?"

"No not that."

"What then."

"The question is about you and Millie. Can you ever be happy with her, will she make you happy?"

"Say it Rosie!" He threw away the last of the cigarette and turned back to her.

"You mean will she make me as happy as I was with you?"

"I didn't say that." She rose to take her leave.

"No you didn't but I deserve that. Even on our wedding night..."

"No Thomas don't speak of that, it's not right."

"Because you knew how it would be. I have been so blind. So stupid..."

He reached out outwards her and finding her, pulled her to him and held her. Her body folded into his. His hand cradled the back her neck so that her cheek rested against his, and he stroked her hair softly. And then turning her face towards him he kissed her, his lips closing on hers, and feeling her warmth relishing his touch he pulled her harder into him, passionately clinging to her as a man drowning. She could feel the urgency of his desire as he trembled. And she could not resist him; her mouth sought his and again she drank him in as they stayed locked in their embrace of mutual longing.

He was the first to speak. Still holding her close his warm breath caressed her cheek.

"God what a mess Rosie. What I have got us into? Why did I ever doubt you? It was unforgivable. You must have hated me. What a fool I was. Still am. What have I dragged you into?" His ragged hot breath warmed her head.

She held him close as he raged at himself, trying to comfort him. She could feel the pain of his confusion as he wrestled with his emotions.

"And is this is what love is? It just feels so right."

He was seized with doubt. "But it is hopeless isn't it! What am I to do...I'm in love with you. Why did it take me so long to see it? I want you to be mine. I need you..... you do know that?"

She pressed him to her.

"I must have you Rosie."

"I know. You will."

"Really. You want me too. Do you really love me?"

"Of course I do. As if you have to ask. I always have: you are such a dolt."

Her words suddenly freed him. They laughed, delighting in each other, before he once again drew her towards him to kiss her, crushing her lips to his, exploring her mouth with his tongue and savouring her, hardening against her until her breath came in harsh sharp bursts and her longing flooded her.

"So what are we to do?"

"We'll find a way."

He stroked her face. "You are so beautiful, my beautiful Cassandra." His grave voice still trembled with his passion.

She roused herself, shaking off the niggling warning.

"I need to get back, walk with me?"

He took the torch from her and together they made their way back to the drive. She took his arm as they slithered and slid down the path holding each other for support until they reached the lane and found more even ground.

Before they rounded the corner to the village pond he stopped pulling her back.

"Can we do this? Is there a way through for us?"

"Just trust me Thomas."

He caught her up to him and kissed her gently. "I do."

She could hear her own fear rising as she sought to reassure him.

"You need to be with your wife and daughter for now. The child is innocent in all of this, she deserves a father…. you as her father. Don't let your anger come between you and her. "

He withdrew from her aghast at her words.

"Thomas listen to me!" She shook him.

"We are all players in this life. Sometimes our roles are compromised… complicated. If you do something rash now we may not be able play our parts. Millie needs you to love her daughter. Accept the child. Yes she was stupid and she has paid the price for her stupidity. We all make mistakes."

The cold night seeped into them. Thomas struggled, torn with a desire for her but knowing that he had to accept her terms and confront the reality of his life.

"But where does that leave us, you and me Rosie?"

"You have to be patient. There will be a way."

"But I must see you before I leave. When can I see you?"

"I said to trust me Thomas. Go home now. I'll get word to you. Leave it to me."

She pulled away from him. He watched her making her way round the pond towards the Papermakers Arms before he then crossed the road to Ivy Leaf Cottage with only a waning half crescent moon to light his way.

The next morning he woke, stiff from lying in their cramped bed and tired from the constant demands of a hungry child forcing him from his sleep through the night. Millie lay exhausted her cheeks were pale. The little cot had been squeezed between their bed and the window. He walked around the foot of the bed to look down on her. She was rosy in her sleep. Her little arms held up at each side as if she were waiting to be held. A soft bonnet of black hair contrasted with her translucent skin. In the morning light he could see a tiny milky bubble on her lip. She was quite exquisite, a beautiful child. He felt a rush of love for her. She was so helpless and vulnerable. What had the world in store for her?

328

He was torn between the desire to hold her or to leave her undisturbed in the warmth of her cosy cocoon. She fidgeted as if knowing that she was watched and kicked her little legs before sighing and settling down to a deeper sleep, her short breaths causing her delicate nostrils to widen and close imperceptibly with each quiet breath.

The room was cold. He reached across the cot and raised the curtain. A hoar frost had painted crisp leaf patterns on the window, he could not see out.

He padded back to the chair where he had placed his clothes and started to dress quietly. Once on the landing he listened to see if anyone else has stirred. The house was silent. Carefully he tiptoed down the stairs, pausing only when a traitorous creak threatened to proclaim his descent.

The door into the kitchen was ajar. A wooden clothes horse by the table was covered in little garments.

He went into the front room. A small tree had been placed by the window. The decorations were too big for it. They had been purchased in the past for a tree of greater proportions. A wreathed fairy sat astride the tip holding her wand aloft as if to grant a wish. He smiled at her. He was in need of her magic; to be a child again and to believe in the magic of Christmas and fairy tales! What he would give to turn the clock back and to be that little boy again. When he believed that the world was safe and he knew his place within it.

The fire had been set with kindling ready for the day but the house had been chilled by the night and the air seemed clammy and damp. He walked back to the kitchen, momentarily hesitating, feeling his intrusion as a stranger, before deciding to go ahead and boil the kettle. He walked to the window. There were no curtains at either side just a suspended lace curtain that hung horizontally from a narrow pole.

The leaf patterns were not so well defined. He was able to see though their shapes and look on the garden. The path was white

329

and the bushes rigid with their mantel of ice. As he looked out, his breath melting small patches, he could see a few faint flurries of bewildered light flakes not knowing whether to continue falling or swirl upwards back from where they had first come. The kettle announced that it had boiled the water and he poured the water into the teapot and sat the cosy on top to allow it to brew. But he could not settle and returned to his watch at the window. The uncertain flakes were continuing their irregular dance. His own inactivity was tormenting him. He needed to stay but wanted to be gone. Making the tea allowed him a distraction. It had kept him to a task. But as soon as he had swallowed the scalding liquid he was once again wracked with indecision.

Rosie had told him that he must play his part but he didn't know how to begin. The previous evening on his return, Beatrice and Ronald had been wary of him, Millie used the child as a defence; the duties of feeding, and changing the baby allowed her an irreproachable occupation and negated the necessity to talk. But they were all uncomfortable, attempting to be cheerful. The artifice was all too apparent.

Ronald had been the first to succumb to silence as the stilted conversation limply petered out. They had resorted to banal pleasantries and small talk. Beatrice had at first been able to act as hostess, busying herself with food preparation until she finally excused herself and was able to escape into her kitchen. The faint clattering of the dishes provided the opportunity to remain out of sight. Ronald had stoked the fire petulantly savaging the coals with the poker.

The sound of a tread on the stair woke him from his reverie. Millie appeared at the doorway. She glanced across at him. Dark shadows accentuated her pale skin. Her hair hung about her face.

She was carrying the child. He went across and wordlessly took the baby into his own arms. Then he indicated the kitchen chair with one free hand.

"Sit down Millie. I've made a pot. It's still warm."

It was the first morning that they had been on their own without either Beatrice or Ronald being present. Millie poured her tea. She looked across at him as he settled the child on his lap. He cradled her head in the crook of his arm and she looked up quizzically at him and frowned, the bubbles lingering on her lips.

"She is wondering who this strange man is," he smiled down at her.

Millie watched them as he rocked her gently. "Mother always said that you had a special way with babies. You could always settle Dulcie even when she had colic." Her voice was faint as if she were speaking to herself.

Thomas looked across at her. "And am I to know whose child I am fathering?"

She swallowed and looked down. "I can't Thomas. I'm sorry. I just can't." Her voice started to break.

"So you do know who the father is?"

"Thomas!" She jerked upright and tears which had threatened to spill flowed unchecked.

He remained unmoved. "So what is the story that we follow with the rest of the village. That we…. that she was conceived before we were wed… is that the line that they have been given?"

"Something like that, yes." She held her head in her hands.

"And the baby was premature no doubt." She shook her head "No not that."

"So when exactly was she born?"

"July, July the third."

"My word so you were four, no nearly five months pregnant when we were married!"

She nodded again.

"So why couldn't you marry the father of your child. What was stopping you? Was he married already?"

"No, nothing like that." A note of bitterness crept into her voice. "I couldn't tell him. I knew that he wouldn't have anything to do with me if he found out. I always hoped that...that we would have a future. I don't know what I thought. And then it was too late. Mother guessed. And he...,"she trailed off.

"Don't ask me any more Thomas it breaks my heart. She's all that matters now. She's everything to me."

"And what am I to you Millie? Did you never think about what I had wanted?"

"I always thought that you wanted me!"

"But not that I should be loved in return? What kind of marriage did you think we could have...one of convenience, for the sake of the child and your reputation? And what would you say if I said that I gave up someone I loved for you?"

"Who!" She rounded on him her eyes blazed.

"So suddenly you have realised that I may have had a life of my own, one that did not, does not include you!"

"Who is she? I demand to know!"?"

"Yes you may well ask Millie. But I don't think that you're in any position to demand. Besides it was a hypothetical question. And you have answered it. You did not consider my feelings in this matter when I made my vows to you in good faith."

He looked at the baby still sleeping in his arms.

"We will carry on with this charade for the sake of this little one, but only on my terms."

Millie looked across the table. The boy whom she had always been able to manipulate had turned into his own man. His easy affability had been replaced with a severity that she had not realised he possessed.

"I see that I have little choice." A note of petulance crept into her tone.

"Your choices became limited on the night that you decided to conceive an unwanted child, and the day that you made your vows in church. I could walk away even now, and believe me when I say that it is still a temptation. So don't drive me to it"

"So I live with that threat do I?

"No I have not made threats. I have promised to support you, for better for worse and I will. Just don't give me reason to regret my decision.

He stood up and handed the child to her. He stretched and shook himself as if to rid himself of his worries as a dog shakes off the water on its coat.

He walked towards the window. Whilst they had been sitting there thick snow had started to fall. The world had turned white.

∞

When Rosie turned over she realised that she felt as if a weight had lifted from her; she was happier than she had expected to feel. She stared at the ceiling. The old cracks in the plaster seemed more delineated there was a different glow on the faded wallpaper. She didn't want to stir. All night she had dreamed of Thomas. He had consumed her thoughts and now as she lay wrapped tightly in the heavy bedclothes his words came back to her. "I'm in love with you...I want you to be mine."

And so you shall! She smiled, and pulling back the clothes she tested her feet on the cold linoleum before slipping them into the slippers that had been cast aside the night before.

She dragged the nightgown from the hook and hugged it around herself.

She went towards the door but could not resist looking outside. She drew back the curtains. There were a few light flakes tumbling. She could see Thomas watching a similar scene and sensed his apprehension. He would soon be gone. They would only have a short time for now, but it would be enough.

333

Ethel would catch the bus to Cranbrook. The morning would be theirs. She ran a shallow bath, trying unsuccessfully to sink under the water that lapped inadequately at her sides. *When this war is over I'm going to fill the bath to the very brim!* she thought.

Back in her bedroom she considered her clothes, none of them fitted her well and she was disappointed at her reflection in the mirror topped dressing table. No matter which way she turned she could only see a small portion of herself. The snowflakes had thickened and whitened the paths, *But it will stop soon*, and she reassured herself.

"I'm off now Rosie d'you hear!"

She heard the door open and close and putting her face close to the window she could see her mother carefully walking up the road before disappearing from view to wait at the stop by Simmons shop.

A fluttering of excitement caught in her stomach. She turned back to the room and started to tidy it up. She stripped the bedding, bought fresh sheets from the cupboard on the landing and made the bed smoothing down the quilted covers. When everything was in order she went downstairs and waited. The door from the kitchen led out to the back yard. Impatiently she watched the hands of the clock move slowly to the next mark and then the next. Finally she opened the door and looked out. The bus had left. There was no one waiting. She went into the bar, the roads still tinged white were deserted. Thomas came out from Ivy Leaf Cottage and walked up towards the pond. She ran back to the kitchen. She waited until he had started on the lane to Mote House before she opened the door. She waved to him to go around the back skirting the tall frozen bulrushes that screened the worn path. He turned to make sure that there was no one about before he walked swiftly behind the bushes and came in. She closed the door behind him.

Ivy Leaf Cottage 2009
Rosie

And that was the beginning and the end of it. We greedily snatched the brief moments, clinging to the joy of our love before the war summoned him back to London. The memory of that wonderful Christmas is still as vivid as if it was yesterday. Using the cloak of winter's anonymity we stole away finding our old isolated secret childhood haunts uninhabited by the constraints of perceived morality. In that short time we were in awe of the depth of understanding that came so speedily to us. We delighted in that knowledge. We felt that no one could have loved more deeply than us. It was impossible to believe that any other love affair could have been as magnificent as our own. Our world revolved around us; when we were together we denied the existence of the outside world. We blotted it out, impervious to anything that did not relate to us, guarding our love so jealously.

I still found it incredulous that Thomas believed me to be beautiful; that in his eyes I had achieved some kind of perfection. I was dazzled by his worship. When we lay together I could hardly believe that I could have captured the heart of a man who had fulfilled my dreams.

Although we shared hopes and dreams and made plans for a life together he did not, and could not, speak of the world of subterfuge that occupied the other part of his life. He didn't need to because I knew enough to know of what that world entailed. I didn't tell him that. His secret world that he thought he had kept guarded from me was evident in his thoughts that I could read. I didn't need to ask or probe. I could see it all too clearly.

The awful espionage and outrageous plots discussed in gloomy offices with such cold calculation appalled me, that, and the knowledge they would be willingly and dutifully executed by expendable men and women. I hated the fact that Thomas

335

played his part in it all. I knew of the raid on Berlin before the newspapers published their version of the events, I knew that Thomas was be party to the planning of the Greek guerrillas and our own agents blowing up the Gorgopotamos railway bridge that month, that they were working on the details of the commandos destroying the ships in the Bordeaux harbour in the new year. And I knew of those whose lives had been ended after interrogation, desperate to keep their comrades safe. But I said nothing of this to him. It was sometime during the following month when I dreamed of the people trapped in the ghettos. The visions of their hell would not leave me for days.

However I am going ahead of myself.

I had said nothing to him of my meeting with Lady Faversham and of her wishes after Kilndown Manor had been sold. She had believed that Thomas and Millie had produced a child. It had not quite been as I had led her to believe. But more importantly I needed to be able to secure a strand of my love of Thomas, to cherish when he would finally be taken from me; that there would be a legacy of his life.

Our time that Christmas was so very brief. I have to admit that our illicit meetings led to an extra frisson of excitement. The tension of ensuring that our relationship would remain secret gave us the same pleasure as that of consuming forbidden fruit. It heightened our senses; our awareness of our fragility and of possible exposure. We were intoxicated with each other.

All too soon he had to return to London, disappearing back into the shadows, but not before we had talked about Millie. I needed him to accept that for a time he had to play out his part as a husband; that in trapping him she had also trapped herself by engineering their marriage. To heighten her unhappiness served no purpose. Despite having been so spoilt throughout her childhood, and being so immature as a young woman, she was devoted to Katharine and appeared to be a loving and responsible mother. She displayed a maternal nature that had even surprised me. It brought out the very best in her. I felt an uncomfortable compassion and sympathy for her that I had not experienced before. It did not sit easily with me. It made things more complicated. It meant that there were more strands to control. I had to justify the means to meet the desired end.

Jack had, as usual suffered nothing. He had escaped scot-free. I knew that he would, come the end of the war, continue his charmed existence and would one day secure a fortune. Jackdaws are programmed to feather their nest. But I was determined that he would not do it at my expense or theirs. There would be a child, a boy. I wanted Thomas's child and to still retain a part of him, but I knew that I could not be the mother. I suffered agonies of knowing that it all had to come to an end.

∞

I left what I had to say until the night before he went. We walked past the old village hall down the hill towards Mallington. The hop fields looked forlorn. A few untidy strands of string hung suspended around the poles. The frost had whitened and straightened the grass that had grown at the base of each pole. They had a neglected look about them. At the entrance to the field the short row of deserted hop-pickers' huts could be seen set at a parallel to the tall fences. We turned in at the unfastened gate and walked towards them.

Pushing the half-opened door and stooping inside Thomas pulled me to him. Bending down he cupped my head in his hands and he kissed me gently. We looked around the little room. There was an old bed with worn webbing and a chair. A few battered pots and pans were piled up in one corner of the room.

"Welcome to my abode fair damsel." Thomas swept his hand around the room as if to display the magnificence of the accommodation.

"Wonderful! You have surpassed yourself. It is exceedingly magnificent."

I pushed him and he pretended to lose balance and fall upon the bed that alarmingly creaked as it threatened to collapse.

"Careful you idiot...you'll hurt yourself!"

But he just grinned and made to pull me down with him, catching my coat. I shrugged the hem from his grasp.

"I'm not that sort of girl Mr Fulwood..... I have my reputation to think of."

"Let me take care of that," his grin widened, and he stretched out to grab me again.

"Not so fast mister." I stepped back. He lie still, closed his eyes and sighed loudly.

"You misunderstand me young maiden. I merely meant to shelter you from the cold from without. Come to me and I will show you how honourable I am."

"Shh...you are daft! I'll sit with you if you promise to be good."

"Oh I can be good, very good!" His rakish smile indicated the innuendo of his words.

"Oh really?"

"Come and see." He invited, patting the side of the bed.

"Oh just for a while then."

I made to sit chastely next to him before he seized me and covered my face and throat in loud smacking wet kisses.

"Sir, you undo me!" My own laughter weakened me and I allowed myself to be held against him.

His fingers undid the buttons on my coat and his hands felt his way around me. I tingled with the feel of his hand on my breast.

"Your hands are freezing Thomas!"

He rolled me over and I lay beneath him giggling helplessly.

"Perhaps this will help to warm you." His hands stole under my blouse and he began to make love to me.

∞

When we had finally satisfied our desire we sat together in the warm glow of our happiness.

"I could never have believed it possible to have found such contentment Rosie". He held my hand in his own, smoothing my palm with his thumb, before bringing it to his lips.

"My God this blasted war. I can't bear that it takes me away from you."

I looked up at him. His face was serious.

"I need to say something Thomas. It's about you and Millie.

He frowned. "No don't spoil this moment Rosie."

"I have to speak about it now Thomas. There's never going to be a right time."

"Go on then what is it?"

"Well it's difficult to explain. I know that you will think that I am mad."

"I think that anyway!" he attempted to humour me but saw that I was unresponsive. "Go on then…. out with it."

"You can see how Millie dotes on Katharine."

"Yes…uhmm." His eyes narrowed slightly.

I tried to find another way.

"I think that she needs to feel that you still care for her, despite it all. She needs you to be a proper husband to her for now. That's all. Not to feel rejected."

He looked suitably stupefied.

"Do you really think that I could…after what we have…"He shook his head unable to find the right words.

"No," I interrupted, "Just listen! We have each other we will always have that, but for her it is only this moment, this time. She has no way of knowing what the future holds for her and Katharine. Is that too much to ask? Just be a little more generous. It takes nothing away from us."

"How can you expect me to be so base, to act as man and wife when you know that I don't love her, that I'm in love with you?"

"Part of you will always love her Thomas admit it. All these years you have held a candle to her. I'm not asking you to fall in love with her, just give her some comfort, some natural affection. Is that too much to ask?"

"And where does that leave us?"

"As I said it leaves us just as we are. It changes nothing. If anything it helps me come to terms with the future; that she will lose what we stand to gain. Does that make any sense to you?"

He stared at me. "Only partially…. I have this strange niggling feeling that there is something more that you could say, but you're holding something back but I can't for the life of me fathom it out. What have I missed?"

"Nothing at all." I assured him. "You are just imagining things Thomas."

As we walked back towards the road the chill of the late afternoon penetrated and caused me to shiver.

"Are you cold?"

"No, no I'm fine. Let me walk on now, don't come now, follow on later when I'm out of sight."

I could feel him watching my slow progress up the hill. I knew that he was bewildered and that he would be turning over the things that I had said, worrying them like a dog with a bone. But I dare not explain any further. I had to wait for another time.

All too soon he had gone. During the days that followed I felt a huge void in my life. It was as if a huge part of me was missing, that I was incomplete… a shadow that had lost its identity. Some days it felt like a real physical pain, an ache that settled somewhere in my stomach, querulously complaining of a strange hunger.

I wrote to him but received nothing back. I knew that he was still safe but it did not stop the sense of loss. I ached to be back in his arms and to feel his skin against mine and to breathe his special scent. How evocative a smell can be; it can bring into vivid focus a moment of the past far more than a visual stimulus. In that

340

instant we relive that gossamer moment. I expect it is because we are somehow caught by surprise when it happens. It creeps up without warning and suddenly we are transported back to a time and a place, remembering the emotion, the heat or cold of the day, the feel of an object….it peels back the multitude layers in an instant and then, fleetingly, it disappears and we wonder if it was just a dream.

The winter always kept us close to home. Cold and the darkness kept us close to our firesides and the blackout ensured that we all remained hidden from each other. And that winter was especially miserable. Not just for me but for all of us. Since the beginning of the war we had had one bad winter after another. When the snow came again that winter it brought back all the horrors of the winters before. We remembered too well the treacherous ice and the snowdrifts of the year before. The older villages blamed the bombing.

 "We never had winters like this before all the blitzes."

The children delighted in the days of missed school, and tobogganing on the snow slopes but for the adults it meant extra misery and hardship. Supplies were disrupted. Transport networks on both rail and road regularly came to a standstill. Fuel shortages mean that heating a house became a luxury. We just resorted to piling on more clothes and having extra layers of bedding. We became bundles of clothing that had to be unwillingly peeled off each night. The war had dragged on. People remembered the First World War; the war to end all wars and began to worry that despite the advances that were being made by the Allies there seemed to be no end in sight.

Finally by March the winter petered out. It retired sulkily providing us with prolonged periods of miserable rain followed by biting winds. But it also brought Thomas back to us. He came and went as before. One moment as large as life and then a distant shadow again. It was to be the last time that he came down to Cranesbury but not the last time I saw him. That came later.

Little Katharine was growing fast. She was taking notice of everything around her and although unsure of Thomas at first, his special gift with children soon had her in raptures. She was delighted with his bounces. His act of throwing her into the air at first had her taking a sharp breath of surprise until she realised the glory of weightlessness and of being smothered in kisses at her descent. Millie was alarmed, adamant that harm would befall her daughter begging him to stop until she saw the rapture in the child's face and the gurgles of happiness.

Thomas was captivated by her as I knew he would be. Her attempts to babble and point and her wobbly determination to haul herself upright amused him. Beatrice had been a devoted mother to both Millie and Dulcie and Millie had inherited those same maternal qualities. Thomas was impressed by the change that he saw in her. Her maturity and lack of artifice brought him closer to her. He saw the best in her. Her happiness in his acceptance of her child melted her reserve. She stopped being fanciful and diffident.

∞

When he came to their bedroom that night she saw that she still had the power to attract him. Motherhood had not diminished her charms. She was still young. The mirror reflected a woman in her prime; she had the colouring of her mother but she now had also developed a graceful beauty that spoke of her connections to her paternal grandmother.

Any man would have been captivated by such a woman. She smiled up at him as he made his way to the bed. He looked at the rounded curve of her full breasts and her glorious golden hair that framed her face and his desire enflamed him.

He bent to kiss her and she reached up to take him into her arms.

∞

I knew that he would be tormented with guilt when he came to me.

"How can you not be disgusted by me?" He was angry with himself needing to have his own culpability assuaged by my censorship.

"Do you love me Thomas?"

Of course I do." His pain was apparent by his hurt protestation.

"Well then. She is happy. And we still have each other."

"I don't understand how you can be so…. so accepting. I have betrayed you."

"No Thomas. There is no betrayal. Because what we have is too special to be invalidated. You and I have a love that cannot be diminished. This war has made things complicated, that's all."

He took me then with an urgency that surprised us both. It was if he knew that we would have such little time left. He was crestfallen afterwards, apologetic at his need to take me so quickly.

"I'm so sorry. You didn't have time to…."

I shook my head. "I love you… you ninny!" I poked him hard in the ribs.

"Next time I expect the full works. No short cuts next time Mr Fulwood."

He propped himself up on his elbow. "Will there be a next time then."

"Of course there will. There will always other times. We will have a lifetime together." I lied.

Rosemount Villa 1942
Roland and Sylvia

"I never expected anything but I thought at least she would think of Ronald." Sylvia indignantly waved the papers at Roland.

"There wasn't going to be much left was there anyway after the death duties." Roland attempted to placate her.

"And that's another thing!" she came back. "It's theft, government licensed theft...sixty five percent. It was bad enough when it was fifty. They might as well have taken the lot and have done with it!"

Roland reached out and took her hand, wrestling the papers from her.

"Don't get yourself worked up. We have managed to do without all these years."

"Yes and you've had to prostitute your art to keep us from starvation!"

"There's lots that are far worse off." He stroked her arm.

"We couldn't even go to see what was left there. Sold in private auction!" She jerked her arm away from him determined not to be swayed from her resentment.

"And what about this trust fund that we are not to privy to...why has that been kept from us. Why are we not entitled to know who it is?"

"It's not a secret dear. The remainder of monies from the sale of the estate will go into a trust fund for Katharine and for any other subsequent child or children of Millie and Thomas. There's no mystery. She must have heard that Millie and Thomas had had the little girl just before she died, that's why the Will speaks about legitimate direct descendants."

Sylvia sat down and one of the dogs who had been watching her got up and came over, placing its chin gently on her lap, its eyes gazing into her face. She looked down and smiled, stroking its head and soothing them both.

"If only people could be as faithful as these hounds."
Roland smiled to himself and looked across at her ignoring the innocently implied insult.
She nibbled at the side of her thumb frowning in concentration. The room was still, waiting for her to speak.
"And that's another thing. Another mystery. Why was Rosemary Minton appointed as an executor? How the hell did mother know that young woman?"
Impatiently she brushed the dog to one side and went over to the cabinet and picked up her cigarettes, worrying the packet until one slipped out. She glared at the cigarette holder lying next to the discarded packet and distractedly inserted the cigarette.
Ronald watched her pacing the room for a while waiting for her anger to abate.
"And anyway what would you have done with the crumbling pile?" He attempted to humour her.
"You seem to forget...it was my childhood home." She was irked at his attempt to pacify her, not yet ready to accede to his reason.
"And it was Ronald's inheritance that we are talking about."
"Yes dear but remember he did have a substantial sum all those years ago when your father was alive."
"That was just a fraction of what they had then."
"It may well have been, but it secured this place for us thanks to him and dear Ronald."
"Mmm." She considered his words dragging deeply on her cigarette as the image of Ronald came into her head.
The echo of a door banging startled them both and set the two dogs barking and racing from the room.
Ronald came striding in brandishing some papers in his hand.
Startled Sylvia went over to him. "Goodness we had only just been talking about you....your ears must have been burning and she went to kiss him but in his irritation he shrugged her away.

"Have you seen this!" he waved the Will at Roland.

Good grief...like mother like son,' he thought wanly, 'absolutely impossible at times.' But he did not reply and just nodded his response.

"But have you read it!" Ronald spoke as if it were a challenge.

"I have."

"Yes indeed we have." Sylvia picked up her own copy, resentful that it had been left to her to voice their disapproval.

"An insult from the grave, that's what it amounts to." Mother and son nodded their agreement and both turned to Roland to confirm their perceived injustice of the situation. He smiled at them both as they impatiently waited for his pronouncement.

"You speak as if there was a fortune at stake. The place was in a hell of a state, and what with death duties, creditors having to be paid back and the like, I doubt if there was much left."

"You seem to forget that father acquired some very valuable pieces, and there were the paintings. You of all people could hardly forget those!"

"No you're right, he did have a good eye I'll grant you that. But what's done is done." He shrugged his shoulders. "No good crying over spilt milk."

"Well I for one think that this Will," and Ronald shook it vigorously, "should be contested."

"On what grounds?"

"That mother and I are the rightful heirs of course." He laughed harshly. "Would have thought that it was blindingly obvious!"

"So you could afford to engage a solicitor?"

Ronald chose to ignore the question, chewing his lip, before another though sprung into his head.

"It's not just that is it? The old biddy had a new Will drawn up just before she popped her clogs, who's to say that she was in her right mind; that she hadn't gone a bit doolally living there on her own huh?"

346

"I think that you will find that it was drawn up by that solicitor of hers and was witnessed independently though I do grant you they must have had to swallow a dictionary of gobbledygook to qualify." He sighed. "I have read it, but I have to say that I can't make head nor tail of most of it; think it's a way of keeping it all a closed shop!"

Roland grimaced involuntarily and Sylvia seeing the gesture became alarmed. "Is it that pain again?" she went over to him, a wave of fear washed over her.

"No, don't fuss it's nothing it will pass."

"You've said that before." She looked down at him anxiously. "I think that you should see someone. It can't be right. Last time you said it was indigestion but you haven't had anything since breakfast, and then that was just a piece of toast because you said you weren't hungry."

"I'm fine." He attempted to find a more comfortable position. "Its fine, don't fuss."

"What's this?"

"Your father is being very stubborn Ronald. He's had a couple of funny turns but he will not see anyone. I said to call out Dr Sutton, but no, he keeps saying to me that it's nothing to worry about.... as if he knows anything about it."

His denial of seeking help together with her own fear made her indignant, "and he thinks that I can't see when he's in pain!"

She stubbed her cigarette out and went into the kitchen where she proceeded to clatter the pots and pans as she dried them and put them away.

Ronald and Roland listened to the onslaught.

"Try and leave some of them intact my dear!"

But she was in no mood to listen or be humoured and closed the door firmly so the sounds became muffled.

Roland closed his eyes and the two men sat together but distanced by their own thoughts

"Then there's the situation at home." Ronald began. A sense of renewed grievance grew.

Roland reluctantly opened his eyes and focused on Ronald.

"Had no chance of a good night's sleep for months now!" His voice was petulant.

"The baby." Roland nodded.

"I have not only my work at the bank but also my responsibility as Air Raid Warden for this community. They rely on me. My men all require my leadership. They look up to me. It's understandable; a man with my kind of experience in the last show. I said to Beatrice, I need to be on my toes, alert to any danger and that means that I need to get a decent night's sleep." Roland gazed across the room as Ronald's words washed over him but he nodded again to demonstrate that he was still listening.

"Then she has the blasted cheek to say that she has her work down at Mote House. Hardly in the same league!"

He tapped his fingers on the arm of his chair and one of the dogs believing that he had summoned it, came to put its nose by his hand. He pushed it away.

"I got covered in hairs last time I was here!"

Sylvia came back from the kitchen catching the tail end of the conversation.

"What happened last time you were here?"

"I was just saying to father that I've had a devilish time of it these last months; the baby keeping us awake no end of nights."

She looked surprised. "Oh I thought that she'd been settling well. The last time I saw Beatrice she was singing her praises saying what a happy baby she was. Mind, with your Beatrice she likes to think that everything is perfect."

"Oh the two of them are besotted all right. Terry towelling nappies and washing hanging all over the place; place is like a Chinese laundry at times." Ronald distractedly ran his fingers through his hair.

Sylvia was delighted at his description.

"Oh so not such a pristine household these days then? And she was always quick to find fault, look down her nose when she came here."

She glanced over to Roland who shook his head disapprovingly so she turned back to Ronald for approval.

"Well it's quite true Roland as you well know and it's not just me that has noticed either."

Mother and son were united in their grievances, they raised their eyebrows at each other but Roland refused to take the bait and merely smiled back at them. He could not find it in his heart to condemn; they were both so dear to him. And he was concerned that things were not right; once or twice he had experienced such an agonising tightness across his chest. It had taken his breath away. He knew that he ought to see the doctor but then there was the fear of having something serious confirmed. He wanted to blot it out and to make it go away. He was fearful of what the future would hold for Sylvia if she was left alone to cope. He knew that she would never manage alone and his own anxiety kept him awake at night waiting for the pain to subside, willing himself to survive. He could not discuss it with her. She had given everything up for him and he was damned if he would let her down at this stage of their life.

They had lived from hand to mouth for years. He had made up his mind that he would try to see if Parsons could put his remaining canvases for auction. She could hardly be expected to live on a widow's pension. He had scanned the papers for the details in the Beveridge Report but there seemed to be so much opposition to the proposals that he felt that it would be watered down. He had hoped that Sylvia would have had something from the Kilndown estate, it was a cruel blow. To her it represented pure spite but for him it merely confirmed their poverty.

It was a blessing that Ronald had a secure job at the bank with a confirmed pension, but then he too had financial responsibilities, he had the demands of a wife and daughter, well two daughters. He hadn't asked how much of a contribution Thomas was making to the household, but the wedding small as it was, that and having a child so soon into their marriage must have eaten into their resources. He had even considered the sale of Rosemount Villa, but the war had depressed the market even if there were buyers to be had. The thought of moving house with all the upheaval was too traumatic he knew that she would be devastated to admit to an even lesser lifestyle. She may have lived in reduced circumstances all these years but she couldn't escape her keen sense of superiority. It had been inbred. She had inherited a proud view of her family's history of wealth and privilege. Even as they had battled to meet the tradesmen's bills she still held firm to the belief that somehow she was above mere commerce. Might and right; just as the ancient kings had clung to power so she clung to the vestiges of her upbringing. He had loved her then and over the years his love had matured and deepened.

"When are we to meet Katharine? I've heard that she takes after you and your mother with her colouring. She'll be a beauty if she takes after you my love."

He smiled at Sylvia and was rewarded by a look of sudden pleasure that lit her face. It melted away the tension of the afternoon.

"I'll get Millie to bring her over. It will be good for her to get out of the house. She had such a time of it one way and another." Ronald rose to go.

"We can sort out this other business another day I dare say."

"Tell Millie to come one afternoon. She can stay for tea."

Sylvia followed him to the door.

"And don't overdo it Ronald. You can't be expected to do so much without proper rest. Make sure that Beatrice understands that. You should put your foot down."

She waved to him from the door and watched him walk away.

Kilndown Woods 1943
Rosie and Thomas

It was an Indian summer that year. The summer had been a washout but finally the days remained dry and the evenings mild in the late autumn sun.

I walked down to the woods and waited for him at the lodge. It was showing all the sad signs of abandonment. The small latticed windows, only just visible, were mottled with dusty cobwebs whilst the rest of the crumbling masonry was swathed by an invasive Virginia Creeper which threatened to envelope the entire house in a profusion of tendrils and red leaves.

Small birds had returned to the lower branches of the sweet chestnut tree lulled into a false sense of security, as I had stood so quietly taking in the air of the early afternoon. The gregarious sparrows chattered to each other in the hawthorn bushes whilst a blackbird carefully stalked its buried prey at the grass verge. Wood pigeons kept up their insistent whooping calls, periodically ending with a half enquiry before beginning again.

I watched a bee laboriously explore the speckled foxglove trumpets and then, forgetting that it had already visited a bloom, begin the process again, each leg coated in a rounded bubble of yellow pollen.

The blackbird was startled, it crouched and then flew away proclaiming its displeasure at being disturbed.

Thomas appeared.

He walked towards me and my heart jumped. He wore a light shirt and had turned up the sleeves; his jacket was slung carelessly over one shoulder. He had lost some weight but his tall frame still showed the magnificence of his figure. He strode towards me and in one moment had held me fast. I was lost in his embrace and his long kiss.

"I haven't got too long."

He looked forlorn as if his own statement had betrayed him.

351

"I know."

He twisted his fingers in mine and we walked together along, deviating off the path to step around the tall grasses and nettles at the beginning of the wood. As we followed a trail the nettles thinned out and then there was just a carpet of mossy grass and patches of blackberry bushes with immature fruits.

He laid his jacket down beside the horse chestnut tree. Above us the branches bore the clusters of new prickly conker cases. We lay looking at the sky through the branches. The surrounding blackberry bushes had provided a secluded bower.

Wordlessly he took off my blouse and carefully folded it to form a pillow. I unbuttoned his shirt. We watched each other undress. His long legs caught mine as he turned over to me. He tenderly stroked my face, my throat and then my arms before caressing my body; his gentle hands offering just the lightest touch as of a soft downy feather. My body responded to the intimate pleasure of his touch. I felt utterly adored. Our bodies were in perfect accord with each other's needs. We fitted together so naturally. I melted into him and when he finally took me, restraining himself at first to give me my pleasure, I felt his shuddering desire peak and then his delight at our mutual satisfaction. I lay pulsating as my climax slowly ebbed away leaving me completely fulfilled.

I turned to look at him. He grinned back, the tension of his life had lifted and he was that uncomplicated boy of our childhood. I traced the fine lines at the edge of his deep brown eyes that looked back at me.

"I am all yours." He groaned dramatically as if I had made him an unwilling conquest. "No more! You have drained me! Enough!"

I smiled down at him and kissed his lips. We lay quietly together our bodies slowly regaining a state of tranquillity. I moved a strand of hair away from his brow before kissing him again. My lips moved over the lids of his eyes and down his nose before finding his mouth again which opened to accept mine.

The silence of the woods was only disturbed by the call of a bird overhead. It was if we were cocooned in our happiness. I didn't want the moment to end. I couldn't bear to think that this beautiful moment would never be repeated, that our love would be just a memory.

The thought of not ever having him make love to me again brought me to an intense longing for him. I needed to feel him as an intimate part of me, to reclaim that ecstatic ecstasy. I wanted to drink him in.

I moved to hold him closer to me. He closed his eyes and smiled as I caressed him, smoothing my hands over the soft down of his stomach and down to his loins. His breathe caught sharply as my tongue explored the contours of him. He panted as I brought him to a state of desire. Finally he could not deny the urgency of his arousal. He turned over to me crushing his body to mine and we began a frantic rhythm of love as he hotly entered me again; both straining against our desire to reach our climax too soon. We both fought desperately against it; the peaks of juddering pleasure grew closer and closer together until in one shattering eruption of rapture we came together.

He gasped trying to catch his irregular breath as he rolled from me as I took in desperate gulps of air. As we slowly recovered from our ordeal of passion he breathed in more deeply and evenly. His voice seemed to come from a long distance away.

"When this show is over I want you to be my wife. I can't live this way."

I didn't want to break the spell and said nothing.

"You know of course that Millie's pregnant again."

I nodded and rested my head against his chest so that I could hear the thudding of his heart.

"Yes....December." I placed my arm across him.

"What must you think of me?" He drew my head up so that he could look at my face and studied it anxiously.

"It should never have happened. It just makes such a mockery of everything. I have made things ten times worse. I know what you said last time but it does take things from you…. from us both. You know it does. How can you believe in me Rosie? I seem to sleepwalk from one disaster to another; a complete basket case!"

"Shh… don't spoil the moment. Don't say another word!" I put my hand over his mouth. "Just say that you love me, nothing else matters."

"I will always love you; you know that don't you?"

"Be still. Shh…. now."

The sun flitted between the branches casting light and shadow over his body. I watched mesmerised as his skin changed hues. The coarse dark hair of his loins contrasted with the softer down on his pale belly. His upper torso showed the curves of his ribs and the definition of well-honed muscle. He was beautifully formed.

He watched me watching him, bemused by my study. I couldn't resist the pleasure of running my hands over him, feeling the dips and depressions and the curves of his body. I wanted my hands to have a tactical memory of him. I wanted them to be imprinted with his shape and form as a blind person understands an image conveyed by their ability to interpret the sensations of touch.

He was in his prime. His thick brown hair was untouched by grey, his skin taut and firm; he was my Adonis. I caught up his hand and turned it towards me. The long fingers were strong, the palms quite hard. I put my hand against his to measure them. My fingers barely reached the second joint of his. He brought my hand to his lips and kissed it.

"I don't want this moment to end." I sighed. "Shall we just stay here forever?" I grinned up at him.

"Okay then my turn now." He smirked playfully as he rubbed his nose against mine and before pushing me down attempting to tickle me as I squirmed and wrestled from his grasp. But he was too strong. As I weakened, helplessly laughing, he began to take his time to pleasure me again. I finally lay there languidly, allowing his intimate caresses to bring me to my own individual flooded ecstasy.

∞

It was later than we had intended, by the time we had gathered ourselves together.

I knew that I would not see him again. We walked back along the lane and when we parted I willed myself not to look back. I would always see the image of him smiling down at me as the weakened rays of the sun flicking through the trees played peek-a-boo across his face. I would remember our walk hand in hand. I would not watch him leaving me.

As I continued my solitary walk back to the village my mind crowded with jumbled thoughts. They stormed into the void that his leaving had created.

He would be pulled into a world that took no prisoners and I willed myself to not think of the end that he would meet. Throughout the summer desperate French saboteurs had been blowing up supply lines, destroying vital equipment, and there would be heavy fighting ahead in the winter months. The Resistance had already lost one prominent leader. Betrayal and death awaited others. It was inescapable.

And so I had greedily taken the time that we had together and blotted everything else out. A lifetime of pleasure snatched in one final blissful afternoon. I had no regrets that we had consummated our love with such urgency, only that it had to be carried out under a cloak of secrecy. I was only too aware of all the lives that were inexorably linked to ours. I could have cheerfully allowed some to be exposed for their selfish disregard and their betrayals but in doing so it would have brought to bear a light on those who were innocent of wrong doing. It would be the unravelling of a string that once undone refused to be bound so tightly again.

It was no easy task to judge those who were merely led or those who would lead. There was Jack who had been both a friend to Thomas but then had ultimately betrayed his trust. To have exposed his culpability to Thomas would have destroyed something precious in Thomas; a faith in the framework of his home, his family and his friends. It was the very something that he was seeking to preserve. His determination to defend all that he held so dear made him the person that he was and the person that I loved unreservedly.

My own father had shaped so much of what we all had become. Remove one small stone from the base of a tower and watch it slowly crumble. His clandestine love affair with Beatrice had made her so frightened of exposure. His liaison with Roseanne, his violence towards Ethel and his love of drink had tarnished his reputation. He could have removed so many obstacles had he been true to his better nature. Arnold Parsons would have fought his corner if he had made a clean breast of it and told Ethel that he wanted a divorce before it got so complicated. As it was he was so frightened of losing Beatrice that it clouded his judgement. He never believed himself worthy of her.

But by bringing another child into the world it merely allowed the tragedy to continue. It ensured that Beatrice had even more reason to be frightened of public censure. It would eventually lead her to collude with Millie, supporting her in a wilful deception. With some imagination they could have declared her confinement. Many girls had received proposals of marriage only to find their men snatched from them, lost on the battlefield on land and sea. Together, using a little ingenuity, they could have lessened the shock with a story of the death of an imaginary fiancé. People were more willing to compromise their previously held concepts of morality; they accepted that war brought with it a different set of rules. The uncertain times had made them less censorious.

Instead her own history shaped her, and she used Thomas as a willing sacrifice. Had she been more courageous she and my father could have perhaps shared a public life together eschewing convention to divorce to become man and wife. They would have made a good life together. I would have felt safe. They would have provided me with an anchor. I missed the father that he could have been. Perhaps I could have even loved myself and in cherishing my gift I could have been less vindictive and judgemental; perhaps I could have even grown old and grey with Thomas. Now that would have been a life worth living.

They said it was the shock of hearing that Thomas had been killed in action that brought about Millie's early labour. She had been due towards the end of the month but it was on the fifth of December that Thomas's son was born. There was no doubt that Thomas was the father. He was a beautiful child. He came into the world without a fuss. Within days he settled into a routine. Millie could feed him and then he would sleep. He would make just the smallest protest when bathed or changed but otherwise he would accept being passed around and admired, gazing up at his admirers with a look of contentment.

"He's such a good baby," Beatrice was proud of her grandson.

I had held him in my arms and felt such an overwhelming sense of love. I wanted him to be my own.

It was a dark afternoon when I visited Millie. The clouds which had hung low throughout the day threatened to bring rain. When I rang the doorbell it had started to drizzle. The house smelt damp with washing. Millie sighed when she saw me.

"I've only just got Katharine down, she's been grizzling all day." Reluctantly she led me into the drawing room. The small fire struggled to keep alight throwing out little heat; a few live coals sat amongst the grey ash. Millie had placed Katharine's cot close by. She saw me look towards it.

"It's too cold upstairs during the day. Father brought her down here for now."

The new baby lay sleeping tightly swaddled on the settee. Millie had wound round a blanket to keep him tucked safe in one corner. She sat next to him. I went to pick him up.

"Don't wake him up, it'll disturb Katharine!"

I glanced at her and she recoiled from my gaze. I picked him up and held him close.

"I will be a guardian and his Godmother." I said as I stroked his soft cheek. I heard her sharp intake of breath but didn't look over to her. Standing and swaying slightly to rock him I spoke to him.

"Your name will be Samuel. Samuel Thomas Fulwood"

"Whatever are you saying Rosie!" Millie went to stand and take him from me but I waved her away.

"We need to set a date for the Christening."

"We! We! What are you talking about?" She was irritated but my look made her suddenly nervous.

"You can speak to Reverend Martin and set a date in February."

"Who do you think you are Rosie!" A flush of indignation made her pink.

"You can choose your own Godparents for Jack's daughter," I said coldly,

"Whatever do you mean!" She hissed.

"Just as I said, I thought that I had made myself quite clear. You can choose what you wish for Jack's daughter but you will announce that I am to be the godmother for this little one and you will make a will that in the event of your death I am appointed as his guardian"

Millie made for the door, but she hesitated when she heard me speak again.

"Call your mother and see what she has to say."

"I will!" She flounced out.

I waited, listening to their urgent discussion. They came in together to present a united front.

"Rosie," began Beatrice, "whatever has got into you? What have you been saying to Millie to upset her so? She is still grieving over Thomas, has just given birth and she tells me that you are flinging around wild accusations. Have you no shame! It really is quite outrageous. And you call yourself a friend!"

"I merely informed Millie that she will invite me to be the child's Godmother and I that will accept."

Beatrice stared at me.

"I also said that I have no claim or hold over the decisions that she makes on behalf of Katharine, Jack's child."

She drew herself up. "How dare you Rosemary!"

"I dare because I must."

"And what gives you the right to say such things!"

"I have Thomas's letters telling me that he knew that he was not the father. He told me that he knew that Katharine was Jack's child." I lied.

"He told me that he went along with the charade because he would not see Millie being humiliated. Did you think that he would not find out? He didn't want to believe it at first but then Jack finally admitted that it was true."

"I don't believe you!"

"Then you leave me no alternative. I will show copies of my letters to Thomas's father and to your own parents Mrs Latterbridge. He will believe me and so will Mr and Mrs Parsons although I would be sad to see them being reminded about Dulcie's parentage."

Beatrice sat down heavily on the settee.

"Your family have ruined ours!" Her voice was husky.

"Sadly the opposite is true. I lost my father because of you."

"It was an accident." She murmured.

"You may well wish to believe that it was an accident..... that he followed you that day....that when you met on the train and he tried to tell you how much he loved you.... you walked away. He was killed because of you."

Millie looked at her mother, her mouth hung open. She shook her head slowly.

"My father adored you and his child Dulcie and he lost his life because of it." I was gratified to see that she flinched.

"Mother it's not true? Mr Minton and Dulcie....never!" She was aghast

"And now you," I turned to look at Millie, "we have another deception Millie. You used Thomas when it suited you. You had

360

your fun, and then decided to reel him in. He always took care of you even when we were children…. so you decided to allow him to think that you needed him and loved him."

I looked into the little face. His mouth twitched and his eyes fluttered before he succumbed to sleep again.

"I promised Thomas that I would take care of this little one and I intend to keep my promise."

"I think that you should leave this house at once." Beatrice moved to towards me, but hesitated when she saw that I had not moved.

"You may not believe it Mrs Latterbridge but I was sad that you and my father didn't stay together. You were good for him. You made him happy. You brought out the best in him."

She brought her hand to her mouth.

"You also may not believe that, despite everything I have always liked you. That's why I think that we should settle this business together."

She looked across at Millie before turning back to me. She had composed herself ready to take control. I admit that I admired her for that flash of boldness, but I knew that it was just that. She had still not realised how strong my position was.

"You have a very strange way of showing it then. Do you really you think that we would be dictated to by you?"

"Well perhaps we should ask Mr Latterbridge, but then again you may not wish to drag up the past. It might be better that he never found out. I imagine that it would be quite shocking news for him. There could be nasty repercussions. I wouldn't say that he was a very forgiving kind of man. He values his reputation too much for that. Perhaps that's why you were so persuaded when you realised Millie's predicament."

Millie had turned her face away.

"Then of course there is the matter of perjury on not one but two birth certificates, making you both in danger of being prosecuted for fraud."

Millie burst into tears which startled Katharine setting her off and her sharp cries awoke Samuel. His lips quivered. I turned and walked out into the hall and into the kitchen with him. Beatrice followed me. She attempted to reason with me.

"Why are you doing this Rosie?" Her awful agitation made me almost sorry for her, but my heart had hardened against Millie.

"Thomas did not deserve to be treated this way by either of you. And now that he has gone it is time to put things right. You will take Millie to the registrar and say that she has realised that she had made a mistake in registering Thomas as the father of Katharine and instead have Jack's name inserted. You can, in mitigation say that she was still recovering from major surgery at the time and had been confused during her long convalescence… if it comes to that…… otherwise it will be a mere formality to correct an error made in good faith."

"But…."she began and I knew what she wanted to say.

"Nobody will ever know. If you do this my lips are sealed. Jack will not find out from me what has been done, he need never know… agreed?"

She nodded.

"All I want in return is that you both agree that I will play a major part in Samuel's life. As his Godmother and guardian I will be consulted on any decision that is made; that I will become as close as his own mother as to his welfare and his upbringing. I am not asking to replace Millie but to be just as important to him." Her anger was beginning to subside, as she considered my terms.

"You or Millie have nothing to fear from me if you meet me on this. Had it not been for Thomas and this child of his, all your secrets would have been safe, I would never have said what I have known all these years."

Beatrice breathed in deeply as a sudden thought came to her and she looked into my face.

"Why of course…why did I not see it before? You loved him!"

I smiled at her. "Of course I did."

∞

And so it was agreed. Millie and Beatrice went to see the registrar in Maidstone and a new birth certificate for Katharine was issued. Millie saw a solicitor and I was named as Samuel's legal guardian. The Christening was set for the beginning of the New Year. Dulcie and I accepted our invitations to be Samuel Thomas Fulwood's godparents, together with two men from the village who had been in the same class with Thomas and Jack, Peter Renshaw and Frank Peters. As they were away in the army Ron Ticehurst and Joseph Simmons were asked if they would stand in as proxy godfathers, if their leave couldn't be obtained.

The war found us at home that year. Although we had all suffered the usual difficulties of shortages of fuel, of coal, clothing coupons and food rationing, had lost some of our nearest and dearest who were fighting on foreign soil, the in village we were still immune from the direct results of war. We were not in the big cities of Hull, Coventry, London, Liverpool, Plymouth or many other places which had suffered from constant bombings. We had not experienced the torment and agonies of the Blitz in our part of Kent. Often bombing raids in the capital had been aborted and the Luftwaffe had jettisoned their bomb loads on their way back home but we had always been lucky.

In January we heard that London had been hit again and we read about the heavy losses suffered by the RAF during the Nuremberg raid but in June there was a new weapon, the V-1 Flying bombs which were attacking the capital. We called them the Doodlebugs. During the first few years of the war stray bombs had hit first Hawkhurst, then Paddock Wood and Canterbury, with craters opening up huge holes in the streets of Maidstone with few casualties unlike the terrible loss of lives during the Blitzes in London and around its suburbs, but after Ashford had been hit by the new Doodlebug we realised that nowhere was safe in Kent. Then there was the V-2.

It was on a Monday when the sky was clear and the washing was fluttering in the breeze drying nicely when we heard the first drone of the Doodlebug. It seemed as if it was going to pass us over until the sound cut out. And then we heard the explosion. Later we tried to piece together parts of story, but there was no one left to tell the whole tale.

Roland had just left their house to walk the two dogs, walking past the oast house towards the Red Cross Centre which had been our village hall. He had looked up when he heard the drone. The dogs had strained at their leads. He had to wrestle with them to keep them close to him, and when he looked up again and realised that it was quite quiet there was an earthshattering explosion. The dogs broke from him pulling him to the ground. He had lain on the road not knowing where he was, and then as he painfully raised himself he looked back along the road and saw the huge pall of black smoke.

Rosemount Villa had suffered a direct hit. He tried to get to his feet but a crippling pain gripped his chest in a tourniquet. He looked up and saw the clear blue of the summer sky and then nothing.

Ronald returned later that night. It was as if he had seen a ghost. He had shrunk. All his bravado and bluster had deserted him. He could hardly bring himself to repeat any details of the day's events. A small section of the house had remained strangely untouched immune from the destruction. There were even pots and pans in the kitchen, which still had walls intact, still sitting on the draining board waiting to be dried, but the rest of the house including Roland's studio had been reduced to rubble; Sylvia's portrait torn and buried along with all the other shredded canvases. There was no way of telling which room was which, just a pile of blackened brick and mortar. They had eventually found Sylvia and took her to the mortuary in Tunbridge Wells. Roland was found afterwards; the two dogs cowering alongside him. They retreated away racing through a gate into the hopfield as soon as the ambulance team arrived. They could not be coaxed so they had had to leave them there.

Ronald heard that they were still missing and went back to fetch them but it was too dark and despite his calls they did not respond. When he returned again to the house he slumped into a chair in the drawing room. He refused offers of tea shaking his head.

"I have to go and officially identify them tomorrow. There's to be a post-mortem. They have to find out how he died, he wasn't in the house you see." He looked up and laughed at them.

"Imagine! The Boche still managed to kill him and he wasn't even there!" His laughter rose to a long uncontrollable whine before he took his head in his hands and sobbed.

The village was in sombre mood then next morning. Both dogs had been found by Alice Fulwood. She had gone to check on their three hens in the makeshift coop that Samuel had constructed, to see if they had laid, and found the dogs waiting at the door. They seemed to respond to her timid encouragement. At first they were wary but she soothed them and they finally allowed themselves to be led into the house. Alice had always had a way with animals. When she and Samuel had first courted he always said that she could charm the birds from the trees. Animals instinctively seemed to know that they were safe with her. Even as a young girl she attracted them, nursing back to health those who had suffered injury. She had a knack and a deftness of touch. Despite any pain they would be stilled and allow her to handle them. She had no fear of them whereas people made her uneasy and shy; she never knew how to make conversation and would withdraw into herself. People used to wonder how Samuel and Alice had come to be married. They were 'chalk and cheese' as some locals would have it, with others sages wisely remarking that 'opposites always attract'.

Whatever the case they were happy together. Their marriage was successful. The one sadness was that despite wanting a large family Alice had been unable to bear more children. She had suffered two miscarriages and one pregnancy had almost gone full term but she had lost the child in the seventh month. Thomas had been their one treasured delight, but was never spoilt. As with animals Alice was confident with children. She introduced Thomas to the natural world, played with him and kept fair boundaries. Thomas was loved and cherished.

Their loss at Christmas cast such a pall of despair over Alice that Samuel thought that she would never recover. It shocked her into a silent world. He did not know how to reach her. She went about the everyday duties as in a trance of misery. She hardly spoke to him, only to her cackling hens, which strutted around displaying their glorious shiny plumage, and to the thin stray cats that sidled around the kitchen door asking her for scraps.

When Samuel found the dogs in the house he took them up to Ivy leaf Cottage. To his surprise and dismay Beatrice was horrified.

"We can't have the dogs here!"

"Well what do you expect me to do with them then?" He was annoyed. He had not expected such rudeness.

"If it hadn't been for Alice goodness knows what would have happened to them." He expected some gratitude, not to be kept standing on the doorstep. His sense of propriety was upset. But she continued to stand as a gatekeeper to the house. He waited for her to resolve the situation.

"Well?"

"Well I don't know what to say Mr Fulwood but with two young infants here we can't possible take them in. You must understand that."

"I'm sure your husband would have another view Mrs Latterbridge." His anger made him stiff with formality.

"As your late mother in law's dogs I might remind you that they are your responsibility now, not mine." He held out his hand in exasperation to offer her the leashes. She recoiled from them.

"I'm sorry but until we can sort this business out I think it best if you take them back with you for the present. Of course I'll make sure that you are not out of pocket with feeding them."

He turned red with the implied insult. "I don't think that will be necessary! When exactly are you expecting Mr Latterbridge back?"

367

She shook her head. "I can't say. He has gone to Tonbridge Wells….the identification process…..both parents…it has hit him very hard." She was piqued that he did not offer his condolences. He turned on his heel and went to walk away but then turned again, stiff with anger.

"My poor Alice may never recover from the loss of our only son. I'll tell her that you asked after her. Don't worry about these dogs of yours; we wouldn't want to see them come to any harm."

He strode down the path, and flung open the gate so that it swung wildly back and forth on its hinges.

By the time he reached home he had worked himself up into a rage. Alice was surprised to see him back with them.

"Weren't they in then?"

No she's in all right…. said that she couldn't have them there because of the children. Didn't ask what we were supposed to do with them, and then had the cheek to say that she would pay for their upkeep as if we were beggars! I never even mentioned anything about money, Damn cheek of it all! Giving herself airs and graces as if they were the only people that matter. I will not have it!" He puffed loudly suddenly feeling quite giddy.

"Calm yourself dear. Here come and sit down and I'll make a pot of tea."

She patted the seat of the chair and took the dogs with her into the kitchen closing the door behind her. He heard her talking to them.

"What are we to do with you then? Now don't you fret….there there… thirsty are you? Let's find a bowl and we can sort you out."

"My, my, you were a thirsty pair weren't you?"

He heard the cupboards opening and closing.

"Not sure that I've got anything for you in here. We'll have to take a trip to old mister Drew see if he's got a bone or two left over. Now what's this in the larder? Bit of gravy left over. Soak a bit of bread in that? Should tide you over for now, poor lambs....there we are, is that nice?"

As he listened he realised with a shock that he hadn't heard her say so much since Christmas, *it's taken her mind off things for the present* he thought. As he thought of her, thankful that she had had a few moments of respite from her heartache, his own grief washed over him as the image of his young handsome son came into his mind.

∞

I had been the one to break the news to them about Thomas that last Christmas. When I knew that Millie had received the telegram I went straight down to the station. When Alice had opened the door to welcome me, with a faint hint of surprise, I could see how quickly it faded when she saw my face. Her polite smile remained but her eyes widened. She was alert watching me intently. She did not need words to understand, she had an animal instinct for seeking out the truth of a matter. Her hand flew to her chest and then to cover her mouth.

"It's Thomas!"

I reached out and held her close. Her small birdlike frame shook in my arms. I could hear her calling out to him; her silent cries too afraid to make themselves audible. All her babies had gone, he was the last. I was heartbroken for her. They had not deserved such tragedy, but then who does? Who can say why some live such gilded lives and others are called upon to suffer not just once but many times over. Alice had lived such a blameless life and yet she had been subjected to such anguish. Her kindness and fortitude had been thrown back at her. Her little life had been placed on a rack. Was it to test her to see how much she could bear? I was angry for us both. We had loved so well and yet it had not kept him protected from danger.

I think it was then that I promised to redress the balance.

I led her into the front parlour and she sat stupefied staring into the distance as if to try and reach out to him. I felt my tears well up for her; they washed over me, for us both. I knelt down and held her small hands in mine. Her beating heart fluttered trying to escape the confines of her breast. There were no words of comfort that could ease such misery. We clung together trying to make sense of the senselessness of the day.

Samuel arrived back home for his midday meal. I was in the kitchen making a cup of tea when I heard his step and he opened the door.

"Why, hello Rosie what are you doing here." He said in astonishment seeing me in their kitchen and then he started to panic, "Is it my Alice? Whatever's the matter?"

I put down the teapot and shook my head.

"No but there has been some bad news I'm afraid." I began slowly. He had always been such a pompous, self-important man but I was aghast that I would be the one to break that shallow bubble of conceit; that I would be responsible for bringing him down so hard. I did not want to witness his grief or his horror and mortification that I would think him weak or unmanly. As master in the house he had to be able to hold his nerve and keep a stiff upper lip. It was his duty as a husband.

I led him to the parlour and turning my back half from him so that he was shielded from my gaze I said, "I'm afraid to tell you that Millie has received a telegram. Thomas has been killed."

I heard his gasp before I saw myself out and quickly left the house.

∞

Alice understood that day what Thomas had meant to me. Mr Fulwood remained an awkward man retaining his officiousness and love of bureaucracy, but to me, he finally proved that he had a better side to his nature. His care for Alice almost endeared me to him. I had not seen much of that before. Perhaps her meekness and timidity had forced him to be strong for them both; his arrogance a way of sheltering her. Perhaps his pompous manner had just been a way to cope with that responsibility, a cloak to sustain him in his position.

Two weeks after the birth of the child and in almost in a state of denial about Thomas, still trying to not to drown in waves of grief, I decided to let Alice into my confidence. I still had some reservations about Mr Fulwood.

I knocked on the door and waited, feeling her desperate unease before she finally opened it, to let me and the cold air in.

"Oh it's only you." she said with some relief, standing back to let me pass.

"Oh it's so cold today. I can hardly feel my nose." I touched it to see if it was still there. The action made her smile wanly.

I unwound my scarf and hung my coat on the hook behind the door. She motioned for me to come into the kitchen. The range was alight but the rest of the house was freezing if the hallway was anything to go by.

We sat close to it. The kettle on the top whined querulously. I nodded towards it. "A watched kettle never boils."

She made to move it.

"No its fine...the tea can wait. I wanted to speak to you about something."

She raised her eyes to meet mine and then lowered them again. It was difficult to know how to begin. She was still so fragile, so raw.

"You know that Millie has had their little boy," I began slowly, watching her reactions to gauge how to proceed.

"Well...I hope that you'll agree with what I propose. We live in such uncertain times. Who's to say what is round each corner. I want to be a part of his life, to be able to offer some guidance and support." She had not made any sign that she was still listening but I could feel her weighing up on each word.

"I want to be his godmother." The silence hung in the air.

371

"And I'm going to ask to become the child's guardian in case something happens to Millie. I feel...there just needs to be someone of my age who could be called upon...."

I found it difficult to continue. Our world no longer made sense and here I was trying to govern the future. I waited until I could speak without breaking down. I tried to swallow away the restriction that had settled in my throat, trying to force the weight in my airway to clear. Several times I tried. It returned with a vengeance. I admitted defeat and wearily sat back in the chair.

She looked directly at me.

"If only he had married you." she spoke so softly.

"Things would have been so different."

∞

Apart from the day of Samuel's christening earlier that year they hardly saw their grandson. Alice remained almost a recluse, only going up to the village when it was unavoidable and Samuel was still massaging his resentment with Beatrice. The christening had been an awkward affair. Samuel had been adamant that they would be in attendance to witness the naming of his grandson. Alice had pleaded with him that she couldn't face it, but on the day she finally gave way to his persuasion. She held on to his arm and he responded on her behalf when she was spoken to.

I was horrified that Millie and the Latterbridges had treated them so shabbily. That spring and into early summer Millie had still not taken the baby down to the station house.

A week after the post-mortem on Roland I went to Ivy Leaf Cottage. The coroner had announced the verdict. Roland had suffered an aortic-aneurism probably brought on by the stress of the air attack. He had died instantly. The family were assured that he would have felt no pain. Plans had been made for the funerals.

The dogs had remained with Alice and Samuel.

When I knocked on the front door the curtain in the drawing room had twitched. I waited. A game was being played. I waited and then knocked again. Reluctantly Millie came to the door and before she could stop me I pushed her aside and walked from the hallway and into the kitchen. The back door was wide open to let the cool air in. Little Sam was outside in his pram that had once been Millie's and Dulcie's.

Beatrice was at Mote House and Ronald was out. Millie picked up Katharine swinging her heavily onto her hip. The toddler had been playing on the floor with a collection of saucepan lids and a wooden spoon. She had a head of black curls like Jack but she had her great grandmother Sylvia's striking violet eyes.

"She's quite a stunner isn't she?"

When I went to speak to her she turned away, hiding her face into Millie's shoulder.

"She's going through a shy phase." Millie explained, pleased with the compliment but still wary of me.

"Mother says that she's exceptionally forward for her age; she chats away and she's toilet trained." Millie could not resist the boast. It gave her status, proving her to be a good mother.

I walked outside and Millie followed. She placed her on a little trike but the child sat unmoving, watching me, weighing me up. I went over to the pram. Sam was fast asleep; his little chest rose and fell rhythmically.

"You do know that Thomas's parents have hardly seen him Millie."

Her lips thinned in annoyance. "Well they know where to come. I can hardly traipse all the way down there with the two of them. Have you ever tried pushing a pram back up that hill?" She was indignant at my interference.

"You now that's not what I mean."

"Well I can't think what you are saying. They certainly haven't asked after him!"

373

"You know that Mrs Fulwood has not been well. She was hit so hard with losing Thomas."

"You forget. I lost my husband too! I don't suppose that means much to you. And I have to raise two children on my own. Not being a mother I can't expect you to understand!"

I allowed her the jibe.

"It would be nice if you could take Sam to see her when your mother is here to look after Katharine. Otherwise I could take him."

"You!" She shook her head. "I don't think so!"

"Well perhaps we could go together then." I kept my tone even.

She looked across at Katharine who had started to peddle and wobble down the pathway.

"Steady…..be careful now!"

"Anyway they've still got those the dogs there." She said over her shoulder as she walked behind Katharine.

"Yes Millie…the dogs that once belonged to your father's parents!"

She shrugged her shoulders, "well they're still there."

"What did you expect them to do with them? Really you are all impossible at times."

"They might attack the baby." She shrugged her shoulders again.

"Well I see we are getting nowhere here. You seem determined to dig your heels in."

"Everything that I have said is perfectly reasonable. Mother thinks the same."

"In that case you will have no reasonable objection to deny me, as his godmother, the right to take him to see his other grandparents. I might also go and pay Mr and Mrs Parsons a visit since I believe that they would also be pleased to see him.

She caught hold of the trike as it neared the gate.

"Have it your own way Rosie. We'll go together."

"An excellent idea Millie."

I took another peek at Sam and walked down the path towards her.

She opened the gate for me placing herself between it and Katharine before closing it firmly.

"See you soon!" I called and waved my hand as she turned sharply leading Katharine back up the path.

Papermakers Arms 1945
Jack

Jack arrived back at the end of June. Ethel could hardly contain her delight. He dumped his kitbag in the hall and strode into the kitchen.

"I need a bath." He stretched himself and looked around the place seemed smaller and shabbier than he had remembered. A fly encrusted paper hung at the window. Ethel followed his gaze. "We've had a real problem with them this year," she apologised. "I need to get the boiler going if you want some hot water, it might be quicker if I boil up a kettle."

"I'll want more than a kettleful mother."

She smiled encouragingly at him. "Oh silly... I didn't just mean that. I'll get some pots going on the stove as well. Oh it's lovely to have you home at last."

He accepted her enthusiasm and turned to go up the stairs, before remembering his kitbag.

"Half a mo...." he fished inside, "here you are."

He held out a packet of stockings waggling them in front of her.... for her to take them from him.

"Go on take them," he said with some irritation at her seeming reluctance. "You don't have to thank me straight away!"

She was cowed by the strangeness of his tone, not sure whether he was joking.

"Goodness I didn't expect anything dear." She tried to bat away her doubts.

"How did you get hold of these?" She turned over the packet in her hand inspecting them.

"Ask no questions, hear no lies."

The staircase squeaked as he went up. "I'll shout when I want the water," and he turned at the landing to disappear into his bedroom.

Later that evening he went out.

"Just popping out for a quick reconnoitre!" he called over his shoulder. Ethel was disappointed; she thought that he would spend the rest of the Sunday evening with her.

He started to walk across the road towards Ivy leaf Cottage. The sky was just beginning to darken. Light clouds had taken on a crimson rim and the air was still. As he reached the other side of the road he heard a shout and saw Ron waving to him.

"Heard you were back....how's things?"

Reluctantly Jack turned and walked up towards the bakery.

"Not bad Ron, not bad at all...pleased to see the back end of this show though."

"I'll bet."

They shook hands and Ron patted him on the back. "Good to have you home son... and in one piece.....many didn't make it."

Jack squinted up the road. "No. Just luck of the draw I reckon."

"So ready for civvie street then? You'll find things have changed lad, and not for the better I'm afraid to say. Shortages everywhere, things will get worse before they get better so they say."

Jack nodded his head, "I'm sure you're right Ron."

"Did they say they'd hold the job open for you?"

Jack considered the question, "Well I don't think that'll be a problem."

"Well since you've been away there's many a girl who has turned her hand to mechanics you know. They've been doing all kinds of men's work, farms, factories and the like."

Jack smiled slowly, "Well I don't think they'll be a problem for me."

"No? Well there'll be a few young men who'll be surprised. Some of them in really skilled work, good workers too by all accounts."

"I'm sure the government will do something about that like the last time around. Get them back to the kitchen sink; make way for those of us who made their homes safe for them."

"I don't know lad. I don't think they'll be so easy to shift this time."

"They will soon enough when they find themselves in the family way!" Jack grinned back at Ron.

"Ah well you could be right there!" he smiled. "Anyway I must be getting along. Good to see you back in one piece." He turned to go and then turned back.

"I suppose you have heard about our young Thomas." His face suddenly sombre.

"Tom? Why what's up?" Jack's expression of surprise dismayed Ron.

Ron swallowed. "Well didn't Ethel say anything?" he tried to avoid the inevitable.

"What about Tom....no, why?"

"He copped it in France. A month before Christmas."

Jack's face grimaced. He took a step back trying to recover his balance."

"What!"

"Thought you knew lad! Did no one write to say?" Ron was astounded, horrified to be the bearer of such news. "Surely your mother wrote..." He tailed off. A muscle in Jack's cheek twitched; his lips were set in a thin line.

"Never knew why he was over there. All secret and hush hush according to my Betty." Ron waited anxiously for Jack to speak.

"No, I didn't....I hadn't......" He forced the words out. At his side his hands clenched.

"Murdering bastards!" And he went to walk away.

Ron caught hold of him. "No, wait up."

Jack tuned back "What?" He went to shrug him off.

"A couple of other things..... well you might not have heard." Jack looked at him with seeming indifference.

The Latterbridges at Rosemount, suffered a direct hit. Killed Sylvia Latterbridge; husband was out walking the dogs. He heard bomb going off, died of a heart attack."

378

Ron looked sadly at him. "Not much of a home coming is it!"
Jack turned to walk back, "Thanks Ron, catch up with you later.
Say hello to Betty for me."
The gloom of the night followed him home.

∞

The next morning Ethel heard him in the kitchen. When she went
downstairs he was sitting at the table already dressed.
"My you're up early, going anywhere special?" she smiled.
"Going into Maidstone, see if my old job's still there."
She was taken aback at his cold tone.
"Is there anything else anything wrong? Has something upset
you dear?"
He didn't answer her. She felt strangely disquieted by his
stillness.
"Jack love?"
"Why should there be anything else mother?" His question was
more of a challenge.
"I don't know what you mean." She was upset.
He sat trying to quell the riot of confusion in his head; the
questions that had been going around and around.
"Why didn't you write and tell me!" He barked at her.
"Why didn't you tell me! I had to find out from Ron!"
"Find out what? Tell you what?" His anger frightened her.
The rage hit him. "About Tom for God's sake! I didn't know!"
She stared at him in shock. Her face was pale. "Of course I wrote
to you!" She was pained by the accusation. "Why would you
think that I hadn't! I wrote straight away as soon as we heard!"
They stared at each other, each unwilling to believe the other.
"Then why didn't I get it. I had other letters!"
"How do I know Jack?" He was determined to challenge her. She
was hurt to find that she still had to explain herself.

"All I know is that I sent all my letters to you to the address that you gave me…. look."

He watched as she took her little address book from the cupboard, turning the worn pages until she reached one with the corner turned down.

"See!" She produced the evidence for him. ""This was the right one wasn't it?"

"Well I don't understand it mother." He sat back tipping the chair on two legs. "I just don't know." He scratched his head.

Suddenly he stood up looking at his watch. "I need to get going, I'll miss the bus."

When she looked around the quiet kitchen her eyes narrowed as she tried to recall the moments of the past; trying to think back, retracing the past.

∞

It wasn't until Millie was half way up the road that she saw Jack waiting outside Simmons shop for the Maidstone bus. By the time she had realised that it was him it was too late for her to turn back. She saw him look up. Despite Katharine being held fast by her reins she still managed to determinedly lurch from one side to the other.

"Katharine stop pulling you naughty girl." The child looked up dismayed at the sudden reprimand and her bottom lip protruded.

Knowing that he was watching them unsettled her. She was annoyed to find that she had spoken so sharply to the child. It was an irritation knowing that she looked dishevelled. All morning things had gone awry. First she couldn't find one of Katharine's shoes and then her purse wasn't in her shopping bag. By the time both had been found Katharine decided that she needed a wee. It had been quicker to carry her upstairs where she had left the potty in the bath than bring it downstairs. The child was becoming so heavy. When they came downstairs she realised that there were a few small wet stains on her skirt. It must have when she had bent down to empty the potty into the toilet and it had splashed back. For a moment she considered changing or sponging it down. In the end she had decided to leave it.

Now she was also aware that her hair had not been washed and that she felt and looked harassed.

With relief she saw that the bus was making its way down the hill. She slowed down enough to make sure that there was no way that they could meet before he caught the bus.

She heard him shout as he stepped onto the bus.

"Catch you later Millie!"

The bus waited before turning right and going on its way. She watched it disappear.

Katharine looked questioningly up at her to see if she was still in trouble. Her little forlorn face reproved Millie's unfairness.

Millie bent down to comfort her, giving her a quick kiss.

"It's alright, silly mummy got in a tizz."

The child was still uncertain.

"Tell you what let's go to see the ducks." She smiled at the child and was rewarded by a look of delight.

They crossed the road and went over to the pond. The ducks scattered at their approach.

∞

Jack watched the familiar scenes of fields and hedges, houses and farms as the bus wound its way round the narrow lanes towards Maidstone. It was strange to see such familiar sights when he felt so different. There was an unsettling feeling of doubt too in the pit of his stomach. What if he wasn't wanted? What if there was no job to go back to? There was always the black market but his contacts had scattered after they had been demobbed. He wasn't sure that he could set up anything so profitable again on his own. He had done nicely during last couple of years. The stores had provided a nice little earner. Always someone ready to take supplies and no questions asked. Once a requisition had been enhanced it became easy to off load the surplus. Leaving the army had cast him adrift.

He glanced out of the window. In the orchards the branches of the apple trees were bowing down, laden with their fruit. In the distance he could see the South Downs, indistinct in the summer haze, but he could see gold patches of the ripened corn in the fields below them.

The bus laboured up the hill below in low gear before it started its descent to Loose Valley and the town. Houses took the place of fields and then the fire station and shops as they neared the town.

He swung off the bus at Bishops Palace and walked across the road to the garage, his easy smile and casual manner at odds with the grip of unease in his stomach. He felt a stranger in his own land. The familiar building where he had worked now seemed peculiarly foreign. Yet there it was, in no way different than as he had remembered it. The large garage doors were shut. He went around to the side entrance and up the stairs to the little office. It seemed more cramped than it had done before; the stairs more scruffy and worn. He breathed deeply and pushed the little brass bell on the counter. It was suddenly as if he was transported back to the time when he had, as a young lad, been asking to be taken on. He felt the same uncertainty, the same insecurity flooding through him. A rejection as a young lad was one thing but could he recover if he was subjected to the ignominy of being cast over now that he was a man?

"My word if it isn't young Jack!"

The relief of the friendly greeting threw off his self-doubt. Of course he was needed. Why had he thought otherwise?

On the way home he relaxed. He took in the views with a new absorption. He was home now and he would make up for lost time. An image of an immaculate young woman wearing grey gloves and two-tone shoes came into his head. He smiled to himself. 'I wonder where you are now'. A well-heeled existence beckoned, he smiled at the simile of her shoes and his future. He needed to formulate plans.

As the bus bumped along his thoughts turned to Millie and then Thomas. A heaviness sat with him. He could recall as if it were yesterday the days of their childhood. An image came of them scrumping apples in the field; making dens by the stream and then constructing the swing which broke and dunked them both unceremoniously in the water. Such happy carefree times before things changed and they grew up and things got a bit complicated.

He swallowed uncomfortably when he thought of Millie. What a saucy minx she had been. Devilishly attractive in her uniform; quite a woman of the world when they had met casually in Chatham when he was billeted there and just before his lot got moved on again.

The silly sixteen whom he had been able to charm so easily had matured; she was well aware of the effect that she was having on the men around her. Quite irresistible.

It had been quite a shock to have heard that she had been ill and then the next moment the wedding was announced. She and Thomas! He hadn't thought that Thom was her sort. She never had shown any interest in him as far as he could remember, far too intellectual for her, and then there they were getting married and Thomas asking him to be best man. Even at her own wedding she could flirt with the best of them. Thomas didn't seem to notice her carrying on. Mind Thomas always saw the best in people, he even got on with Rosie, and she was a hard one to like; seemed to have a big sulk on at the wedding for some reason or another. Mind she looked a sight in the dress, hanging off her like a scarecrow. She never was a looker at the best of times. No chance that bridesmaid upstaging the bride that day! Thomas did the honours and took her for a twirl on the dance floor although he didn't look as if he was enjoying it much, couldn't wait for it to end if his memory served him right.

Still he did feel a twinge of guilt when the nuptials were announced, especially as it was only a few months before when they had been having a bit of a fling. They hadn't written to each other afterwards. There wasn't really any point. They both had a bit of fun and that was the end of it. He was never one for putting pen to paper at the best of times.

It was still a bit a shock to see her with a child in tow. She never seemed to be the maternal sort, too much of a good time girl for that. Thomas obviously didn't waste much time though. The little toddler must have been about two or three; he was never any good at guessing ages. He hadn't thought to see her with a child so soon though. He had always made it quite plain that he wasn't going to get tied down with a wife and kids. Certainly not the marrying kind. Free and easy that's the way he liked it. He wanted a chance to make something of himself. All that malarkey could come later. If a girl started on about net curtains, choosing engagement rings and the like, that was the time to scarper.

The bus stopped outside Drewe's shop. The blind was drawn half way down but he could see him cleaning up the place through the open door.

"Afternoon Mr Drewe. Still busy I see."

Drewe turned towards the door. "Oh it's you ....made it back then...all right for some."

"Yes as you can see, all in one piece."

He turned and walked away. 'Miserable old sod', he thought some things never change. He wondered whether to go straight home or to call over and see Millie. He was intrigued and restless. His mother had jangled his nerves that morning. He wasn't ready to face her.

He stepped back across the road and carried on down to the cottage. At first he was going to go around the back of the house as he had done in the old days but a new kind of reserve held him back. He knocked on the front door.

Mrs Latterbridge stood silhouetted in the doorway. He couldn't make out her expression but he had an uneasy sense that he was not welcome.

"Yes?" Her voice was sharp and curt.

"Hello Mrs Latterbridge is Millie in?"

"Why!"

He took a step back from the door. "I saw her this morning when I was catching the 8.30 and didn't have a chance to say hello." She stood looking beyond him blocking the view into the hall; her mouth pressed itself into a thin line as if to stop up any words that might escape. And he waited as the silence hung between them, irritated by her manner. What was the matter with these people!

A noise in the hall made her turn back and he could see the little girl dragging something along the floor. On seeing him she suddenly moved behind her grandmother folding herself into her skirt.

"It's not a good time Jack." Beatrice did not attempt to disguise her annoyance. The child's presence accentuated her sense of irritation, clinging to her; making a demand upon her that she did not wish to display in front of him.

They stared at each other. Jack heard the coldness of her tone.

"Sorry I must see to her. I'll tell Millie that you called" and she went to close the door.

"Hold up!" Jack moved quickly. He put his hand against the door and his lips formed the shape of a smile.

"No need to stand on ceremony Mrs L. With only just getting back home I thought it only right to say a quick hello that's all. I'll come back later if it's all the same to you."

The innocence of his manner jarred against her. He had wrong footed her, made her look small-minded. Her dignity was ruffled, her sense of grievance deepened. Who did he think he was, just

385

waltzing back as if nothing had happened? Got off scot free more like! Men like him always did.

The light tone of voice made Katherine curious. She peeped out at him considering him whilst still clinging on to the security of her grandmother.

Jack leaned forward, his wide grin offering reassurance, "And who's this then?"

"Katharine. Millie's eldest." Her sense of propriety overrode her aversion to his presence. The answer came of its own accord betraying her desire to keep him at a distance.

He saw the child's dark hair framing her little face; the deep violet blue eyes, recognising that already the child showed the promise of future beauty.

"Mmm... such a pretty little thing. And Millie...she's had another?"

"Yes she and Thomas, they have....they had a son. Now I really must get on Jack." She made a determined effort to face him down.

"Not to worry. I'll call again. See you around Mrs Latterbridge. Be sure to tell Millie I called." He gave a little wave to Katharine and strode back down the path seemingly oblivious as the door closed immediately behind him without her offering a goodbye.

Jack seethed. A hitherto unknown feeling of uncertainty had cast a cloud. He was peeved to not know the cause of her resentment. It compounded his sense of wellbeing; a sense that had overshadowed his homecoming. He had looked forward to his idea of being the centre of things once again and yet at every turn he felt diminished; that he had no idea of how things stood. They had closed ranks on him. Shut him out. He needed to re-establish himself, but first he had to find out the cause. A niggling doubt arose, one that he had buried deep. But he couldn't bring himself to examine the past. His nature would not tolerate introspection. He worried at the problem, scratching at the irritation, resenting the need to probe deeper.

He found himself edging the pond and continuing down the lane to Mote House. It was as if his feet knew more than his head. He followed their lead, unconscious of the thickening green of the hedgerow and the wind caressing the pale heads of cow parsley. He didn't see the cherry sized apples just beginning to take shape, the browned decaying blossom collecting like discarded confetti at the base of each tree or the hover flies that had yet to decide where to alight.

He felt the sun on his back but paid no heed to the clear blue sky that contained only a couple of circling hawks with their outspread fringed wings, catching the air currents as they choreographed their effortless ascent. He was at odds with the world and took no pleasure in his surroundings.

Mote House came into view. It was at once familiar and yet different. Again he experienced the same feelings that had come upon him at home, at the garage, then at the Latterbridges and now once again it was as if a new world one had taken the place of the old one, pretending to be the same as before, but not quite able to replicate it. It was an illusion of familiarity and he was on the outside trying to find a way back in.

As he came closer to the lion guarded entrance he could see that much had changed since he had last been there. There was an unkempt look about the place. No water played in the fountain. The wind had diligently collected small twigs and dusty old leaves and left them to settle against the corners of the porch way. The once immaculate lawns were in need of some work. Patches of daisies and dark fairy circles replaced the once unblemished green.

He pulled at the bell and glanced back at the grounds. A blackbird turned its head sideways, stamped vigorously on the blades of grass before suddenly lunging and then straining back to pull at the worm.

Then it took flight, its staccato calls loudly complaining that he had witnessed the assault.

Rosie opened the door to him. She was wearing an apron. At least she had not changed he thought. Still as thin as a rake, her hair in need of a good brush, and her eyes fastening upon him as if she could read into his soul.

"Well, well what can we do for you?" she turned back into the entrance hall leaving him to close the door behind him before following her.

"Millie's at home and won't see you. You've upset mother and now you want to know what's up I suppose. Thought you might have worked it out by now. Slow even for you Jack, the war didn't sharpen your senses did it?"

Her direct attack took him by surprise. He had not heard her speak so dispassionately. As children they had squabbled but he had never found himself so belittled. She was actually looking down on him; his own sister!

"I have a lot to do today the last patient left last week and we are trying to pack up the bedding."

He shook his head. She sighed at his incomprehension.

"The sheets and blankets. Now that the beds have been removed."

He followed her into the dining room. Where there had been thick carpets and fine furniture there were upended iron bedsteads stacked against the scarred wood panelled walls. The parquet floor showed unsightly deep grooves.

"The beds.....damage wasn't deliberate...they were difficult to move being so heavy."

"Mr Parsons volunteered the place as a hospital for wounded officers. All of the downstairs rooms were requisitioned. Some rooms upstairs have hardly been touched. A lot of them enjoyed the library when they were well enough to use it. Really the place has fared well considering, just a few careless cigarette burns, no pictures used as dart boards, or names carved on the walls...."

Rosie put a pile of sheets into a packing case before turning back to him.

"She knows why you want to see her. Things have changed Jack. You caused enough trouble in the past, and then left other people to clear up the mess."

Jack started to speak.

"Go home Jack. You're only in the way here. Go home and apologise to our mother. She worships the ground you walk on and you've done nothing but trample on her feelings." She shook her head as he continued stare at her.

"Just go home" she sighed, "And leave things be."

Cranesbury Village 2009
Rosie

I knew that he would stir up another hornets nest. He couldn't bear the thought that he wasn't in control; that he hadn't got his own way. Even though he had set his sights on Diana for his future prosperity he had to go meddling and stirring things up for Millie. But then she always was her own worst enemy. It was the usual tale of playing with fire. Her mother had warned her, and I told her what would happen, but she was so convinced that she could play him at his own game and finally pay him back for all the hurt that he had caused. As usual she hadn't begun to think of the consequences; being so determined release all the pent up emotion that she had kept in check.

Of course he eventually found out about Katharine. The evidence was there, staring him in the face. But then he was always so oblivious to the consequences of his actions, only believing that which suited him at the time, but that came a little later.

On that June evening when he came across Millie by the duck pond I think that even he was shocked at first by how guilty he felt when she confronted him about their past affair. She accused him of his reckless betrayal and how careless he had been with his friendship with Thomas. Once Millie made him realise that he lost a true friend he finally began to grieve for him. But then, true to form, it wasn't long before a warped self-pity set in. It became more about his loss and how he felt, rather than any consideration about Thomas. And his self-pity made him feel deprived; that somehow he was owed some compensation for his loss.

∞

It had been a warm night otherwise Millie would have gone home sooner. The day had been hot without a breath of air to cool the village people, and both toddlers had been out of sorts.

Katharine had settled much later than usual and Millie felt stifled. Even Sam, usually so easy to put down had squirmed and struggled against his covers, fighting against his overwhelming need to sleep. His red cheeks glowed with exhaustion; his hair lay wet across his forehead. Millie had taken him up and pulled off his vest in an attempt to cool him down but as soon as she tried to place him back into his little bed he became a state of misery; desperate to sleep but still fully awake. Finally Millie decided to try and place him in the pram, and take a short stroll around the village hoping that it would lull him to sleep.

She didn't see Jack leaning against the railing at first, being so preoccupied to settle Sam. When she glanced up he was there right in front of her. Even in the twilight his familiar handsome frame was unmistakable. But that same evening light gave her a confidence that daylight scrutiny would perhaps have denied her. It did not disclose the dark circles under her eyes but added a certain air of mystery to her appearance. She had washed her hair that morning and knew that she presented a better picture than she had on the previous morning when she had seen him catching the bus.

"Well, we meet at long last." Jack drawled, removing the cigarette from his lips and blowing the smoke away from them towards the pond. He chewed at the tip of his thumb and the tip of the cigarette continued to glow as he deliberately held it between two fingers close to his cheek. The posturing action suddenly reminded her of the heroes in the films that she had once adored. Now it just seemed to resemble an awkward cliché. He peered into the pram. The little boy had finally surrendered to sleep and was lying spread-eagled on top of the covers. Millie was proud of her child. He was so quick for his age, everyone said so, already quite able to chatter away with Katharine. They were as thick as thieves, quite inseparable. Katharine always wanted to mother him, and he allowed her to cuddle him, not protesting even when she held him too tight.

391

"Who's this then?"

"Samuel."

And he heard the fierce pride in her voice.

"Thomas never met his own son." She turned to face him. "He was killed in action…. we never found out where exactly. Somewhere in France we were led to believe."

She drew herself up and turned her head away from him.

"Yes…we lost all our best men in the end."

Her words stung him. He had not thought her capable of such a rebuke; to penetrate his confidence so easily. This was a world away from the silly empty-headed girl who had so easily succumbed to his charms. He was shocked at her maturity, leaving him floundering to regain control.

She turned back to see the effect of her words and was satisfied to see that he was struggling to respond.

"So how was your war then Jack?" Again the brittle tone of her voice disconcerted him. She had placed him squarely in the firing line and he felt unable to dodge her accusing words. He had not prepared himself; had not thought it possible to be in such a position.

"Nice to be home safe and sound no doubt."

"I didn't know about Thom. No one thought to write and tell me." It was his turn to attack. "He was my friend too y'know." She ignored the implied grievance; his need for some kind of recognition.

"Perhaps no one knew…well…knew exactly where you were. You always were difficult to pin down. Something in stores was it…?" He flicked his cigarette away.

"Well I won't keep you Millie. See you around no doubt. Always knew how to enjoy yourself if I remember rightly."

He sauntered away without a backward glance making towards The Papermakers Arms.

She stood watched him go and felt a pulse throbbing at her throat.

∞

The next day Jack took up his old position at Rootes. It was during the dinner break whilst he and another mechanic sat outside with their sandwiches that he found out that the firm had lost their salesman. "Poor sod. Joined up for the navy, first off, sailing round the Med no problem at all, and then bought it when he was home on leave. Direct hit in Campbell Road, got his house and half of next-door too. Good job he had no kiddies." Jack commiserated with him, whilst his heart soared. His thoughts raced. How to convince them to offer him the position? He needed some kind of leverage, some contacts, something that they couldn't turn down. All afternoon his mind was busy.

On the way home on the bus he turned over ideas, rejecting some, until he finally settled on a plan. It would be through Rosie. The Parsons had always had a soft spot for her, and now that she had been so close to them being at Mote House it gave him a way in. He would infer that she had wanted him to take up the opportunity. That it would improve things at home for Ethel and her. Parsons knew the right sort of people. He always had. But he also needed to find a way of making the Parsons somehow beholden to him. He had to make them believe that he was acting in the best interests of them all. What could he offer as an inducement that would interest the old boy?

The problem, far from being solved, seemed to spin around and around. He decided to bide his time and wait for the right moment. A thing like that could not be rushed.

∞

The early hot summer continued and by July the earth was parched and dry. The little stream that had flowed from Mote House down through Kilndown Woods to the old manor house dried up completely. The leaves on the apple tree started to curl up, and small un-ripened fruit fell under each tree. Even the hops slowed in their progress up each pole.

Millie had provided a tin bath of water in the garden for the children. Stripped to their knickers and pants they happily splashed and paddled in the galvanised vessel, stepping in and out, filling plastic buckets and pouring water over themselves and each other. Then tiring of that game Sam found it more fun to attempt to sink the toy boat whilst she tried unsuccessfully to rescue it. It was before long that she became exasperated.

"Stop it Sam. I'm going to tell on you if you don't stop it."

"It's mine!"

"It's not yours. I had it first."

"But it's mine…. I got it."

"It's not your one!" She made to grab it from his grasp but he was too quick for her, and grinning he held it behind his back. His legs planted wide apart to show off his victory.

"Mummy!" She shrieked. "Sam won't play fair!"

She stamped across the burnt grass as Millie appeared at the doorway with a beaker of lemonade.

"Goodness me what is going on here?"

Katharine was pink with indignation. "Sam's pinched my boat and won't give it back."

"Well you come and sit over here and have this nice lemonade, and we'll sort it out." She tried placating her.

Katharine stuck her tongue out at Sam and settled herself on the canvas deckchair. Her little legs stuck out at right angles to the ground.

Sam watched her enjoying the drink, torn between wanting one himself and not wanting to give up the toy. Katharine delivered the decisive blow as her mother went back to fetch a drink for him.

"Well I don't want it no more, and I'll drink your drink an all."

Sam threw the boat down into the tub and rushed towards her. In her attempt to ward him off she emptied the contents of the beaker over herself.

Millie came back to find Katharine screaming and Sam standing a little way off looking sheepish.

"Goodness me why can't you play nicely? And all that lovely lemonade that granny made for you spilt. Sam I think you need to come here straight away and say sorry to you sister, young man. Here! Come on!"

Sam heard the authority in her voice. She rarely spoke so crossly to either of them. He was shocked into obedience.

As he made his way over to them his bottom lip trembled and Millie held out her hand to guide him to them.

"Now what do you say?" He felt her lovingly comfort him as she held him close to her, enabling him to deliver his apology whilst knowing that she had already forgiven him.

When Jack came home from work he heard the children playing as he walked down the road. Their happy shrieks of laughter drew him to them. Peering over the fence he watched as they danced around the tug attempting to empty the contents of their buckets over each other. The innocence of their play suddenly took him back over the years to when they had played as children and he mourned the loss of that time when things had been so simple; before they grew up and the war took so much of it away.

The little boy reminded him of Tom in so many ways with his large brown eyes and the way he held himself, but Katharine was quite different. She was a pretty child there was no doubt but quite unlike either Millie or Beatrice Latterbridge. Her dark abundant curls and deep blue, almost violet eyes made her look quite exotic. She must take after her great grandmother he thought.

Millie appeared. "Time for tea now, that's enough now. Who wants some jelly for afters?"

The toddlers threw down the buckets and ran towards her.

"Oh no, not so fast, you two. I'll have the buckets and the boats if you please. We tidy up don't we, bring them here."

She looked up and saw him standing watching them. The children followed the direction of her gaze. He smiled at them and the boy's curiosity got the better of him. Sam went over to the fence holding aloft his boat.

"My boat...." He offered it for Jack's approval.

"Well it's a good one at that." He inspected it with due gravitas before handing it back. "And what's your name then. No let me guess. You must be Samuel!"

Sam beamed with pleasure at the recognition and nodded his head, stretching out his hands to receive the toy back.

"What's yours?"

"I'm Jack, an old friend of your mother's." He didn't look across to see Millie's reaction.

"You comin in to play?"

"No not today I'll come another day is that all right?"

The toddler shook his head slowly considering the agreeable suggestion, before offering his idea. "Katy's got a birthday we're having cake."

"Really... when's that then."

The child looked up to the sky for inspiration before solemnly announcing, "Yesterday tomorrow. She's three now. You comin?"

"Mmm I'm not sure!" He grinned at the child.

"You'll have to ask your mother."

Millie came across quickly, leaving Katherine to keep her distance from the stranger. "Come along young man...time for tea." She caught hold of his hand to lead him away.

Sam looked up at her, "He can come can't he?"

Millie involuntarily grimaced before she adjusted her smile.

"Goodness we'll have to see, he may be a very busy man." She turned and glared back at him.

"No problem Millie. I'd be delighted." He touched his hat and waved to the children before turning back to cross the road. When he reached pushed the door open the gloom of the bar caused him to pause and adjust to the new light. He considered the little scene, before a thought took hold. The lad said that his sister was already or going to be three, but that couldn't have been right. He must have misunderstood.

He walked towards the kitchen door. Had it been four years ago when she and Tom had got wed? He tried to recall the wedding. It had been a cold day, must have been early in the year. He hadn't thought that it was so long ago. It niggled him that it wouldn't come to him. There was something amiss and he couldn't think what it was.

Ethel was in the kitchen her mending things strewn across the table. She smiled when she saw him in the doorway. "Sit down lad I'll put the kettle on."

He allowed her to fuss over him.

"Just saw Millie and her kids over the way." He began.

"Oh uh huh." She placed the kettle under the tap and turned to the stove.

"Seems as if they're having a birthday party for the little girl soon?"

"Oh yes that's right dear....tomorrow I think. She was three this Tuesday. I saw Dulcie the other day asking if Ron could make a little cake for her. "

Her back was to him as she took the cups from the cupboard. He was pleased that he could question her without it being obvious.

"Oh that's nice......Didn't he do the cake for Millie and Tom's do too?"

She set a space on the table for the cups, pushing the sewing tin to one side.

"He did, made a nice job of it considering the rush. Mrs Parsons got some extra eggs for him as I recall. Mind, the icing had to be thin."

"What do you mean the rush?"

"Well, it turned out that she wasn't as white as the driven snow that March after all...so much for all the Latterbridge's swanky ways and fuss. She and Thomas....well it was the difficult times.... not that I blame poor Thomas of course. Just let's say that little Katharine came along sooner than was expected that year!"

Jack sipped his tea. So that was it! That was the answer, the reason for Mrs Latterbridge's evasion and the way Millie had been. They were ashamed to admit that Millie had been pregnant when she got married! Who'd have thought it! She and Tom...and he mused over the idea. He idly counted the months. March, April, May June, July....just five months that meant that....and he breathed in sharply. Nine months took it back to...just before the Christmas...that was the time when...and he put his hand to shield his eyes as the image of Millie swam into his head.

"Are you all right dear?" Ethel saw his taut face and his half-closed eyes.

"Is it too warm in here?"

Jack had to wait until the following week before he found the opportunity to corner Millie. He wanted to catch her when she was on her own and unable to evade an interrogation. She had either been in the village with the children or with Beatrice. It was on the Sunday afternoon when he had seen Beatrice and Ronald taking the children out. He watched them from the upstairs window that overlooked the pond as they made their way down the lane towards Mote House. Ronald was angrily gesticulating and pointing to the sky with his free hand as he struggled to carry a heavy bag with the other. Jack smiled to himself. Some people never change. Ronald was just as priggish as he had always been. Such a pompous man.

He heard Rosie banging around in her room and he came onto the landing.

"I've just been watching the Latterbridges going down the lane", he spoke to the interior of her room.

"Wonder where they're off to."

"Beatrice said that she would treat the children to a picnic at Mote House and give Millie a break. Mr Latterbridge wanted to watch the cricket match but she insisted... so I shouldn't think that he was best pleased. Mind the Parsons won't be too happy to see him either. Last time he went he told Mr Parsons that Forrester was being difficult. That went down like a lead balloon." Rosie laughed.

She poked her head around the door. "And don't you go stirring things up either Jack."

"What makes you think that I'm going to do anything of the kind?"

"Because I know you."

"You just think you do Rosie that's all."

He clattered down the stairs and went out through the kitchen.

Rosie rushed to the window and saw him quickly crossing the road and taking the back path into Ivy Leaf Cottage.

"Damn him!" Rosie sighed. "There goes another Sunday's peace!"

∞

Jack knocked lightly on the kitchen door. As Millie opened the door to him it she was so startled at first to see him standing leaning against the door jamb that she stood quite still before attempting to close it again.

"Now that's not very friendly Millie." He pushed his way past her. "No way to treat an old friend at all."

"You're no friend of mine Jack Minton."

"There's others that might think otherwise." He smiled down at her.

"What about a cup of tea then."

"I'm not making tea for you. I think you had better leave." She opened the door and indicated the exit.

"No Millie I'm not in the mood to leave just at present. I think you and I need a little talk. Mind....come to think of it you had a lot to say last time we met as I recall. A lot of...what shall I say....not what I would have expected from an old friend."

"You long since gave up that position...if you ever were a friend."

"Well you were friendly enough in Chatham. We seemed to rub along very well. Quite close you and I were then."

"Yes and haven't I had cause to regret it ever since!"

"Really Millie, whatever can you mean? I seem to remember that it didn't stop you from getting what you wanted."

"What are you trying to say?"

"Well it all turned out nicely for you didn't it you married Thomas and then had two lovely children."

He spread his hands out, "Unless there is something else that you haven't thought to mention."

Millie stared at him her mouth gaped open.

"Mmm now I wonder if I knew what you wanted to tell me...was it something about Katharine. Could that be it?"

She shook her head unable to speak.

"Yes I reckon that it could be that. Well, well, fancy that. Not Thomas's child... no? Perhaps somebody else's.... no surely not, not when you accepted Thomas's marriage proposal. Not when you knew that you were already carrying another man's child. Not the well brought up daughter of Mr and Mrs Latterbridge Millie!"

He banged his hand on the kitchen table.

"Did Thomas ever know that she was mine?"

Millie shook her head again. She had never seen him consumed with such a cold rage and his anger frightened her.

"So no denial then? So she is mine?"

She sat down heavily at the kitchen chair trying to hide her face.

"The truth will do Millie."

"The truth...what do you know about that? You would have never stood by me. I was just one of many to you. I didn't find out until it was too late, too late to do anything."

"Except to plan a nice white wedding."

She heard the sarcasm and winced at its directness.

"So what's to be done?"

"What do you mean?"

"I mean what's to be done? Who else knew about this beside your parents? And did Rosie guess? Yes I bet she did, there's not much that goes past her. No wonder she looked as if she lost a shilling and found a sixpence that day. Who else knew Millie?"

"No one knew."

"But Rosie knew."

"Yes she guessed."

"Guessed that it wasn't Tom's or guessed she was mine?"

"Knew it wasn't Tom's."

"Did she know the child was mine!"

"She knew."

"How?"

"She just knew. I don't know Jack, she just knew!" She stared at him.

"She knows more than we do about lots of things."

"What do you mean?"

"I'm not saying Jack."

"Tell me!"

"She's your sister, you ask her!" Suddenly she found some courage to stand up to him.

"How dare you come into this house and start throwing your weight around. I've never asked you for anything. You got off scot free and now you suddenly want to be a father... well it's not going to happen. It's always been about you but it isn't, it's what best for the children not you. Fathers are there for their children, they put them first. You've never done that in your life."

"Is that the line that your mother took?"

"No it's what I am saying. Me, little empty-headed Millie who you could always push around. I'm their mother and I know what's best for them and it doesn't include you!"

"So Katharine is going to be deprived of knowing her true parentage?"

"I'll tell her when the time is right."

They both turned in unison when Rosie came into the kitchen.

"I told you not to come Jack."

"I know what you are after." She sat by Millie and held her hand.

"Really? And what a lovely picture you both present, true friends." He laughed at their discomfort.

"Jack I know what you want." Rosie repeated. "And it's not about Katherine is it? You want to use whatever means you can to better your position. You think that this is a way to get to the Parsons. Do you really think that some kind of hare-brained blackmail is really a sound way to gain some leverage with Mr Parsons? Throwing all this dirt in their faces? Oh Jack what would our father think of you?"

"Don't throw that old chestnut back at me Rosie. I know you never thought much of him."

"He was a good father to you Jack, for all his faults."

Jack narrowed his eyes, "Oh yes, I remember now was this the man that used to knock our own mother around and left us with a mountain of debt. Is this the father we're talking about?"

Rosie sighed and breathed out slowly.

"Look," She tried again, "I know what you want Jack. If you stop fighting me and upsetting Millie I can help you. Just for once trust me and let me sort things out my way.

He shook his head, his mouth turned down in disgust.

"Why should I suddenly start trusting you?"

"Because I understand what you want and it'll benefit us all, and you'll have nothing to lose if you choose my way."

He threw himself down on the chair.

"And if I don't?"

"You'll lose the chance to come up in the world.....the chance to buy a certain lady another pair of dove-grey gloves."

She laughed at the seeming flippancy of her phrase, but her eyes locked into his and with a shudder he felt as if she knew all his secrets, and had always known them.

∞

Rosie met Beatrice and Ronald coming back up the lane as she made her way down to Mote House.

"I should have taken the pram with us. I think their little legs are quite worn out!"

Ronald was perspiring. "Proper planning and we wouldn't have had this problem." He transferred the picnic bag that was threatening to cut off the circulation to his fingers, to his other hand. Beatrice was carrying Sam on her hip and had a listless Katharine in tow.

"Let me help."

Rosie held out her arms and lifted Katharine up. The child wrapped her arms around her neck and her head lolled against her shoulder.

"My word you are a sleepy head!"

Beatrice started to politely protest, "We're taking you out of your way."

"No problem. It's only a few minutes for me."

Beatrice transferred the weight of Sam onto her other hip. "Goodness this child is growing fast. I'm sure he shoots up another inch every day." She felt awkward accepting Rosie's offer of help so quickly.

"Did you have a nice picnic?"

"Lovely, the children did enjoy themselves."

"Except for the damned wasps." Ronald breathed heavily.

Rosie and Beatrice exchanged glances and to their mutual astonishment they actually found themselves smiling at each other.

"Except for the wasps of course," agreed Beatrice, and she turned her head away from Ronald so that he wouldn't see the look of merriment on her face.

∞

Leaving the little party at the pond, Rosie turned back to continue on her way down to Mote House. She knew exactly what she was going to say and that Arnold would understand the need to settle Jack's ambition.

She was shown into Arnold's study. It still had boxes piled up at walls waiting for the military records to be transferred to London. He waved towards them disapprovingly.

"Thought they would have taken then by now. They said that they would definitely be gone by the end of the week and here they are still clogging up the place. I'll be glad to see the back of them and all their regulations and whatnot." His smile belied the sense of his statement. He was only too pleased to be back in his rightful place to be ruffled by such trifles.

"And what brings you here Rosie on a Sunday...thought you would have had enough of the place! Come and sit down my dear."

"It's a matter that involves my brother and your Millie Mr Parsons."

He frowned and took time to examine the buttons on his waistcoat before looking up.

"Go on with what you need to say."

"Some time ago you were kind enough to give Jack some good references. Without your say so he wouldn't have got the position at Roots and I dare say would not have been welcomed back."

"Mm...well?"

"Jack's forte lies elsewhere. He'll never make a good mechanic and when the firm has the pick of men they'll be pleased to let him go."

"So what's this got to do with Millie?"

"History has a habit of repeating itself with our families Mr Parsons." She waited to see the impact she had made. He breathed heavily and nodded slowly.

"Go on."

"She and Jack were close in the past. It could cause trouble for her."

"Trouble?"

"Jack has an ambition to better himself, but there is no possibility of that as it is, so he is looking around for a diversion.

"And our Millie is the diversion."

"Well in a way yes. But it's more to do with her reputation.... he has taken upon himself to ask questions about Katharine."

"Katharine, what's the child to do with it."

"History repeating itself."

He sat upright.

"You're surely not suggesting...!"
She interrupted him.
"No I'm not.... but he could cause people to question how things were. Gossips like to take one bit of news and before you know where you are the story has spread like wildfire. Millie could be very hurt by such rumours."
"Damned gossips! Folk are too fond of tittle-tattling; putting two and two together and making five."
He placed his large hands over his desk as if to smooth away creases of distress.
Rosie waited. The air in the study had taken on the scent of his masculinity once more. She could smell the beeswax of his recently polished desk.
"Mr Parsons. I want to ask you a favour. At Rootes there is a vacancy for a salesman. As it stands Jack has no chance of getting it. But I know that given the opportunity Jack would make more than a go of it. He is able, when he puts his mind to it, to be very persuasive. But there is more than that. If he had that first opportunity he could climb very quickly to the top. His ambition would leave us all behind here. He wouldn't give any of us a second look and we would be free to get on with our lives. He would be so wrapped up in his own life."
"So why have you come to me?"
"You know the families. You know the Pembertons and the Rootes family. You still have connections, Reggie in the Hawkhurst, and then Tunbridge Wells lot."
"You want me to put in a good word for him?"
"Yes there's that of course, but I also want to ask for a business loan. If he could offer some inducement to take on the position, without pay, on a profit sharing basis there would be no risk to them but in time he could build up a really good customer base. I know that he could do it."
Arnold shook his head slowly and sucked in his teeth. "Margins are very small at present Rosie, very tight. People have different

priorities at present, like just putting food on the table. The car trade is a luxury one."

"Yes I know." Rosie agreed. "But there are some who have had a good war, they still have money and some are still making it."

"Quite the little business woman aren't you." He smiled at her. "I don't know where you got your brains from Rosie. You are a one off an' no mistake. How much are we talking?"

"Well Dagenham is taking on more men and the Ford Anglia seems to be doing well. Rootes won't be dealing in the top end as yet so I'm thinking £400."

Arnold pursed his lips. "That's a tidy sum Rosie. And when will I see it repaid?"

"If Jack gets the position…. in five years… if you don't charge interest."

"No interest…on an unsecured loan…."

"It will be paid back…you have my word."

"I don't doubt you Rosie……but your brother is a different kettle of fish as you have already said."

"Exactly, that's my point…..he can charm the birds from the tree. Whereas…well…. I haven't that same capacity."

They smiled at each other.

"Well you strike a strange bargain… but I'm willing to take the risk I suppose."

"Do you think that you could speak to your contacts this week? I want to tell Jack as soon as possible."

"I'll do some telephoning around, might even pay William a visit to speed things up, take him out for lunch….how does that sound?"

"It sounds good. It has taken a weight of my mind too."

"You seem to spend a good deal of time thinking of others rather than yourself Rosie. You need some fun as well. Put some roses in those cheeks."

"Oh I'm fine Mr Parsons."

407

"So what are you going to do once things have been sorted out here? Take up nursing as a career, with all the experience that you've gained being here?"

"No, I haven't the vocation, besides there is a lot to do in the pub. We need to look at ways of encouraging more custom than just passing trade. The locals just make it tick over but there's no real profit in that….to be absolutely truthful I haven't given it much thought. I think the war made us focus on the here and now."

He nodded his agreement. "I think we've all been like that…what is the phase? In suspended animation…that's it!"

She went to stand.

"Mind Rosie, you really ought to use that brain of yours."

She smiled at him. "It's nice for you to say so, but I haven't any special talents, chamber-maiding and waitressing are rarely recognised as formal qualifications even in these enlightened times!"

They laughed easily together.

So that's how it came about. Jack's enthusiasm for the latest gleaming vehicle enticed those all who were quibbling about a purchase. He was the archetypal salesman. The acquisition of a good suit, his good looks and a genial manner soon attracted admiring glances. He was in his prime, confident and successful. Even William Rootes had to admit that sales were booming and his profits were looking healthy. That's when Diana was drawn in.

She watched him laughing with a customer, noted his easy charm and as she passed the showroom he raised an appreciative eyebrow and tipped his hat towards her.

Within three months they were walking out together. He met her family. Within six months he was a frequent visitor to their grand and imposing house, charming her mother, impressing her father. His acquisition was within reach. A year later their engagement was announced, and within two years by 1947 they were married.

Jack never deviated from the path that he had set to follow and he never took a step out of line. He had imagined that he had captivated her, but in fact it was he who was completely entranced by her, although he would not in those early years ever have admitted it.

He loved her carefree manner and her confidence of her well-placed position in the world. She brought glamour and prestige to his life and he never looked back. He flirted with his customer's wives and girlfriends but only enough to enable him to close the deal. The flirtation was merely a part of the business plan.

Diana may have been his quarry but he was her prize. She brought out the very best in him, and he became the brother that I had hoped he would become. Finally the two warring sides of his nature became reconciled. She achieved the almost impossible, undoing the years of cunning and malice that Ethel had encouraged in the child.

They say that a leopard never changes its spots. Well perhaps his were just camouflage because he did change. His success made him generous.

Jack and Diana had a sprawling place on the outskirts of Tunbridge Wells, bought with the proceeds of his car dealership business. By then he was only dealing in the classic car trade; big money and even bigger profits to be made.

I saw little of them in the intervening years. It's not that we lost touch by choice just that their lives and mine went in different directions.

There was just one time when things changed. It was a shock to them all. It could have been disastrous. It was a difficult time that took some time to heal.

Diana, as an only child kept close to her parents and they had always treated Jack as their own. He had made their daughter happy; provided them with three lovely grandchildren and they continued to enjoy a comfortable lifestyle. Jack had no reason to look back. He always looked forward. He still had ambition but it was tempered by an overriding sense to value the present. He was no longer driven.

∞

It should never have happened, but then the sixties were a time when things changed in many people's lives.

Katharine was living in London in a comfortable flat. Her inheritance from Lady Faversham had long gone by then but it had given her the chance to move away from the dreary country life that she despised and cultivate a new set of friends. At first she had studiously attended the art college course in Maidstone for the first year, travelling back and forth from Cranesbury, but that soon began pall. Once her fellow students had introduced her to the city scene it gradually began to draw her in. At eighteen she was too young to handle money but too old to take advice. Ronald had tried to intervene but the talk of investments bored her. At last she felt that she was free, and her many friends encouraged her expansive lifestyle.

She was always going to be beautiful, her genes had determined it. Jack's and her own grandmother, it was a striking combination. The fashion scene beckoned, and she followed. Within months she acquired an agent and work poured in. Within ten years she had reached the pinnacle of her profession but then her age started to slow down the amount of offers. The world wanted new fresh faces, quirky, different. Her classic beauty was not as highly prized. Younger, thinner girls sashayed down the walkways, their anorexic faces defiantly facing the flashing cameras.

It was at the jazz club in Soho in 1968 that she first met Peter. The smoke haze that hung suspended in the air provided a filter of mystery. She was sitting with a girlfriend and two young men in a corner of the crowded room. They had ordered more drinks. Their voices were raised as their consumption of alcohol diminished their inhibitions. She looked bored. She had only gone because Belinda was so insistent.

∞

"Come on it will be wild! Anyway I'm doing a shoot in Brixton on Friday and then I've got to be back in boring Bruges. You remember… that magazine job…come on …I told you about it ages ago? Ghastly cheap stuff…bloody awful clothes. Nothing fits and you end up being pinned into the things."

"Oh I don't know…. who going?"

"Damien and Roger."

"Oh God not that pair of queers!"

411

"It'll be fun. They sold some stuff the other day and have been flashing the cash ever since."

"Last time, as I remember they bickered all evening, it was dreadful."

"Don't be such a misery Kate. You'll enjoy it, promise!"

∞

"Remind me not to believe you next time you ask."

"Aw...Kate, lighten up....there's some seriously good talent out there. Just look around"

She waved a hand to indicate the bodies swaying together. The space was too cramped to do otherwise.

"It's unbelievably hot. I can hardly breathe."

"Wow ...neither can I... will you just look at him...!"

Katharine looked at the young man standing at the bar. He took a cigarette from his shirt pocket, lit it, and as he drew in the smoke he lazily surveyed the scene. As she watched him he turned his head and looked across at her.

She couldn't resist a smile in response to his nod of appreciative acknowledgement.

"Wow...now that's one fanciable young man....and I saw him first sister," breathed Belinda.

She rose from the table and walked towards him. Katharine watched as she whispered something into his ear and drew him onto the dance floor, twisting her arms around his neck. They swayed together; his hand rested across the small of her back.

By the time Belinda arrived back to the table Katharine had decided to leave.

"Oh no...don't go, the night's still young."

"And so was that young man that you were trying to eat...cradle snatcher!"

"Don't be so mean....you're no spring chicken yourself!"

"Thanks for that...who needs enemies when friends....."

She trailed off as she became aware of him standing by their table.

He nodded down at her.

"Your friend forgot to introduce us. Fancy a dance?"

She rose to accept quite aware of Belinda's furious face. He led her to the centre of the room...squeezing them between seemingly inseparable groups.

"And what do you do with yourself when you're not here." She was amused as he held her close to him, pleased with the effect that she was having.

"I'm at the LSE"

"Oh..... a student....and what are you studying?"

"Law...for my sins..."

"And do you..."she smiled up at him.

"When the occasion arises."

She felt the pressure of his hand move to her lower back and smelt the beer on his breath.

"Does this law student have a name then?"

"He does," he grinned "But you have to tell me something first."

"Oh... do I? Like what?"

"What you do...and where have you been all my life?"

She tutted. "And you were doing so well...but now a little cliché...shame on you young man." But the delight in her laugher demonstrated her pleasure at the compliment.

"So what do you do?"

"Oh this and that.... I model... for various fashion houses." She shrugged, "I go to the theatre, frequent bars and sometimes meet young men, students....." she teased.

He was captivated by her confidence; aroused by the scent of her body so close to his own. The evening of heavy drinking was starting to affect his ability to focus but her boldness still drew him on.

∞

When he finally awoke he was confused by the unfamiliar surroundings. His head felt tight and as he went to sit up he could feel an unpleasant sensed of gravity pulling him around. One arm was completely numb; it didn't feel as if it belonged to him, he had no feeling in it. As he moved again he realised that he was sprawled out on a hard couch too short for his length, his legs were tangled in a blanket.

A moment at the door caught his attention.

"Ah you're finally awake then!"

He shook his head trying to recall the night.

"It's okay kid, you were completely blotto by the time we got here. An' you're worried; I think you're still a virgin as far as I know!"

He felt the taunted by her words; humiliated at her seeing him in such a helpless state.

He suddenly had an overriding need to find a toilet as his stomach threatened to reject the previous night's contents.

She saw his distress and quickly opened a door.

"Try not to miss....I've got a long day ahead."

Later that morning he watched covertly from the kitchen as she dressed, thinking that she would not discover his vantage point. Every deft move that she made fascinated him. She drew on her stockings clipping them onto the suspender belt. Her slip slid over her body clinging to her curves. He saw how she expertly twisted each small pearl button on her lilac blouse before drawing up the skirt zip.

She laughed at his quiet study. "You learn to dress and undress fast in my world."

He blushed as he realised that she had been aware of him watching her.

Brushing her hair she replaced the brush back on the dressing table before she theatrically turned her back to him moving her head to glance over her shoulder.

414

"Time you were going kid. "She imitated the low tone of Katharine Hepburn.

"Can I see you again?" He heard his own desperation in the request.

"Sure...you might, if you go to the right places in town."

"I still don't know your name." He felt suddenly immature; concerned now that she obviously realised how gauche he was.

"Katharine you can call me Kate." And she went to show him out.

"No I mean your real name." He understood that she had alluded to the film star.

"It is Katharine, my mother named me after Hepburn, she was into films in a big way back then when she had me." She shrugged.

"Cary Grant, James Stuart.... in those days that's what they did, a trip to the cinema every week she used to say."

∞

Of course it ended in tears, thankfully ending before it had a chance to begin.

She had eventually decided that a day out in the country would be fun. He had pleaded with her and as she had nothing better to do that weekend she gave in. It amused her to know that she had such a constant admirer. In one way she was curious to see the place where he lived. She could see that he was used to having money and was not afraid to spend it. Anyway she was bored and thought it would be a nice diversion.

They motored down to Tonbridge Wells on the Saturday afternoon. He had wanted to make an early start but she laughed and told him that she didn't do early mornings at the weekend; said that he could come and pick her up after lunch.

When they swept into the drive she was impressed. The old warm red brick and Tudor styled Victorian house boasted six bedrooms and five reception rooms. A trimmed flowering wisteria followed the line of the porch and lower windows, draping its heavy blossom in a profusion of blue-lilac.

As he swung the car to a halt at the front door she heard the sound of gravel crunching under the wheels.

She went to walk towards the front door.

"No this way," he walked ahead of her circling the bow window as he followed the path to the back of the house.

She was amused to find that she had followed him, allowing him to lead her, as he demonstrated a new confidence, being on home ground.

Jack was sitting by the back door and turned his head at their approach. He saw her trim figure and the cascade of dark hair falling around her shoulders. She was quite a looker, older than he had thought she would be, but still quite stunning. He was proud that his son had such good taste.

"Hi dad."

He rose to meet them and held out his hand.

"Kate," she extended the tips of her fingers, and looked at him with some appreciation.

He indicated the table still holding his small tumbler of gin, and then turning to Peter he gave him a hug.

"Would you young folk care to join me... coffee, a cold drink, something alcoholic perhaps?"

"Just a coffee for me." She slid into the seat opposite to him.

He could not see her eyes. They were hidden behind her oversized glasses, but he was aware that he was being scrutinised.

"Pete, do you want to see to that?"

"Sure dad." He disappeared into the interior of the house.

"How was the journey down?"

"Uneventful." Her mouth turned up amused by his opening gambit of small talk.

"So you live in the city."

She nodded. "Hampstead Heath."

"Nice area to live."

"It has its compensations." Again there was her slow smile.

"Nothing like this of course."

A bee landed heavily on the table. Its legs were swaddled with thick bands of yellow pollen. They both watched it in the silence that followed and watched its ascent as it suddenly decided to take off.

"Peter tells me that you work in fashion."

"I model... yes."

He could imagine her swaying on a catwalk. She knew the effect that she had. It amused him to see her playing with him. Quite captivating he had to admit.

Peter came back placing the cups carefully on the table.

"Drat I forgot the sugar!"

He walked back to the house.

"For a fashion house?"

She shook her head. "No-one that you would know. Some stuff goes into the women's mags, My Weekly, Good Housekeeping.....
I did a shoot for Cosmopolitan, but that was a while ago now. My agent did say that Vogue could still be interested but we shall see. It's a fickle industry."

She took a cigarette from her handbag and lit it, blowing the smoke away from them, and resting her elbow on the arm of the chair.

"The photographers have their favourites... you wait for the right opening and then..." She shrugged, "well, it pays the rent."

"So an independent woman then?"

They watched as Peter came back.

"So what are your plans for the day Pete?"

"Thought we might check out The Pantiles, see if there is anything to catch her eye. Come back for some grub and then leg it back again."

"Sounds irresistible!"

He finished his drink and stood up. "Well I won't keep you. See you later then."

"Actually Kate's folks are from around there too."

"Really?" He turned back arrested by an awful thought. An image two children playing in a garden came into his mind.

"I might know them... what's their name?" He tried to steady his voice.

"Oh it's just my mum now, well my mum and gran now. My father was killed in the war, I never knew him. Fulwood, my mother's Millie Fulwood." She sipped her coffee.

He waved his arm to say goodbye and walked quickly back to the house. There was a pounding in his ears. He felt his chest tighten. In his panic he didn't see the edge of the hat stand and felt the corner drive sharply into his hip.

Katharine! She was his Katharine, the child that he hadn't seen for over twenty years or more. His past had suddenly tumbled into the present. He couldn't breathe....what was to be done? Had she and Pete already...it was unthinkable! And to think he had actually found her...attractive, his own daughter! He was aghast. He had even flirted with her! But what if Katharine and his Peter...he choked as he tried to subdue his fear. How could it have been possible for her not to have known? Had Pete never told her his name for Christ's sake! It was incredible! What a bloody mess!

But it had to be stopped. He had to find a way to end it all.

There was an incessant ringing in his ears. A phone was ringing in the hallway. He walked towards it as if in a trance.

"Hello?" He couldn't think straight.

"Jack...it's me, Rosie. I need to see you. Don't ask now, just come over. I'll explain when you get here."

He put the phone down, replacing the receiver onto the cradle, wondering if it had actually happened. It was like a bad dream. Surely he would awaken and it would all go away. Things like this didn't happen to people like them. He gazed around him; the beautiful house, a loving wife, his wonderful children, a successful business, and more money than he had first thought it possible to have.

Then anger replaced his bewilderment. He would not see it all destroyed but he could not see a way forward. It would all come out. How could he prevent it?

He tried to think what Rosie had said. Did she say she was coming over? No, he was muddled... he was to go over there. Why did she want to see him now...at this time when he had enough to worry about? But then she often seemed to be on the button, perhaps she had had an inkling of all this. Perhaps Millie had mentioned something to her.

He would leave a note for Diana. She would be back at five. He could be there and back even before then if he went now. He locked the doors and ran to the car.

∞

I waited for him to calm down before I said anything.

"We'll go for a walk it will help clear your head."

"I just don't know what to do. The lad is smitten with her, Christ his own sister!"

"Half-sister." I watched him trying to steady himself, my words not leaving a trace.

We walked together following the road down the hill towards the station; away from prying eyes. He looked so distracted.

"And what if they've already...you know, done it!" He appealed for me to understand the inference without having to spell it out. He could not bring himself to say the words.

I shook my head. "She's just amused by him. It's like having a pet: she likes the adoration, those puppy dog eyes of his....nothing more."

"How can you even know that?" He hunched his shoulders in desperation, "Anything could have happened."

419

"Yes it could have but it hasn't. She has enjoyed keeping him at arm's length, tantalising him. Remember she is aware that she is not quite in the first flush of youth….. he's, well he's still just an impressionable young boy in her eyes."

"I hope that you are right." His breath was short as he tried to quell the panic.

"This can be sorted out. There's the carrot and the stick. He shook his head "I don't know what you mean exactly."

"Money talks, opportunities are getting harder for her. There are a whole set of new thin Twiggy girls on the block. Her looks aren't the ones in demand now, and she's used up all the money she had from the inheritance.

"Inheritance… who from?" He looked up and his eyes narrowed.

"A trust fund set up by Lady Faversham. Katharine came into the money when she was eighteen. That's why she gave up the art college; took herself up to London.

But he was still thinking about what I'd said.

"She got an inheritance off the old lady huh? Well well….."

His eyes narrowed.

I ignored him. "Money can so easily drip though your fingers if you don't make it work for you. Anyway it's long gone. You need to get some distance between them…..a one way ticket to Hollywood f'instances. Who could resist the glamour of that? All her life she's modelled herself on those old film stars. And over there they still appreciate the classic type of looks that she has."

He sucked at his teeth, worrying over the problem. I could tell that he was thinking about his son; the explanations to be given, the questions that could be asked.

He signed deeply. "It won't work. These Hollywood types….the girls are young…starlets in the making….eighteen year olds…"

"Perhaps, but you have to admit that she has style, she knows how to promote herself."

"And what to say that she'll come back after a couple of months when it doesn't work out, and we'll be back to square one. And what do I tell Pete?

"Nothing…. you don't need to explain."

I went to continue but he was too insistent and interrupted me.

"No hear me out Rosie. First we have to find God knows how much money, then she has to agree for God's sake and then what do we tell her…that suddenly we're going to sponsor her with no guarantee that she'll find work or will even stay there. It's all fantasy!"

"She'll agree." I said. "When you see Beatrice and explain, she'll agree."

"Me?"

"Oh yes she'll make sure that Katharine goes….carrot and stick."

"What am I to say? Tell her that I think my daughter and my son are…she'll…I don't know!"

"You forget it's her granddaughter too. She cares very much about her and she'll not want another family scandal."

"What other scandal…Millie and me?"

"Well yes." I allowed his ignorance "you and Millie."

∞

And that's how Katharine went to America. Jack paid for the tickets and Beatrice asked her father for some extra funds. Katharine was mortified when she was given her birth certificate and immediately applied for a passport; she didn't need to be told not to contact her step-brother and her flat was quickly sold. Peter just assumed that she was away working away somewhere until he came to painfully realise that she had simply walked out of his life. After a few days when he had not seen her he went to her flat. That's when he saw the For Sale sign.

Katharine never did make it into the film industry. Despite several promising screen tests and some bit parts she ended up meeting a flamboyant film executive and they got married. As it happened it was 'happily ever after' for a while but then Hollywood finds a way of destroying relationships. Finally she found his womanising too difficult to handle. They divorced and she ended up marrying a construction manager, had two girls and they moved up to Washington. He was a reliable guy, solid and dependable, a world away from the lifestyle in California. Sadly apart from an annual Christmas card there was little contact with her family in Kent.

Peter met Caroline in his final year at university in 1970 and they had enjoyed a casual fling, but it wasn't until ten years later that they finally got together. Both had been in long term relationships that hadn't worked out. When they finally met up again they were both wary of repeating past mistakes and both knew what they wanted.

Peter had already established a successful business and later that year in 1980 they were married. Their son Adam came along two years later.

Peter previously had pursued a variety of jobs with law firms but although he had been making good money he felt restless. He had an embryonic entrepreneurial talent that needed to be released there was the inherited flair for communication from his father and he was good with people, but he didn't want to be in the motor trade despite Jack's offers of a partnership. He needed to find his own way and it came about just by chance.

It happened when he was talking to a friend over a long liquid lunch. The rambling discussion meandered aimlessly until the subject of the boom in the American antique trade came up. It immediately caught hold of Peter's imagination.

Within the year he had found a suitable small shop in Tunbridge Wells and by the late 1970's he was shipping container loads of distressed bric-a-brac to Maine, New Hampshire and Vermont. Caroline had a keen eye for quality which suited the home market. She organised the shop side whilst Peter happily trawled around auction houses and house clearance sales finding what could only be described as second-hand junk. Old mangles, rusty pots and pans, old door handles, Victorian cracked chamber pots and distressed Welsh dressers sold over there just as well as Caroline's exquisite Art Nouveau Royal Dux figurines and vases, her Dresden china, French bronzes, Tunbridge ware and her ubiquitous Staffordshire China dogs did at home.

Minton Antiques; it was just meant to be.

Many customers were attracted by the name; bemused when they found that it was not just a clever marketing ploy but his actual name over the shop doorway.

They decided to put Adam's name down as a day boy for Dulwich Preparatory School and later at the age of eleven he attended Cranbrook School as a boarder. Adam was described as an all-rounder and fitted in well. He enjoyed all the sporting opportunities that were offered and, although not zealous in his studies, he always managed to attain sufficient grades to satisfy Peter and Caroline.

"Education is an investment." Adam was told. "Spend the time well and it will reap its own rewards."

He happily accepted the mantra but paid very little attention to it. His tutors found it difficult to chastise him for his lamentable efforts since he possessed such a cheerful gift for appeasement. He was an archetypal hare; bounding to the finishing line just behind the tortoise but always managing to complete the race. Perhaps if he had been more studious he could have achieved far more, but he was happy in his own skin and attracted a set of loyal friends.

There was a period during his final two years at Cranbook when he realised that if he wanted to continue his studies and apply for a place at university then his nonchalant approach to the course work needed to be amended. He did buckle down and found to his surprise that he had actually enjoyed the experience.

Once he was accepted into Kent University he moved to live in student accommodation in Canterbury. The years of boarding made it difficult to accept the constraints of home life. In moments of sober reflection he said that he found himself a stranger to his own family. Not sharing everyday experiences with his two sisters made him feel an outsider whenever he went home. It was as if they spoke a coded language which he could only finally penetrate when it was almost time to leave them again.

They enjoyed family holidays, skiing in the Alps and hot summers in Lake Garda, but his gap year spent travelling around the Antipodes gave him a real sense of being his own man. The open spaces of Australia, the beauty of New Zealand and experiencing the colourful cultures of Vietnam, Thailand and Burma almost convinced him that his future lay in in those distant lands.

It was only when he came back and met Ellen that summer that his wanderlust abated.

He and Ellen….. Ellen and Adam.

But there is more to tell; more to explain. The parts that have been hidden in the past.

The Papermakers Arms 1950
Millie and Dulcie

Millie's life was so very different. She became introspective. She imagined slights where there were none. She even bickered with Beatrice over the way the children should be governed, and it irked her that Ronald, who had always doted over her, became so quickly irritated by the children. He became more petulant and childish himself. The children had become her focus so she defended them even when she knew that they need to be censured. Of course it did not help her mental wellbeing that I was so determined to keep Sam close to me. It was all I had left of Thomas. I was jealous of their relationship. I wanted him to be mine. Dulcie saw the two sides. She saw the danger of possessive love and tried to act as mediator, to mitigate the worst excesses. She helped me through those early years, easing us all through our petty squabbles. She saw my plans and coaxed me to be more reasonable.

Lovely kind and generous Dulcie.

She had been my sister in birth and was my sister in spirit. We had such a shared understanding. There was no need to speak, we just knew each other. Her gift was as strong as mine but she allowed it to guide her whereas I fought against it, trying to bend it to my will.

When she met Graham Sumner I knew that they would be happy. He was like her, open-hearted, but was a far simpler, uncomplicated soul. What you saw was what you got. He accepted his lot and made no demands. I liked him as soon as I met him. He was working for the Gas Board They were laying another pipe- line, bringing gas pipelines to a farm near Iden Green

He was a quiet man, shy at first before he got to know you, very practical and willing to lend a hand. He came into The

425

Papermakers Arms early one evening in 1950 and asked if we were serving meals.

∞

"Well we have meat pies but nothing fancy."
"I'm not looking for fancy just some plain good grub." His grin lit up his face. You could not help but take to him.
I led him to a spare table by the window.
"We get them fresh from our baker up the road. He does beef and kidney or just the beef."
"Reckon I'll have the beef and kidney then."
"And what will you have to drink."
"Just a half. I'm catching the 6.44 back to Paddock Wood, and then on to Charing Cross."
"You've not got much time then, it's a mile down the road to the station."
"I know… I'll have to get my skates on."
As I walked back to the kitchen to warm the pie I willed Dulcie to come. I could see them together. There was such a feeling of brightness about the image that I held. I felt such warmth wrapping around me, hugging me; enveloping me in a layer of peaceful calm.
Dulcie knocked on the kitchen door and came in
"He's in the bar." I said and she unquestioningly took the pie from me.
I went to the bar and reached up for a glass, watching her as she bent down to speak to him.
He had looked up and I could see the attraction that passed between them. He had such an easy way.
I beckoned to Dulcie to take the beer glass from me and she went back to him. They exchanged small talk; more was communicated than the words themselves.

Then in no time he stood up, it was time, he had to go. He knew which direction to take but still allowed Dulcie to accompany him to the door. They stood closely framed in the doorway as she pointed down the hill.

Of course he came back the next day and the next. He was to get some lodging in Hawkhurst to save the journey but I told him we had a spare room and we could do with the cash. He took it for the week, and then the next. Soon he was a familiar figure in the village, getting to know the locals, exchanging pleasantries.

One evening he was especially late coming back. I had saved him some supper as he was always ravenous after a hard day at work.

"You're looking a bit peaky tonight, difficult day?"

"No more than usual just the blues I reckon." I smiled at his concern.

"Y'know when you do that you just remind me of Dulcie."

"Do what?"

"That look you both have. I dunno it's difficult to describe. When I first knew you I thought that you were sisters! You both have a way of knowing a chap I suppose.....getting under your skin. It's a bit unnerving at first!"

I shook my head as if to find this news bewildering.

"Surely folk have said that to you before!" he looked bemused at my reaction.

"No never."

He held my gaze. "You're dark horse Rosie......if I hadn't fallen for Dulcie then who knows?" He joked but then he caught hold of my hand, suddenly quite serious.

"I hope there's a good chap out there for you too," and patted my arm kindly.

∞

Three years later in June of that year there were two marvellous celebrations to relieve the austerity of the times. First we squashed into the Latterbridge's front room, gathering round the

427

television to watch the coronation of Queen Elizabeth. Millie sat with Sam and Katharine on the settee, Beatrice and I used the kitchen chairs, Dulcie sat on Graham's knee whilst Ronald commandeered the other arm chair. The rain pattered against the windows that morning as the flickering black and white images of the young Queen tucked inside the royal coach, appeared on the small screen, but it couldn't dampen our enthusiasm. We were delighted to witness such a significant piece of history.

Graham was there too.

"My folks camped out all night. I bet they're soaked to the skin!" He was worried about them. "Wonder if we'll see them. They should have got a good spot. They said that they were going to The Mall."

We watched the possession passed the waving crowds and then held our breath as she proceeded slowly up the central aisle of Westminster Abbey.

Later that day after the street party we watched the fireworks lighting up the sky.

Graham leaned into Dulcie, wrapping his arms around her.

"We shan't need fireworks on our day love."

∞

By the end of that month the normal June weather returned. It was warm and dry. On the day Dulcie looked radiant. Her unfussy short white dress had a sweetheart neckline with a pinched waist and her short veil was held in place, hiding her brown curls, with a circlet of cream roses.

She chose Katharine and Graham's niece to be her bridesmaids much to their delight. She knew that Sam would have been mortified as a pageboy despite Ronald's helpful suggestion to them both when they were first planning the day. I think he would make an excellent usher she told him firmly, and for once Ronald did not pursue the idea.

Later the reception was held at the village hall. Dulcie was determined not to make too much fuss.

"It's enough that we are together," she said.

The two bridesmaids were secretly delighted with their dresses although they both affected an air of grown-up nonchalance. Katharine was as dark as Graham's niece was fair, dark and light, day and night; a pretty combination.

Ronald was his usual stiff self, holding court to whomever he managed to corner. Beatrice watched him as he rose to make his speech, clearing his throat noisily. Her eye caught mine.

He droned on, offering a plethora of mundane platitudes as creative gifts to the assembled guests....welcoming Graham to their family....not losing a daughter but gaining a son.... it seemed only like yesterday when Dulcie was just starting school...where had the years gone....trust that Graham would be able keep her in the style in which she had become accustomed. Beatrice was embarrassed by his faint insinuations that Dulcie somehow had not made a better match, and hoped that Graham's family would not notice.

Graham rose to give his speech. His cheeks were red-tinged as he proudly glanced down at his bride.

He started quietly first complimenting the two pretty bridesmaids and thanking the two families for their support, and then, as he realised that his first joke had gone down well, his confidence grew and he was able to turn to his bride and question how it was that she had chosen to make him the happiest of men.

"Just think if it hadn't been for Ron's wonderful steak pies and the Gas Board bringing me to this part of the county I wouldn't be here now celebrating the very best day of my life with you all. I still can't believe my luck."

After all the speeches people settled down to catch up on family news and gossip. Graham came to sit with us. Sam was gleefully just finishing his second piece of wedding cake and was eyeing up the trestle table which still held some the remains of the buffet.

"Go on lad," Graham encouraged him. It'll be a while before you see a feast like that again.

He turned to me.

"When I was his age my mother could never fill me up..... said that I must have hollow legs!"

We watched him hover over the table. "Rationing hard for everyone but I think it's hardest for these kids of today not to have had the things that we took for granted when we were young 'uns."

He gazed unfocused into the distance.

"My mum was always a good cook and she can still put things together to make a good meal, more than can be said for some around where she lives. Kids by her, well best grub they ever get is a bag of fish and chips from the local chippie."

I looked at his profile and thought of Thomas. He would have approved I thought.

Graham watched three older couples who had spontaneously risen to dance. Their steps were well rehearsed as they held each other comfortably together moving as one.

"You and young Sam are close too aren't you? Spend a lot of time together."

I nodded.

"Even thought that he was yours when I first came here."

I didn't reply.

"You need to let people in Rosie. You're still a very attractive woman you know. I think that it's time for you to come out from those shadows. We both think so, Dulcie and me."

He grinned down at me as he stood up.

"Take my advice Rosie. You look after number one for a change.
Well I need to find my wonderful wife and give her a whirl
around the floor."

I could hear his delight at being able to acknowledge that she
was his at last.

"I'm so glad that she found you Graham. You'll both be very
happy."

He turned back to her.

"Funny that's exactly what she told me" He laughed easily and
went off stepping carefully around the dancers to find his bride.

I went to find Arnold and Louise. They were watching the
dancers too as his hand rested on her arm.

"Ah... hello young Rosie. Saw you talking to Graham just now.
Nice chap I must say....a good sort. I was only saying to Louise
wasn't I my love?"

She turned and agreed.

"Yes a nice young man. Sensible. I'm very pleased for Dulcie.
They make a good match."

"Fancy a little turn around the floor then Rosie. I think I can still
remember how!"

I nodded. "Still remember how! You're still in your prime Mr
Parsons!"

He held me lightly but firmly guiding me around the other
dancers with practised ease.

"And how's married life suiting your brother Jack these days? All
very fast wasn't it? You certainly had your finger on it and no
mistake. And they have a son I hear. How old is he? Must be one
or two years old by now?"

"Yes they are all very well. Peter will be three soon."

"Good grief where does the time go! They grow up so fast.
Seems like only yesterday that Sam was a little nipper and now
look at him. Soon to start at Cranbrook?"

"Yes next September."

"Mmm... clever just like his father."

I swallowed hard and momentarily lost the rhythm of the dance, until his guiding hand brought me back to the music.

"And then there's Katharine, already trying to be a young lady." He sighed.

"I think that once they reach double figures they think they're grown up these days!"

And what about you Rosie?"

"Me?"

"What's keeping you here? And don't say the pub. Your mother could find help."

"It's not as easy as that."

"You're wasting your time there. You should be thinking of yourself for a change."

"Funny that's what Graham's just been telling me."

"The lad's right."

"Perhaps he is."

"What if I asked you to come and work for me?"

"Me?"

"Take over the reins; help me consolidate the business, keep things on track so to speak. Louise keeps saying that I should slow down, take it easier. She may be right."

"I haven't any business training."

"You have a brain Rosie. That's what I see, what I've always seen....even when you were just a scrap of a thing. I watched you when you were with those poor wounded boys. No training for nursing either but you just had an instinct for finding the right way. "

I shook my head.

"I wasn't in charge I just followed orders."

"Come and see me tomorrow Rosie.....and keep an old man happy."

Mote House 1954
Rosie and Arnold

And that's how I ended up back at Mote House. It was a magnet that drew me to it. I was so busy learning about Mr Parson's businesses that I almost didn't see what was happening right under my nose. The days flew past so fast. I heard Beatrice talking to Louise.

"I think she's not coping anymore mother. Katharine is becoming more spoilt by the day, Ronald snaps at the children and then she just takes herself off. Even Sam keeps his distance"

I heard Louise murmuring indistinctly, trying to soothe her fears.

"You're making more of it than it is Beatrice."

"It's not just that." There was an irritable note in her reply.

"Once the children are at school she sits doing nothing, just stares into thin air."

"Perhaps she's tired....needs a bit of a tonic to buck her up."

"No!" She tutted. "It's not that. She doesn't look after herself all day, doesn't bother to dress, and then, once the children are home from school she'll suddenly, without so much as a by your leave, decide to go out."

"Gracious! Where does she go?"

"Nowhere...that's the whole point. She walks around the village, goes down to the station, up to the church, just aimlessly walks around."

"Perhaps the fresh air does her good after being cooped up in the house all day.

"Mother I think she needs to see a doctor."

That's when I knew I was going to finally intervene; once Beatrice had realised how serious it had become. Millie had always been fragile and frivolous. When the children had been young Dulcie had been there in the background always being supportive, providing the invisible shield. But Dulcie had gone. Millie knew how to be a good mother she had found her natural place caring

433

for them as babies but as they grew and developed personalities of their own it was as if her own role was being stripped away. She had been shocked to find that her youth was transitory. Her thirtieth birthday had signalled an age that she had not been prepared to accept. All her life she had revelled in her power to attract and be admired. She had come to believe that she would be impervious to age. When she stared in the mirror she did not see the strikingly attractive woman staring back at her. She saw the faintest of lines, the skin no longer quite so taut at her throat; her lips not quite as full.

Most women would have revelled in her, still evident, beauty, but Millie had moulded herself on the impossible images of the Hollywood stars who never aged; captured as they were on film, always to remain desirable sirens of the silver screen.

When Dulcie left she felt abandoned. Their happy marriage only confirmed her worst fears; that she was no longer eligible. Her widowhood wrapped itself around her and suffocated her. Her mental health began to fail. It was the start and I did absolutely nothing to assist her in those early years.

I watched her deterioration and kept Sam close; his wellbeing was far too important. He came to spend more time with me. I helped him with his school work. He had a natural ability to absorb new information, but more than that, he could actually apply his knowledge and reason with me. We shared in the enthusiasm of discovery. It was an utter delight to see him blossom. It was such a happy time for us both.

I also loved the challenges of Arnold's business interests and even developed a taste for finance. Stocks and shares suddenly took on a life of their own. I could see that it was driven, not only by hard sound commence, but by the vagaries of whim, gossip and innuendo. One indiscreet word in the confident bull market shattered all confidence on the trading floor causing the nervous bears to take to their heels. I quickly understood that my gifts could prosper in such a setting. It was about intuition and foresight not merely adding up the figures.

I found myself advising Arnold on my hunches. He took me at my word and within the year his investments grew exponentially. One morning as we consulted the Financial Times together, Arnold leaned back in his chair shaking his head in utter disbelief. "Do you know Rosie…. I'm making more money now in real terms than I've ever done in all my years of trading. You seem to have the Midas touch my dear!"

"Well it never worked for us in the pub."

"No." He became subdued, "No, I'm sorry that you had such a hard time of it one way and another."

"Gosh, don't apologise for that! You have always been more than generous. My father had good reason to thank you for your kindness; we all have been in your debt, especially Jack."

"He smiled waving away my thanks. "No need…no need at all."

"Do y'know, I still have that Russian doll that you gave my father all those years ago? I've always treasured it. It meant so much to me, you have no idea."

"Well, well," He was delighted. My words had struck a chord as they were meant to do. It was a simple as pinning down a butterfly. He pressed his fingertips together. "I can remember that day as if were only yesterday. Strange that those times seem to be more vivid now than the present…..must be something to do with my age."

He rose slowly from his chair and rubbed his back "Well I think we deserve a cup of tea, what say you?"

∞

I knew that there would come a time when he would reconsider his will. It had been playing on his mind. So much had changed since Archie's death. Now Millie had two children to consider and Dulcie was married. We spoke about them. Arnold was quite open. He had learnt to rely on me. He did not need to take me into his confidence; I was already there, at his right hand, to guide him.

"I've been thinking about my will Rosie. Louise says leave it as it is but I'm not so sure. I'm not happy with it."

"Does it do what you want it to do?"

"Ah well you see that's just it." He drummed his fingertips lightly on the leather surface of his desk. That's just it. I don't believe that it does."

"There's not just the investments, I need to consider this house as well. Time will come when I'm gone that it will be too big for Louise. Dulcie's married and no doubt will soon be producing a family and then there are Millie's two. We always thought that Millie and Dulcie would eventually inherit this house jointly. Beatrice has the cottage of course, but we need to think about the grandchildren now."

He considered his words, and then looked across at me.

"And then there's you Rosie."

I knew that he would finally realise it.

"You have been more like a daughter to us. We have come to think of you as one of our family."

I murmured my confusion and allowed him to continue.

"I want you to be a beneficiary too."

He held up his hand at my mild protest.

"I have asked my solicitor to come to the house on Friday so that we can work out the details."

∞

The new will was written. I was named as the executor and one of the main beneficiaries too. He had complete faith in my ability to manage the assets of his estate. There was even an opportunity to make a deed of variation and I knew that I would take full advantage of that.

436

Knowing that he wanted to simplify his investment portfolio I made a suggestion that perhaps my counter signature should be required on the accounts. He needed to look at tax implications on the interest that was accumulating. He decided to open accounts and transfer some of the funds to a joint account just as a temporary measure.

I always urged him to make sure that Louise understood the steps he had taken but he waved my concerns.

"I don't want her to think that I have interfered."

"Rosie she has never understood my business and never will. It would only worry her. Besides If I can't be a judge of character now I never will be."

So who was I to question a man who had spent his entire life building up a business empire? I had given him the opportunity to rein me in and he had not taken it.

I had secured the future for Thomas's child and his children. Millie was of no consequence. I had done what I had to do.

∞

The following year Sam started his secondary education at Cranbrook thriving in the challenging atmosphere. By comparison Katharine showed absolutely no aptitude for academic study. She became bored, spending most of her time trying to find an easy route and then becoming quite adept at not being available when any chores needed to be undertaken. Meanwhile Millie had twice been accommodated at a secure place in Coxheath for some 'recuperation'. Her family learnt to be wary of her spells of exuberance and then the low periods of depression. She swung between the two states and they had little idea how she should be treated. Her 'mother's little helpers' amphetamine medication seemed to just subdue her and then she would sit staring into space, stupefied, unable to rouse herself.

Beatrice became mother to her grandchildren during the worse moments of Millie's illness, whilst Ronald refused to accept that anything was wrong. He was furious that it unsettled his routine and somehow implied some inherited instability.

"Certainly not on my side of the family!" His indignation was all too apparent, and he was carelessly oblivious of the effect his outbursts would have on the children.

"She needs to pull herself together."

Also he was afraid of what people would say. The stigma of mental illness was too awful to contemplate. Beatrice was left to pick up the pieces, whilst Dulcie did her best to smooth things over.

I must admit that I was sorry for her and ashamed when I met up with Dulcie on one of her flying visits.

"She seems to have more and more episodes these days, and all the pills that she takes! Mother said the doctor was even suggesting her having ECT treatment. Rosie it's barbaric!"

She looked so sad.

"Every time I come back she seems to be getting worse. Have you seen her recently?"

She knew the answer; I didn't need to tell her. She looked at me.

"Rosie they need your help. They all do. Not just Sam."

I promised to do more and watched as her eyes narrowed as I tried ignore the urgency of her plea in my head.

She caught hold of my hand. "Do it for me then?"

"Okay I promise Dulcie. I'll try." I shrugged my shoulders, guiltily trying to shake off the burden of my own procrastination.

∞

By the time that I did do something, Dulcie and Graham had moved further away. They had rented a small flat in Hounslow and then as Graham gained promotion they moved over to Reading. With the new boom in the building trade and the Clean

Air Act he decided to set up on his own installing gas boilers and took on an apprentice.

I did set up an expensive consultation for Millie. Beatrice took her to London to see a consultant. A different kind of treatment was offered and for a while she seemed much better.

To salve my conscience I wrote to tell Dulcie the good news.

And so we carried on. My work at Mote House provided me with the independence that I had always craved. Although there was still so little choice in the shops we were pleased to finally see the end of rationing.

I knew that Jack and Diana had had Peter by then and he hardly ever came to visit Ethel unless it was her birthday. Eventually it was decided that she should move out and Fremlins installed a new licensee whilst Ethel and I moved to Kilndown Lodge, rent free, near the railway station close to Samuel and Alice Fulwood.

Oxford 1965
Sam and Anne

Jack and Diana did not attend Sam's wedding. I had helped draw up the guest list and offered to post the invitations on Millie's behalf. Graham and Dulcie came with their little one David, who looked exactly like a smaller version of his father. Ronald walked with a stick and leaned on Beatrice's arm for support. He looked frail and unsure of himself. His collar seemed two sizes too big around his thin neck.

Thankfully Millie was in good spirits. She was pale but cheerful and had taken Beatrice's advice about her costume.

Katharine looked glorious in her Anne Klein sheath dress. She turned all the heads as she walked elegantly up the aisle accompanying her mother to the front pew. They sat together, one pale blonde head next to a mane of magnificent jet black. Whispers went around the church. Those who read the fashion magazines recognised the pouting looks of Jean Shrimpton, Joanna Lumley and Patti Boyd and proudly noted the tall model in their midst. She easily outshone the other guests and the bride.

Sam heard the whispers and turned round and found the congregation staring in her direction. He grinned and turned back to face the stained glass panels. She had provided a moments respite from the nerves that had fluttered all morning around his stomach.

As he waited exchanging looks of increasing panic with his best man there was a rustle and bustle as the congregation stood as one and the organ puffed itself to proclaim the entrance of his bride. He had to turn to see her and found himself having to swallow hard as she progressed up the aisle towards him.

I saw his look of adoration and my heart contracted. It was as if my Thomas was there, standing in his place by proxy. He would have been so proud of the young man that had taken on his mantle.

Later at the reception he stood with his new wife as they welcomed and accepted the congratulations of their guests. He took me to one side after the wedding breakfast.

"I don't know how to thank you Aunt Rosie. I couldn't believe it when I had such a large inheritance. Anne and I have been looking at some places. Only small mind, but we reckon that we could put down a sizable deposit. It will be such a great start, to get a place of our own."

His boyish enthusiasm made me smile.

Katharine wafted over to our side.

"Well little brother, congratulations, you see, you can look the part when you make an effort." She pulled at his waistcoat.

"Well you seem to have everyone eating out of your hand sister dear."

He looked down at her.

"Is London still where it's at?"

"Of course darling, where else......anyone who's anyone...you know what they say. Tell me where did you two hook up?"

"They met at the Oxford Debating Society." I said.

"Gosh did I tell you that? He smiled at me.

"I don't remember saying that. Yes we did actually," and he turned back to Katharine.

"Oh good Lord don't say that you are actually surveying the talent!"

"A girl can look."

She turned back to him. "Debating Society huh? Sounds like fun."

"Go away and bother some other poor unsuspecting soul." He punched her arm playfully.

"Careful you idiot I bruise so easily!"

"Only your ego."

They watched as she walked away.

441

"Some things never change." I said. "Actually before you go, there was something else. When do you think you will come down to Kent next?"

"Well it won't be until next month why?"

"Oh that'll be fine. Do come and see me I have something for you both."

"Mmm sounds mysterious."

"Lovely to catch up with your Aunt Dulcie isn't it? The boy is certainly a big lad for his age."

They looked across the room as Dulcie turned to raise a glass in our direction.

"So you're going to stay in Oxford then?"

"Well yes. Anne's doing her doctorate now and with my work at the law firm. The only downside is being so far away from mum. And she misses us both I know she does. And then there's gran, she has her hands full with granddad. And he's not looking so good is he. Can't believe how he seems to have gone down since we last saw him."

"Age is like that Sam. We tend to plateau for a while and then step off the cliff edge!"

"You don't look any different."

"Ah well I've taken the elixir of youth."

"Oh.....didn't know that they are selling it down there then."

"It's a well-kept secret. If I tell where... then the spell is broken. Anyway love, I want to go and speak to Dulcie and you need to get back to your lovely wife. She's a nice girl. I approve."

∞

When Sam came down to see us Ethel was out shopping.

"Oh you've only just missed her." I was pleased to be able to time things so well.

"Have you seen your mother?"

442

He frowned, "she's not as good as she was a bit ago….seems very agitated."

"I think Ronald doesn't help matters."

"You're right there. I don't know how gran puts up with him."

"Years of practise I suppose."

I led him to the sitting room. On the sideboard sat the two Clodion bronzes.

I heard him draw in his breath in admiration.

"They are by Clodion. Two of his best I believe…. Bacchante aux raisins."

I indicated the young woman on the right holding aloft a bunch of grapes and then the other leaning against a tree trunk as the ivy twisted around the base at her feet.

"Your father always admired them."

"Phew… they must be worth a bob or two!"

"You could say that. They are your wedding present…for you and Anne. They need to be insured. I haven't had them valued recently so you must see to that. They need to be valued both as a pair and then separately."

"Where did they come from…..Mote House."

"Oh no….here at Kilndown Manor. They belonged to Lady Faversham. She left them in her will to your father to then pass on to a male heir. I was waiting for your marriage. It seemed the right time. They have found a home at long last."

"I didn't even know that dad knew her.

"Oh gosh yes, she was very fond of your father. He reminded her of the son that she lost in the First World War. She took it very badly when they lost their son and heir."

"But I thought that grandad was their grandson. Why didn't he inherit the estate then?"

Lies come so easily when there is no one to refute them.

"Your grandfather was given a sizeable amount that was in trust to him when he came of age, and he gambled it all away I'm afraid. Then he went to her pleading with her, after just a few months to give him more money to pay off his creditors. Even your grandmother still doesn't know the whole story. And then his mother, your great grandmother Sylvia, and her husband Roland, had a huge falling out with her when they found out that she had refused to see him.

He shook his head sadly.

"Families huh?" he sat on the corner of the seat still staring at the bronzes.

"Well I imagine that they thought that they were going to inherit the entire Kilndown estate. Your great grandmother Sylvia didn't speak to her mother again, not even at the end when they knew she only had a few months left at most.

"That's really sad."

"Mmm....yes you're right... so really there was nothing for it. She decided to write out another will and then sent for me, asking me to be an executor. Your father had always been more of a son to her you see. They could talk together. Anyway I don't know why but she decided to send for me, as a friend of your father's, to ask me to ensure that you, as his heir, would be properly provided for after her estate was sold. And then, if anything happened to Thomas, to also make sure that there was a small provision for his daughter Katharine. Of course I said yes, what else could I say? And I promised that I would. She had wanted your father to inherit everything but of course the last war changed all that."

"So who paid off Grandad's debts then?"

"Your other great grandad, Mr Parsons. He forked out all the money that he owed and then paid for Ivy Leaf Cottage."

"Blimey!"

He wanted to avoid a scandal and some of the creditors were not the type to say no to."

"I just can't imagine grandad being mixed up with people like that. I thought he was born in that bank!"

We smiled broadly at the shared vision of Ronald sitting sedately behind his desk at the bank, surrounded by stylized cartoon gun-toting gangsters. Sam was caught up in my web of deceit. If you wish to spin a web, make sure that the strongest strands are made of genuine material and then continue to weave the rest of the thinnest threads through them.

"The 1920's were strange times Sam. The war led to some unsavoury characters coming out of the woodwork. People were still surprised to still be alive. Everything was topsy-turvy."

"I still can't imagine it though….Grandad in dens of iniquity, blackjack and Russian roulette, smoking fat cigars and peering through a smoke haze!"

"Well I don't think it was quite like that. Probably more like a few high stakes at the races or in a couple of poker games! He just got out of his depth that's all."

I protested mildly. "Then he didn't know how to recoup his losses and I think he panicked."

"That sounds more like him."

"Anyway I would rather that all this just stays between us Sam. Old wounds et cetera. And can I ask you not to mention these gifts to your mother or Katherine. It would be like rubbing salt in especially as Lady Faversham did not make any other special bequests other than these to your father and you. I would be uncomfortable having to explain her reasons to them, even if I knew everything that had passed between her and your grandfather."

"Right-ho you can rely on me. A soul of discretion." He placed his hand across his heart and my own heart skipped as I saw Thomas in his place, an image that lingered for just a split second before it was replaced by his young son.

"Gosh you are the image of your father you know!"

I had to explain my momentary glance of confusion, even though I knew that he had not observed my lack of composure.

Always I needed to vigilant, always the exhaustion of living the lie; of being ever watchful.

"Well I suppose you had better get off. How is Anne... keeping well and making preparations for a new addition?"

"Honestly Aunt Rosie, we've only been married a few months!"

"Exactly...."

He beamed at me. "Well we might have to make some alterations to our plans."

"Tell her to look after herself."

"You are unfathomable at times."

Glastonbury Festival 1984
Rosie, David & Lauren

It was on that very day, as Sam stood in the hallway of Kilndown Lodge and bent down to kiss my cheek that I finally sensed how it would come together: a daughter for Sam and Anne. Watching him stride away, unintentionally mimicking his father's walk, before turning back briefly to wave his goodbye, I waited until he disappeared up the hill before I closed the door. And in shutting the door I closed out all other sights and sounds too, allowing myself to be completely immersed in the reverie of my vision. So many times in the past I had feared my gift as it so often came accompanied by sadness and heartache but this was completely different. A feeling of euphoria and warmth unexpectedly enveloped me. I was transported by a rush of happiness. I waited for some clarity; some explanation for the wonderful contentment that had very rarely accompanied my visions in the past.

The knowledge that Sam and Anne would have a child was just part of it. I knew that it was, or would be a happy event of course, but hardly the reason for me to have such an overwhelming sense of serenity. There was more to it than that. I emptied my mind and waited, trying not to be impatient.

I could hear music in the distance and people laughing and chattering together, they seemed to sway as one; a lake of bodies caught up in the beat, hands rhythmically waving in the air. I knew she was there. It was the child but then no longer a child. And suddenly it was gone, and I could only feel the beat of my own heart.

But I knew that it was the start, the very best coming together.

∞

The field was strewn with sagging tents surrounded by untidy piles of belongings and baggage. Lauren struggled into her wellingtons holding on to a guy rope which threatened to part company from the tent. Helen's head appeared at the opening, and she squinted up at Lauren.

"You'll pull the whole thing down at this rate!" Yawning she pulled the flap to one side and before struggling to stand upright, puffing with the exertion.

"My head feels as if it's too heavy!" she moaned.

They stood together looking across the field. A faint haze of mist surrounded them.

"My God it knows how to rain around here."

She held up one sock that dripped down her arm.

"Everything is wet through."

Lauren put a warning finger to her lips and pointed to the tent next to them.

"Think they're still in there...shh..." her hand went over her mouth to stop the laughter that threatened to escape.

"Look..."

They could see a rounded large bulge pressing against the strained fabric of the tent.

Helen mouthed an O of approval and smirked at Lauren.

"Fit or what!" and pointed to herself, then at the tent and back again, indicating a direct line of attraction.

"Phwoar...!"

Lauren tried to subdue a giggle and waved her hands helplessly in front of her.

"Stop it they'll hear you...you wanton hussy!" She hissed.

There were sounds of muffled groans and then a loud explosive fart within the recesses of the tent.

"Better out than in as the vicar said."

"Bloody hell you fired that one off without warning Dave!"

Helen and Lauren turned to each other facially demonstrating mock outrageous indignation before doubling up in a fit of giggles.

Suddenly a bearded face appeared and peered up at them.

"I see we have company. Obviously we can't keep the fans away mate.

"We happen to be here in this tent, and I think you'll find that we pitched it well before you came on the scene and started claiming squatter's rights to the whole field." Lauren spoke loudly to ensure that her words penetrated the hidden occupant.

"Oh I say….pardon moi mademoiselle."

"I can't find my bloody pants!" A muffled voice came from within.

The bearded face suddenly withdrew and there was a muted exchange of words before they both struggled from their tent.

"Good morning young ladies." Dave bowed before them sweeping an imaginary hat that he had doffed from his head. The exaggerated address seemed to have no effect on either girls who now stood contemplating both lads with folded arms and arched eyebrows.

"Now they find their manners." Helen remarked to Lauren, "and bet they can't remember a thing about last night either."

"Now that is where you are quite wrong young miss; a night of unbridled delights, beer and music. Was that not so Steve?"

"Well you got the beer bit right…and I think the inebriated doesn't quite do justice to that state you were in."

"Oh dear…. censorship at such an early hour Steve…..these delightful ladies appear to be somewhat aggrieved." He spoke to the back of the head of his companion who was now lamely attempting to lug a bag from the tent.

Lauren looked up at David and saw him smiling at her. "Can we humbly beg your forgiveness; we don't get out much you see. This is all new territory for us country lads."

"Really? You seemed to be very forward from what my friend and I can recall."

"Well as you seem to have a better grasp of veracity can I only apologise for whatever we did or didn't do."

Steve gave the bag an extra tug and stumbled backwards as it suddenly came free of its confined quarters.

David dug his hand into the pocket of his jeans and then finding nothing he searched his jacket. Triumphantly he produced a ticket stub and then a pen.

"Ah ha!.... writing implements and papyrus. Here is my telephone number." He wrote the number on the underside of the ticket, squinting surreptitiously at her to gauge what effect that he had made on her.

She grinned at him and her open face showed genuine interest. He was instantly delighted and surprised by his own reaction. He noted her blond hair held in a loose ponytail that the morning sun seemed to turn a shade of warm amber, and the escaping strands that fell forward to frame her face. Her violet eyes that had looked so boldly into his face averted their gaze when she became aware of his scrutiny.

Suddenly they were both shy. He clumsily thrust the paper towards her and she attempted to affect a casual manner as she took it from him.

"Thanks." She couldn't think of what to say next. Only that she was aware that her face was probably betraying her fervent wish to look calm and in control.

Helen who was oblivious to either of them, having been watching Steve's vain attempts to restore order, unwittingly saved their moment of acute embarrassment.

"Tell you what. If you two help us get this tent down we'll let you buy us a drink. And we might even accept an offer of a packet of crisps."

"Phew...strike a hard bargain don't you!"

450

Steve found a drier patch of ground to dump his bag and turned back to her.

"Okay ladies….and what if we offered a lift into the nearest town. Would we be completely exonerated?" He scratched his beard.

"Well can't go that far, but we'll consider our next move."

"Sounds fair….don't it?" Steve turned to David for confirmation. "So where is your preferred destination? We're heading off to Shepton Mallet."

"That suits us fine we can get the train to Bristol from there. First things first, though I need to brave the loos before getting back to civilisation, or even Shepton Mallet."

David and Steve started to spread their belongings out over the wet tent before rolling everything together in an untidy bundle. Lauren shook her head at their clumsy attempts to gather up the escaping items.

"I think we'll do it our way."

She disappeared into the tent before finally emerging with a slightly damp bag, which she placed on the corner of the listing tent.

David watched her as she once more struggled to move inside the tent on the brink of collapse.

"What did you think of The Smiths this year?"

"Yeah not bad I suppose, though I was surprised to see Elvis Costello, didn't realise that he was appearing."

Lauren fought her way back out of the tent, being acutely aware that her rear end was being scrutinised as she came out shuffling backwards.

"No… a very surprising appearance……"

David nudged Steve as they affected innocent surprise when she turned to face them.

"What did you say?"

"We were just talking about last night."

She put the two bags together and proceeded to untie the ropes. The tent imploded on itself, defeated by a lack of tension.

451

"Must have been a Girl Guide too I reckon."

They knew the effect they were having, and were amused by her air of superiority.

Helen returned. "It was worse than ever."

She breathed in deeply. "The smell, well ugh…..indescribable! Next time we're bringing surgical masks."

She saw the tent and bags, "oh good we're done then?"

"Nearly, just give me a hand to pack this away."

"Oh no Lauren…let's just leave it."

"We can't do that!"

"Others have…. look around."

"Yeah but it's not my mine. I borrowed it. I can't not give it back to them can I!"

They looked forlornly at the splattered tent.

Steve and David stood slightly apart watching their confusion before Steve nudged him in the ribs.

"Okay girls…stand aside," and he rolled the tent up tightly and waited as Lauren opened the bag. He wiped his hands up and down his jeans.

"Now who's owed a favour eh?"

Together they walked ungainly across the field having to stop every few paces to pull their boots from the mud and adjust the weight of the bags. David took Lauren's from her, swinging it over his shoulder with his own bag.

"Here give it to me. You'll end up tipping over at this rate." And his free hand steadied her as they made their way to the gate.

Their car showed the same lack of care as they shoved the camping debris into the boot and then attempted to find a clear space in the back. Crisp bags, crushed cigarette packets, empty bottles, odd socks, a glove and other items of miscellaneous clothing seemed to have all found a resting place on the floor. There was a distinctly unhealthy smell of unwashed bodies as Helen and Lauren climbed into the back struggling over the front seat that refused to tip forward from its original moorings.

David watched as they finally managed to squeeze in.

"Not often that we have four in here...."

"Oh yeah...we believe that don't we Lauren!"

David pulled out the choke and started the car. It faltered and backfired before deciding to tick over noisily, and with a grinding of gears and a jolt they set off accompanied by alarming rattles that seemed to emulate from various parts of the car.

Lauren pulled a face at Helen as they lurched uncomfortably from side to side as the car bumped along the dirt track before coming to the main road.

"She's never let us down yet has she?" David yelled to Steve when he saw their faces in his rear view mirror.

"Goes like a dream." Agreed Steve, turning round to see how their passengers were coping.

"More like 'Nightmare on Elm Street'!" Helen grabbed the front seat to stop herself being jolted.

"Have you seen that...great film..." he became animated.

"No that was a euphemism for what we are experiencing at the back here. It's called irony."

"Oh..." He turned back and grinned at David.

"Reckon they're experiencing a sense of humour failure back there."

Once they were on the main road they could finally relax and take in the views of the countryside. Clumps of poppies sporadically lined the verges and mingled with the golden crops at the edges of the fields.

"Fancy a drink first before you catch the train then?" Dave stared ahead as the traffic ground to a halt.

"I thought that was the plan." Lauren shook her head at Helen and they all leaned forward to see what had caused the delay. Steve leaned out of his window trying to see around the bend. The engine idled and faltered once they had stopped causing David to apply pressure on the accelerator as it threatened to stall.

"Think there's cows ahead….. yeah…I can see them. Blimey there's loads of them……must be moving them to another field."
"Hold on…yep…they are going in through the gate…oops one's gone the wrong way! Oh it's turned…. there's a sheepdog rounding them up. Hello…nope now there's another one turning back….now its decided to stop and eat …..no… no… it's on the move again…at 'em boy…that's the way to go!" His animated narration caused David to shake his head.
"He can get very over excited when he has a bovine experience."
"And they're off!" Steve accurately mimicked Peter O'Sullivan, "now Daisy is overtaking Buttercup as she retakes the lead with Gertrude now easing her way through…it could be neck and neck…a photo finish…. and yes! Daisy blocked that move and it looks as if she's home and dry! A triumphant day for Spot the dog who was with them all the way….. and now back to the studio…Dave?"
"Don't give up your day job Steve."
He eased the clutch and they began to move slowly forward again.

∞

At the pub they all became self-conscious after the confines of the car had provided some degree of anonymity. Now they were exposed sitting in the corner of the bar with just a small glass ringed table between them. They were aware of how others might view them. The girls had been aghast at their dishevelled appearance after glancing at their distorted reflections in the toilet's unforgiving mirror.
Suddenly they were no longer the spontaneous free spirits at a music festival who had engaged in some seriously enjoyable flirting. They were themselves again, back in the real world, bound by codes of acceptable behaviour. They felt slightly crushed by the return of normality. They were aware of hearing the sound of their own voices in the quiet bar where even the

bartender appeared to be eavesdropping. Their natural banter petered out and the banality of small talk took its place, with alarming silences. They had exhausted attempts of engaging topics of mutual interest, naming bands, gigs that they had attended, and places where they had visited, but the girls were only too conscious that their experience of the wider world was severely limited despite their attempts to sound sophisticated.

"What do you do then Dave?"

Helen reached for her glass to take an awkward sip at its contents.

"Would you believe chemical engineering? Yes it's a bit of a conversation stopper isn't it!" he laughed ruefully. He rubbed his hand down one leg trying to ease the tension.

"Four years at uni and then out in the real world." He added as the silence threatened to descend once more.

"And you, are you a student?" He turned to Lauren.

"No, not now....I'm a nanny, a live-in nanny I mean.... I look after three children at the moment. They are... well... they are all young, one is just a baby, the middle one is three just starting morning nursery and the eldest, a boy, is six." She nodded at them as they listened to her.

"They're really good kids, easy to like.....not like some." She smiled

"How long have you been with them?" David leaned forward. She looked at him and started to relax.

"Oh I only started six months ago with them. It's my first family.....before then I was in nurseries and of course I did some work in the paediatric wards and a special school when I was training to be a Nursery Nurse."

"And did you always want to work with children?"

She laughed. "Well I wanted to be a vet when I was little; we more or less had a menagerie at home, hamsters, cats, dogs, goldfish, rabbits, a gerbil that we inherited from a friend and I used to volunteer to look after the school pets during holidays…so there was always a full house.

"And did they all get on!"

"Well we had to keep an eye on the cats especially when they first met the hamster, but they didn't bother with the rabbit at all, he could hold his own…quite a feisty individual."

"What about them with the dogs."

"No trouble at all, great friends, even slept together…they got on like a house on fire."

"So why not a veterinary college then?"

"I didn't get the grades and to be honest don't think that I could have handled some the work anyway. You have to be focused; to see what the animal needs, rather than just thinking about how you feel about it. It's not about being squeamish, I can cope with blood and sick and so on…I have to in my job…but it's the idea of not doing harm, of having all that responsibility and then perhaps getting it wrong." She shrugged not quite knowing how to explain and conscious that he seemed to be watching her intently.

But he just nodded and smiled at her. She was so young and earnest, refreshingly open when before, the previous evening at the festival they had all played the game; playing roles that suited the occasion. Now they were exposed, brought back to their everyday lives. He had fancied her as soon as he first saw her but now, listening to her talk he wanted to know more.

"So this is your first job?"

"Mmm…finally I get paid! It's still a bit of a novelty… to have my own money!" Her face lit up.

"Of course it was a kind of probationary period at first. They had to know whether it would all work out, there has to be trust, that kind of thing…especially when you're all under one roof, and then they leave first thing and are not back 'til late so…"

"So they are getting a lot for their money Lauren!" Helen turned to David.

"She's still in denial but they take advantage of her good nature! No..." She held up a finger in front of Lauren, "let me say my piece....this is the first time that she has had any time off."

"No that's not true Helen."

"Well apart from an odd evening here and there....and you do their cooking, and housework, always running errands, taking stuff to the dry cleaners...more like a Girl Friday than a nanny. They saw you coming. No mistake!"

"I only helped out because their au pair left....it's only temporary."

"And we all know why that was!"

"Helen you don't know anything."

"I know that you don't see what's in front of your own eyes because you've got too close to those children, and they know that.... that's all I'm saying."

David felt a strange sensation of wanting to protect her watching her struggling to defend herself.

"Sorry." Lauren turned to David and Steve.

"Helen and I see things differently. She thinks that I am too soft."

"No I don't just think you are; I know you are. You believe everyone is as nice as you...and they're not."

Helen turned to Steve and narrowed her eyes "Whereas me, well I'm just the opposite...don't imagine that people are always as good as they would have me believe."

Steve raised his glass to her. "I'll second that. Who's for another?"

∞

Looking back David knew that he was captivated that day all those years ago. If anyone had said that there was such a thing as love at first sight before then he would have dismissed them as just plain mad. That they were talking absolute rot, but when it hit him it was as if there had never ever been anyone as wonderful as her. She was perfect then and was still the only woman for him. He couldn't believe it when their whirlwind courtship resulted in their marriage. He had been the luckiest man alive then and was still blessed.

Lauren wasn't just his wife she was his partner in life. Then when they had Ellen he felt that he had been blessed again.

He supposed that every parent believed that their child was superior to any other child, but in his heart of hearts he felt that in their case it wasn't just a figment of their imagination; she really was a lovely child, so bright and such a happy little thing. Sometimes at night he couldn't breathe thinking that something bad could happen to her. It was the stuff of nightmares that he wouldn't always be there for her. She had walked before any of their friends' children. He watched her contentedly playing with her toys, repeating the little rhymes and songs that Lauren sang to her, pointing to the pictures in her little books, naming animals and her colours, following her order of her numbers as she counted one, two three. By the age of two she could hold a conversation, not just indistinct babbling, and she had a really good vocabulary, even the district nurse had said so when she had checked her development.

"My word, she's quite a little chatterbox isn't she!" as Ellen gravely asked her if she would like sugar with her tea as she carefully passed her a cup of water from the plastic tea set.

His mother found his wonder in his child quite amusing.

"She takes after you. You were exactly the same at her age. Into everything and always asking questions…why, why, why…if I had a penny for every question I would be a rich woman by now!"

Dulcie watched Ellen and Lauren as they sat together at the dining room table, their two heads close together as Ellen drew her shapes on the paper.

"Then there's your Lauren always stimulating her, such a natural with children. You can see why she thrives."

"I was hoping that Aunt Rosie would finally be able to come up and stay over this year. I can't remember the last time we saw her." He turned as the telephone rang in the hall.

"Oh hang on I'll just get that." He heaved himself from the chair. Dulcie watched him walk away and smiled to herself.

"Well...would you believe it? That was Aunt Rosie on the phone just now...amazing! I said that we were only just talking about her!"

"Mmm....strange how those things do happen." Dulcie turned away to watch Ellen.

"Well they seem to happen a lot in our family. Dad's right, you're both a pair of mind readers, that's why we never get away with anything.!"

"No that's just your guilty conscience giving you away." Dulcie laughed at his rueful expression and leaned over to tousle his hair.

"Hey mother..... leave it out!"

"So she's not coming."

"Well I don't need to tell you then do I!"

"It would have been lovely to have her up here and be together this Christmas after all the upset of last year."

They both sadly considered the changes that the last year had brought. Poor Beatrice had been quite unable to cope with Millie's longer bouts of depression. Increasingly she had turned to Rosie to help. At first, losing Ronald had given her increased vigour, freeing her at last from his childish petulance, but then, perversely, she found that Millie seemed to turn against her, as if she was somehow to blame for Ronald's long drawn out illness and finally his death.

It was if Millie needed to lash out those who were closest to her and blame Beatrice for her unhappiness. Rosie reluctantly accepted the situation was becoming too difficult for Beatrice to manage. She left the Lodge and had moved in with them.

Finally during the early onset of winter Beatrice could not shake off a bout of bronchiolitis and by the beginning of December pneumonia had set in.

Dulcie knew that she would not see Christmas and they were just thankful that Beatrice had known Ellen for that brief time.

By Christmas Millie had been placed in a secure unit for her own safety. When Dulcie had gone down for the funeral and to visit her she saw how her illness had finally robbed her of her identity. Her decline was rapid. Millie no longer had any interest anything around her. She refused to leave her room, muttering and shouting at the staff, refusing food and then proclaiming that she was being starved. They said that she could no longer be safe on her own.

As Dulcie made the journey back up to Reading, she realised with a pang that it would not be long before she returned for another funeral.

∞

Rosie had sent up a large luxury hamper containing champagne, truffles and other delights from Fortnum and Masons, with her profuse apologies for not being able to be with them, together with a huge soft teddy bear for Ellen and a generous cheque for David and Lauren. David had been staggered by the amount.

"Five thousand pounds! We can't accept it."

But Dulcie had insisted on her behalf.

"She will be so upset if you refuse it. She wants it for you all and little Ellen. Just spend it wisely that's all."

"But she's never even met her. It's such a shame. There always seems to be a reason why it's not convenient for her to come. Something always comes up at the last minute."

"She's turning into a recluse."

"No she's more comfortable on her own David that's all." Dulcie stared into the distance. She's always been very solitary even when we were young."

"But dad said that as kids you were all really close...that he remembered that she was more like a mother to Sam than his own mother."

"Well that's not quite true. Your aunty Millie was always very caring, she doted on both your father and your cousin Katharine when they were little but she did have some problems even then. Lots of upsets; I'm afraid my sister was always quite fragile."

∞

Ellen climbed down from the table and came over to Dulcie proudly holding out the paper and offered it to Dulcie.

"It's for you." she announced.

Dulcie looked down at the childish drawing. There was Lauren and David, standing closely together on one side of a house, and then Ellen, with three other women. Two with brown hair holding hands and the other, as fair as Ellen, her yellow hair shoulder length standing slightly away at the edge.

Dulcie breathed in sharply before she smiled and thanked her.

"Lovely thank you, can I keep it?"

"Of course." Ellen nodded firmly.

David came over to admire her work.

"And who is this?" he pointed to himself and Lauren.

"You know who they are...it's you and mummy silly."

He smiled at her.

"And who have we here?"

Granny and her sisters....."

David shook his head. "No sweetpea, granny's sister was your great Aunt Millie. She only had one sister."

"And Rosie too!"

He shook his head. "No just great aunty." He laughed as she frowned up at him.

"Rosie was their friend who helped out when your great aunty was very poorly. They all grew up together when they were little like you."

Bewildered she turned to Dulcie, but before she could speak Dulcie held out her hands and brought her little face close to her covering her in kisses making her squirm in delight.

"It's just perfect Ellen, thank you."

Later that night Lauren put out the light and turned to snuggle into David. The bedroom was cold after leaving the warmth of the fire downstairs.

"Wasn't that strange?"

"What....what was?" David was drowsy, he could feel sleep lulling him gently into his dreams.

"Strange that Ellen drew Rosie in the picture"

He grunted and turned back to face her.

"No...not really... she send up the hamper....we were all talking about it...that's all. Nothing strange about that...quite the opposite I would have thought."

He kissed her cheek and went to turn away.

"But she's never seen her."

"So?" His voice was muffled as he drew the covers around himself.

"But she looked like Rosie."

"Yeah... well she looked like a grown up."

"No it wasn't that...they looked exactly the same, Dulcie and Rosie, like twins."

She nudged him as he involuntarily jolted; his limbs grew heavy as he allowed sleep to claim him

She nudged him again.

"Ouch ...I was nearly asleep then!"

"You were asleep."

"Well thank you Mrs Sumner! Go to sleep." He sighed loudly before drawing in deep breaths that slowed to a steady rhythm.

Lauren stared into the darkness.

"I still think it's odd."
But the room only heard the sound of gentle breathing.

When I heard from Sam that Ellen had met a young man by the name of Adam Minton it confirmed my worst fears. I hardened my heart against him despite all Sam's protestations that my fears were completely groundless.

Jack had caused so much heartache in the past and I was determined that his family should not once again hold sway over the future. I would not see all my endeavours go to waste.

I had felt so finally alone when Dulcie died at a ridiculously early age. She had always been my voice of conscience which I had chosen on so many occasions to ignore. Her death was an accusation; I had carte blanche to advance in my Machiavellian schemes but now there was no restraint, no gentle voice of reason, it was as if I dare not allow myself that freedom. Her death caused me to grudgingly accept the free will of the living.

I always knew that Dulcie would not see an old age and it was as if she had packed as much as she could into her quiet life. She had delighted in her growing family and played a full part with her grandchildren. I pitied Graham for his loss. He was a man cast adrift when she died aged just sixty. There he was, looking forward to sharing their retirement together that year and suddenly in a matter of months all his plans and hopes were dashed. David did what he could to lessen the blow for his father but when a soulmate is lost there is no adequate balm to completely soothe the heartache.

I sent flowers but did not attend her funeral. It was a cowardly act I know, but I couldn't face his desperation and see him realise that, of the two of us, the best one had been taken.

But I haven't actually admitted to myself why I carried around such guilt and still do to this very day. Why I cut myself off from those who were part of my past.

It had started all those years ago with Archie and Beatrice; my careless role in their affair that led to my own father's death. Perhaps if my relationship with my mother had been different, well who's to say what could have been. And then there was my awful all-consuming jealousy of Millie. Was it her fault that Thomas worshipped her from afar? Why did I allow her beauty to overshadow everything? My interference had led to the tragedy. Jack would have still found his fortune as he was destined to do and I could have found happiness with Thomas without snatching such brief illicit moments. We may not have had much time together but we would have been able to take full advantage of the times that the war allowed us to spend together.

If I had not have thrown Mille and Jack together they would probably never have given each other a second glance. Then there was Katharine. I certainly dealt poor Katharine a rough deal. First there was her illegitimacy and the shock when she found out that Jack was her father. Secondly, I knew that her small inheritance would cause her all kinds of problems, providing her with the independence that she was certainly not ready to cope with and propelling her so quickly, as it did, into a pretty mean world.

I was so caught up with her brother, Thomas's son, that I disregarded her right to have a normal life. It suited me that she was out of sight and out of mind. I knew that the film world would gulp her in and spit her out. I pretended that she had the life that she craved but I knew that it was all fantasy. If I was so able to control lives why did I at least not try warn her? Her abusive marriage was something I foresaw and yet I did nothing to prevent it.

And money. Once again it rears its head. I had ensured that Sam had his inheritance from Lady Faversham with a token amount in trust for both Katharine and him when they reached eighteen. I had the lease papers for Kilndown Lodge which she put in my name, and then there was Ivy Leaf Cottage. When Arnold bought the property his name had remained on the deeds even after he gifted it to Beatrice and Ronald. We had long talks about Millie and Dulcie. He confided in me speaking of his fears for their future and Ronald's interference. He was adamant that Ronald should have no interest in any of the properties.

"That man is a scoundrel. Why our Beatrice took up with him I shall never understand until my dying days."

I listened as he poured out his frustrations, allowing him unburden his fears. I became his sounding board; a vessel to receive his confessions.

"You are more of a daughter to me than….well… my own flesh and blood my dear. Millie might take after Beatrice in looks but by Jove she inherited the brains of that idiot father of hers and no mistake. Just cotton wool between those ears of his. Blasted man!"

He twisted the stem of his fountain pen petulantly.

"I want to make sure that if anything happens to Beatrice that Millie and Dulcie each have half the proceeds of the cottage. Then there's this place. You can't imagine what this place means to me Rosie. You love it too don't you? It's everything that I ever dreamt of…..me….just imagine… starting out with nothing….had to make my own way and then, my word, I did it Rosie. Your father knew it too. There was a man after my own heart. Louise would have fifty fits if I said this to her… but he was the man for our Beatrice right enough."

He examined my face.

"You knew about your father and Beatrice didn't you?"

I smiled at him and reached out my hand to touch his.

"Course you did. Nothing gets past you does it?"

He held my hand lightly and stared across the room at the Hooker prints, speaking to himself more than to me.

"Dulcie was the best thing that happened to them. You knew that too didn't you?"

I shrugged and nodded.

"Yes, two peas in a pod...that's what my Louise said. She saw it before me you know. But..." he sucked at his teeth.

"Folk can be so quick to judge and then there was Ronald. He had a cruel streak you know. Led Beatrice a merry dance right enough. There was even talk about him and that barmaid of yours... Rita... Rosalind something like that as I recall.

"Roseanne."

"Course it was." He waggled his finger at his ear.

"Memory's not as good as it used to be. "Getting old and befuddled."

His sad smile caught my heart.

"So what's to be done Rosie?"

"It depends on what plans you have for the future I guess."

"There's not much future left for me now."

"I mean what do you want to just think of Millie and Dulcie or do you want to look further down the line.....a future for Mote House for example?"

We sat quietly together as he leaned back into his chair breathing in deeply.

"Your investment portfolio is considerable and still growing. That needs to be managed. Some could be set aside for the upkeep of Mote House. I think that you want this house to remain in the family so you need to decide who should inherit it. Millie's eldest Sam...his children? Dulcie's children? On one side the property and the other side the profits of your portfolio, there's some equality there. You could set up trust funds..."

"You're right Rosie. I don't want Mote House sold when Louise and I have gone. Not if there is a chance that the family could live in it. I want someone to love it as I do."

I spoke about a deed of variation and wills, and promised, that when he asked for his solicitor to call, that I would be on hand.

∞

And so there you have it…
'The King was in his counting room counting out his money
The queen was in her parlour eating bread and honey...'
Perhaps you think I should be eating humble pie now that you
are privy to so much of my history. I am relieved to have it out in
the open but there is still the matter of Ellen.
Ellen and Adam.

∞

I hardly need to explain Ellen do I?
 When I saw her coming up the path it was if I saw the vision of
Millie once again, until I looked into her eyes. I felt a fleeting
touch of Dulcie then, reaching out to me and then it was gone as
quickly as it had come.
I knew she shared our gift. It had the same warmth and intensity
of Dulcie but there was something more, still not quite fully
developed. Not a sharpness like mine but a kind gentle intellect.
She had the capacity to reason without condemnation;
acceptance of human fragility, but a capacity to be hurt.
I had kept my distance from her family all those years hoping
that my isolation would protect her; keeping her fingers away
from spinning wheels during all those years when she was
growing up. She was safe I thought, up there first in Cheltenham
and then in Oxford; family life, friends, opportunities, plenty of
good old established universities to choose from. No good
reason at all to come to Kent. Then I heard the news. She had
met him at the Graduation Ball in her last year.
He had come back for that one evening.
Five years since his own graduation. Five years after leaving that
very same university he went over to Canterbury, to escort a
friend's young sister to the ball. How perverse was that! When I
found out that Ellen had embarked on a history course over
there it had given me such a painful jolt. I kept seeing them

468

together, two heads pouring over the same books although I knew that it wasn't possible. That they had both studied history was strangely coincidental but nothing more. I kept ignoring the insistent voices; reassuring myself that for once my fears were groundless.

He had long left and gone back home to Tunbridge Wells. His new business venture was thriving. There was no reason for him to go back. And even if he did the chances of them ever meeting were so slim. I supressed my fears and after a while they began to fade until last year.

Adam. As soon as she saw him she would have seen what I saw in my mind's eye; a gregarious, engaging carelessly handsome young man. A man who took you into his confidence; a man you felt you could trust, a man who was comfortable in his own skin. He was a man who appreciated life and what it had to offer him; a man who valued both intrinsic beauty for itself alone whilst understanding the monetary value that it represented to others. He was an auctioneer. Throughout his life whilst growing up he had been surrounded by objects of age, rarity and beauty. The names of artisans and artists were as familiar to him, as the names of football teams and pop stars were to his contemporaries. The marks on precious china or a signature on a canvas held no mysteries for him. He had a feel for quality. He had been a willing student, eager to learn from his parents' careful appraisal of pieces that had come into their showroom. His quick and accurate acquisition of knowledge gave his father huge satisfaction that he had been able pass on his interests to his own son and his willingness to pursue a university course served the same purpose for his proud mother.

His life had been comfortable.

A private education had allowed him to mix with children of parents who had themselves amassed objects of art and furniture of quality in their own homes. Familiarity had not made him careless of their value or of the skills of the craftsmanship that they exhibited. Indeed he was often perplexed by their cavalier attitude to their own possessions. It pained him to see new careless scratch marks on dining table inlaid with fine veneers or a valuable vase that had been placed too close to the edge of a sideboard, as much as it puzzled him when he witnessed their thoughtless and often offhand treatment of their own children.

Adam had been loved, but not spoilt by either of his parents. Although they were busy people they were generous with their affection and time and they all shared an infectious sense of fun. His mother was a good mimic and his father could keep a straight face when telling the most outrageous and comical stories. Despite living close to both sides of the family it was his mother's parents who popped in from time to time, or they would share holidays with them at home or abroad. Adam was very close to his maternal grandmother and she doted on him. As he grew older he saw less and less of his father's parents and they featured very little in their conversation or thoughts from one year to another. As a child Adam gave no heed to the difference in the relationships and it was only years later when he recognised that they had been almost strangers whilst he was growing up.

Once he left home to stay in digs near the university he enjoyed the camaraderie of his fellow students. He embraced the social life that it offered and all the new experiences that it opened up. Attracting the attention of the girls he was able to pick and choose at will. During his second year two of his friends decided to rent a house together and, when one decided to move out, they put a notice on the campus board asking for two more house mates. They were inundated with calls before they decided on two girls, both of whom soon became rivals for Adam's affections which finally led to an end of term fracas. Both girls were vociferous in their claims and at first Adam had quite enjoyed the novelty of being a Casanova, but the constant squabbling and threats of personal details going viral created too much tension.

When they left, Adam and his remaining house mate Chaz decided that it would be a blokes only zone as they sat on their much abused and uncomfortable settee, providing their own commentary for Match of the Day with only a couple of beers for company.

During the summer he decided against going home for the vacation and instead teamed up with Chaz to go to Italy. The original plan had been to start at Lake Garda and end up on the Amalfi coast, but the charms of Florence and Venice captivated Adam.

He had seen many works of art, but coming up so close to the breath-taking work of Michelangelo, strolling in the Palazzo Strozzi and gazing up at the cupola in the cathedral made him dizzy with wonder. He marvelled anew as he stared up at David wondering how one man had been able to fashion cold hard marble and turn it into the rounded softness of warm flesh and fine delineated muscle. It was nothing short of miraculous.

Then he was fascinated by the lavish splendour Venice. The cruel glittering bejewelled ball masks: the intricate swirls, fashioned lilies and roses entwined in the opulent Murano glass chandeliers, twisted stemmed goblets, and ornate mirrors edged in reflecting etched glass and lacy scrolls. At night he felt lightheaded he walked alongside the swirling dark waters and gentle arching Renaissance bridges over the canals.

The summer came so quickly to an end and suddenly he was unwillingly thrust back into the familiar world of academia and study.

He was still too unsettled to apply himself and the first term came and went. It was during the time spent at home at Christmas that he was acutely aware of how his parents' hopes had been pinned on his success. It was as he listened to their innocent chatter that he felt a faint twinge of remorse that continued throughout the festivities. He went back in the New Year with a determined resolution to shut out all other distractions and work hard on his thesis.

He almost kept to his promise.

Canterbury 2003
Adam

If Amber had not cried on his shoulder that night saying how
Lucas was an absolute bastard it would never have happened.
Caitlin had texted her but she just couldn't believe it.
"She's such a cow….I thought that she was just stirring up trouble
but then I heard him on his phone. He didn't even say sorry or
anything; even then, even when he knew I knew……didn't even
try to deny it. And with her! How can I face any of them? They all
know now. I look like a complete idiot!"
She had knocked on his door late that evening saying that she
had been locked out and couldn't find her keys. He had first
offered coffee while she waited and then, as the evening went by
and they talked, he found that they had almost consumed two
bottles of chardonnay. It was getting late. She still showed no
sign of going.
He was acutely aware that her mascara was running down her
face and despite her attempts to wipe her nose with the back of
her hand he could feel a small irritating patch of wet shirt sticking
against his chest as she clung to him.
He tried to reassure her, patting her back in awkward pats before
becoming aware of her lithe body pressing hard against him as
she sobbed. He felt a slight firming of his loins. She really was a
very attractive girl.
Holding her a little tighter he gently kissed her forehead, and
then her cheek and her neck, before moving his hand slowly
down her back and finding her unexpectedly relaxing into his
embrace. She offered her salty wet lips to him and parting her
mouth with his tongue he found that she was returning his kisses
with surprising urgency.
Then they were down on the floor. He had knocked his hip
sharply against the side of the kitchen unit as he endeavoured to
prevent her from falling. Pulling up her loose jumper he

unclipped her flimsy bra which sprang apart with surprising elasticity. She moaned as he coupled her tiny undeveloped breasts.

Then he was aware that she was struggling to undo the belt at her jeans. She strained under him, pushing him to one side and kicking off her shoes so that she could wriggle out of them. He decided to undo his own trousers but before he could execute the plan she had started to unzip them and unfree his member. Her action took him by surprise. Suddenly she was in charge. She pushed him over and as he turned she straddled him. Her boyish torso bore down on him as she lowered herself brushing herself against him.

He had not quite experienced such vigour and enthusiasm before. Although a little unsettling at first he quite liked the idea that she was expertly divesting him of his clothes. He was also aware that he had not uttered a word since the performance had begun. He could hear his own rasping breath and was aware that she had fixed herself securely upon him so that she could mount his manhood, and then rising and falling with quite a pronounced bounce she allowed herself to enjoy a rigorous copulation.

Her eyes closed as she gave herself up to the sensation and he lay beneath her happily pinioned to the hard floor watching her small pointed breasts hardly moving despite her vigorous activity. Then abruptly with a series of jagged gasps of satisfaction it was over for her, and she athletically rolled off sighing heavily.

"That'll teach the bastard," her words floated through the air. He experienced an acute sense of grievance that somehow he had been an irrelevance. Used as a kind of hobbyhorse. It was an unwelcome novelty. He had been so used to adoration that the idea of being somehow used as a kind of balm against someone's bruised pride was disturbing. He didn't quite know what to do next. He was faced with an unexpected dilemma. She had certainly cooled any ardour that he had at first felt but he wasn't sure that he could actually ask her to leave so soon after such an intimate act. It would seem unchivalrous at best and downright rude at worst. Anyway would she want to stay?

She solved the problem for him. She bent down to retrieve her bra.

"I'm not sure if I can completely commit to us right now, you know... me and you... not right now...it's still too....well raw I suppose... you know?"

She had expertly replaced her underwear and began pulling on her jeans.

He tried not to show his utter surprise. He had thought that she had shown quite a bit of commitment just a few minutes before. It seemed best now to just murmur his reluctant agreement. Somehow he felt required to state some disappointment.

"No quite.....you're quite right.... do what you think is best...its early days as you say, perhaps we need to step back...it's no big deal... I agree...just leave things the way they were before."

He knew as soon as the words were spoken that it was definitely not what she wanted to hear.

She sharply turned back to face him.

"Well...you could show a bit more enthusiasm than that!" Her stained face took on a peevish look.

"I'm not some kind of cheap shag you know."

He swallowed uncomfortably. Again she had caught him off balance.

"Anyway with your reputation perhaps I shouldn't have come here in the first place."

"My reputation...I don't..?"

"Oh come off it...don't come the innocent with me...I'm not buying that. Do I look as if I just stepped off some kind of high school bus huh?"

He wasn't sure where it was all heading but had a nasty feeling that it wasn't going to be good.

475

"I thought that you and me had some kind of connection but it seems as if you are like all the other bastards around here. You took advantage when my head wasn't where it should have been."

She bent down to put on her shoes with a slight wobble and then stood up to face him.

He was at a disadvantage still pulling on his trousers before straightening up.

"Advantage of you!" he pulled at his zip suddenly annoyed.

"Well what do you call this then?" she swept her hand around the kitchen before pointing to the empty bottles and their glasses on the small dining room table.

"Cheap wine… just so you could get inside my pants….well screw you Mr. You're not getting off the hook that easily." She glared at him.

"I think you have some serious issues Amber…..you called all the shots tonight not me."

"Serious issues…serious issues…I'll tell you what's serious…you'll find out how serious this can get."

Snatching up her bag it fell open and a set of keys fell to the floor. Without a word she picked them up. He stared at them in her hand and shook his head. Her eyes flickered in his direction; a faint look of discomfort crossed her face before she resumed control.

"To think that they were there all the time…if only I had known I wouldn't have had to come here and suffer all this….this dreadful humiliation!"

Pulling at his door it swung open and she swept out.

The hallway echoed with her accusation before he was able to shut them out. He stared at the closed door.

∞

476

It was on the second day after he had returned from a morning lecture that he found two policemen standing on his doorstep.

"Mr Minton?" One enquired.

"Mr Adam Minton?" He spoke again.

"Might we have a word inside?"

∞

Later when he came from the station he felt as if he could hardly breathe. A tight knot of anger held his chest rigid. He felt maligned, and shamed, but worse there was a desperate despair of his own stupidity and a bewilderment that it could have ever happened to him. Things like that only happened to other people. And what was he going to say to his parents? How could he begin to tell them? Already he could imagine their hurt and disbelief that their son could be involved in something so sordid and terrible.

He came to his digs and almost walked on by. It represented a crime scene; no longer a place where only a few days ago he was happily working, oblivious of how his world would come crashing down around him.

He wanted it all to stop. Just go away. He didn't know what to do.

"Hey Adam!"

He looked up and saw Chaz walking towards him. His instinct was almost to turn and run but he stopped and waited.

"You look grim mate!" Chaz laughed at first and then drew back concerned as Adam just stared blankly back.

"Blimey what's up mate?"

∞

As Chaz made coffee Adam sat biting the fingers of his clenched fists.

He came in and set the two mugs down finding a space amongst the scattered papers on the desk.

"Christ she's toxic...surely you knew that?"

Adam didn't raise his head.

"Didn't you ever see that old film...The Life and Loves of a She-Devil? Why do you think Lucas dumped her? She is seriously weird. Some really big mental health issues"

"Try telling that to the police."

Chaz's head snapped up.

"The police...... what are you on about ...what's happened...what the hell's she done now?"

"There's been an accusation." He couldn't bring himself to say it.

"What kind...drugs, assault..?"

Adam shook his head clenching and unclenching his fists.

Chaz blew out his cheeks in relief.

"I thought it was going to be really bad..."

"Rape! She's said I raped her!" The words flew uncontrolled from him. His shoulders started to shake.

"Christ no! Not again!"

Adam looked up trying hard to swallow. "What do you mean... again?"

"She told Caitlin that she was attacked...oh...I don't know... years ago, but she was made to withdraw the charges or something like that. Anyway Caitlin says that she's a drama queen. Can't bear the limelight not to shine on her....there's always something going on. Caitlin didn't believe half of it. Lucas said that she's a Jekyll and Hyde...up one minute and down the next...what's it called...manic depression...no....bipolar disorder that's it...she has to take stuff to control it and when she's doesn't it all kicks off."

Adam felt drained. His body just wanted to rest.

"Mate you need to tell them. They probably have records that kind of thing."

"It's not going to make it go away....I'll still have to go to court."

"Not if she withdraws the allegation mate."

"She's hardly likely to do that."

"Look Lucas knows a lot of stuff about her. She's been using stuff...not just prescription drugs. He found that she had a stash in his flat. Went ballistic when he found it and then she said that it wasn't hers. And she hangs out with some weirdos. I think mummy and daddy have had to bale her out a few times too. Let me go and see him. I won't mention names or anything. Just so as I know....you did have sex right?"

"Yeah....but she came on to me really strong...one minute we were drinking and she was saying what a shit Lucas was and then next...well she came on to me. She said that he had locked her out or she'd lost her keys, and we'd had a quite a bit to drink while she waited 'cos I thought that she was in a bit of a state. You know...really upset about him.... so I was like trying to calm her down and listen to her, and the next minute she jumped me."

Chaz shook his head.

"Then afterwards she was on about commitment and that she wasn't ready for another relationship, and neither was I... so I thought that was that. That's when it all turned nasty. She said I was trying to get her drunk then I said that I thought she had some problems, the way she was going on and then it kind of really kicked off. She made some kind of threats... something about...oh I don't know...!"

Distractedly he massaged his forehead.

"How do people expect you to remember all this? I told them everything that I could think of...oh yeah...that's right... that she did have her keys all the time, so she lied when she said she was locked out... and they just wrote it all down."

He breathed heavily.

"They said, 'was it consensual?' I felt like saying well I didn't have a chance to say no!" He laughed at his lame attempt of humour.

"Christ what's going to happen Chaz?"

479

"Leave it with me. I'll come back tonight. Just sit tight and don't speak to anyone....least said and all that."

∞

It wasn't until the following week that he received an official letter. He opened it with fumbling trepidation. The words danced about on the page. It confirmed that they had received a full retraction; that it was deemed not in the public interest to prosecute but that the allegation would remain on the police files.

He had to re-read the typed paragraphs before he made sense of them, and even then he was fearful that there had been some kind of bureaucratic error; some callous joke played on him, teasing him as a cat with a mouse; letting him go only to snatch him back again.

It was hard to return to his studies at first but the idea of having any social contact was even harder. He attended lectures, wrote up his notes, buried himself amongst the history of art pages of his books and prayed that he would get a good enough degree. His faith in his fellow man had been severely shaken and he found that he no longer took things at face value but wondered if there was an ulterior motive behind an innocent remark or action.

His cynicism was noted by his old friends who secretly wondered if the exam pressure was proving to be too much for him. Chaz remained loyal and discreet and understood only too well why he eschewed the company of women, kept the door of his digs locked and rarely participated in impromptu outings.

The end of the final year finally arrived. His parents were delighted to find that he was awarded a first class honours degree in History. For Adam it was a huge relief to find that he could put his university days behind him and immerse himself in the business of auctioneering. Objects d'art were refreshingly

480

uncomplicated. As time went on he relaxed and he began to regain his confidence. The familiar surroundings of home and old friends not connected with his university days allowed him to settle back, and he began to enjoy small social gatherings once again. He had always been a good conversationalist but as time went on, although he still could be interesting and amusing, he became far more adept as a listener.

Chaz announced that he was coming home for a few months after his travels.

"Think I've had enough of the backpack life mate. Reckon it's time to get myself sorted."

They both expertly flicked open another bottle and drank the contents thirstily. Adam shifted back on his chair tipping it onto its back legs and stared back at him.

"Yeah?" The question hung in the air inquisitorially.

"Yeah...I reckon." Chaz leaned forward and punched him playfully on the arm unsteadying Adam.

"Watch out you wuzzer...nearly cracked a tooth!"

"Yeah well...questioning my integrity or what?"

"Just that you've said it before and then gone off again."

"Yeah s'pose," He sucked his tongue against his teeth.

"Just that I feel that I've done that now.....it doesn't give me the same buzz. Don't get me wrong. Great places out there...Thailand, Laos, Vietnam, Cambodia, Philippines...I've seen a lot. Really different, great places, great people. But...oh I dunno....feel that life is passing me by somehow.

"What, at the great age of thirty...the big three o?"

"Hey twenty-nine thank you!" He attempted to push Adam again but missed and nearly toppled himself out from his own chair. Adam grinned at his uncoordinated assault. A blackbird flew across from the tree and over the hedge complaining about their intrusion. They watched its flight and sat for a while contemplating the sun as its rays flicked in and out of the branches.

"So what's brought this on?"

Chaz chewed his lip. Oh I dunno lots of things really...Alice getting married, parents going on about a proper job...you know...

wasting my life, wasting my education, 'why get a degree if you're just going to bum around' type of stuff."

He looked slightly defeated.

"And I s'pose they're right. Opportunities slipping away... I've got no real experience to speak of."

He sighed heavily.

"I look around, see people like you. Making a success of your life. I envy you mate. You knew what you wanted to do and you did it. Whereas me, well...what do I want to do...that is the question!"

"I thought that you and Chloe were still an item."

"Noo...not any more mate...no... long gone..." he pressed his lips together ruefully.

"Can't blame her....plan was one year...an adventure before real life began... and after a while she knew that I didn't have a clue."

Adam watched him as he passed his hand over his tanned face. His freckles and blonde hairs on his arm were highlighted by the sun as his attempted to stroke his wild crinkled ginger hair into some kind of order. There was an awkward brief moment of silence, which would have been hardly noticeable to any bystander.

"Anyway...let's not talk about me old mate. I've come to see what you are up to and ask a favour." He shook off his melancholy as a dog would shake off water. Already his eyes had a new light shining in them. The transformation was a well-practised act.

"And what exactly is the favour?"

"Ah...straight for the jugular I see. Not an onerous one at all actually I'll have you know." He adopted a piqued air.

"Well it will make a change."

"There is a friend of my dear sister Alice who is about to graduate and she has just split up with the beau who was to accompany said lady to the ball."

"Where?"

"No wait until you have heard the full story. She is a lovely girl. No complications. It's just that it could prove to be somewhat embarrassing for her to scout around for a partner with all her friends already fixed up as it were."

"I'm not going on any blind date Chaz."

"This is not a blind date mate...just getting her out of a scrape for her big night...she's not going to ask you to marry her! All she wants is a half-decent looking bloke for the night. That's it. And I promised Alice that I would scout around for her. "

"So you've already said that I would do it."

"No! I just said that I would ask around…. and as my best mate I thought of you first."

"And where is it?"

Chaz took a breath and spread out his hands in supplication. Adam stared at him. "No way!.... I'm not going back there!"

"It's just one night mate."

"Don't put that on me Chaz… no way!"

"Look. It was a long time ago...nobody would even know who you were over there these days. And what does it matter, nothing happened, nobody knew."

"Except all those… that you had to get to say what she was."

"They've long gone."

"Look she's a nice girl and I told Alice that I would ask you."

"So it was me all along then...you couldn't think of anyone else?"

"Look, I would do it myself….but…."

"So what's stopping you?"

"Alice said that she wanted someone more presentable. The girl needs…."

"The girl needs what?"

Chaz tutted and sucked in some air. "Her guy, well her former guy was a kind of a good catch and I...well I just don't measure up. Alice said to be sure to get a handsome dude...like you mate. She likes you....she always has! She says that you're one of the good guys...she thinks that I'm....well that it's about time I took

some responsibility and couldn't I just do this one small thing for her."
"Yeah…but that's just it …you're not doing it…I am."
"Semantics…just semantics….I'll never ask for another favour, promise mate.."
He placed his upturned hands in front of him.

∞

It was strange to see the familiar roads again as the taxi cornered bends before finally slowing down and becoming caught up in the melee of other cars stopping to disgorge their contents on the pavement. Swirls of long dresses and dapper suits were deposited on the pavements. Their owners anxiously checked possessions, patted pockets, positioned hair back into place before affecting an air of nonchalance and slight boredom as they greeted friends, air-kissing the space between them.
It was Canterbury meets Hollywood without the paparazzi; a celebratory evening for the extras determined to party the night away.
Ellen turned and smiled at him. "Don't we just look great? You and me huh...knockout!" She beamed.
"You can't think what this means to me. I just thought that I couldn't face anyone and then Alice managed to persuade you. I owe you one!"
She gave him a friendly squeeze.
He couldn't help but be pleased. Her enthusiasm was infectious.
"Now you understand the back story right?" She whispered and giggled nervously as they walked towards the entrance.
"We met last month. No… two months ago. You are besotted with me. We met on the London Embankment. You are a chartered accountant in the city…it was a lunch break. You live in…,"she turned to look at him considering the idea. "You live in… where would you like to live?"

485

"Staines."

She turned her nose up.

"No...we need something far more upmarket."

"I'll have you know Staines is a very marketable area."

"Okay...Staines." She intoned the word elongating the vowels and laughed happily.

"Anyway...so you live in absolutely stunning Staines and your company is what...what can we call it?

"Riverside Accounting Solutions"

"Yeah...like it! You're really good at this. Anyway I'll point out my ex-partner just in case we need to go into avoidance mode....we'll dance the night away and I'll be eternally grateful to you and name my first born after you."

"Shame if it's a girl."

She had put him at his ease. Her easy chatter emboldened him.

"Let me do the talking if need be...you can just play the strong silent type okay?"

"I thought that I would get a speaking role...just a few lines."

"Oh no...you'd become a screen stealer...I have to protect my assets mister. I call the shots is that clear!"

As the evening wore on Adam found that he was having an unexpectedly good time. Ellen was everything that Alice said that she was. Good natured, intelligent, kind and very amusing. A perfect companion for the night. It was evident that she was well liked by a couple of friends whom she introduced, and he was suddenly very pleased to be with her. He looked down at her head as they danced and saw the lights playing across the room, over the moving couples, over her hair.

She looked up at his serous face.

"It's turned out okay hasn't it? Not as bad as you thought after all. I knew that we'd get along as soon as Alice suggested it. I have a kind of gut instinct for that kind of thing."

"Instinct?"

"Well call it intuition. I always have had it you see. It's stronger with some people than others. Now with you…"

"Yes?" Strangely it seemed important to him that he made the grade; that she thought him somehow special.

"Nope…not very good at all I'm afraid."

She laughed as his face fell.

"Of course with you silly …don't worry, I can read you like a book!"

His happiness was suddenly swept away. A haunting warning of rejection came over him.

She squeezed his hand gently, reassuring him.

"You're one of the good guys….oh don't worry, I'd sure know if you weren't. Now don't get all serious on me, come on we're here to have a good time!"

She reached up and pecked his cheek, and then wrinkled up her nose in amusement at his surprise, before gazing into his eyes.

"You and me mister…" She held up her finger to listen to the music.

"Let's boogie!"

∞

If someone had said to him that it was possible to feel as if you had known someone for a lifetime within in a few short hours he would have dismissed them as being somehow seriously deluded. But that evening by the time they hailed a taxi and made their way to the station he felt as if they had always been together. Silly things made them double up with laughter. He felt fresh and alive. Everything about her entranced him. He could not remember a time in his life when everything seemed to make sense. When the train drew away taking her with it he felt that it had stolen a part of him. And later that night, when he had not heard from her to see if she had arrived home safely, he could not stop looking at his mobile willing it to ring and to hear her voice again.

If this was how it felt to fall in love it was accurately described as a kind of madness. He could not think, he could not settle to anything. He walked around the room picking things up and then putting them down again in a stupefied state. Finally his mobile rang. It jolted him back into the world.

"Hi there." Her voice. He could feel her close once again.

"Hi."

"Well we had a blast didn't we? Just wanted to say thanks for everything… for being a stand in….great job by the way!"

He had panicked. Was this a 'thank you but goodbye' call?

"Great. Yes. Really good evening, anyway thanks for the invite." He squirmed as he stumbled over the platitudes.

"So….well…I know that it was supposed to be just a one off….and I don't want you to say yes, when you really mean no… but say we meet up again somewhere soon. How does that sound?"

She waited for his answer.

He cleared his throat. The relief was overwhelming.

"Wow…No… well that'll be great. When can we…when are you free?"

"Saturday?"

"Where?"

"How about the London Embankment?" She laughed as she heard him considering it.

"No only joking! Meet me at Piccadilly Circus. We could pop into the Royal Academy, go across and have a lunch in St James Park, stroll down the Mall. Whatever you fancy."

∞

It was the same feeling in the pit of his stomach. Fluttering pangs of excitement mixed with fear. He remembered the first time he had been given a bike and peddled unsteadily until he found his balance, and when he knew that he could swim a few strokes and not be sucked under the water in the vast bathing pool. He

488

waited by the steps of the Statue of Eros. That it actually represented the winged Anteros appealed to his sensibilities; a Greek god of selfless, not romantic, love. Despite the tourists who had gathered to take pictures by the fountain he still felt quite isolated as he waited impatiently for her. He looked at his watch for some consolation but each time it merely informed him that he was well over ten minutes too early. He shook it slightly to see if the hand had got stuck. When he glanced at it again it showed that another thirty seconds had passed. There were still ten minutes to go. He wondered if he was in the right spot and that she would see him amongst all the people that thronged around him.

He wondered if there was a better vantage point where he could be seen and still be able to watch the coming and goings of people, and to see her arrival.

Self-consciously he held the small bouquet of pink roses. He had thought red roses to be too ostentatious. Then after buying them from the flower stall he realised that she would have to carry them around with her all day but he couldn't think of anything more suitable. A gift might be too presumptive.

He looked at his watch again. There were still five minutes to go. He could feel his heart beating; his throat seemed to be constricted. And then suddenly he spotted her weaving her way around the crowds and he just managed to quell the desire to shout out to her.

Then she was in front of him beaming widely; her lovely blonde hair gently being wafted away from her face by the breeze.

"For me? Oh how lovely?"

She took them from him, delighted by them and pressed her face amongst the petals.

"Goodness they even smell good. Most cut roses don't seem to have any perfume these days."

She reached up and gave him a peck on his cheek.

489

"Very thoughtful of you. Now do you want to do inside or out? It's such a lovely day, almost seems a waste to be in doors."
She turned and indicated her small backpack.
"See if they can go in...but don't squash them!"
As he carefully placed the flowers stalk down with just their heads peeping out, he was conscious of her slight perfume. It felt wonderful to be close to her again.
"Great now we are hands free!"
Casually she held out her hand and caught his in hers before they set off, walking side by side, their synchronised strides already imitating the easy gait of a couple well used to each other's pace.
"So mister...art or park?"
He delighted in the feel of her hand and squeezed it lightly before answering.
"Park and then lunch?"
"Perfect just what I thought." She smiled looking ahead; already knowing that he was looking down at her, and then she glanced up.
"And a blue sky....what more could we possibly want!?"
And they both knew the answer.

∞

Ellen sat close to her grandmother. Dulcie lay in bed, with her head propped up against the pillows. Graham had rearranged the bedding to make her more comfortable.
"Well so what is he like....your young man?" She moved her hand from the covers to hold Ellen's loosely in hers.
"Tall dark and handsome I'll be bound."
They both grinned at the cliché.
"Well he has dark hair and blue eyes and of course he's gorgeous."
Ellen produced her mobile.
"I took a selfie for you gran so you could see for yourself."

490

Dulcie studied the two faces smiling towards the camera. Ellen's grin was wide whilst he looked slightly bewildered. His eyebrows were raised in query. She saw at once Millie and Jack, Archie and Beatrice staring back at her. Happy. Comfortable. In love. It was just as she had hoped it would be.

She indicated the drawer of her dressing table.

"Open it...there's something I want you to see."

Ellen spread the small black and white photographs on the bed cover, turning them and discovering names and dates that had been written on the back.

Millie and Thomas 1942. The bride looked radiant holding a large bouquet as her husband looked down at her, his face slightly obscured in profile.

"My sister Millie and your mother's grandparents. She was always stunning. A real head turner just like a Marilyn Munroe! And then dear Thomas. He died in the war. Such a lovely man, such a waste. Tom Fulwood."

Dulcie sighed and stroked the photo lightly with her finger.

Next Ellen picked up a tattered picture. She squinted at a strangely familiar face smiling back at her, standing in front of a lion statue by an entrance and read the name.

"Beatrice 1919 Mote House"

"She looks like mum too."

"Yes, your great grandmother Beatrice Parsons as she was then, just before she got married to Ronald... my father."

She pressed her lips together pausing briefly, and Ellen heard the lie. Dulcie quickly gathered up another picture.

"Now this is a lovely one." She gave it to Ellen.

"Dulcie and Rosie. Ivy Leaf cottage 1940."

The two girls stood together on a small pathway with a flower bed behind them just visible. The taller girl held a protective arm around the younger girl's shoulder and the younger girl held out a flower as if to give it to the photographer.

"I was ten then...Rosie would have been..." She screwed up her eyes to do the calculation." Yes...eighteen then."

Ellen took it from her. Her mind swirled with images. She looked at Dulcie who smiled back at her and nodded slowly.

"Your sister too?"

"Uh huh....yes...Rosie was my half-sister." She nodded again.

"Such a long time ago now....a lifetime away.

"Ronald.... Beatrice's husband he wasn't your father was he?"

"No he wasn't dear....my real father was Archie Minton. It would have been a scandal if it came out. He was a publican and Ronald worked at the bank....different as chalk to cheese. Rosie and I were like two peas in a pod. It was very difficult...there were always rumours. But then Beatrice's father, Arnold Parsons, held a lot of sway in the village and people liked him. So I guess people just looked the other way. And they felt sorry for Rosie."

"Why Rosie and not you?"

"Dear me...where to start love. My father Archie was a complicated man. His wife Ethel was a difficult woman to like and she certainly didn't want Rosie. Then people said she and Archie used to fight like cat and dog. The word was that he used to hit her when he'd had too much to drink."

"Abused his own wife!"

"Yes...it was all very sad. A nicer man you couldn't meet when he was sober. But behind closed doors, well he was a tormented soul and he lashed out. Didn't know how to cope with her. But he loved me and worshipped the ground that my mother walked on. He should never have married Ethel. They ruined each other's lives. So sad. I know there are no excuses but I loved him too, and Rosie tried to, but he just wouldn't let her in."

"So is that why people felt sorry for Rosie. Because of him?"

"Well that.... and Thomas of course."

"Millie's husband?"

"Rosie was always sweet on him even when they were children. She adored him, but Millie always played the victim, the

492

archetypical damsel in distress but Thomas never saw it. If Millie snapped her fingers he would come running. Some men never see the bigger picture even if they are clever. And Thomas was very, very bright but she dazzled him. Rosie could never compete. It wasn't until it was too late that he saw how things were. We all saw how it was with Rosie. When she found out that he had been killed it was like the end of the world for her. It was only little Sam his son that kept her going. That's your mum's dad, your grandad Sam Fulwood."

"Have you got a photo of Rosie's dad?"

"Archie? No I don't think there is one. Now there is one of Jack and he was the spit of his handsome father especially as he grew older. There should be one when he married Diana. Have a look through."

Ellen turned the pictures over. There were postcards among the photographs, and letters still in their small envelopes addressed to Miss Dulcie Latterbridge and then she found a wedding photo. She stared at the picture. Adam stared back at her.

"He's just like your Adam isn't he?" Dulcie said softly, and stretched out her hand to her.

Mote House 2009
Rosie, Ellen and Adam

I came back from the dining room with the box of papers. It was time.

"Here we are, the proverbial Pandora's box," and I placed them on the kitchen table in front of her.

Ellen opened the box and looked inside. She saw the exposed documents and the red ribbon bound wills. A slight old musty smell wafted up from them.

"It's all there…. Wedding certificates, leases, deeds, share certificates, dividend statements, wills, letters ….they're yours to take, or look at them here….whatever you choose." I shrugged my shoulders.

She glanced back at me and then replaced the lid.

"We don't have to do it all now. We can just talk. I'd like to know more, you know, just chat……if that's okay with you."

"What do you want to know?"

"Well I spoke to my gran before she died and she told me about this village and your life here, when you were all growing up together."

I watched her casually brush a stray hair from her face. It reminded me so much of Beatrice. No artifice about her actions; not really knowing how beautiful she was.

"I wanted to see the house, this house where she grew up and to meet you of course."

"And is it how you imagined it to be?"

"Of course it is!" she smiled at me. "How could it not be?"

"And you found out about us?"

"Well some of it. My gran had kept photos, pictures and some letters that kind of thing. She showed them to me. She knew she hadn't got long. I miss her."

"So do I. She was all I had left…of that past life I mean."

"What was it like growing up here?"

"Oh very different to nowadays. People talk about the halcyon days. They think about their childhood and how uncomplicated things were but they are so wrong. We were locked in by a set of rules, moral codes that were set in concrete. Perhaps in a large city there was more freedom, I don't know but in a village like this...well there was always someone who knew something and before you knew where you were it was common knowledge. Spread around like wildfire".

"Did your family ever know that you had a gift like Dulcie? Or did you always keep it a secret?"

"I don't know what you mean."

She sat back in her chair and her lips twitched.

"Come off it. You've got that sixth sense just like me and Dulcie, I can feel it!"

I shook my head.

"It's not a gift it's a curse."

"Okay...well did anyone else know besides Dulcie?"

"No not really. I suppose it frightened me in some ways. Anyway let's not talk about that."

"Okay. So what was it like here in your day?"

"That's a big question. There was our childhood. We went to the school down the hill, played around the orchards and woods. Then when we were teenagers there was all the talk about war and then war broke out and all our lives changed. It changed everything. It took away my dreams. Suddenly we were all grown up. People moved away, I came to live here to look after Beatrice and I'm still here!"

"But you worked at Mote House didn't you?"

"Yes when it was used for the wounded officers. I was never properly trained like Beatrice, she was a VAD, whereas I just helped out."

"But afterwards Dulcie said that you worked for Mr Parsons."

"I did some general bookkeeping, that kind of thing."

"So you never went back to live at Kilndown Lodge."

"It was only on a short term lease and once mother died I gave it up."

"And you stayed here."

"It was left to Millie and your grandmother by Mr Parsons but he said that in the event that either Millie or Beatrice need care that I should remain. And now it passes on to you."

"Me?"

"There was a codicil drawn up. The property should pass on to an heir of Dulcie's choosing. She chose you."

I smiled at her, "It's yours whenever you want it."

Ellen's lips trembled slightly before she took up her own papers. "On the land registry for Mote House it had two names listed .... Dulcie Sumner and a Rosemary Minton"

I nodded letting her lead the way.

"And now it appears there has been a recent change there is just one name .... Adam Minton of Tunbridge Wells, Kent."

"Yes you are quite right."

"So can I take it that you ....."

"Dulcie told me that I should let things take their course. She had more faith than I did and I decided to take her advice...quite simple really. It's called putting things right"

Ellen rose and stood by the window, her back towards me.

"I'll come back on Saturday."

"Of course my dear."

∞

We walked up the drive. Adam held my arm. It seemed much steeper than I had remembered as we rounded the bend before the house came finally into view.

Lime trees provided us with some welcome shade with their profusion of large leaves hanging limply from each branch as if attached by some careless artist. We followed the line of sunshine on the path which led up to the defunct fountain. The dolphins no longer spewed jets of water from their bulbous lips, but the lions had remained on sentry duty and stood passively watching our approach.

I gave Adam the key and he opened the door. It needed another firm push before it swung open to admit us.

We entered the large entrance hallway and our feet echoed as we made our way across to the study.

"Mr Parson's…. he loved this room almost as much as the garden."

Although his desk was bare I could still see him sitting there happily surrounded by his papers. I went behind the desk and sat in his chair, something that I had never done when he was alive.

"Everything is still well looked after, really neat."

I followed her gaze around the room.

"Well he really was a very wealthy man and as his executor I have used some of the assets over the years to maintain the place. It's done via an agency. Why don't you go and see the rest of the house I'll catch up with you. I'm not so good at stairs these days and there are a lot of them in this house." I waved them away.

"I'll be fine….take your time."

I knew that they would fall under its spell and love it as I had always done. Ellen had been so adamant that I should stay in the cottage. And I have to admit that it would have been hard to have gone through the process of removal. I had dreaded the idea. She had been very thorough in examining the papers. I was very surprised that she had managed to assimilate such a lifetime of confusion…but then I suppose that her gift had filled in the gaps. She was able to see the bigger picture whereas I had always concentrated on the details.

The more I watched her the more I felt at ease with myself. She relaxed me, calmed my concerns when I thought that she would have had reason to condemn.

"You lost so much." Her words caught at my throat. It was so unexpected to be in the receipt of such kindness, when I had steeled myself for final retribution.

I could hear them as they passed by the open door as they made their way to the dining room.

"So many opportunities in a place like this. So much space! The rooms are so light and airy. Weddings, photo sessions, antique fairs, concerts.......wow...the list is endless. Oh god...don't you just think it's wonderful? I just want us to live here... always"

I heard his laugh; amused by her enthusiasm. They went down the hall and her heels clattered on the tiled floor.

I just wanted to see one room before I went into the garden. I eased myself up. The walk had been more strenuous than I had thought it would be. I made my way to the library and opened the door.

There they were. Two figures caught together in a tender embrace; his dark head bending down to hers. My father and Beatrice.

A shaft of faint sunlight played with the dust particles in the disturbed air. I watched transfixed as it created a circling halo around her golden curls.

Adam and Ellen: finally the circle was complete.

Hourglass Tree of Archie Minton

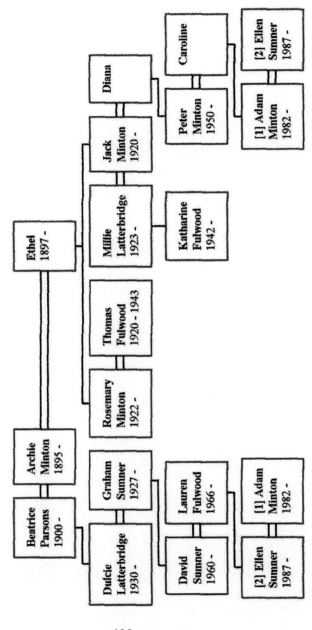

Hourglass Tree of Ellen Sumner

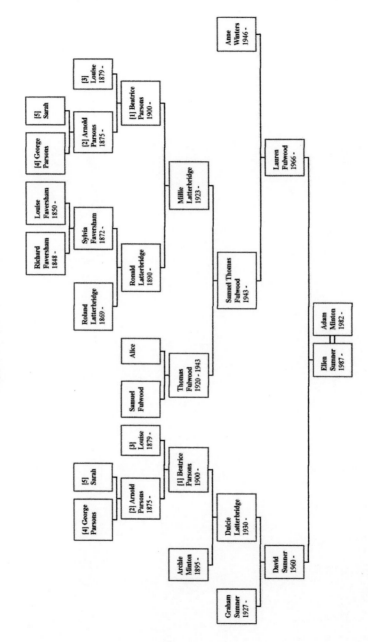